REND

Necrotic Apocalypse Book Three

D. PETRIE

MOUNTAINDALE
PRESS

ACKNOWLEDGMENTS

This book is dedicated to Paul Campbell. He was a good friend, beta reader, and fellow author.

He will be missed.

PROLOGUE

A month ago, Mitchell Carter's biggest worry was figuring out which of his coworkers filed a complaint with HR on him. According to some oversensitive jackass, he had made an offensive joke during a team-building exercise. The whole thing was stupid. He said offensive shit all the time, so why any one comment was suddenly deserving of a complaint was insane. Not his fault people couldn't take a joke.

He chuckled to himself as he stared down at the guardian ring on his finger.

Lot of good it all did. Whoever filed that complaint had to be dead by now. Probably torn apart by zombies or drank dry by revenants.

Good. A smile worked its way across his face. "Fuck 'em."

"Fuck who?" Miller, the guardian standing beside him at the base's front gate, stared at him in question.

"Nobody." Carter grumbled and glanced at his HUD.

Guardian: Level 15 Fighter

Things had worked out well. In fact, the apocalypse was the best thing that had ever happened to him. Sure, he'd nearly been killed a dozen times the first night, but he wasn't some weak-ass sheep begging for protection. No, he was one of the strong, and in this new world, it was the strong that came out on top. In the beginning, he'd fought and killed his way through the following week until Skyline showed up looking for recruits. They were his kind of people.

He'd enlisted the moment they brought him back to the base.

Carter relaxed, feeling the comfort of the sword on his back. A month ago, he was worried about HR, and now… well, now he was a mercenary. That was how things should have been from the start. In Skyline, he never had to worry about offending some oversensitive waste of space. No, if a civilian so much as looked at him funny, he could punch their head clean off their shoulders and no one would bat an eye. Not even those Autem guys seemed to care as long he respected them and he didn't kill any kids.

Not that he would, of course.

No, kids needed to be protected now more than ever. The world had been wiped clean, with all the old arguments and complaints dying out practically overnight. With that, kids could finally be raised right.

That was probably why he liked the recruiters from Autem. They seemed to have a good plan for things. There was something noble about taking charge and rebuilding. With a little luck, he could work his way into a position with them.

Then he'd be golden.

Skyline was all well and good, but seeing as his current rank had him capped at level fifteen, he would have liked to move up. Unfortunately, the brass was strict about who got a pass and who didn't. Even worse, after the shit that went down in California a week ago, it didn't look like Commander Bancroft had any intent of processing his request for advancement anytime soon. Not with him focused on hunting down that necromancer that had slipped through his fingers along with an entire group of survivors.

Carter couldn't believe how angry the man had been after returning empty handed. Not that he could blame him. If some smart-ass zombie had caused him that much trouble, he wouldn't be able to think about anything else until he had the dead man's head on a pike. In fact, a big part of him wished he'd gotten selected for that operation. They really should have sent their best. Who knew, he might have made a difference. It wasn't like this necromancer causing problems sounded that strong. At the very least, he could have stomped a few zombies into the dirt and proved himself enough to beat his rank's level cap.

Sadly, he'd been on guard duty at the time.

That just left Autem as the path to more power. They didn't seem interested in taking on anyone his age since they preferred to train their guardians early, but he figured he could convince them to make an exception. All he had to do was be a good guardian and remain strong. They would have to take him after seeing his potential.

He'd make his mark eventually.

Granted, Autem had some sort of belief system that seemed to be a requirement of everyone that joined their forces. It was another reason to recruit young. Kids were more pliable when it came to that stuff. Carter didn't see that as a problem in his case. After all, he had no issue telling them whatever they wanted to hear. If they said he needed to pledge his allegiance to a pet rock, he would do it as long as he got stronger.

Hopefully that would be enough.

If not, he didn't know what he would do. Carter wasn't a fan of being excluded. That part pissed him off. Then again, he didn't have much to complain about. Level fifteen wasn't anything to sneeze at and guarding the front gates was an important job. Plus, there was something to be said for being a part of the world's only surviving military force.

Carter sighed and glanced at his HUD again to remind himself of the power he'd gained. It was still hard to believe how strong he'd become. He felt like a god. He couldn't help imagining what life would be like at level thirty.

"What the hell is that?" Miller tore him away from admiring his stats.

Carter squinted into the night, having trouble seeing far. After letting his eyes adjust, a familiar boxy shape became clear in the distance, heading straight for them. "Is that a truck?"

Familiar or not, a cargo truck shouldn't have been anywhere near the area. Located in the middle of the Mojave Desert with only one road leading to its front gates, Skyline's main facility was normally surrounded by nothing but flat emptiness. The location had given the military contractor the freedom and privacy to grow without unwanted observation as well as the ability to see for miles.

Overall, the base was over three square miles with a mix of barracks, aircraft hangars, runways, and a literal army of personnel. Carter took a step back from where he stood at the main gates. Behind him, just within the entrance, was an open space that housed a processing area. That was where they took in survivors before they were sent off to either recruitment or to Autem's colony on the east coast. Currently there was no one there, as they hadn't taken in anyone new for the last couple days.

"Were we expecting anyone?" Miller moved toward the guard house to the side of the gate.

"Don't be stupid, there's no reason why a cargo truck would even have a use anymore." Carter reached for his radio. It was obvious that the truck didn't belong there.

That was when the base's alert siren went off, accompanied by an announcement from Commander Bancroft. "All Skyline personnel, report to defensive stations."

"Looks like the brass is way ahead of us." Carter released his finger from his radio's call button. The cameras mounted along the outer walls must have already alerted the commander.

"Shit, are we under attack?" Miller glanced back as every guardian assigned to the night shift filtered out and climbed to the gunner towers that lined the base's ten-foot wall.

Carter wasn't sure what to make of it. Surely Bancroft didn't need to mobilize all of the gunners to handle one truck. He rushed to the guard shack and reached for a pair of binoculars. Raising them to his face, he got a better look at the vehicle. It was an eighteen-wheeler, the kind that used to handle long haul transport. Again, he questioned why something so basic would merit so much firepower.

That was when a second truck pulled out from behind the first, kicking up dust from the dry clay that covered the ground around

4

the road as it drove up beside the lead vehicle. His eyes bulged as a third and fourth tractor trailer moved from behind the first to join the line. More vehicles spread out into a row one after another, each barreling forward alongside the rest. Dust clouds filled the horizon as the vehicles made it clear they had no intent on stopping.

Behind, the men stationed in the gunnery towers opened fire, filling the sky above Carter's head with streaks of white-hot lead. The guns thumped in a steady rhythm as sparks flew from the oncoming trucks. Sweeping his binoculars across the scene, Carter found plates of scrap metal welded to the front grill of each vehicle like armor to protect the engine. None of it was enough to stand up to a full-scale war. Instead, the defenses seemed like they were only meant to last long enough to reach the base before giving out.

Carter watched as bullets shattered windshields and peppered each driver through cracks in the armor plating. Confusion washed over him when none of the men showed any sign of injury. They each wore helmets and kept their hands at ten and two.

"My god. They're going to sacrifice themselves." Carter dropped his binoculars and retreated back inside the gates to prepare for the incoming assault.

"No they won't." Miller did the same before slamming his hand on to a big red button to raise the bollards that lined the gate's opening. "Did you see their hands?"

Steel pillars slid up from the pavement to block the gates as Carter raised his binoculars again. Focusing on the lead driver's hands, he struggled to understand what Miller had meant. Their fingers were filthy. Actually, they almost looked... rotted. Carter gasped as a bullet slammed into the knuckles of the driver he was watching. His hand simply exploded, yet he didn't even flinch. Instead, he curled what was left of his shattered fist, just a pinky and an index finger, around the steering wheel to keep the truck moving in a straight line.

"Christ, they're all fucking dead!" Carter recoiled in horror as he realized the row of eighteen wheelers couldn't be stopped. "How is it even possible? Zombies can't drive."

"Tell them that." Miller cast a Barrier spell to protect himself from the inevitable assault that would hit their gates before thrusting a finger at one of the vehicles. "Who the hell is that?"

Carter flicked his eyes back to the oncoming truck, finding a hooded figure crouched on top of the lead vehicle. He couldn't tell who it was or if they were alive or dead. A long coat flapped in the wind behind them. His blood ran cold.

Is that the necromancer that ran away from Bancroft a week ago?

Would he really be that crazy to attack us head on?

Bullets impacted all around them, causing the figure no more distress than a fly buzzing in their ear. Staring at the dark presence through his binoculars, he felt like they were staring straight through him even if he couldn't quite make out their eyes across the distance. A swell of fear rose in his chest, worse than a million HR complaints.

With hands shaking, he looked away as the gunners on the wall ceased firing. A second later, a dozen rocket propelled grenades fired into the sky. They streaked through the night, a plume of smoke trailing behind until they slammed into the vehicles in a last attempt to slow the assault before it plowed into their walls. Detonating in a staccato of rapid blasts, the explosions lit up the landscape.

Some of the haphazardly welded armor held, though a few of the vehicle's cabs erupted into flames. The damaged trucks weaved, bumping into the ones on either side, but ultimately, they remained in line, forced to continue forward as the other vehicles kept them moving straight. Even when they began to fall behind, with their current momentum, it was clear that they would still reach their destination.

Carter searched for the figure, hoping they had been hit by the barrage. He found them, standing right where they had been, their coat trailing them like a cape as smoke billowed past. For a moment, they seemed to flicker in and out of existence.

That was when another siren sounded, this time along with orders to hold the line. Carter snapped his eyes back to the nearest speaker in confusion. It was too late to push forward. They should have been retreating to a defensive position.

"Fuck that." He cast a Barrier spell and retreated into the processing area where he might survive what was coming.

"Where are you going?" Miller shouted over his shoulder.

"Staying alive, and you should too." He waved his hand to tell him to follow. Miller hesitated for a moment before taking one last look at the trucks and following Carter.

The siren continued to blare as several kestrels lifted off from the airfield on the other side of the base. Dozens of aircraft took to the skies, each heading for the vehicles, guns blazing to cut a swath through the surrounding desert. Clouds of clay and earth filled the air, blocking everything from sight. Carter held his breath as he waited for the dust to settle and the night to return to the usual calm he was used to.

It didn't.

Over a dozen trucks emerged from the cloud of debris, traveling well over a hundred miles-per-hour. The kestrels had only stopped a couple. The figure on top stood tall with their arms out wide.

"Oh shi—" was all Carter could get out before the lead truck slammed into the bollards at the main gate.

The eighteen-wheeler crashed to a stop in an instant, sending its trailer flying up into the air, tumbling end over end. The figure leapt as the crash launched them forward. They hit the pavement in a tumble, rolling to a stop in a maneuver that would have left even a high-level guardian broken and battered. They stood back up just as the trailer they had rode in on crashed down to the pavement behind them.

Before anyone could react, another two vehicles slammed into the wall, bursting through the concrete. The mounted guns ceased their continuous fire as the trucks obliterated their defenses, along with the men that manned them.

The figure vanished into the chaos as both trucks jackknifed and slid into the center of the processing area. Seconds later, another three cargo trailers flipped over the wall to spiral through the air, like the first one. A squad of guardians scattered as another semi-truck plowed through the building they were positioned beside.

It was like something out of a disaster film. All carnage and devastation.

Carter cursed the order that had told them to hold the line. They must have lost over two dozen men already, with more meeting their end every second.

One after another, zombie driven vehicles exploded through the wall or flipped over it in a cascade of destruction. He couldn't believe his eyes. Skyline had been prepared for almost anything, but this, this was all out madness. Even with the power he and his fellow guardians carried, how could they have expected such a dead stupid assault? It was just too barbaric to think possible.

The siren finally cut off as a few guardians lobbed Fireballs and Icicles at the wrecked vehicles.

"Hold your spells!" one of the higher-ranking men shouted from behind.

A sudden stillness fell over the base with nothing but the sound of flames spitting to fill the silence. For a moment, Carter relaxed.

"Is it over?" Miller started to stand up from where he'd been ducking for cover.

"I don't..." Carter started to speak before a strange sound drifted over the base. "What is that?"

It almost sounded like music.

A calming bass strummed through the air accompanied by a peaceful guitar and piano. Carter spun around, searching for the source, only to find nothing. It was as if the sound was being sent directly into his ears. His mind struggled to place the tune as the wreckage of the trucks settled.

Then came the vocals.

And now the end is near...

The voice was smooth, like velvet.

"Is that..." Miller furrowed his brow. "Sinatra?"

Carter snapped his eyes back to the nearest overturned cargo trailer as a horrid scratching merged with the music. A howl came from one of the other box trucks before the door on the back popped open.

It wasn't over.

As the vocal stylings of Frank Sinatra sang the lyrics to *My Way*, a zombie the size of a bull exploded through the side of one of the vehicles like it had been made of tissue paper. Armor of bleached bone covered its body, culminating in a horned headpiece. Two dozen zombies poured out behind it, crawling over each other all at once to spill into the processing area. One by one, the other vehicle's doors popped open as the dead poured out. Some were already injured from the crash, but most were still fully functioning.

The sound of a raven cawing overhead mixed with the orchestra from *My Way* that was being broadcast directly into Carter's head. Several more armored brutes shredded their way from within the other cargo trucks along with dozens of zombies.

Carter clenched his fists as he sent a surge of mana to pool around his knuckles. The order to attack blared from the base's speaker system as Sinatra's voice swelled to drown it out.

The dead marched forward, their numbers growing exponentially as each truck released its deceased cargo. A few zombie soldiers rushed forward, their hands deformed into wicked claws, while others howled, their jaws splitting open to brandish a hideously wide mouth of jagged teeth.

Carter's legs trembled as he analyzed the army of the dead.

Zombie Glutton, Uncommon.
Zombie Lurker, Uncommon.
Zombie Brute, Uncommon.
Zombie Leader, Uncommon.

There were dozens of each mutated abomination and so many more regular zombies behind them. This was it, a chance to fight. His chance to show his power and prove to Skyline and Autem what he was capable of.

So why wasn't he moving?

Fear rumbled through his body along with the vibrations of the unsettling crooning of Sinatra that flooded his mind.

Every instinct told him to run.

To hide.

To survive.

Before he could act on the impulse, the last two of the cargo trailers burst open as two hulking forms emerged like a stripper from a cake. Both of the creatures were over two stories tall and covered in even more thick plates of bleached bone than the smaller ones. They were reminiscent of the armor of a medieval knight. A skull-like helmet protected their heads, each bearing a pair of horns that reached toward the sky. Standing at their full height, the shadows of the two behemoths stretched across the pavement to fall on the guardians that stood in their path.

Carter choked on his fear as he analyzed each of the undead titans.

Zombie Destroyer, Rare.

His eyes bulged as the horde marched forward in pace with the swell of Sinatra's orchestra. Carter shrank away from the fight, panic filling his mind. Skyline had seemed so powerful. Powerful enough to make the world bow down to it, but yet, someone out there was still willing to fight back.

Someone… had declared war.

Fighting consumed the base as the shadowy figure that he had seen earlier drifted through the chaos and flames. A tattered hood covered their face in a shroud of darkness like an all-consuming void. The figure held their arms out wide as they revealed in the destruction that they had wrought.

Carter ran.

It was too much.

He wasn't ready.

Fire, magic, bullets, and blood raged through the night as he fled, leaving the destruction behind. Glancing back, he caught sight of Miller falling beneath the horde, his scream blended into the final crescendo of *My Way*.

The Chairman of the Board's voice reverberated across the battlefield.

I did it my way!

CHAPTER ONE

ONE
WEEK
EARLIER

Digby shoved through the cockpit door of a kestrel and leaned over Rebecca's shoulder to place both hands on the controls so that he could press his noseless face against the window.

"It's beautiful." He could hardly believe what he was seeing.

"Welcome to Sin City." Alex leaned back in his seat beside Rebecca as their craft flew over the land known as Las Vegas.

Digby had trouble focusing on any one point. The buildings were so strange and extravagant. It was like nothing he could have imagined. A pyramid sat next to the sphinx with a castle across the street.

A literal castle.

It was even larger than Hearst's Castle that he'd left behind just that morning. He'd been grieving for the loss of his previous home since they left after it had been attacked by Bancroft and the rest of his goons the night before.

Now, Digby didn't even care about the place.

Not when there was somewhere so much more impressive to

claim as his new domain. In fact, there were so many palaces on the strip below that he could have his pick of the litter. Digby thrust a claw at the cityscape.

"What's that green woman?"

"That's the Statue of Liberty." Rebecca shoved his hand away with her elbow. "It's a replica built as part of a hotel."

"Replica?" Digby flicked his eyes back to her.

"Yeah, the real one is across the country on the East Coast. The casino down there is themed after New York City where the original statue is."

"What is a casino?" Digby returned his gaze to the buildings below.

"It's a place people go to gamble." Alex leaned forward. "I've never had enough money to be able to go though. It didn't seem responsible when I could potentially lose my rent check in a matter of minutes."

"The house always wins," Rebecca added.

"What's that now?" Digby pulled away from the window to lean on the side of the cockpit door.

"Simple, Vegas is a place where almost anything can be won or purchased." She clicked her tongue. "Down there, anyone could make all their fantasies come true, but in the end, it's only temporary. You play the odds long enough and everyone loses eventually. It's inevitable."

"So is death," Digby smirked, "and I beat that."

"Yeah, but the point of Vegas is knowing when to quit. They don't call it Sin City for nothing. People overindulge and end up regretting it." She glanced back at him. "Think you have the willpower to walk away when you're coming out on top?"

"Oh certainly not." He shrugged. "Biting off more than I can chew is pretty much all I do."

"Maybe don't admit to that so easily." Alex eyed him sideways.

"What? I know my flaws."

Digby turned back into the passenger compartment and checked on Asher. The deceased raven sat, huddled up on one of the seats. She had certainly earned a break after all her hard work. Without her ability to command a horde, none of them would have been able to give Bancroft the slip the night before. After reaching the master's mutation path, the feathered zombie had taken over control of the dead during the battle after their previous master had sacrificed himself to create an opening for everyone else to make a break for it.

A memory of Rufus passed through Digby's mind. The decrepit, old zombie had used his final moments to protect the human survivors that had now become Digby's responsibility. The last thing he had said to him echoed back.

Against a force as powerful as Skyline, heroics won't do. That's why the world needs someone as sneaky and underhanded as you.

Everything had been placed on his sneaky and underhanded shoulders. Digby struggled not to collapse under the weight. Especially after last night when all he had done was hide. Literally.

Using Rebecca's illusion magic to convince Skyline's forces that himself and everyone else back at Hearst Castle had died, they had all snuck into an empty swimming pool. Once there, they just waited until the coast was clear beneath an illusion of water. After luring Bancroft, Skyline's commander, away with a half-baked declaration of war, Digby and the rest of the survivors had quietly skulked away.

The three soldiers, Mason, Parker, and Sax, had taken the rest of the humans with them to set up a temporary camp while Digby and his Heretics scouted out a new home. They had taken the sun goddess statue with them to keep the revenants at bay, just in case. Digby groaned at the thought of the horrid creatures.

Whatever Henwick had done to the curse that animated the dead, the revenants had nearly stolen the world from his zombified brethren. Now, a simple bite could do far more harm than simply pass on the curse. If it happened at night, or if the sun went down before a person stricken with the affliction succumbed, then they would become another of those vampiric monstrosities.

Unlike the dead, a revenant survived off blood alone, leaving behind more bodies to join their ranks. Not only that, but they were stronger, faster, more vicious, and… oh yes, they could heal most wounds. It wasn't all bad though. The creatures did at least have one weakness. The sun. Or more accurately, the shift in balance that daylight caused in the ambient mana that they absorbed. The result rendered them as weak as the common dead while the sun shined down.

Of course, Digby had a similar weakness. When the life essence contained in the sun's light flooded the land, it left less death essence for him to power his necromancy spells with. It was still possible to fill his mana pool, just slower and more frustrating. No amount of meditation was going to change that. About the only thing he could do was dig himself a grave and dive in beneath the soil. At least then he could access a mana balance containing a higher percentage of death essence.

Digby shook off his concern and ran a hand across Asher's wings, receiving a calm yet appreciative feeling across their bond. Her intelligence value was nearly as high as his had been when he'd first woken up in this new world, though she hadn't seemed to have reached the level of thought that he had gained back then. According to the Heretic Seed, everyone had a limit. She just might have reached hers already. It was alright, though. Digby didn't need Asher to become a genius. No, she was perfect just the way she was and there was still a chance she would learn how to make the most of the intelligence that she had.

Hell, he wasn't that smart either.

Digby had reached his limit as well, leaving his cognitive functions above average, but still falling short of anything close to genius. Now, if he wanted to improve his mind, he would actually have to learn things the old-fashioned way. Granted, he still intended to drop all of his extra points into intelligence anyway. It was the main stat for his class after all, and it gave him the greatest boost to his mana pool.

It seemed his problems were only piling up.

Grand work, you idiot. Just look at the mess you've made. Digby shook his head. He hadn't come close to being able to fight Bancroft on equal ground, so how was he supposed to go up against Henwick? The man had eight more centuries to grow stronger than he'd had. Not to mention Skyline and their mercenaries were only the tip of the iceberg. On top of that, Henwick was building some sort of new world order.

Autem.

The name of Henwick's empire sent a shudder down his necrotic spine. He still didn't know much about them. From what little he'd been able to learn from Easton, Rebecca's spy within Skyline, Autem was a mysterious organization that had hid in the shadows, waiting for Henwick to make his move. Now the bastard's trap had been sprung, Autem had swooped in to take over while the old world crumbled overnight.

How do I stand up against something like that?

Digby sunk into one of the seats that lined the passenger compartment of the kestrel and buried his face in his hands. It was too much. Even worse, he had committed himself to the fight. Like a fool, he had gone so far as to declare war. After that, the rest of the survivors seemed to think he was actually up to the task, despite the fact that he'd merely bumbled his way through the last few weeks.

How dumb could I be?

All he had wanted was for everyone to fall in line long enough so he could get them through the night alive. As to what came next, well, he hadn't thought that far ahead.

Too late now, I suppose.

He raised his head. What was done, was done. He had tried running away before, and that hadn't worked out any better. All that was left to do was to play the hand he'd been dealt. If he had to lead his people to war, then so be it. He just hoped he wouldn't get them all killed in the process.

There was going to be a lot of work to do, it seemed. Work that he couldn't do without finding new allies.

Digby picked Asher up and placed her in his lap before glancing to the translucent circle that floated at the edge of his vision. The shape snapped out, front and center, expanding as text filled it from top to bottom.

STATUS
Name: Digby Graves
Race: Zombie
Heretic Class: Necromancer

Mana: 253 / 253
Mana Composition: Pure
Current Level: 26 (4,860 Experience to next level.)

ATTRIBUTES
Constitution: 24
Defense: 30
Strength: 28
Dexterity: 28
Agility: 30
Intelligence: 44
Perception: 37
Will: 38

Not terrible, all things considered. Digby relaxed, letting the realization that he was stronger than he'd ever been bury some of his doubts. Sure, he wasn't quite super human yet, but he was above average on all fronts. Next, he brought up his list of available mutations finding just one remaining.

MUTATION PATH, RAVAGER, AVAILABLE MUTATIONS:

SHEEP'S CLOTHING
Description: Mimic a human appearance to lull your prey into a false sense of security.
Resource Requirements: 10 flesh

Digby let out a sigh as he checked the contents of his void.

AVAILABLE RESOURCES
Sinew: 20
Flesh: 14
Bone: 17
Viscera: 4
Heart: 22
Mind: 16

He certainly had enough resources to claim his final mutation, but as much as he wanted to have a nose again, he had been holding off on it. Considering the fact that Henwick, Bancroft, and the rest of Skyline knew him as a walking corpse, restoring his human appearance would serve as a helpful disguise when he needed it. Henwick might still recognize him, but he hadn't seen him alive in eight hundred years. The odds of the man remembering his face over the centuries were slim to none.

Actually, now that he thought about it, he had slipped away from Skyline back in California. It wouldn't do for someone to spot him in Vegas. With Skyline and Autem still sending squads out to find new recruits, it was entirely possible that his location might get back to them if he showed his deceased face out in the open. In fact, it was downright certain. Not to mention, if he was going to have any luck convincing potential allies to join his fight, then he was going to need to be able to approach them without sending them running for the hills at first sight.

That settles it.

Digby moved Asher back to the seat she had been resting in earlier and stood up to traverse the kestrel's compartment to where a reflective piece of plastic was mounted on one wall. He took in his deathly visage one last time.

A formation of bone formed what looked like a horned crown resting on his brow, though, in reality it was attached to his face as part of his bone armor. Looking at his right arm, more bone covered his wrist and hand to form a clawed gauntlet. It too, was fused to his deceased body. The skin of his face was a shade of ashen gray and locks of ghostly white hair covered his head down to his shoulders. Even his eyes were inhuman, with each of his venomous green pupils floating in a pool of milky white. Then there was his nose, or lack thereof.

For clothing, all he wore was a simple shirt and trousers beneath a long, black coat. One sleeve was rolled up to accommodate his gauntlet. The outfit had been looted from a shop the day before. The only part of it that wasn't was the pauldron on his shoulder, held in place by a series of leather straps. It wouldn't do much to protect him but, being a part of a fictional Goblin King's ensemble, it held the power to increase his influence over those with lower intelligence than his own. It also granted him an extra fifty points to his maximum mana.

Tearing his attention away from his reflection, Digby brought his mutation list up and claimed his final option. *Let's see what Sheep's Clothing can do.*

Regret filled his mind as discomfort surged through his entire body. He didn't feel pain the same as he had back when he was alive, but if he were to describe the feeling, it was as if his skin and fingernails were being shaved off little by little. A weird gurgle emanated from his mouth as he stood, spasming in the kestrel's passenger compartment. Digby craned his neck to one side to make eye contact with Asher, who simply cocked her head at him. Rebecca and Alex talked amongst themselves in the pilot's compartment, clearly unaware of his plight. That changed when he fell flat on his back with a hard thud.

"What the hell, Dig?" Rebecca looked back. "How many times do I have to tell you to stay seated in a moving aircraft?"

"Crap, are you okay?" Alex got up from his chair to rush to his side.

That was when the sensation of having his body peeled vanished.

"What happened?" Digby sat up with a start.

"Whoa." Alex stopped short, his mouth hanging agape. "What did you do?"

"Jesus." Rebecca stared at him from her seat before snapping her attention back to the horizon.

"I claimed my last mutation. The one that said it would make me look human." Digby slapped his left hand to his cheek to fondle his face. "Am I handsome?"

"Ahh…" Alex's mouth hung open.

"Thank all that is holy." Digby pinched a pointy bit sticking out from the center of his face. "I have a nose again!"

Wasting no time, he sprang back up and checked his reflection. He froze the instant his new visage stared back at him.

"Oh…"

He would have cried if he had been able.

It was just so beautiful.

"That's me." Digby pointed at his reflection. "That's what I looked like before I died. I mean, this is my face."

Sure, his skin was pale, his cheeks were gaunt, and his hair was still white, but it wasn't anywhere near as bad as not having a nose. He stared into his eyes, finding the cloudy layer gone, leaving behind two piercing emerald irises. They still held an unnatural quality but that only served to give him an air of mystery.

"What do you think?" Digby stepped into the middle of the passenger compartment and threw out both arms wide to present himself to his apprentice. That was when his armored gauntlet flew off his hand and landed in Alex's lap.

"Ah god!" His apprentice flung the bone glove away like it might bite him.

"Wait, what just happened?" Digby raised his right hand, finding five normal human digits where his claws had been. His eyes widened. "I have fingers again?" Reaching down to pick up his gauntlet, Digby shoved his hand back inside. The bone glove practically pulled his hand back in as if becoming a part of him again. It released him when he attempted to pull his wrist back out. "Oh, that is weird." The mutation had somehow converted his gauntlet into a removable piece of armor.

That was when he realized that the horned crown on his brow was no longer attached to his skull either. Lifting it up, the formation of bone slipped off his head, leaving his hair a bit disheveled but nothing more in terms of traces that it was there. Digby placed it down on one of the seats next to his gauntlet before marching around the aircraft with pride.

"Not so bad, if I do say so myself." He gave his fellow Heretics a twirl so they could take in his true form. "I'll admit that I may not turn many heads, but just look at this nose. I'd say I've practically rejoined the land of the living."

Rebecca glanced back. "I don't think any living person is that pale. You're like a member of the Addams Family."

"I don't know who they are." Digby glowered into the cockpit. "And you're not one to talk, Becky. You barely go outside. A little sun would do you well. Less people will think you've gone revenant."

Rebecca scoffed and tipped the kestrel to one side with a flick of her wrist.

"Hey!" Digby threw one foot on to the wall to stop himself from falling over. "Nice try, but that's not going to work anymore. My agility is high enough to handle your immature—" His words were cut off as the craft lurched in the opposite direction to throw him into the other wall.

"I keep telling you to remain seated while the kestrel is in flight," she added in a sing-song voice.

"Yes, yes, you have mentioned it." Digby folded his arms and remained seated. That was when he noticed a message at the bottom of his vision.

New mutation path available, Emissary.

Hmm, let's see then. Digby focused on the circle floating in the corner of his view and willed it to show him his options. A list of four mutations filled the shape.

MUTATION PATH, EMISSARY, AVAILABLE MUTATIONS:

APEX PREDATOR
Description: You may consume the corpses of life forms other than humans without harmful side effects. Consumed materials will be converted into usable resources.
Resource Requirements: 50 viscera

BODY CRAFT
Description: By consuming the corpses of life forms other than humans, you may gain a better understanding of biology and body structures. Once understood, you may use your gained knowledge to alter your physical body to adapt to any given situation. All alterations require the consumption of void resources. Your body will remain in whatever form you craft until you decide to alter it again.

Resource Requirements: 200 mind
Limitations: Once claimed, each use requires the consumption of void resources appropriate to the size and complexity
of the alteration.

OVERPOWER
Description: Similar to the Ravenous trait, this mutation will
remove all physical limitations, allowing for a sudden burst of
strength. All effects are temporary. This mutation may cause
damage to your body that will require mending.
Attribute Effects: strength + 100%
Duration: 5 seconds
Resource Requirements: 35 flesh, 50 bone, 35 sinew

MEND UNDEAD
Description: You may mend damage incurred by a member of
your horde as well as yourself, including limbs that have
been lost or severely damaged.
Resource Requirements: 50 mind, 100 heart.
Limitations: Once claimed, each use requires a variable
consumption of void resources and mana appropriate to
repair the amount of damage to the target.

Happy hunting... this might get weird.

Digby cringed at the requirements for each mutation. They
were higher than any he'd seen so far. If it weren't for the fact the
Revenants were technically human, he would have to kill hundreds
of people to reach all of them. Overpower was certainly a good
choice, and Apex Predator would open some options for future
feeding.

Mend would have been vital if he wasn't a Heretic on top of
being a zombie, since it gave him a way to heal the damage he
sustained. Though, considering he already had a spell that did the
same thing, he didn't see much value in the mutation other than
the fact that would allow him to repair his minions.

Looking over the list, Body Craft was the clear winner. Digby thought back to the Revenant bloodstalker that had torn him in half just days ago. The thing had sprouted wings and took to the skies. It was hard to see the downside to that. Wings would increase his mobility ten-fold and that was just one of the possibilities. Granted, if he was understanding things correctly, the mutation seemed to require that he take Apex Predator first to allow him to eat animals without side effects. Actually, he hadn't realized there were side effects to begin with. He simply hadn't tried to eat anything other than people and revenants. He didn't have an appetite for much else.

"Hey handsome," Rebecca called back from the pilot's seat, pulling him out of his thoughts. "I'm taking us down for a landing, so get ready to head out. There's a parking garage down there that I think I can slip into and keep the kestrel hidden. It's off the main strip, but I figure we can still get a read on the situation down there and find a place to stay for the night."

"Sure. I'd like to take in the area before choosing which palace will be our new home anyway. Might as well keep a low profile until we make a decision."

"Agreed. If it's clear enough down there, we can secure somewhere for our people to spend a few nights." She tilted the craft forward to bring it down.

Digby watched from his seat as the kestrel lowered into a stone structure similar to one he'd been in back in Seattle. The roof was built to contain a ramp that led to the floor below. It was just wide enough for Rebecca to slip the aircraft in. A mechanical sound came from the rotors on both sides as they adjusted their position to accommodate the opening. A grinding noise followed as the entire airship shook.

"Oh shit, sorry." Rebecca winced in her seat. "I bumped the ceiling. But, ah, I think we're good."

"Let's hope so." Digby gave her a sideways look as he stood up from his seat and tapped his shoulder. Asher responded by flapping to her perch and settling in.

Rebecca hopped up from the controls as soon as the kestrel's engines shut down. She grabbed a backpack containing a few necessities and slung it over her shoulder. Alex did the same as he hit the open button for the airship's ramp. He grabbed a machete on the way out, just in case.

Digby stepped toward the opening and picked up his staff from the floor where he'd left it when they boarded. The weapon had given him a new level of respect for his apprentice. Alex's value as an artificer was quickly becoming clear.

The staff wasn't anything fancy, just the handle of a shovel with a steel diamond shape attached at the top that Alex had crafted with the help of Parker back in the forge they had built together. The item may not have looked like much, but it had the effect of saving him twenty percent of the mana needed for any spell while holding it. Of course, he'd needed to implant thirty points of his total supply into the staff through Alex's imbue spell to create the enchantment, but the benefit had already proved worth the sacrifice.

"When we get a new forge set up, I'll make you a new staff." Alex gestured to the weapon. "We can destroy that one to get your donated mana back and imbue a new one with the same enchantment. I'm not sure how long that one will hold up."

"Indeed." Digby ran a finger along the dark burns that covered the weapon's shaft. Skyline's commander had really done a number on it. "Who would have thought Bancroft was able to pull lightning from the sky?"

"At least we know what class he is." Rebecca stepped up to his side to peek out into the parking garage from the kestrel.

"Yes, I can't say I would have thought something like a tempestarii was even possible," Digby added as he crept down the ramp, hoping the parking structure was empty.

Alex followed behind, reaching into his pocket to produce an iron key that he'd found a few weeks ago. With his blood sense, Digby felt the artificer move a small amount of mana through his body as the key glowed.

"We should be good." Alex shoved the item back into his pocket. "Detection spell says there's nothing hostile around."

"Pity." Digby sulked. "I was hoping for at least a zombie or two. After losing the horde in the fight last night, I could really use a couple minions on my side. Hell, I'd even settle for a revenant, at

least then I could kill it and reanimate it for some temporary help."
He shrugged. "Oh well, I suppose I'll just have to settle for
Tavern." Digby pulled the large diamond from his pocket that
served as a storage vessel for his infernal spirit as he opened his
maw on the stone floor and cast Animate Skeleton.

The shadowy portal to his void appeared to reveal a small pool
of black fluid as a trickle of green energy drifted from the
gemstone in his hand. A moment later, a skull rose from the dark
puddle followed by a collection of bones. Each individual piece
snapped into position to form a skeleton, dripping with necrotic
blood.

"Need something, brah?" Tavern swept their empty eye sockets
around the parking garage as if trying to figure out where they
were.

"Please refer to me as Master or Lord, anything but brah."
Digby sighed and rubbed at the bridge of his new nose. The
infernal spirit had been formed by merging the lingering traces of
several deceased fraternity brothers into one. Digby didn't fully
understand why that made the skeleton so irritating and obsessed
with alcohol, but Rebecca and Alex seemed to find his frustration
amusing.

"Sure thing, boss man." The skeleton gave him a halfhearted
salute.

"Close enough." Digby cast Blood Forge to turn the remaining
black fluid that coated his bony minion into a glossy shell of additional protection, complete with spiked knuckles for offense. "Stay
here and keep an eye on our airship. There's bound to be survivors
out here somewhere and I don't want anyone touching my stuff."

The skeleton nodded and marched over to the kestrel to stand
guard.

"And if someone does show up, try not to kill them or make
any enemies. We are going to need able-bodied fighters on our side
if we're going to have a chance against Henwick, and it won't do
to start any fights with anyone else."

Satisfied with his orders, Digby checked his mana before
leaving.

He made a note to use his magic sparingly. During the day, it would take twice as long to absorb more, and it never hurt to be cautious. With nothing left to do there, Digby tapped his staff on the floor and started for the nearest stairwell, leaving his crown and gauntlet behind.

"Let us be off then. We have no shortage of things to do."

Rebecca glanced back at the kestrel. "Everybody remember where we parked."

Alex chuckled at her comment, though Digby wasn't sure why it was funny. He decided not to ask.

From there, they went straight for the nearest casino, a place called the Never Say Die. The sign bore the image of a lone die rolling across the letters. Digby found the name appropriate for the dead world they inhabited. Before heading inside, he sent Asher off to survey the area and to let him know if any threats were approaching. With her in the air, he strolled through the doors of the casino. His enthusiasm waned as soon as he entered the building.

"Is it me, or is this a bit of a dump?" He twirled a finger in the air to indicate their surroundings.

Alex let his machete hang limp at his side. "Yeah, compared to the places on the main strip, this is kinda—"

"Shitty." Rebecca finished his sentence as she strode past a row of strange machines. "But if we want to keep a low profile, it's as good a place as any."

Alex followed. "We should raid the hotel's shop while we're here."

"Yes, yes, a little looting always serves to brighten the mood." Digby nodded as he wandered into the building.

The casino floor was wide with several rows of the same boxy machines. Digby pulled down on a lever sticking out from one side, feeling disappointed when nothing happened. From what he could tell, it was some sort of gambling device. The rest of the place was less interesting, just a guest check in area next to a small shop containing trinkets and the like.

"Do you think we should disguise ourselves or something?" Alex drew his attention away from their surroundings as he tugged on a lock of his hair.

"What's that now?" Digby cocked his head to the side.

"You know, now that you look different. It might be a good idea for us to do the same." He shrugged. "I'm not going to grow a new nose or anything, but maybe some hair dye or something would help keep us under the radar."

"I was thinking that too." Rebecca pointed to a tiny black dome embedded in the ceiling. "With the power grid down and the internet all screwed up, we don't have to worry about facial recognition, but Skyline must have my photo on file. So it makes sense to do what we can. Besides, Alex is getting a little shaggy." She finished her statement by placing a hand to the artificer's head and messing up his hair.

Alex sighed, looking disheveled. "You're not wrong. It's been at least two months since I've had a haircut."

"Want me to give you a trim?" Rebecca offered. "I cut my own hair for years while I was locked up in my apartment. I can probably manage yours."

"Sure." Alex nodded and headed for the stairs that lead to the guest rooms.

"Great, we'll get settled in, then we'll stop by the nearest store and pick up some scissors and dye." Rebecca followed close behind, leaving Digby alone on the casino floor as they disappeared into the stairwell.

Approaching a table covered in worn green felt, he picked up a small disc that resembled a coin. The words Never Say Die were printed along one edge with, Las Vegas, Nevada, on the other.

"So this is Sin City?"

He closed his fingers around the disk.

"Let's hope we come out on top."

CHAPTER TWO

Digby pulled on a few more levers sticking out of the boxy machines that filled the casino's main floor while he waited for Rebecca and Alex to break into a couple of the rooms upstairs. A sign above the gambling devices labeled them as dollar slots. None of them were currently functioning but after kicking one over and impaling it with a blood spike, he was able to figure out how it worked.

"How boring…" Digby frowned, finding few gambling options besides the basic machines.

He'd enjoyed the games they had played back in the cafe they had spent the night in during their time in California. It was a pity to discover that most of what the establishment offered were nothing more than simple games of chance that lacked any form of skill or strategy.

Eventually, he lost interest in the machines and headed off toward a bar that sat off to one side of the room. Grabbing a few bottles of cheap alcohol would go a long way in terms of keeping Tavern happy. Of course, his minion couldn't disobey an order regardless of their wants, but it seemed like good business to keep the infernal spirit content. There may come a time where he needed the skeleton's absolute loyalty and bringing them a gift every now and then would be worth it. Granted, Tavern would only dump whatever Digby gave them on the floor when they tried to pour it down their nonexistent throat.

"That's odd." Digby slowed to a stop as he reached the bar, finding most of the bottles missing. Clearly someone had already passed through and claimed the majority of what there was to offer, leaving nothing but bottom shelf swill. Looking around, he noticed another strange detail.

There were no corpses.

With the curse spreading through the world, it was highly unlikely that there would be no bodies in the building. Sweeping his eyes across the room, he spotted signs of a struggle through the space. A tipped over table here, a spatter of dried blood there. Based on the evidence left behind, it was definitely strange that there were no corpses. It was as if someone had already removed them.

"Definitely odd indeed." Digby frowned as he inhaled a whiff of a strange, unnatural scent that seemed to cling to the space. It was like it had somehow permeated the building's yellowed walls. Then again, his nose may have looked better, but his sense of smell was still a bit out of tune. It may have just been him.

"It's smoke." Rebecca walked casually up to the bar while tying her hair back.

"What?" Digby cocked his head to the side.

"That's what you're smelling. It's cigarette smoke." She nodded. "It was illegal to smoke inside a building throughout most of this country but the casinos here still allowed it on the main floor."

"Really? It doesn't smell right, even with my distorted senses." He furrowed his brow. "People smoked back in my day but I don't remember the scent being so acrid."

"Yeah, there's a lot more chemicals involved now." She shrugged and followed. "I remember the smoke bothering my eyes last time I was here."

"You've been here before?" Digby arched an eyebrow at her.

"Yeah." She hopped onto one of the stools that sat in front of the counter. "It was a long time ago, back before my parents sold me off to Skyline. I lived in Arizona and they took me here when I was a kid."

"Is Sin City really the place to bring children?" Digby eyed her sideways.

"Probably not. But we didn't have a lot of money and it was in driving distance, so, you know, we made do." She looked to the floor before adding, "Parts of the trip were fun."

Digby didn't press the subject further, though it was starting to make sense why she chose the city as their destination. After being imprisoned by Skyline for a decade, she probably wanted to try to reclaim something from the past that she'd lost. The moment was interrupted when Alex hopped down the stairs that led to the guest rooms.

The artificer had changed into another floral shirt and pants. Digby suppressed an eye roll, wondering how many of those ugly garments his apprentice had left at this point.

"We ready to go?" Alex cast his detection spell on the key he carried and shoved it in his pocket so he would feel it grow cold if a threat approached.

"Indeed." Digby grabbed his staff and led his Heretics out into the street.

Once outside, he caught a glimpse of Asher flying overhead. A sense of freedom drifted across their bond. She must have been feeling a little trapped being cooped up in the kestrel all morning. He sent a supportive thought back, letting her know it was alright to enjoy herself. He got a warm, *thank you*, in return.

Much like the casino, the street outside was quiet. There were a few wrecked vehicles littering the area, but nothing so bad that it would block the roads or completely hinder travel. Digby kept his eye peeled for corpses, hoping he might pick up a new minion. According to Alex's key, there were a few threats in the distance, but they weren't anything significant enough to worry. Though, his key did grow cooler as they moved further down the street.

After fifteen minutes of walking, they came to an apothecary that could possibly hold what they needed. Unfortunately, they found the place mostly empty.

"Looks like someone beat us to the punch here." Digby kicked at a crushed bag of potato crisps.

"There's still a few things left." Alex collected a small assortment of canned food that hadn't been looted as of yet.

"It might actually be a good sign that the place has been cleaned out." Rebecca picked up a plastic basket from a pile near the door and wandered over to where the personal grooming products were stored.

"How so?" Digby followed her.

"It would have taken a decent crew to loot this whole place, meaning that there may be enough survivors in the area to stand up to Skyline. If we explain things clearly, they might help, considering it's only a matter of time before Henwick's new empire shows up looking to order them around like they did to us back in California."

"Yes, and time is a factor." Digby tapped his staff on the floor. "If we can recruit a group of organized survivors, then we might be able to stand a worthwhile offense before Skyline and Autem grow any stronger."

Rebecca grabbed a plastic basket from the apothecary's front counter and returned to the shelves. "My guess is that whoever looted this place is the same group that moved the bodies from the casino."

"Noticed that too, huh?" Digby eyed her.

"Yeah, if anything, that's a good sign too." She scavenged a few bottles of shampoo that had been left behind. "If they cared enough to remove the corpses, then they have an intent to reclaim and protect the area."

"Sure, but that might also mean they won't take kindly to our lot showing up and invading their territory." Digby poked at a few products that had been left on the shelves.

"True, we'll just have to be careful not to make any enemies." She shot Digby an accusatory look.

"What?" He feigned innocence. "I assure you that I will be on my absolute best behavior."

"I'm sure," she added in a tone dripping with sarcasm. Her point made, she returned to scavenging. "At least they didn't take any of the hair color products. I guess there's not much need for them in the apocalypse." She held a box with a picture of a blonde woman on the front up to her head. "What do you think?"

"Lovely," Digby commented through a layer of sarcasm, not caring what color she picked.

"You could always update your look too." She bent down to grab a jar from the bottom and tossed it up to him. "I think we've found your color."

"No thank you." He caught it to find it full of a thick pink liquid before tossing the container over his shoulder.

"Suit yourself." She shrugged before walking into one of the other aisles. She stopped short a second later and ducked down to grab a couple items that had been knocked off the shelves and left behind. "Oh, thank god."

"And, what are those?" Digby furrowed his brow.

"Necessities." She smirked. "Can't survive the apocalypse without tampons and condoms."

"I don't know what those are." Digby narrowed his eyes at her.

"Yeah, that's not surprising." She dropped the boxes in the basket she carried and headed toward the front of the store where Alex sat on a counter opening a can of stew.

"Want some?" He peeled the lid off. "I have beef stew and, ah..." He looked at the other label. "Beans."

"Ugh, cold stew and beans. No thanks." Rebecca turned her nose up at the offer despite the fact that she was probably starving, not having eaten since early that morning.

"Think again." Alex placed the can down on the counter and held his hand next to it as Digby sensed mana flowing through his blood. The artificer took his hand away as the contents of the can began to bubble. He tore off the lid of the can of beans as well. "Just let that sit for a minute, then stir it good."

"Is that the cooking spell you discovered back in California?" Digby held his hand close to the can, feeling the warmth radiating from its surface.

"That is shockingly useful," Rebecca added. "How did you learn it?"

Alex tore open a package of plastic cutlery and shoved a spoon onto the open can before casting the same spell on the other. "I did all the cooking for us the whole time we were hiding out up north and continued to help out once we picked up more people. Eventually, the Skill Link threw me a bone, I guess. I've ranked the spell up already too, which doubled its max temperature. It's not the fastest ability, but I can get something up to around six hundred degrees if I keep it going. Warming food is pretty quick though."

"Really, now?" Digby nodded and considered the possibilities. "Think you could warm a corpse to about body temperature?"

"Gross, Dig." Rebecca, snatched the can of stew off the counter and stirred the contents before shoveling a spoonful in her mouth in direct contradiction to her previous disgust.

"What? Even zombies enjoy a warm meal every now and again." Digby gave her his most innocent shrug. "I know it's easier to shove corpses directly into my maw, but sometimes it's nice to eat the old-fashioned way."

"Just as long as I don't have to share a table with you." Alex started in on the beans. "You're not exactly a pleasant eater when you're gnawing on a severed limb."

"Plus you talk with your mouth full," Rebecca added, whilst also talking with her mouth full.

"Would either of you like to lodge any other complaints while we're on the subject?" Digby glowered at them both.

"Oh shit, hey!" Alex hopped off the counter he was sitting on and set his can of beans down before shoving his hand in his pocket. At the same time, a single word flowed across the bond that Digby shared with Asher.

Threat.

"Something's coming." Alex pulled the iron key he carried from his pocket. "My enchantment just went cold." His statement was immediately followed by the sound of screeching coming from down the street.

"Something's afoot." Digby ducked low and made his way around the counter so he could look out the window behind it. "Rebecca, can you—"

"I'm on it." The illusionist was casting a concealment spell before he had even finished his sentence. "Stay close together and don't make any sudden movements or noise. The spell won't work if you draw too much attention. That means no shouting, Dig."

"Oh, I hardly ever—"

"Shhhhh." She brought a finger to her lips. "At least try to whisper."

"Fine, fine." Digby groaned and turned back to the window as a pale, screeching form dashed past it.

Active Revenant Lightwalker, Uncommon, Hostile.

"Looks like I don't need my apprentice to warm my food for me, after all." Digby chuckled. "A live meal just showed up right at our door."

Before he had a chance to pursue the creature, a gunshot rang out from the direction it had come from. The bullet slammed into the revenant's back, throwing it off balance as a group of men rushed into the street in front of the store where Digby and his Heretics watched from. A second bullet struck the creature in the leg, slowing it down as it struggled to regenerate the wound.

"Hold your fire!" one of the men yelled.

He was black and wore a leather jacket underneath a simple bulletproof vest, with a plain pair of denim trousers. In his arms, he carried a rifle. Approaching the revenant, he raised his weapon. The other men spread out to surround the creature. Digby counted six of them, each wearing a durable jacket and chest protector. Taking in their appearance, one detail stuck out. Each of the men had a playing card stuck to their chest armor some-where. Digby eyed the leader of the group, noting a two of clubs tucked into a strap.

Armored Human, Uncommon, Neutral.

Digby analyzed the rest of the group to make sure none of them were guardians. He'd made the mistake of not checking potential threats before and ended up regretting it. It was a mistake he'd decided not to make again. He relaxed when the Heretic Seed labeled them all the same.

"At least they aren't with Skyline." He leaned closer to the window.

"They look well-equipped though." Rebecca peeked out while still eating stew from the can in her hands. "Their gear is mismatched but it's all quality stuff. Some of it is military grade and the rest looks like law enforcement."

"They must have scavenged it over the last month." Alex stepped to Digby's other side and shoved a spoonful of beans in his mouth as if the scene outside was nothing more than dinner theater.

Glad they're both getting used to this world, Digby commented to himself sarcastically as they ate quietly and watched the situation unfold.

"Fire!" The man with the two of clubs on his chest called out.

Strangely, only two of the men obeyed, firing one bullet each. It was if the order had only applied to them, while the rest of the group was meant to stand by with their rifles trained on the revenant just in case.

"Let it heal." The group's leader held up a hand.

Interesting. Digby raised both eyebrows in approval of their tactics. The revenant lightwalker differed from the rest because it lacked the weakness to sunlight like the others, making it one of the most dangerous types to a regular person. Despite that, the group controlled the situation. In fact, it looked like they were trying to force the creature to exhaust its mana supply. They probably weren't aware that was what they were doing, but they must have fought enough of the monsters to know that their healing ability would only last so long when sustaining continuous damage. On top of that, they were also keeping their distance, clearly aware of the threat that a bite could present, even during the day. Without an enchanter, there would be no way to cleanse their status if any of them were to be cursed.

"Fire!" The group's leader repeated as the same two men shot again, each only expending one bullet as if conserving ammunition.

The revenant screeched in protest, but they kept it down in

place. A moment later, its movements began to slow and its wounds ceased their regeneration.

"That's it. Take it down." The man in charge called out as one of the group fired a single bullet through the revenant's eye.

"How effective." Digby nodded at their capabilities.

"Yeah, that was practically surgical." Rebecca finished off her can of stew. "Whoever they are, they've definitely learned how to handle themselves."

"Think we should go out and make friends?" Alex asked before eating another spoonful of beans.

"Let us not put the cart before the horse." Digby shook his head before turning to Rebecca. "Can you keep us hidden if we move?"

"Yeah, what are you suggesting?"

"We follow them and try to gauge if they are possible allies." Digby tilted his staff back and forth. "They are currently listed as neutral, and that could go either way. We should try to get an idea of who they are and if there are more of them around. Once we have a better handle on things, I'll make contact." He sent a quick thought to Asher to tell her to keep watch from above just in case there were more men in the area that they hadn't seen.

"Sounds good." Rebecca headed for the door. "Just stay close to me and be quiet. We should be fine as long as we keep our distance and don't draw their attention."

"I remember." Digby followed her to the door. "No shouting."

Alex shoveled a few more rapid spoonfuls of beans into his mouth before setting his can down and joining them.

"I'm glad I don't have to share a room with you tonight." Rebecca eyed him as he struggled to swallow a mouthful of beans.

He choked it down. "I don't care, I was starving."

Digby shook his head at them both before peeking out the door. The men outside made sure the revenant was dead before heading back in the direction they had come from. Digby glanced back to Rebecca to make sure her spell was still in place to conceal them. She answered back with a nod and he skulked out the door, being careful not to make a sound.

From there they kept their distance, following the group as they made their way down the quiet street. Rebecca made sure to refresh her concealment spell whenever enough time had passed for her to absorb enough mana to get back to full. Digby couldn't help but feel grateful for the ability and the fact that it lasted long enough for the delay in mana absorption to pass before it wore off. As an added bonus, Rebecca gained a new rank to the spell in the process.

Taking a few turns here and there, they reached a wide-open area with a few more hotels and casinos, nowhere as large or as grand as the buildings that lined the main strip that Digby had seen on his flight into the city, but there were still a few interesting details and a few long stretches of grass.

Digby made a note of the area, as access to bare earth could be used for his burial spell in a pinch. It was a strong attack spell, as well as a good way to replenish his mana supply since he absorbed more essence while resting in the comfort of a grave.

Ahead of them, the men continued their progress through the city. Other than some simple chatter, they seemed to be well disciplined. They walked in formation and kept their rifles at the ready as they moved.

"They must patrol the area regularly," Rebecca whispered from the sidewalk where they observed the group from the shadows fifty feet away.

"That's probably why there's so few threats around. I shudder to think how vigilant they must have been to have done so much in only a month," Digby added as he stepped up behind her.

"There must be more patrols like this one." Alex slipped around a wrecked vehicle that had driven straight into one of the buildings. "No way six guys cleaned out this whole area."

"Agreed." Digby nodded. "Plus, they left the revenant's corpse behind. Not that I'm complaining, since I could use the resources. But it does raise the question: if they aren't the ones moving the bodies, then who is?"

"They must have another team or something that's in charge of clean up." Rebecca stopped for a moment to refresh her concealment spell. "If that's the case, then they might have a lot more people. I'm glad I kept the kestrel camouflage when we arrived. They might have seen us coming otherwise."

"Wait." Digby held up a hand as the group they were following did the same, stopping in front of one of the smaller hotels on the street to have a discussion. "I wish I could hear what they're saying."

"Let me." Rebecca stepped forward and crouched behind an abandoned car. She closed her eyes for a moment before speaking again. "They're going to check in on someone inside that building. There's a group of survivors in there."

Digby ducked down beside her. "How do you know——"

"What they're saying?" She finished his question for him. "I'm an illusionist, so my main stat is perception. It was already high to begin with, probably because I started out in surveillance. But I've been putting most of my additional points into it as well. It's had an impact on my senses."

Digby arched an eyebrow as he willed the Heretic Seed to display Rebecca's status.

STATUS
Name: Rebecca Alvarez
Race: Human
Heretic Class: Illusionist
Mana: 294 / 294
Mana Composition: Balanced
Current Level: 26 (650 Experience to next level.)

ATTRIBUTES
Constitution: 38
Defense: 33
Strength: 32
Dexterity: 36
Agility: 33
Intelligence: 38
Perception: 54
Will: 34

"Impressive." Digby pumped his eyebrows in approval. "So you can hear them from this far away?"

"So you're like a dog then?" Alex scooted up behind them.

"My senses aren't quite that sharp yet, but you're partially right." She nodded. "I hear most things and my sense of smell is much stronger. Hence my reluctance to be around you after a can of beans. I've gotten used to foul odors mostly from hanging around this guy." She hooked a thumb at Digby. "But still, your farts aren't something I want filling my sensitive nose."

"What do you mean being around me has gotten you used to foul odors?" Digby tried to smell himself, only finding the same earthy aroma that he'd gotten used to.

"Dig, you're a corpse." She stared at him blankly. "You don't smell like flowers."

Digby scoffed. "Well, I'm certainly no worse than Alex's flatulence."

"Hey."

Rebecca leaned her head from side to side. "Actually, you do smell a little better since taking that Sheep's Clothing mutation."

Digby tried to smell himself again. "Really? That's good to—"

"Crap, guys, they're leaving." Alex interrupted their banter by thrusting a finger at the group as they entered the building.

"I say we follow them." Digby stood up and started toward the hotel's entrance.

"Hold up." Rebecca stopped him. "We can follow them, that's fine. But we will need to be a little more careful. It's harder to keep people hidden in an enclosed space since there's less distance. If even one of them notices us, the spell will unravel. So we'll have to try to make use of natural cover and move slowly."

"Got it. Stealth mode." Alex led the way to the door, crouching as he walked.

"Indeed." Digby made sure to hold his staff so that it wouldn't drag on the ground and followed his apprentice whilst also crouching for added concealment.

"You two are so gonna get us caught." Rebecca refreshed her spell and continued on toward the entrance.

Digby pried the door open with the tips on his fingernails,

wishing he had put his clawed gauntlet back on before leaving the kestrel. Then again, if he intended to introduce himself to a group of ordinary humans with the aim of recruiting them to his war, it would probably be better to leave his more monstrous features out of the conversation.

Once inside, Digby found the men talking to a pair of less heavily armed survivors. Instead of rifles, they each carried an axe. They must have been guarding the casino's entrance. Digby led his Heretics as they snuck inside to eavesdrop on the group as they spoke to the guards.

"We're here to see Elenore. Mr. Rivers wants an update." The leader of the group with the two of clubs on his chest let his rifle hang off his shoulder as if the building was considered safe.

"Ah, okay, I'll let Ms. Sharp know you're, um, here." One of the men carrying an axe fumbled with a walkie-talkie on his belt before bringing it to his mouth and thumbing the button. "Hey, this is the front door. We have a patrol from the strip here looking for Ms. Sharp." The radio chirped back along with a voice that acknowledged the request. The person with the axe waved the group in. "Just head to the bar, she'll meet you there."

"Thanks." The leader of the group took a few steps before turning back. "Oh, we killed a shrieker a few streets over, make sure you guys send out a clean-up crew before it attacks zeds or something."

"Oh, okay. We'll get to it." The guard nodded as the group continued on their way.

Interesting. That explained where the bodies are going. The armed groups must protect the area while the lesser equipped survivors handle the rest. Digby furrowed his brow. It certainly explained something but it didn't tell him enough about their leadership dynamic to know if they would be sympathetic enough to his fight to help. He shook off the concern as the group of armed men continued further into the casino.

Digby glanced back to Rebecca to make sure her spell was stable enough to pass in front of the two guards. She shooed him forward with a sense of urgency, telling him to move before they lost sight of the others. He slipped by while the guard's backs were turned just in case.

Further in, Digby surveyed the interior of the building. Similar to the Never Say Die, the casino-hotel combination had clearly aged over time, though it had been maintained a fair bit better. The main floor was full of the same slot machines, providing Digby and his Heretics with no shortage of places to hide. Together they skulked down a row of the boxy machines while keeping the group of armed men in sight as they traveled through a maze of twists and turns. It was as if the place had been designed to be confusing so that gamblers would have a hard time finding their way around without running into more ways to lose their money.

I'm starting to see what Becky meant when she called this place Sin City.

Finally, after doubling back once when even the group they were following got lost, they found their way to the center of the hotel. Digby stopped short as the maze of slot machines opened up into an atrium. It must have been two dozen stories tall. Windows lined the walls on all four sides. He took a second to stare up at the space, realizing that it was the hotel's guest rooms looking down on him. The floor of the atrium was just as interesting. Instead of more gambling machines, trees and stone pathways filled the space, surrounding the guest check in area. A circular bar sat at the atrium's center.

Digby made his way across the room, using the trees for cover as he followed the group of armed men. Reaching the middle, Rebecca crouched behind the counter of the bar while the leader of the group sat down on the other side of their circular counter. Digby and Alex ducked down beside her so they could peek over at the group without risking too much attention.

A walkway wrapped around the first few floors that made up the atrium. Digby noticed a few people moving back and forth with urgency, as if the visit from the armed group had not been expected.

After a few minutes, the man wearing the two of clubs got impatient, standing back up and wandering toward a strange stairway that led up to the second floor. Digby hadn't seen a set of steps like it before. They were black and seemed to fit together in a strange pattern. The stairway was bracketed on both sides with a thick barrier topped with a black rubber railing that curled down toward the floor at the bottom. The design was odd, as if there was a function that he was missing.

Maybe it is supposed to move? Digby arched an eyebrow as he put two and two together. A part of him found it hard to believe that the people of the modern world have been so lazy to require stairs that did the walking for them. Eventually, his judgmental thoughts were interrupted when the leader of the armed group started shouting.

"Elenore!" The man held both hands to the sides of his mouth as he shouted up the stairs. "We don't have all day!"

"Yeah, I hear you!" an annoyed voice answered from above as a statuesque woman appeared at the top of the steps, wearing a simple pair of trousers and a sleeveless shirt. A pair of thick glasses sat on her nose.

Human, Common, Neutral.

"What do you want, Munch?" She leaned on the rubber railing to her side as she stared down at the playing card tucked under a strap on the man's chest armor. "Looks like Rivers has himself a new Deuce of clubs. What happened to the old one?"

"Expired," the man answered back up.

"That's sad, I was starting to like him." She tilted her head to one side before locking eyes with the man below her. "So what brings you around our humble establishment, new Deuce?"

"Munch is fine, and you know why we're here," he called back up.

"Nah, I like Deuce better. And your take is right there on the bar." She folded her arms in a defiant manner. "Feel free to pack it up and see yourselves out."

Digby flicked his eyes to a pair of boxes full of canned goods sitting on the counter. He ducked as Deuce looked in his direction.

"That's it?" Deuce glanced back up to Elenore standing at the top of the stairs. Digby could feel the tension rise in the room as a few survivors on the second floor watched the scene unfold below. Something about it felt like the two had a history of some kind.

Elenore gave an exaggerated shrug. "What do you want from us? This area only has so many stores to scavenge. That right there is twenty percent of what we've found since the last time Mr. Rivers sent his goons over here. If you want more, you're going to have to clear more of the city so my people can scavenge safely."

Deuce's jaw tightened. "Rivers isn't going to like that answer."

"Well, I don't know what to tell him then." Elenore held out both hands empty. "My people need to eat too."

"Fine." Deuce blew out a sigh. "But, you're sure that's all you have to send?"

"Yup." Her tone came off as antagonistic.

He groaned. "Do you mind if I take a look around upstairs then?"

"I do." She leaned to one side making a point of shifting her hips so the handle of a revolver was visible sticking out of the back of her pants.

Digby froze, realizing that he might have snuck his way into a gunfight without realizing it. Rebecca and Alex held completely still as silence fell across the room. Then, as if on cue, a quiet rumbling came from Digby's side. Slowly, he turned to his apprentice, finding the artificer's face drained of all color.

"Don't you dare." Rebecca mouthed the words at him as his stomach rumbled again.

He winced before mouthing an obvious response back. "The beans aren't sitting well."

"Oh really? You think?" Digby rolled his eyes, entirely unsurprised at the timing.

Fortunately, the armed group on the other side of the bar hadn't noticed anything. Digby just hoped Alex could hold whatever was brewing in his gut long enough for them to get somewhere safe. The tension in the room ramped up as the rest of the men shifted their weapons from their shoulders to their hands. That was when Deuce finally diffused the situation.

"Okay, look, I get it." He reached into a pouch and retrieved a flask. "Why don't you come down here and let me treat you to a drink? There's no reason why we have to be so adversarial here. We're all just trying to get by."

"You're still not going upstairs." She remained where she was.

"Sure, whatever." He beckoned for her to join him. "Just come down here and talk to me."

A few more tense seconds passed before she dropped her hands to her sides and begrudgingly stepped down the stairs. "Fine, but you wouldn't have to treat me to a drink if you guys hadn't taken all of our booze."

"That's fair." He reached over the counter and grabbed a glass.

"So you're trying to be the good cop then, is that it?" She dropped onto one of the stools making a point of leaving an open seat between them as a buffer.

"No." He poured her a glass of brown liquid. "I just want everyone to get what they need without conflict."

"That's a tough job when the needs of some people seem to be more important than others." She leaned on the counter, looking unimpressed.

"I realized that, but sometimes things just are what they are." He gave her a sympathetic shrug and took a sip from his flask. "I realize that your people need food and I would love to walk out of here with just these two boxes. But the fact is that Mr. Rivers is the reason why there are so few shriekers or zeds wandering around out there. It's also a fact that he isn't as understanding as I am about your people's needs, and there's nothing stopping him from sending his high-cards out here to do what I couldn't."

"And what makes you think we're afraid of his high-cards?" She tipped back a mouthful from her glass.

"You really think that's enough?" He gestured to the revolver sticking out of her pants. "'Cause it's not. I'll be honest here. You probably have a few more handguns upstairs, maybe even a rifle or two, but I assure you, it will never be enough. Seriously, you literally wouldn't believe the amount of ordinance Rivers has at his disposal."

"So how about you just head back to the strip and tell your boss that we don't have anything more to give? If you really do understand where we're coming from, then you shouldn't have a problem backing us up every now and again." Elenore locked eyes with him.

"I would if I could, but there is a reason the previous Deuce expired. Rivers isn't a man you get to say no to." He sighed, sounding just as trapped as the woman he shared a drink with. "Look, why don't you just grab a couple more boxes of supplies and we'll just keep it quiet that you tried to pull a fast one here? No reason why things need to get ugly."

"And what if I don't?" She remained defiant.

"Then I can't guarantee the safety of the people here." His face grew serious as he glanced up to the balcony above, where a few of the other survivors watched the exchange. "Need I remind you that supplies aren't the only thing Rivers is interested in. If you truly can't part with a few boxes of canned goods, then sending over a few recruits would do as well."

"No chance in hell," she snapped back.

"I know, I know." He held up both hands. "I don't like that option either, but one way or another, Rivers will end up getting what he wants. Neither of us can change that."

"Fine." Elenore gestured to one of the people upstairs who ran off out of sight only to return a moment later with another two boxes of food.

"Thank you." Deuce started going through them.

Digby grimaced, understanding all too well what was going on. Whoever this Rivers person was, he must have been extorting the survivors under his group's protection. It was a story as old as time. The strong taking advantage of the weak. He had certainly conned a fair number of people out of their possessions back in his day, but this was enough to turn his deceased stomach.

Then again, it sounded like this Rivers fellow had some power on his side. It would be unwise for Digby to make an enemy of him. Starting a second war on top of the one he'd already declared was a bad plan. He wasn't an expert on strategy but he knew enough to understand that fighting on two fronts was a good way to end up getting everyone killed. Besides, he didn't have time to start another conflict.

Fortunately, this woman at least seemed willing to stand up to protect her people. She might even be willing to stand up against Henwick. It was only a matter of time before Autem or Skyline showed up in Vegas looking to continue their conquest, so the survivors there would end up having to fight eventually anyway.

Digby began rehearsing what he could say to the woman that might convince her to throw in with his Heretics. His train of thought was interrupted a moment later by another angry sounding rumble emanating from his apprentice's stomach. Digby flicked his eye to Alex as the artificer gritted his teeth.

Rebecca mouthed a threat in his direction. "I am so going to kill you if you do what I think you're going to do."

Digby cringed, expecting the inevitable. Then, Alex simply relaxed as if the urgency had passed. Digby relaxed as well, grateful that the artificer had been able to control his bodily functions. From the look on his face a moment before, an earth-shattering rear trumpet was inevitable. That was when Alex's eyes looked to Rebecca.

"I am so sorry." He placed his hands together as if asking for forgiveness just as a wave of concentrated death hit them.

Digby scrunched his new nose in horror. It was like hell itself had opened up to release centuries of brimstone. He glanced back to Rebecca as disgust washed across her face. Tears filled her eyes as she clenched both fists until her knuckles turned white.

Oh no. Panic surged through Digby's mind as he realized that the distraction might disrupt the illusionist enough to cancel her concealment spell. He placed a hand on Rebecca's shoulder to try to steal her back to the task at hand. He mouthed a few silent words of support. "It will pass, just hold yourself together."

"How is it this bad?" She pulled the collar of her shirt up over her nose and waited. A moment letter she pulled it back down. "Why won't it go away?"

"Because I'm still doing it." Alex mouthed back.

"Good lord, what is wrong with you?" Digby nearly slapped him.

"I know, I'm sorry. I'm trying." The artificer shut his eyes again just as the armed man at the other side of the bar finished looking through the boxes of supplies.

Deuce looked up abruptly. "What's that smell?"

"Don't look at me." Elenore leveled an accusatory stare at him.

"Well, it wasn't me." He turned to look behind him to see if anyone was nearby.

"You sure? You could at least be honest." She didn't let him off the hook.

"Hey, right back at you." Deuce grabbed one of the boxes and gestured for his group to come get the rest.

"Christ, what died over here?" One gasped for air as he picked up some supplies.

"Ask your leader here." Elenore headed back to the stairway to get away from the area of effect. "I think someone dropped a deuce in his pants."

"Hey, it wasn't me, damn it." The man's face turned red. "Fucking grow up, Ellen." He stormed off a second later, followed by the rest of his group.

Digby remained where he was, opting to stay and try to make contact with the survivors in the building once the armed men were gone. Rebecca stared daggers at Alex as the offense began to fade. Elenore watched the group of Deuce and his men leave before glancing back up at one of the people upstairs that was staring down at her.

"What? It wasn't me." She shrugged. "Not my fault that guy won't own up to it."

Digby shot Alex a final disappointed look before turning back to Rebecca, who was wiping tears from her eyes.

"Alright, here's the plan. I'm going to make my way into the bar and hide while you two use the concealment spell to slip behind those plants over there. I'll step out when no one is looking and make my presence known. Hopefully I can talk this woman and her people into taking our side. There seems to be a fire in them that might be willing to stand up against Autem."

Rebecca reached out to grab his arm. "Are you sure? What if they try to hurt you?"

"That's why you two will be hiding. If things don't go well, I want you both to cast your Barrier spells and help me fight my way out." He shrugged. "Just try not to kill anyone if you can help it."

"What if they won't join us?" Alex opened his eyes, apparently getting his situation under control.

"We'll have to leave empty handed." Digby shook his head. "I don't like the sound of that Rivers guy, or those high-card people that Deuce fellow mentioned, but they sound stronger. We might need to make a deal with them if things fall through here. The fight against Henwick is more important than whatever is happening in Vegas anyway."

"Okay, we'll get in position to back you up. It doesn't look like these people are heavily armed and we shouldn't have trouble getting out of things go bad." Rebecca turned away to glower at Alex. "Come on Toots McToots, let's go hide."

Alex rolled his eyes and followed as Digby crept around the bar to find a spot that couldn't be seen from the walkways above. Fortunately, it seemed that with the armed men gone, there wasn't much reason for the people upstairs to keep watch. The only person still on the atrium floor was Elenore.

Waiting until his fellow Heretics were hidden behind a row of fake plants, Digby snuck back out of the bar and stepped into the open. He hesitated before approaching the woman, remembering the revolver sticking out of her pants. He shoved down his worry a second later and proceeded regardless. He was a powerful necromancer after all, what could a revolver possibly do to him?

Not wanting to startle the woman, Digby stopped a few feet behind her. He stood tall with his staff at his side and waited for her to notice him. After an awkward moment of him standing there, she started for the stairway without turning around to see him. He cleared his throat as she climbed the first few steps.

Elenore reached for her revolver before she even turned around.

"Wait. Wait!" Digby shielded his chest on instinct to protect the Heretic Seed's shard as she spun and pulled the trigger.

The gunshot echoed through the atrium.

CHAPTER THREE

Smoke wafted through the air as the gunshot echoed off the ceiling of the atrium.

"Who the hell are you?" The statuesque woman, Elenore Sharp, brandished a rather inappropriately large revolver at Digby from where she stood, halfway up the black stairway that led to the second floor of the hotel.

"I, ah…" Digby glanced behind him, shards of glass littered the counter after a bullet had shattered the tumbler that Elenore had been drinking from a moment before. He shifted his focus to himself to make sure the bullet hadn't passed through him without him realizing it. Finding his body unharmed, he composed himself and answered her question. "I am Lord Graves and I am here with an offer of—"

"Where did you come from?" She cut him off, thrusting her revolver in his direction to emphasize her words.

"From outside." He gave her a simple answer.

"How did you get in here?" She didn't let up.

"The front door." Digby flicked his eyes in the direction he'd entered from.

"Don't lie." She jabbed her revolver at him like she was dotting the period at the end of her accusation. "I have guards there. You didn't hurt them, did you?"

"No, no, I would never. I just slipped by them when they weren't looking." Digby held up a hand in defense. "I am not your enemy. Listen, my name is Dig—"

"I don't care who you are." She glared at him.

"But that was literally the first thing you asked me." Digby cocked his head to one side.

"What's wrong with you? Are you sick? Infected?" Her gun flicked from side to side with each question. "You're real freakin' pale, buddy."

"Easy now, easy now." He tried his best to defuse the situation. "Elenore… May I call you Elenore?"

"No, you fucking can't." She bared her teeth. "Who the hell are you?"

Digby tilted his head to the other side. "But you just said you didn't care who I—"

"Yeah, well now I do," she growled, clearly frustrated with how she had just contradicted herself.

"And I already answered." He gave her a smile, grateful for his human appearance.

"Okay, yeah, you did. What was it you said, Graves? That a last name?" She started to lower the gun before rubbing at the side of her head with her other hand.

"Indeed, Graves is my surname. It is good to meet you." Digby let himself relax a little. *Excellent, I'm making headway.* He nodded to himself as he got control over the situation. Which, of course, was when Rebecca and Alex ruined everything.

"Hey, watch it."

Digby cringed as Rebecca protested what he could only assume was someone pulling her out of her hiding place in the fake plants behind him.

Alex's voice followed. "Okay, you don't have to shove."

Glancing back, Digby found them both being pushed forward by the two guards that had been by the front door earlier. He rubbed at the bridge of his new nose in frustration.

"What the hell is going on?" Elenore raised her voice, letting her revolver waver between him and his fellow Heretics. "And I better like the answer, 'cause whatever this is, doesn't look good on you."

"I'm terribly sorry." Digby placed a hand on his chest and inclined his head. "These two are my subordinates. I assure you that I mean none of your people any harm and that I am here with an offer of cooperation. However, it would still be foolish of me to neglect to bring back up." He gestured to the pair of Heretics. "Hence, these two."

"This one smells like he shit his pants." One of the guards shoved Alex with the flat of the axe he carried.

"Tell me about it." Rebecca placed a hand to her face.

"Shut up. I still don't feel well." Alex glowered at her.

"Yes, I'm afraid my apprentice had a run in with an uncooperative can of beans not long ago." Digby shrugged. "The results were, well, unhelpful to say the least."

"Oh come on." Elenore deflated. "I was sure that that smell was Deuce because we were the only people nearby and I knew it wasn't me. Which means he's probably just as certain it was me."

"What's that now?" Digby stared up at her with a blank expression on his face.

"Do you have any idea how long I have been rehearsing that conversation about supplies?" She groaned up at the skylights above. "I have to appear strong, damn it. Rivers' goons will walk all over us and take what they want." She leveled her gun on Digby. "Now that jerk is going to go back and tell Rivers that I shit my pants or something."

"Alright, I can see how that would be a problem." Digby nodded, trying to be understanding. "But I assure you, none of that was by design. I truly am here to seek a fortuitous relationship between your people and my own."

"Would you quit that fancy talk." She jabbed her gun at him as she spoke.

"I am just trying to be nice." Digby raised his staff and dropped it back down so that the impact echoed through the atrium. "Now, will you stop pointing your gun at me for one damn second, and let me say what I came to say? If you want me gone afterward, I'll gladly leave the lot of you to your own devices."

"Oof." Rebecca winced. "Probably not the right tone."

"I don't care." Digby cracked his staff down on the floor again and stared up at the woman. "I am here not just to extend a hand in friendship, but to warn of a coming threat. The organization responsible for spreading this curse across this world will not be satisfied with merely killing off the majority of its previous population. As we speak, they are making preparations to bring about a new world order from the ashes of the old, and it is only a matter of time before they set their sights on the people here. I have seen it before. They will arrive under the guise of safety and protection, but they will demand your fealty and they will indoctrinate your young."

"What the hell are you talking about?" The woman folded her arms.

"Skyline!" Digby thrust out a hand before closing it into a fist.

"It's true." Rebecca chimed in from behind him. "You or one of your people might have heard of them. They were a private military contractor with ties to an organization called Autem. I know because I was one of their drone operators. I saw everything. They helped spread the dead through the world and then created the revenants that stalk your people at night."

"Revenants? You mean the shriekers?" Elenore arched an eyebrow.

"Yes, that seems to be your word for them." Rebecca nodded.

Silence fell across the room as Digby became aware of several people on the level above looking down. He remained standing tall with his hand extended to the woman on the stairs as whispers drifted through the room.

Time to close the deal.

Digby turned to address the rest of the onlookers, sweeping a hand out across the room for dramatic effect. "Currently, myself and those who follow me are the only ones aware of the real threat this world faces, and we have vowed to fight back before our enemies grow too powerful to be stopped. That is why, here and now, I ask you all for your aid. I ask for your resolve in reclaiming this world. Together, we will take back what has been stolen."

Elenore remained quiet for a long moment before dropping her hands to her side and leaning against the railing beside her.

"Your answer, milady?" Digby turned back to the woman with his hand outstretched, wearing his warmest smile.

"Don't give me that fedora shit." Elenore waved her revolver in the air as if shooing him away. "You said you'd leave once you said your piece and now you have. So get the hell out of here."

Digby's mouth fell open, not understanding what fedoras had to do with anything. "But what about—"

"What about nothing. I didn't like your pitch, so go." She shrugged.

"Wait, no." Digby dropped the hand he'd been holding out toward her. "That's not fair."

"Look around, this world isn't fair." She tossed both hands out to her sides.

"But what about when Skyline comes after you?" Digby shook his head, refusing to accept her answer. "They will take your people and force them into service."

"We already have Rivers doing the same thing. That asshole runs this city and expects payment for his protection. If we run out of things he wants, he just takes our kids." She sat down on the step she was standing on. "We have enough problems with that, how do you expect us to fight some military guys when we can't even stand up to Rivers? We aren't soldiers. Shit, I was a showgirl a month ago and I just wasted my last bullet firing it at you because you startled me."

"But you were so defiant a moment ago when you held your ground against that Deuce fellow." Digby furrowed his brow.

"Cause I'm full of shit, like that guy's pants." She gestured to Alex with her revolver before dropping it to the step she sat on. "Besides, Deuce used to work security at the casino I performed at and I sort of went out with him once or twice a year ago. He's pretty basic, so yeah, I felt I could get away with a little more without him shooting me."

"Oh, come on." Alex groaned. "I didn't shit my pants. It was just gas."

"A lot of gas," Rebecca added.

"Neither of you are helping." Digby glared back at them before giving his attention back to the woman sitting on the stairs.

"There's no way in hell I'm helping some pale-ass rube fight a war, and neither is anyone else here. Especially not against some organization that I've never even heard of. I mean, who the hell are you anyway to even expect my answer to be different?" She held a hand out toward him. "If you want someone to help you, you have to earn it."

"And how do you suggest I do that?" Digby snapped back, getting frustrated that things were going so poorly.

"Go get Rivers and his deck of cards off our backs." She shrugged. "If you can't do that, then what good are you?"

"Look here." Digby clenched his jaw. "As it is, we only have a small window left to stand against Skyline before they grow too strong to be stopped. I simply can't take the time to fight everyone else's battles."

"Then you may as well find a different city to recruit help in." She leaned to one side.

"Maybe I will," Digby growled back before reconsidering. "Actually, no I won't, I don't have time for that either."

"Okay then, I guess you have my answer." She stood back up. "I'm not going to cause you any trouble, but I'm not going to throw my life away for your cause either."

"Fine." Digby tightened his grip around his staff and stormed off back the way he'd come. He slowed to a stop before exiting the atrium, getting a grip on his frustration before he burnt a bridge that couldn't be rebuilt. "I understand your position. I don't like it, but I understand it." He turned to look at the woman and inclined his head. "My people are taking over the Never Say Die a few streets over. If you change your mind, that's where I'll be." Revealing his location might not have been the best choice, but he hoped extending a bit of trust might buy him some good will.

"I'll remember that." She nodded without saying anything

more before turning and heading up the stairs. "I'm sure you can show yourselves out."

"Yes, yes, I know the way." Digby groaned, despite having no idea if he could actually find his way out of the casino floor's labyrinth.

"Oh, and one more thing. The streets may seem safe for the most part, but keep your people inside at night regardless." Her face grew serious. "And whatever you do, don't let anyone go up on the rooftops after dark."

"What's that now?" Digby turned back to eye the woman.

"Trust me." She pointed to the skylights at the top of the atrium. "You don't want to get picked up by what's up there."

CHAPTER FOUR

Digby dragged his feet the entire way back to the Never Say Die hotel and casino. His first recruitment pitch had not gone well. For a moment, he even wondered if he was wasting his time in Vegas. It might make more sense to move on to greener pastures after all, considering someone else had already staked a claim.

No. He shook his head. *There isn't time to find a new dominion, not while Henwick is growing his empire every day.*

His attention was pulled away by several vehicles sitting in the parking lot of his temporary home. "What the...?"

"It's Mason." Rebecca strolled along at his side while Alex brought up the rear where she couldn't smell him. "I followed the roads in the kestrel on our way here. They were clear enough for everyone to make it here without issue as long as they traveled during the day. The trip was mostly unpopulated desert too, so there was little chance of enemies getting in their way. I sent Mason a map of the best route and made sure to keep them away from areas where those guys were patrolling. Thought it would be easier and use less fuel for him to meet us here than make two trips in the kestrel tomorrow to transport our people and our supplies here. Plus we wouldn't have to leave the cars behind."

"Oh, just great." Digby deflated. "I was really hoping to have a night to myself to wallow in self-pity."

"Sorry. No wallowing for you." Rebecca shrugged. "With a little luck, someone has gotten the hotel's generator and water up and running. I could use a hot shower." She nudged him in the ribs with an elbow. "You might want to start bathing now too. You look human, so you should probably start acting it."

"Bah, I'm clean enough." He waved away her suggestion as they came to the casino's front door.

"Well look what the cat dragged..." Sax met them at the entrance, his greeting trailing off as he noticed Digby's new face. Previously a low-ranking soldier in the now non-existent military of the land, the slender man must have taken the first shift on guard duty.

"Yes, I have a nose now." Digby pushed through the door.

"Damn, that's impressive." Sax gawked at his face. "You're no Henry Cavil, but I'm liking the cheek bones, and those eyes are piercing as hell. I mean it, you have something very regal going on." Sax placed a hand on his chest, lifting it up and down to simulate a beating heart. "It's working for me. If I was a little more goth, I'd take you upstairs."

"Yes, well, I don't know who Henry Cavil is or what being goth means." Digby rolled his piercing green eyes. "Either way, I'm still dead, so not really interested. But I appreciate the sentiment regardless. Today has been a bit of a letdown so I shan't turn down a compliment or two." He continued through the entrance before stopping short. "Where's Mason?"

"He's messing with the sun statue. Getting our goddess set up on the main floor." Sax pointed further into the casino.

"Thank you." He gave the soldier a friendly smile and continued on his way.

Once inside, Digby faced a barrage of questions from everyone that he'd protected back in California. He would have shooed them away, but they weren't stingy with their complements and he appreciated the attention. There was also a notable improvement in their attitude toward him. It was as if they felt more comfortable around him now that he could mostly pass as human. It was nice not to catch them staring when they thought he wasn't looking.

Once the initial shock of his transformation had passed, Digby was able to get a handle on what everyone was doing. James and Matthew, who had helped run things back in California with Rufus, had both taken up administrative tasks.

Together, they had organized the people into a block of rooms on the second floor and set up a pantry for their food stocks. With the supplies they had transported from their previous home, they had enough to last the next three weeks and were already making plans for what they might need to create self-sufficient food sources. James' experience as a horticulturist would come in handy in that endeavor. As far as Digby understood it, the man's previous job had been to grow medicinal plants of some sort. Matthew, on the other hand, had taken it upon himself to get the hotel's basic security systems up and running.

Among the survivors, there were several children. Fortunately, Linda, who had been a part of Mason's group, was capable of gathering the orphans into a manageable herd. A university student named Troy assisted her in the process. Digby watched the pair of unlikely teachers as they kept the children entertained, stimulated and, most importantly of all, out of the way.

Strangely, Digby didn't see Hawk among the other children. Of course, he was pretty sure Hawk wasn't his real name, but he hadn't tried to broach the subject of the boy's background. At only eleven years of age, he'd surely lost whatever family he had within the last month, so if he wanted to make up a new name for himself, that was entirely reasonable.

Still, though, he would have expected the troublemaker to be standing front and center to take in the adoration of the rest of the survivors, considering it was his plan that ensured their survival the night before. Then again, Hawk was an unusual child, so it wasn't that strange for him to run off on his own rather than socializing with the other youths. In the short time Digby had known the child, Hawk had seemed more comfortable bothering the adults than playing with those his own age.

After doing some searching, Digby found the brat in the casino's gift shop, attempting to pry open a glass case full of various trinkets with a screwdriver.

"What the devil are you doing, child?"

"Um, ah… 'Ello, guvna." Hawk responded in the fake accent that he'd been using for the last week as he shoved the screwdriver behind his back. "Nice face."

"Don't try to distract me with complements and that horrid accent, you're clearly up to no good." Digby shoved past him. "Now, stand aside while I show you how a necromancer breaks into a display case."

Digby slipped behind the counter of the small shop and found a simple lock on the back. Without hesitation, he opened his maw in the palm of his hand and cast Blood Forge to command the black fluid of his void to take shape. The shadowy pool responded immediately, sending a thin tendril of necrotic blood reaching from his hand.

I wonder?

In the past, Digby had simply caused the animated fluid to flood into a lock while expanding enough to disable the mechanism within, but now that he had increased the rank of his Blood Forge spell, he had a better idea. Letting the black fluid fill the space inside the lock, he expanded it slightly and hardened it into a matching key. For effect, he formed the shape of a skull sticking out so he had something to grip. As soon as the formation solidified, Digby reached out and turned the necrotic key before pulling it out. He finished by gesturing to the unlocked case with both hands.

"Have at it."

"Woah…" Hawks eyes widened. "Can I have that?"

"This key? Why would you want it?" Digby furrowed his brow at the boy.

"It's cool." Hawk reached out a hand, finally dropping the fake accent.

"You know it's made of dead people, right?" Digby pulled the key away.

"Still cool, though," Hawk insisted.

"Fine, suit yourself." Digby shrugged and tossed the macabre key to the child before opening the display case and grabbing a pair of souvenir flasks from inside. Each bore the words, 'Las Vegas, what happens here, stays here.' He pocketed them both and headed out of the store, turning back for a moment. "Go find yourself a room upstairs and get settled in." He hesitated. "And maybe see how the other children are faring. It would do you good to spend time with your peers."

"Nah, I'm good." Hawk helped himself to a t-shirt from a shelf on the wall. The words 'Oh Craps,' were spelled out across the front above a pair of dice.

"Or don't." Digby continued on his way. "See if I care."

Shortly after leaving Hawk, Digby ran into Parker as she appeared from a door marked maintenance with a bit of grease on her face. Also a low-ranking soldier like Sax, the young woman was one of the group's better fighters. Still wearing the clothes she'd fought Skyline's guardians in the night before, her shirt was missing a sleeve and had several burn marks covering what was left. As it was, she had lost most of the hair on the right side of her head, after taking a direct hit from a Fireball. It would grow back eventually, but she would look a bit lopsided for at least a few weeks.

Like the other soldiers, she had proved invaluable to their survival. After performing labor as a youth at a renaissance fair's forge prior to her time in the military, she had been able to produce a few crude but useful weapons, including his staff. Her knowledge had even helped Alex make full use of his class as an artificer. Together, they had already provided a lot of support.

Digby raised a hand to wave as he approached her. "Hi, Par—"

The soldier responded by throwing a punch at his jaw without warning only to fall when he dodged. She stumbled forward with the follow through and reached for one of the crude daggers she wore sheathed at the small of her back as soon as she regained her footing. "Who are you and who let you in?"

"What the hell, Parker?" Digby threw up a hand in defense, not expecting an unprovoked attack. "It's me."

Her eyes widened as his gravelly voice made his identity clear. "Shit, Dig? Is that you?"

"Yes it's me, you half-wit. I took a mutation that makes me look human." He straightened his shirt. "Didn't anyone tell you?"

"No, I was in the basement getting the generator running. I didn't know you were back." She put her dagger away, before stepping closer to gawk at his new appearance properly. "Where's Alex?"

"I don't know, I'm not his bloody keeper." Digby grumbled, still annoyed at having been attacked. "I think he was doing something about his hair."

"His hair?" She furrowed her brow. "Why?"

"Skyline knows what he looks like, so he and Rebecca thought it would be good to make some changes now that I have adequately disguised myself." He gestured to his face.

"Oh, that sounds fun." She fidgeted for a few seconds before spinning toward the stairs that led to the rooms upstairs. "I'm gonna go help."

"Yes. Yes, you do that." Digby shook his head as he continued on to where the sun goddess statue was supposedly being set up. The mass enchantment of the stone figure had the effect of increasing the balance of life essence in the ambient mana, which resulted in disabling the abilities of most revenants.

The statue was easily the most valuable thing they had found since the apocalypse had begun, which was why Digby had entrusted its care to Mason. Like Sax and Parker, the man was also from the military. As a Private First Class, he outranked them both, though not by much. Still, the soldier had proved a capable leader and had been a significant aid in keeping everyone together.

Mason had also become something of a bedmate for Rebecca, something Digby had found out after walking in on them mid-coitus. He made a mental note to make sure he knocked if he needed to enter either of their rooms. The last thing he wanted was to get yelled at for another twenty minutes like the last time.

Digby found the soldier lugging the statue through the casino on a two-wheeled cart. He wore a simple plaid shirt that was still dirty from the battle in California.

"Careful." Rebecca tried to help as the cart got hung up on a cord that ran across the dingy carpet.

"Don't worry, I got it. I don't want to run over your foot." He gave her a wink before adding, "It's a cute foot."

"Crap, you're not a feet guy, right?" She took a step back as if concerned.

"Don't worry, I'm securely in the butt camp." He pumped his eyebrows at her as he pulled the cart's wheel over the cord.

"Good to know." She nodded to herself.

"Blargh." Digby feigned nausea as he approached the pair. "Can you two bat your eyelashes at each other someplace else?"

"No can do." Mason set the statue upright before reaching in his pocket, only to pull his hand back out with it still empty. He stared down at his palm and tapped at it with one finger. "Yeah, I have it right here in my imaginary day planner: flirt with Becca. So, you know, can't argue with that." His eyes widened a second later as he glanced back to his palm. "Oh, and I'm late for Pilates."

"I'm going to go out on a limb here and say that you don't know what Pilates is." Rebecca folded her arms.

"That is correct." Mason put away his imaginary day planner. "It sounded like something that I could be late for though."

"And that's why you're not in charge of espionage." She let out an uncharacteristic giggle.

"Bah! Enough." Digby waved both hands in the air as if clearing an unpleasant odor. "I get it, you're adorable together. Ugh, I hate it."

"Don't you mean you're happy for us?" Rebecca gave him a smug grin. "Because that's how a human would respond, if you're going to act the part in accordance with your new look."

"Yes, yes, whatever." He rolled his eyes. "Being human is overrated."

Before he could further his complaints, Lana appeared behind him, dragging a brass post with a stand at the bottom. She had a velvet rope slung over her shoulder. "I thought we should block off the statue to make sure no one knocks it over." She glanced at Digby. "Oh hey, nice face."

The nineteen-year-old was still wearing most of her Skyline-issued body armor from the night before, when she'd defected from the mercenary organization mid-battle. Digby had originally met her back in Seattle where he'd helped her and her brother cross the city without being eaten by the dead. They survived, but ended up being taken into Skyline's custody where she was forced to become one of their guardians while she searched for a way to rescue her brother, Alvin, who had been taken in as a recruit for Henwick's empire.

Also, Digby had eaten her father.

It was a fact that he hadn't mentioned to her. Not that it mattered. The man had been dead when he'd found him so, really, it wasn't like he had done anything wrong.

Dropping the velvet rope to the floor, Lana pushed a wisp of curly black hair from her face that had come loose from the tie that held the rest back. Digby couldn't help but notice she wasn't wearing the guardian ring that had granted her the spells Regeneration and Mirror Link. Neither had any value in combat, though, they still might prove useful in a support capacity.

"Casting off your bonds already, I see?" Digby gestured to her hand.

Lana looked down at her naked finger. "Yeah, I took off my ring because I was afraid I might accidentally cast a spell with a stray thought. I can't be sure that Skyline won't get some kind of alert. Don't want to give them any more information than necessary"

"I know what you mean, I set myself on fire one time with an accidental casting." Digby chuckled. "Can you use any magic without your ring?"

Lana tilted her head from side to side. "I still have mana, even if I can't see its readout on my HUD. Now that I'm aware of it, I can feel it. But no, I can't use it without the ring. It's like my access has been blocked."

"Shame." Digby scratched his chin. "Do you think you can still level?"

"I doubt it." She clipped one of the velvet ropes to the post she'd dragged over. "Without a connection to the Guardian Core, I don't know how that would even work. I'm a little stronger than I was, but I probably won't be useful in a fight. Granted, I wasn't that helpful in a fight even when I could do magic, so it's not a big loss. I'm happy to support the people here though. Maybe I can take care of first aid or something. Kind of wanted to be a doctor anyway, you know. Before the apocalypse, that is."

"That would be great." Mason helped to drag over another brass post. "We could really use a med-bay of some kind."

"I'll see what I can get set up, then." She took a deep breath. "It's weird though, without my ring, I feel more like myself. Wearing it made me so aggressive and angry. Plus, I..." She hesitated as if searching for the right words. "...stopped caring. Wearing that thing did something to me, like it was trying to snuff out every ounce of empathy I had. I felt a little numb earlier but, everything came rushing back eventually. Honestly, I couldn't stop crying on the ride here." Lana's eyes started to tear up.

"That's accurate." Mason held up a finger. "She was a mess."

"The Guardian Core might have an effect on the chemical balance of your brain." Rebecca shifted her weight from one foot to the other. "Manipulating their guardians like that would be very on brand for Skyline."

"If so, they probably learned it from those Autem people that have been pulling their strings." Lana wiped a tear from the dark skin of her cheek as a fire grew in her eye. "Whatever they have planned is not good. Which is why we need to get Alvin out of there as soon as possible."

"What's the plan for that, by the way?" Mason finished connecting the velvet ropes that blocked off the sun goddess statue and shot Digby a concerned look. "Not just for rescuing the kid, but dealing with Autem? You talked a pretty big game yesterday when you declared war."

"Yes... I did do that, didn't I?" Digby folded his arms. "Well, the way I see it, we need to hit them hard and fast while they aren't expecting it. For that, we need recruits. I've already approached a group of survivors a few streets over."

"Great, we're off to a good start then." Mason perked up.

"Not quite." Rebecca brought him back down. "It didn't go well."

"Yes, initially they seemed promising, but Vegas has its own problems. Someone named Rivers has been keeping the area safe and free of monsters, but he's also extorting everyone under his protection. Apparently he expects supplies and, similar to Autem, he also wants young recruits, though I don't know why."

"Child soldiers if I had to guess." Mason frowned. "If you're trying to build a quick army of fighters that can't rise up against you, it's a strategy that's proven effective. It's probably the same reason Autem is going for teens and kids. They're easy to mold into what you want them to be, whether it's combatants or citizens of a new empire. Kids have less to unlearn before you can distort them into something else."

"As a woman raised by Skyline since I was thirteen, I can confirm." Rebecca sighed. "Really screwed me up."

"That's in the past." Mason threw an arm around her and rubbed her shoulder.

"I know." She leaned into him.

"So what do we do about this Rivers guy?" Mason brought the conversation back to the question at hand.

"Nothing right now; we don't have time to start an entirely new fight." Digby shrugged. "Actually, if anything, Rivers might be more useful on our side."

"But you just said he was stealing people's kids." Lana's face fell.

"I know what I said." Digby waved away her complaint. "We don't actually know that's what he's doing. What we do know is that he has the fighting force and weaponry to keep this area under his thumb and that's nothing to write off. With an ally like that, we might be able to attack Skyline within a few days. As long as most of their guardians are still low-level, a solid militia might stand a chance. Not to mention, I doubt whoever this Rivers fellow is would stand by while Henwick and Autem move in and take over his territory."

"I don't love that idea." Mason tilted his head from side to side.

"But if this guy has the men and weaponry that you say, it might be worth exploring the option."

"Indeed." Digby let a smug grin spread across his face. "And if Rivers were to somehow lose most of his forces in a fight against Henwick's emerging empire, well then, let's just say the fool would be easy to deal with if he becomes a problem in the future."

"Jesus, Dig, that was about the most villainous thing I've heard you say yet." Rebecca glowered at him. "You want to throw a cackle in there for good measure?"

"Don't judge me, Becky." Digby glared back. "You knew what I was when you joined up with me."

"Damn." Lana deflated. "I just defected from an organization bent on world domination and immediately became a supervillain's henchwoman, didn't I?"

"A bit." Digby gave her a smirk. "And I like the sound of that. Supervillain. Yes, that'll do nicely."

"Oh, quit scheming, Goldfinger." Rebecca rolled her eyes.

"I don't know who that is." Digby glowered at her.

"Either way, you have to beat Henwick first." Mason backed up his bedmate.

"Bah, you're no fun." Digby pouted.

"Someone has to keep you from going off the deep end." Rebecca smiled back. "But as long as you're not going to the dark side tonight, I am going to take a shower and see what I can do about my hair to change my look."

"You need any help with that?" Mason removed his arm from her shoulder.

"With my hair or showering?" She shot him a mischievous grin as she took his hand and dragged him away.

"Oh, so those two are a thing then?" Lana leaned to one side.

"Indeed. It's annoying." Digby furrowed his brow, realizing she had missed the couple's flirting earlier.

"That's nice, I guess." Lana nodded before shoving her hand in her pocket and pulling out the golden band that had been on her finger before she'd defected. "What should I do with my guardian ring? It doesn't do me any good, but is there a way to destroy it?"

"Hmm, destroy it you say? The choice is up to you, but if you wish to be rid of that ring, then give it here." Digby held out his hand.

"Sure." She placed the ring in his palm as he closed his fingers around it.

The Heretic Seed responded in kind, telling him that Lana's Mirror Link spell could be extracted. He hesitated for a moment, debating on if he should take it or if he should save it for Rebecca. It would certainly be a useful spell for her, but if he claimed it, it might evolve into something else. More importantly, it might become a spell that Henwick's forces don't have access to.

After weighing the decision, he extracted the spell.

"There you are." Digby held out his hand to Lana, prompting her to do the same. He poured bits of gold dust into her palm. "Your guardian ring is no more."

"What the…?" She snapped her eyes back to his. "How did you do that?"

He brushed his hand off on his coat. "I extracted your communication spell and added it to my own. I doubt it will function with my mana balance but it will evolve into something else when I try. The process destroys the ring though."

"That's okay." She let out a breath. "I'm glad it's gone."

"Good." He gave her a smile. "Consider yourself officially free of Skyline."

"Thank you." She nodded.

"I try." He accepted her appreciation without actually thinking about her words.

"No really, thank you," Lana reached out and placed a hand on the shoulder of his coat. "I really am grateful that you got me out of there and that you're willing to help rescue my brother. I'm pretty sure a villain wouldn't do that."

Digby hesitated, feeling the sincerity in her voice. There were a number of things he could have said in response that might have secured her faith in him. He didn't say any of those things, obviously. Instead, he turned to the statue of the sun goddess in front of them to avoid eye contact, and got something off his chest.

"I ate your father."

"What?" Lana sucked in a sudden breath.

"Sorry." Digby shrugged. "He was already dead and it, sort of, just happened."

"Ah..." She trailed off, clearly at a loss for words.

"Well then, it's good to have that little secret out in the open." He immediately spun on his heel and walked off toward the stairs that led to the guest rooms. "Try to get some rest tonight, I'm sure I'll see you in the morning."

CHAPTER FIVE

After making sure that everyone from California had gotten settled in, Digby retired for the day. On his way up the stairs, he poked his head outside to call Asher. The raven had kept watch long enough and deserved a break. It didn't take long before she swooped down to land on the head of his staff.

Reaching the second floor, he made a point of choosing one of the furthest rooms down the hall from the others, taking a moment to relax once he was inside. Speaking with everyone had begun to take its toll, leaving him a little overwhelmed. Not to mention, his failed attempt at recruitment was still hanging in the forefront of his mind. After that, he needed his space.

"How am I going to stop Henwick if I can't even convince anyone else to fight?" He deflated and placed Asher down on a small table before sitting next to the door. She didn't have an answer for him.

The room wasn't much to speak of. Just a bed that he didn't need and a table and chairs. Apparently, the owner of the Never Say Die casino and hotel didn't care much for housekeeping. The walls were yellow and the sheets were stained. It would have been nice to have claimed one of the better rooms on the upper floors, but Parker and Sax had limited the generator's power supply to one floor in order to conserve resources.

Digby shrugged and slipped out of his coat. It wasn't the worst room he'd ever stayed in. In fact, compared to some of the places he'd passed through back in his day, it was a cut above the rest.

Taking Rebecca's suggestions into account, he investigated the bathroom. He stripped off his clothes and he fiddled with the knob on the shower until water poured down. He left the temperature set to cold, since it didn't really matter to him either way. Finding a strange pump container attached to the wall of the shower, he pressed down on it until soap came out.

Cleaning himself was easier now that he had a normal right hand. Despite that, a part of him missed his claws. Fortunately, the Sheep's Clothing mutation had only removed his crown and gauntlet, leaving the rest of his armor where it was. Plates of bleached bone still covered his chest and back to absorb damage and protect the shard of the Heretic Seed that resided in his unbeating heart. Although, now that he had a chance to look at his armor, it did seem a little more refined as it fit the contours of his body better.

After giving himself a thorough scrubbing, Digby shut off the water and exited the shower to stare at his human face in the mirror. The initial joy of having a nose again was beginning to wear off now that he'd had it for a day. Now, it just looked weird.

Shoving the thought from his mind, he placed a hand to the reflective surface and cast Mirror Link.

> **Mirror Link cancelled due to incomparable mana composi-**
> **tion. Minimum 10% of each heat, vapor, soil, fluid, and life,**
> **mana required.**
> *Surprise, surprise.*

Digby rolled his eyes at the message and kept casting until he felt a new spell weave itself into his mind.

> **Mirror Link has evolved into Talking Corpse.**
> **TALKING CORPSE**

Description: Temporarily bestow the gift of speech to a corpse to gain access to the information known to them while they were alive. Once active, a talking corpse cannot lie.
Rank: D
MP Cost: 20 (+variable based on extended duration)
Duration: 1 minute (+5MP for each additional minute)
Range: Touch
Limitations: Requires a corpse or a Human that could potentially become a corpse. This spell's duration can be extended as long as it has not yet expired. Once this spell ends, it cannot be cast a second time on the same target. Interactions with Talking Corpses may vary based on your target's previous personality, as well as their feelings toward you. Some may only answer questions while others may be able to hold conversations.
WARNING: While a corpse may always be truthful, it is still possible to give misleading information.
Probably stick to simple questions.

"Simple questions indeed." Digby considered how a corpse might get around the requirement of telling the truth. He shrugged off the thought, hoping the spell might provide a solid lead in a pinch.

Retrieving a new pair of trousers, shirt, and undergarments from one of the containers he'd stored in his void back in California, he pulled them on. He'd assumed he would feel a little more human once he was cleanly dressed, but it strangely didn't have the same appeal he remembered. In the end, he just felt hungry. The thought of a fresh corpse filled his mind. That was about all he enjoyed anymore.

Well… that and watching movies.

Rebecca had introduced him to a plethora of stories imagined by mankind that centered around zombies. Most were quite entertaining, if not a little sad. Unfortunately, Digby had left his tablet in the kestrel and he didn't feel like going across to the parking garage to retrieve it. He glanced out the window at his view of the structure beside the casino. It wasn't that far, but the sun had already set, leaving Elenore's cryptic warning hanging in his memory.

"What's the worst that could happen? It's not like any revenant would have any interest in me." He nearly choked on his words as the silhouettes of several winged forms took to the sky.

Revenant Nightflyer, Uncommon.

"Maybe I shall remain indoors, after all."

The memory of fighting a winged revenant was still fresh from his time in California. He could still hear the sound of Tanner's leathery wings flapping whenever he closed his eyes. The figures in the sky didn't look as big, but still, his tablet wasn't worth pressing his already disappointing luck for. Staring out at the bat-like creatures, they looked to be the size of a normal human.

"Must have mutated into a path that can fly." It wasn't surprising; if Tanner could do it, then it stood to reason other revenants might have the same ability. He made a note to mention the discovery to the others, just in case they hadn't seen the creatures yet.

That was when someone knocked on his door.

"Who is it?" Digby snapped his head to the side and shouted.

"Hawk."

Digby let out a groan before making his way to the door and yanking it open. "And what is it that you want?"

"I found a DVD in the gift shop. Parker, Alex, and me were going to watch it on the big TV in one of the function rooms downstairs." Hawk looked up at him with a hopeful expression.

"I don't know what a DVD is." Digby frowned.

"It's a movie." The child's face fell, clearly surprised by his lack of knowledge.

"And why did they send you to retrieve me?"

"Because you're kind of a jerk, and they thought you would yell at me less because I'm a kid." Hawk explained cheerfully as if he hadn't just relayed an insult.

"Shows how much they know. I yell at children all the time." Digby folded his arms and stared down at the boy as he glanced back up with the same hopeful look in his eyes. He stood like that for a long beat before giving in. "Alright fine, I was bored anyway so I didn't mind coming to invite you."

Finally, Digby smiled. "Alright boy, you don't have to beg. A movie would do nicely right about now."

Calling to Asher, he headed back down the stairs as Hawk rambled on about everything he found in the gift shop. As they reached the first floor, a strange scent wafted toward him. It made his void howl in hunger, reminding him that he hadn't eaten anything—or anyone—since the day before.

"That's popcorn." Hawk walked a little faster.

"That's disappointing." Digby frowned, realizing that whatever it was, it wasn't something he could eat.

"Sorry. Do you need to eat every day or…?" The child left a few steps between them as if a little worried that Digby might be hungrier than he looked.

"I would like to, but no, I don't need to eat as long as I don't use the resources in my void for anything." Digby scratched at his stomach. "Doesn't mean I don't feel hungry though."

"Oh." Hawk let the subject lie, without asking anything more.

To Digby's surprise, nearly everyone had turned up down stairs. Apparently, news of Hawk's discovery had traveled. People had even moved a few sofas into the function hall to get more comfortable. It was actually rather nice to see. Of course, none of them had completely let their guard down after having barely survived the night before, but it was good to see them taking a bit of time off.

That was when Alex entered the room.

Digby burst out laughing as soon as he took in the artificer's new hairstyle. A blue shock of messy locks covered the top of his head, while the sides were nearly bare.

"Why the hell did you let Becky do that to you?" Digby let out a few more chuckles.

Alex ignored the abuse. "Becca was busy, so—"

"I did it." Parker dropped into a sofa nearby, looking proud of herself as she flipped her head to one side.

Having trimmed her hair short to balance out her lopsided

appearance, she was left with an asymmetrical cut of bright pink hair. She gave Alex an approving look. "Don't let the dead guy judge you, I think it looks cool. Besides, I need someone to take the attention off this pink mess." She tapped her own head.

"I like it," Hawk added.

"Yeah, it is the apocalypse after all." Alex gave an exaggerated shrug. "Always wanted to do something wild, and now I don't have to worry about looking professional for job interviews and what not."

"Glad to hear." Digby let a layer of sarcasm coat his words.

"You really shouldn't talk." Rebecca approached behind him. "Not after you dressed like the goblin king for the last two weeks."

"Fair enough, and I do miss that coat." Digby turned around to find her usual black hair replaced by a cascade of platinum blond locks that had been cut up to her shoulders. She'd kept her bangs long so that they covered half her face. "I see you took a more conservative approach."

"Yeah, I'm not trying to stand out like these two jackasses." She hooked a thumb at Alex and Parker. "But at least this hides my face a little and might keep someone from Skyline from recognizing me at first glance."

"Indeed." Digby spun back to Alex. "So what do you have planned for us tonight?"

The artificer grabbed a narrow box and tossed it in his direction. "We're in Vegas, there's only one choice."

Digby stared down at the case of what was apparently called a DVD. A picture of several men wearing suits and standing in a line covered the front while bright lights filled the background. Reading over some of the names listed at the bottom, he looked to his apprentice. "Who is George Clooney? And does he get eaten by zombies in this movie?"

"No, there are no zombies in it. And Clooney must be dead by now, so probably just watch the movie and don't think about it too much." Alex pulled a device with buttons covering one side from his pocket and pointed it at a large screen mounted on a cart with wheels so it could be moved.

The system flickered to life as the same picture on the DVD

case appeared on the screen. Parker flipped a switch on the wall up and down, causing the lights in the room to turn on and off. Digby didn't understand the meaning, but the people in the room quickly found their seats and quieted down. He took that as his cue to do the same.

From the time that Digby had become aware, he had learned so little of the world he'd become a part of. His only glimpse of the society that had once existed had been seen through the lens of zombie movies, watched on a small tablet computer. He simply didn't know much about the people or the figures they considered heroes.

Now, a new kind of story began to unfold before him. Not one of death, blood, and survival, but one of cunning, confidence, and triumph. In two hours, a narrative of a theft played out step by step, keeping Digby on the edge of his seat. It was a heist. He hung on every word, every detail, and every trick. The story spoke to him in a way none other had before.

The reason was simple.

The characters on the screen weren't just con-men and criminals, they were relatable. He saw himself in them and they showed him everything that he could be. They weren't hiding in the gutter like he had all his life. No, they were Lords in their own right, taking what they could without apology.

Something in his mind clicked into place as a realization took root and settled in. Sure, he had accomplished nothing back when he was alive. In his village eight-hundred years ago, he was just a lone peasant with sticky fingers. Now though, well, he had accomplices.

Digby looked around the dimly lit room as everyone watched the movie play out. Rebecca sat beside Mason, while Parker, Alex, and Sax filled out another sofa. Including him, that made a crew of six.

Eventually, the movie ended and the screen went black. Everyone talked for a little longer before filtering out and heading back to their rooms upstairs. Digby pulled Alex aside as he left to ask him to show him how to operate the DVD system. After giving his apprentice an uncharacteristic, "Thanks," he sat back down alone in the dark and pressed play.

In total, he watched the movie three times on repeat. Each time, he sat completely still without even blinking. He remained like that until the sun began to rise. Again, the credits rolled, but this time, he felt a grin creep across his face.

"Have you been here all night?" Alex yawned as he entered the room to flick the lights on.

Digby craned his head to make eye contact with him.

"Gather the crew. I have a new plan."

CHAPTER SIX

Digby stood tall in front of the television that he'd been repeatedly watching the same heist movie on for the last eight hours. Of the five humans that he had begun to think of as his inner circle, four of them sat on the sofas facing him. Rebecca and Mason sipped coffee while Alex yawned beside them. Parker sat at the end of the couch with her head back and her eyes closed. Asher perched on the monitor behind him. The only one absent was Sax who remained on watch at the casino's entrance.

"Thank you all for joining me on this fine Tuesday morning."

"It's Saturday." Alex let out a lengthy yawn.

"It is?" Digby frowned and looked to Rebecca who nodded. "That's not great. I suppose it's easy to lose track when there is no real schedule to the day." He shook his head. "Anyway, I have a plan on how to get the upper hand on Henwick."

His presentation was interrupted by Parker as her open mouth emitted a quiet snore. Digby rolled his eyes and grabbed a discarded bag of popcorn from the night before. The pink-haired soldier woke up with a start when he lobbed it at her head. Asher cawed to assist in keeping everyone awake.

"Hey? What? Okay, I'm up." She blinked as stray puffs of popcorn rained down upon her.

"As I was saying." Digby ignored her confusion and continued. "It's becoming clear to me that, so far, our approach to this war may be flawed. After my failure to sway anyone to our cause yesterday, I simply don't believe that we can build a relevant force that can stand up against Skyline or their partners in Autem."

"That's fair." Rebecca leaned back in her seat. "But what do you suggest we do to keep Henwick's empire from gaining any more power?"

"Simple." Digby reached out a hand and slowly closed his fingers into a fist. "We rob him."

Silence fell across the room before anyone spoke.

"Sure, why not." Rebecca casually sipped her coffee.

"Okay." Alex nodded.

"Wait, what?" Mason shot Rebecca a confused look. "That's it? You're going right along?"

"You're new." She tilted her head from side to side. "This is what Dig does. He comes up with absurd plans. I argued the first time and he proved me wrong. So at this point, I'm turning off my voice of reason and going with the flow."

"There's no point in arguing anyway." Alex added. "He's going to do it no matter what we say."

Mason glanced back to Parker who was trying to eat a few stray pieces of popcorn that had landed on her shoulder by sticking her tongue out so they stuck to it. He turned back to Digby when it was clear she would be of no help. "Okay, Dig, I get that you do things differently. But you can't just watch a heist movie and decide that theft is the solution to our problems."

"Why not?" Digby shrugged.

"Because it's nuts," he responded matter-of-factly.

"Is it though?" Digby countered. "Henwick has hundreds of guardians by now. Maybe even thousands. We can't compete with that, but it won't matter if we sneak in without alerting their forces. While we're inside, we can help ourselves to something that can even the odds."

"What do you even intend to steal?" Mason shook his head.

"Well, I have a theory." Digby started pacing. "Back when I

was dead set on avoiding a conflict with Skyline, I intended to hunt down more fragments of the Heretic Seed's monolith."

"Yeah, and you thought that would help you learn more about your power." Mason nodded along.

"Indeed." Digby stopped for a second. "But to be honest, it was really just an excuse to shut Alex up so I could hide like a coward and avoid fighting Henwick."

"Figured that," Alex chimed in.

"Yes, I thought that if you all thought I was dedicated to getting stronger so we could eventually fight back, you might get off my back and let me be. However, now that I'm committed to this, I'm back to thinking that reclaiming the Seed's fragments might be our best bet."

"So what does that have to do with Skyline?" Mason shook his head.

"Everything." Digby turned to the soldier with a smug expression. "Thanks to the time Lana spent on the inside, we know that Henwick's men hunted down all of the Seed's fragments long ago. So it stands to reason that they still have them all somewhere on the base. Add the shards they have to the one lodged in my chest and we'll have them all." Digby froze the second his last declaration left his mouth, realizing he'd never actually mentioned that detail to the soldier.

"There's a shard in your chest?" Mason arched an eyebrow.

"Umm, sort of." Digby cringed. "I was trying to keep that part secret in case someone got captured. But yes, it's why I can come back from the dead even if my brain is damaged."

"Good to know, I guess." Mason leaned back before getting back to the plan. "So you think Henwick has the fragments on Skyline's base?"

"Indeed." Digby nodded. "And we know from the reports that Easton, our man within Skyline, has given us, that there is a secure building on the base where Autem's people have taken up residence. So my guess is the Seed is somewhere in there."

"But Skyline has other facilities." Rebecca finished her coffee. "The base is the largest, but there are smaller ones here and there all over the world. The Seed could be housed in any of them."

"True, but it stands to reason that they would keep it at whichever location is most secure. I'd still bet that's the largest one." Digby began pacing again.

"Okay, but if the base is the most secure, how do you intend to get in there without anyone noticing?" Mason stopped him.

"I don't know." Digby realized that he hadn't thought that far ahead. "I figured Rebecca's illusions could get us in. Also, we might be able to learn important weaknesses of their defenses that could be exploited later."

Mason looked to Rebecca, then to Alex. Both of them continued to nod along with the plan. "Fine. Why not?"

"Thank you." Digby clapped his hands together. "I knew you'd see it my—" His sentence was cut off by the sound of a woman's voice shouting from outside the room.

"Where's Graves?"

"Hey, stop." Sax could be heard calling after the interruption. "Who are you and what do you want?"

"There you are!" The vaguely familiar face of Elenore Sharp burst through the doors at the back of the room. She stopped short, as soon as she noticed Asher perched on the screen behind him. Digby arched an eyebrow. After declining to become an ally the day before, she was the last person he expected to see.

"Welcome to the Never Say Die." He gave her a polite bow hoping that she might have reconsidered his proposal. "To what may I owe the pleasure of this unannounced visit?" Digby flicked his eyes to Sax who entered the room behind her. "I see guarding the front door is going well."

"Don't blame me, she just barged in like she owns the place." Sax rested his right hand on a pistol holstered on his hip. "What did you want me to do, shoot her?"

"Sorry for being pushy, but I don't have time for manners." She locked eyes with Digby. "Right now, I need your help."

"Oh?" Digby grinned, realizing that he may have just gained the upper hand in his negotiations with the woman without even doing anything. "And what could I do for you on this fine Friday morning?"

"It's Saturday." Alex raised one finger.

"Yes, yes, Saturday, right." Digby nodded.

"Stale popcorn?" Parker held a half empty bag in the woman's direction.

"No I don't want any popcorn." Elenore slapped the bag to the floor.

"Of course, my apologies." Digby glared at Parker as he led Elenore to one of the open sofas. "Why don't you have a seat and tell me what the trouble is?"

"I fucked up." She dropped into the cushions and placed a hand on her head. "I thought that putting up a tough front for Deuce would get him to cut us some slack and leave us with more supplies. I was hoping that it could earn me some respect, but that a-hole must have told on me. I woke up to a team—to a team of Rivers' high-cards at my door."

"I see." Digby stepped away. "Unfortunately, as I stated yesterday, I don't have time to fight other people's—"

"They took my son." She snapped her eyes back up to him.

"I wasn't aware that you had offspring." Digby broke eye contact.

"I do and those bastards took him, as well as two other kids that we had with us." Her face contorted with anger. "You said you want to fight some kind of war, right?"

"I did." Digby nodded.

"Then you must have weapons and soldiers." She stood back up. "I know I blew you off yesterday, but I can swallow my pride enough to ask for help."

Digby hesitated, unsure of what to do. He glanced to Rebecca and Alex for their opinions. They returned his look with one of their own that was clearly conflicted. On the one hand, he didn't like what was happening in the city and putting an end to this Rivers fellow would probably be for the best. Then again, the man could just as easily be an ally that might provide him with fighters when the time came. Even if his plan of a heist went off without a hitch, that would only buy time and give him an advantage. He would still need an army of his own eventually.

"I'm not sure—"

"Please!" Elenore slapped the back of the nearest sofa, her

voice cracking. "I don't have anyone I can turn to, and I can't let them take my boy. I can't lose anyone else!"

"I know, I know." Digby held up both hands to calm her down without committing to anything.

Her eyes narrowed a second later. "Look, when those men showed up at my place, I could have told them about you and your people. You probably have kids here that you care about and Rivers would want them too."

Digby flinched, immediately thinking of Hawk. "But you didn't tell them, did you?"

"No I didn't." She calmed down. "So, please, help me. If you do, then I will pay you back any way I can. I'm no soldier, but if your people can get my son back, then I will fight whoever you want me to. Shit, I will follow you to hell and back if I have to."

Damn it.

Digby let out a long needless sigh, realizing he was trapped. He glanced to Alex and Rebecca again, this time receiving a nod from them both. Then finally, he brought his gaze back to the woman who had just sworn loyalty to him in exchange for his help. He raised an eyebrow. "To hell and back, you say?"

"Whatever, just help me." She gave him a firm nod.

"Very well, wait for me outside while I get some things ready. I'll be there in ten minutes. We'll set out then." Stepping forward, he placed a hand on her shoulder. "I can't make you any promise but this, I will do everything in my power to reclaim your kin."

"Thank you." She paused and let out a sigh. "Why do I feel like I just made a deal with the devil?"

Digby removed his cold hand from her shoulder and gave her a crooked grin.

"My dear, you have no idea."

CHAPTER SEVEN

"Time to pay our new neighbor a visit." Digby dropped into the passenger side of a four-door car that Mason had driven from California. The rest of his coven climbed in as well, followed by Elenore.

"Wait, this is it?" Elenore leaned forward to grab the goblin king's pauldron that was fastened to Digby's shoulder.

"Of course not." He scoffed.

Elenore's hand slipped away. "Okay, sorry, for a second there, I thought you were going with just the four of us?"

"Don't be ridiculous." Digby rolled down the window to let Asher in. The raven flapped down and landed on the center console. "Alright. That's everyone."

"What?" Elenore leaned forward. "But where are all your fighters? And why don't you have any weapons?"

"I don't have any, why do you think I was trying to recruit more?" Digby growled back.

"But what about the people in there?" She thrust a finger back at the Never Say Die. "You had a couple dozen from what I counted."

"Oh, most of them aren't fighters." Digby settled into his seat.

"We have a few soldiers, but we don't have any weapons other than a few crude swords and knives."

"Swords?" Elenore sputtered. "But Rivers has dozens of heavily armed men. What are swords going to do against that?"

"Obviously not much, that's why we're leaving them behind." Digby tapped the dashboard, yelling at Alex to start driving despite sitting next to him.

"But that leaves us defenseless?" Elenore's voice climbed an octave with each word.

"I have a machete." Alex pulled the car out of the parking lot.

"Yes, yes." Digby gestured to his apprentice. "Alex has a machete."

"That's not…" Elenore's eyes bulged as her breathing sped up. "Are you insane?"

"Excuse me for not living up to expectations," Digby added, a mocking tone to his words. "Might I remind you that this was not my first choice either?"

"But Rivers is going to kill us!" she shrieked.

"Oh, bah." Digby waved her concern away. "I figure I might be able to negotiate with him. Maybe he can be reasoned with if I explain the threat that Skyline poses for everyone."

"And what if he doesn't listen?" She dug her fingernails into the back of his seat.

"Then we improvise." Digby shrugged.

"You're gonna want to trust us here." Alex leaned over, clearly trying to sound confident. "We've been through a lot so far."

"I would suggest keeping an open mind," Rebecca added, tiptoeing around the subject of magic.

With that, Elenore dropped back into her seat in the back and stared at the ceiling. Obviously, they could have explained to her that Digby was an undead necromancer and by 'improvise,' he meant murder the closest person and reanimate their corpse, but that would only lead to a longer conversation. One that Elenore might not have been prepared to accept easily. If things went wrong, she at least seemed resourceful enough to go with the flow of a fight and to hold her questions until the dust settled.

Digby enjoyed the rest of the ride in silence, occasionally stroking Asher's feathers.

Las Vegas truly was a sight to behold, making him wish he could have seen it before the world had ended. The lights must have been incredible. The sights only became more grand as they drove onto the main strip toward the fanciest casino in the area where Rivers had apparently set up shop.

As they approached the building, a group of six heavily armed men came into view. Digby recognized the man in front as Deuce, the goon that had visited Elenore the day before. It must have been his group's turn on guard duty.

"Stop the car." Digby popped his door open before turning to Asher. "Survey the area, let me know if they have any more people standing guard on the other entrances. Don't take any chances and stay hidden."

The raven nodded and took flight. As a zombie master, she was too important to let anywhere near a potential fight, so keeping her in the air made the most sense while still making use of her ability to gather information.

"What's the deal with the bird?" Elenore stared at Digby, clearly feeling uneasy.

"Don't worry about it." He exited the vehicle to avoid the subject and the rest of his coven followed. Approaching on foot, Digby made his presence known to the armed men guarding the casino. "Greetings, I—"

"Get your hands in the air," Deuce called out before he had the chance to finish his introduction.

"Alright, alright." Digby raised both hands halfway.

"We just want to talk to Rivers." Elenore stepped forward with her arms held up.

"Shit." Deuce let his aim falter. "Elenore, I know what you're thinking—"

"He took my son, Deuce!" she shouted back.

"Okay, I know." He lowered his gun altogether. "I nearly got myself killed last night defending you, damn it. Rivers has it in for you because your payments have been light lately."

"My son, Deuce! They took him," she repeated.

"I won't pretend I like it, but you can't stop him." The man's voice shook. "So please just go."

That was when Digby cleared his throat, causing the man to raise his weapon again in Digby's direction. "I'm sorry, but leaving is not an option at this point."

"Who the hell are you?" Deuce stepped closer.

"I am Lord Graves and I am here to negotiate." Digby lowered his hands despite the guns being pointed at him. Keeping his movements slow, he held his coat open. "My friends and I are unarmed, and I have information that your superiors will want to hear."

"What about him?" Deuce gestured to Alex.

"I just have a machete." The artificer held perfectly still.

"Yes, see, it's just a machete." Digby let go of his coat and stood tall. "We mean you no harm."

"Oh yeah, why haven't I seen you before?" Deuce kept his gun raised.

"We're new to the area," Rebecca chimed in.

"Okay, and what information do you have for Mr. Rivers?" Deuce lowered his weapon again.

"He will find out when I tell him." Digby kept his answer vague.

"No, you'll tell me now." The man narrowed his eyes.

"No, I won't." Digby stepped forward.

"I hope you know what you're doing," Elenore whispered from beside him.

"Heh, obviously I have no idea." He glanced back and gave her a wink before addressing the armed group again. "I assure you, your boss will want to hear what I have to say, but I will only speak to him in person."

Deuce stared at him for a long beat, letting the tension build before finally speaking. "Alright, fine. I'll take you upstairs. But I make no promises that he'll let you leave. And tell your guy to drop the machete."

"Perfect." Digby clapped his hands together and gestured for Alex to comply before strolling forward like he didn't have a care in the world.

Their guns weren't really a threat to him, and it seemed that behaving unpredictably would serve to keep them off balance. The only question was how many people this Rivers fellow had inside and how well armed they were. A gun might not be able to kill him but a bullet to the brain would put him down long enough to be a problem. Especially since he'd decided to leave his bone crown and clawed gauntlet behind in an attempt to appear less threatening. The down side being that he'd lost the added layer of protection that they provided. Not to mention, he'd left Tavern back at the kestrel to stand guard. He could call the infernal spirit back to the gemstone he carried and resummon them, but that would cost mana and he wasn't sure how much he would need.

Digby checked his HUD.

MP: 253/253

It was certainly enough to do some damage, but still, it would only go so far. Of course, he did have his staff stashed in his void just in case. If things got hairy, he could call it forth and forge a blood blade on its head to make a spear. If things got real bad, he'd consumed enough resources to activate his temporary mass mutation. The suit of necrotic armor would probably be enough to ensure a victory. Hopefully.

I don't love the uncertainty. Digby walked forward with confidence regardless of his fears. *This is not how I wanted to do this.* He had wanted to come from a position of strength when he approached Rivers, but the fact that he needed to free Elenore's child gave his opponent leverage.

I do not like this, indeed.

The armed group surrounded them with two in front to lead the way and three in the back, ready to shoot. Deuce walked in the middle next to Digby, making a point to stay close to Elenore.

"You sure you want to do this?"

"I'm getting my son back." She remained firm.

"Okay, I know." He tightened his grip in his rifle. "I tried, you know. To talk him out of sending the high-cards after you."

"Bullshit," she snapped back. "If you really cared, you wouldn't be following that bastard in the first place."

"Hey, you're not the only one in a difficult situation." His voice sounded sincere. "The world isn't what it used to be. I do what I have to to keep people safe."

Digby arched an eyebrow at the man's response. It almost seemed like he wasn't any more fond of his lord than Elenore was, like he was somehow under duress. He walked closer to the man to do some digging.

"I must say, my associates and I happened to be in an apothecary near where your group took down one of those creatures yesterday." He gave the man a smile to show that he approved. "My apologies for not introducing myself at the time but I must say, your teamwork and organization was impressive. You must have become quite experienced in dealing with these monsters."

"You saw that?" Deuce seemed to relax, accepting the compliment for what it was. "Those day shriekers are the worst that I've had to deal with. I'm just glad the other types only come out at night."

"Shriekers?" Digby pretended like it was the first time he'd heard the word. "I can see why you would call them that. Revenants do like to make noise, I suppose. Especially the lightwalkers."

"What's that?" Deuce furrowed his brow.

"Revenants," Digby repeated. "That's what those creatures are called. There's many different types, but the ones that remain active while the sun is up are called lightwalkers."

"Oh, so that's the name your people gave them." He tilted his head to one side.

"No, I mean that's what they are called." Digby gave him a smug grin. "Like I said, I know things that your lord would be interested in."

"Oh…" Deuce trailed of, looking confused as they approached the front entrance of the casino.

"Let me ask you, why is it that you work for this Rivers fellow?" Digby did his best to appear curious. "You sound like you at least understand and feel for Elenore's plight. Surely you could take a stand and—"

"Are you insane?" The man glanced around. "Don't say shit like that."

"Like what?" Digby feigned innocence. "I just mean to say that you seem to be well trained, judging by how you handled that revenant yesterday, so you might actually stand a chance if you gather together with some of the other like-minded survivors in the area."

"Shut the hell up, right now." Deuce blocked the doors, stopping Digby and the others from entering. "If anyone heard what you just said, all of us would be as good as dead." He flicked his eyes around as if searching for threats. "Rivers is not someone to screw with, and his high-cards are worse."

"I hardly see how they could be that scary." Digby played dumb.

"Haven't you wondered why there are so few monsters around in Vegas beyond those flying ones?" Deuce leaned closer. "I'll give you a hint, it wasn't my team that killed them all. I don't even know how they did it. We're just the grunts. We're the guys that take care of the stragglers and collect supplies. The rest of the guys up there," he pointed toward the hotel above, "they're ruthless and will not think twice about offing you, me, or a bunch of kids for that matter. So whatever you have planned here, better not make trouble, because Rivers will make you regret ever having set foot in Vegas."

"Alright, alright." Digby backed down. "I get your point. I shan't do anything that would draw the ire of your lord."

"Christ." Deuce glared at Elenore. "Where the hell did you find this guy? He sounds like a LARPer."

"We just met, actually." She remained firm. "And he was willing to help when there was no one else to turn to."

"Yes, I'm practically a saint." Digby batted his eyelashes, enjoying the fact that he had eyelashes again. Rebecca snorted drawing an irritated glare. "Do you mind?"

She shook her head and remained quiet as Deuce finally opened the door. He nodded to the rest of his men, signaling them to return to their post while he accompanied Digby and the others the rest of the way. For a moment, he thought they might be allowed to walk in with less guns surrounding them, but unfortunately, another pair of guards came to meet them as soon as they were inside. He noted the pretense of a low-value playing card stuck to each of them. Clearly neither of them were members of the high-cards that Deuce seemed so concerned about. Digby filed the detail away for later as a strong scent reached his nose.

"Is that bacon?" Alex perked up.

"Probably." Deuce continued forward. "The high-cards are at breakfast. They made a special trip out this morning and hit the buffet as soon as they got back. Try not to stare when we pass by the dining area."

"Noted." Digby nodded as they walked through the casino's entryway. Taking it in, he had to force himself not to focus on any one detail for too long. The extravagance was simply unmatched. Ever since waking up in this new world, Digby had been shocked by the opulence that modern people lived with, but this was on an entirely new level. The castle he'd encountered the Heretic Seed in was a mere hovel in comparison.

Decorative filigree and murals covered every wall, as well as the ceiling. Even more impressive was the size of it all. The casino itself covered more land than his village had back in his day. Hell, the place had a larger footprint than most of the buildings back in Seattle. It made sense why Rivers chose it as his palace.

"Keep up." Deuce gestured with his head as Digby began to fall behind.

He picked up his pace only to find himself dumbstruck again as they passed a wall of weaponry. There must have been hundreds of firearms. Rifles, handguns, even explosives, all stored haphazardly against the side of the room. Boxes of bullets were stacked high, along with body armor ranging from police vests and helmets to full military gear. There might have even been enough to give Skyline a run for its money, provided they could find a way to fill out their ranks with some more Heretics to even things out.

Rebecca gave a low whistle. "Deuce wasn't exaggerating when he said they were well armed here."

"If you think that's impressive, you should see what's kept in storage. The first week after everything fell apart, the high-cards hit every possible place where weapons and ammo might be stored." Deuce gave her a knowing look. "There's even a tank in the garage."

"I…" Digby slowed, shaking his head as his mouth curled down into a disgusted frown.

"You have something to say?" Deuce slowed as well.

"No. I have nothing to say," Digby practically snarled back, having trouble keeping himself under control. The sight of their armory sent a surge of rage through his body. There wasn't a need for Elenore or anyone else to hand over their supplies for protection. Not when there were enough weapons for everyone just sitting here.

Digby grimaced. It was becoming clearer and clearer what sort of man Rivers was. The bastard and his men had scooped up every usable weapon in the city to ensure that none of the survivors in the area would be able to use them. Rivers was keeping them dependent on him while ensuring that they couldn't rise up against him. It was sickening. It was vile.

It was downright medieval.

That was what bothered him the most. The situation was the same as it was back when he'd been alive, when lords hoarded all the resources while their subjects worked the land. Except, somehow, this was worse.

Digby clenched his jaw, wondering if he could actually work with a man like Rivers. It was clear that winning him over as an ally would prove useful, then again, he might be doing the world a favor if he simply ate the man. Either way, he was going to have to make a decision soon.

Passing through another opulent room, Digby spotted a dining establishment built into the edge of the casino floor. Within it, over a dozen men spread out across the various tables, each with a playing card stapled to the back of their chair. The ten, jack, queen, and king of each suit marked them all. The only cards absent were the aces.

Digby had only played poker a few times since waking up in

the future, but he knew enough to recognize these men as the high-cards that had been mentioned. Women dressed in white coats stood behind a partition that lined the wall, serving food from dozens of stations. The men got up from their tables and claimed eggs, bacon, bread, baked goods, meat, and a variety of other foods. When their plates were piled high, they returned to their tables and shoveled it all down their gullets.

"Jesus." Elenore breathed the word under her breath. "That's enough food to last my people weeks."

"Indeed." Digby narrowed his eyes at the display.

"They must have taken this casino before the power grid failed and kept its generators running to keep this much food from spoiling," Rebecca added just before her stomach growled. "Sorry, all I've had was coffee and stale popcorn."

"Excuse me." Deuce stepped forward, ignoring their comments. Digby couldn't help but notice that he ducked his head in a submissive manner as he approached the men at the tables. "I have some people here to see the boss."

"And you just brought them in?" A burly man at the end of one of the tables, with a king of diamonds stapled to his sleeve, turned and spoke through a mouthful of sausage and eggs.

Deuce winced. "Well, yes, they have information that Mr. Rivers is going to want to hear."

"Indeed." Digby stepped forward to help, making sure to act as non-threatening as possible. "Though I will only discuss matters with Rivers in person. What I have to say is not for the ears of those below him."

"Fuck that, you'll tell me now." The man shoved another forkful down his throat. "Then I'll decide if you get to see him, or if I'll put a bullet in your head." Bits of egg flew from his mouth as he spoke.

"I certainly will not." Digby stood in defiance. "I assure you that Rivers will understand the need for discretion once I have said what I came here to say."

"Suit yourself." The man pulled a pistol from a holster at his hip and raised it to point a Digby's head.

Both Deuce and Elenore froze.

Digby, however, simply rolled his eyes. "Oh please, you're not the first person to point a firearm at me. You may shoot me if you wish, but the information I carry will only be relevant for so long and Rivers will want to know while it is still useful to him."

A long moment went by before the king of diamonds responded.

"Why the hell is she here?" He shifted his pistol's aim to Elenore. "We made a special trip out to her this morning to get her brat. If you think we're giving the kid back, think again. She needs to learn her place."

Elenore clenched her fist. "I—"

"Relax." Digby held out a hand to hold her back. "I said I would help your situation and I will. No need to escalate things." He gave his attention back to the man pointing the gun at them, exerting every ounce of self-control he had to keep himself from lunging at the man's throat. Keeping things polite was going to be harder than he thought. He tried his best regardless. "The same goes for you; there's no reason why we all can't be allies here. So why don't you lower the gun and let Mr. Rivers decide our fate?"

The king of diamonds stared at him for a few more seconds before holstering his weapon and repeating the same words as before. "Suit yourself."

"Thank you." Digby nodded.

"The boss is back there." The gruff man hooked a thumb toward the back of the dining establishment before turning to Deuce. "Take your new friends back to see him."

He shook his head. "They aren't my friends, just people that—"

"You brought them in here, didn't you?" The king of diamonds gave him a cruel smile. "I hope for your sake Rivers isn't angry."

"I…" Deuce's voice quivered and trailed off as his mouth hung open.

"It's alright." Digby stepped forward, glancing back at the nervous man for an instant. "We'll be sure to make you look good." Deuce gave him an awkward nod and joined him. Once the nervous man was close enough, Digby whispered, "At the very least, I'll make sure you survive if I decide to eat your boss."

"What?" Deuce stopped short.

"What?" Digby continued as if he hadn't said anything, leaving no room for argument before he rounded a corner to find another table with a lone occupant.

Four armed men dressed in pristine suits stood guard, each with an ace pinned to their lapel. A type of firearm that Digby was unfamiliar with hung down under their coats. They were larger than any pistol, but smaller than a rifle.

Perhaps, something in the middle?

Digby pushed aside the question as his gaze settled on the man at the table, Rivers. To put things simply, he was nothing like what Digby expected. Surely a man that had claimed the strip's finest casino as his home and subjugated the entire city would have the presence of a lord. Yet, such was not the case.

Rivers sat, dressed in an expensive but ill-fitting suit that hung from his lumpy form in all the wrong ways. Digby couldn't help but notice the lack of style. In a world where one could simply claim whatever garment they chose, his outfit failed to impress. Hell, from the look of it, Rivers didn't seem to understand how clothes were even supposed to look. The garments Digby wore may not have been anything fancy, but at least they accented his frame in a positive way. In fact, by just comparing appearances, it was clear that Digby was far more lordly than the man sitting at the table.

The aces stepped forward as Digby approached, making sure to keep him from getting too close. He made a point of sweeping his focus across the group of men to analyze them to avoid any surprises. Each of the aces came up as armored humans. As for Rivers himself, he was simply labeled as a common human.

"Who are you?" Rivers looked up from a plate of steak and eggs.

Digby started to answer before he realized that the unfashionable man was squinting at the playing card fastened to Deuce's chest armor.

Does he not even recognize his own men?

Digby tried his best to hide his shock.

He probably doesn't recognize Elenore either.

There was something even more disturbing about that. The idea that the man had abducted the child of a woman that he didn't even know the face of.

"I'm, ah, the two of clubs, sir. I'm sorry to bother you." Deuce lowered his head and gestured to Digby. "But I have someone here that has requested a meeting. He says he has important information and was only willing to share it with you. I have searched each member of his party to ensure that none of them are armed."

Rivers shoved a forkful of eggs in his mouth as he shifted his gaze to Digby's coven, looking them up and down as if judging their clothing in the same way Digby had done to Rivers a moment before. "You look like nobodies. What's with that shoulder thing?"

Digby glanced at the Goblin King's costume armor that was attached to his coat and granted him an extra fifty mana. "It's a pauldron. I'm told it's quite famous actually. I claimed it from a museum that had labeled it as having been previously worn by a king."

"That so?" Rivers sawed through the steak on his plate with a knife. "So what's your name? And why should I care?"

Digby's eye twitched for a second before he got it under control. "I am Lord Graves, and I come with an offer of friendship."

"Lord?" Rivers shoved a piece of steak into his mouth. "Sounds made up."

"Maybe, but I feel it has been earned at this point," Digby answered, trying to make himself sound important.

"Well, I haven't heard of you, so you can't be that important." Rivers chewed on the same bite of steak for longer than what seemed appropriate. "So, why would I want the friendship of a nobody?"

"I come to inform you of an impending threat that will concern this entire city, as well as an offer of cooperation at dealing with it." Digby slipped past the aces standing in his way to get closer to the table.

Rivers glanced up from his meal for a second but didn't argue. "You know, nobody can get steak anymore. I'm probably the only one that has any. I have a freezer packed with the stuff. There's so much steak in there that I can't eat it all. I've done well for myself here. People would kill for a meal like this, but you see, they can't. Not in this city. I have all the guns. I even have a tank. Whatever you say is coming can't be that bad. So what is it that could be bad enough for me to need help?"

Digby arched an eyebrow, having trouble following the man. He wasn't sure if Rivers was putting on an act to throw him off balance or if he was just trying to brag. It was as if he was actually proud of the fact that he was hoarding food while others were struggling to survive.

Fine then. If he likes to boast, I may as well keep him talking and find out more.

Digby pushed the man's question aside and gave him something else to brag about. "Before we get into the danger looming on the horizon, I'd love to know how you were able to take command of this city so effectively. I must say, I know what sorts of monsters lurk out there in the world, and I am impressed that I have seen so few out and about."

"Yes, we did a great job. A better job than anyone else, that's for sure. Those monsters were nothing." Rivers continued to boast.

"Yes, I dare say you acted fast enough to prevent them from gaining a foothold here." Digby helped to prop him up. "Clever."

"Very clever." Rivers nodded at the compliment.

"The people here must be grateful that you've kept them safe." Digby probed a little further, wondering if the man was really as simple as it seemed.

"You would think so." Rivers put down his fork as if the question disgusted him. "There's several groups of survivors out there and none of them respect what I've done. I keep them all safe, and they try to steal from me. Just yesterday I sent out a group to collect supplies, and they barely came back with anything. One of my guys tried to defend them, saying they didn't have any more, but that's bullshit. I know it's bullshit."

Deuce tensed up visibly, though, from the look of things,

Rivers had no idea which of his men he was talking about. He certainly didn't realize that he was standing in front of him.

"That group has more food, and I have a right to it. They wouldn't be alive if it wasn't for me. They're just too stupid to understand that." Rivers shook his head.

"Indeed." Digby nodded along. "It must be difficult to maintain this city when you have to keep them all in line."

"Tell me about it." Rivers gestured for Digby to have a seat, clearly getting more comfortable with him. "Take this one group for example, they've been light on shipments for over a week. So I sent my best men out there at dawn to put their leader, a woman if you can believe it, in her place."

Digby sat down and settled in. "Yes, I heard you took her child."

Rivers looked up from his meal. "Where did you hear that?"

"From her." Digby gestured to Elenore as she stood behind him. "This is Ms. Sharp, the leader of the group you're speaking of. The woman you took a child from this morning."

"What?" Rivers slapped his cutlery down and searched the room for someone to scream at.

"Hold on now." Digby held up both hands. "I didn't bring her here to cause you any problems. And I assure you, I have the best interests of your city at heart."

"And you, what, want me to return her kid? That what you want?" A mocking tone entered into Rivers' voice.

"Oh lord no." Digby responded with a friendly chuckle. "In fact, I have a few brats in my group I could send your way. So no, I would never ask you to return her child for free. Although, after seeing the resources that you have been able to gather here, I'm not sure what I could offer you that you don't already have in plenty. Well, besides information."

Rivers calmed down a little. "That's right. You said you have something to tell me."

"Indeed I do, but now that I've heard more of your situation and the burdens your accomplishments have placed you, I have a better offer."

It was clear what type of person Rivers was. Digby had known enough people that believed themselves better than everyone else. There was nothing he was going to be able to say that might convince his opponent to help anyone. Not when he didn't even see the survivors in Vegas as people. If that was the case, he needed to try a different angle. One that allowed a man like Rivers to feel like the king he clearly thought he was.

Digby leaned forward with a smile, placing a hand on the table. "How about we play a game?"

"A game?" Rivers furrowed his brow.

"Yes, of course. This is Vegas, is it not? And judging by your men here, you must appreciate a game of cards." Digby tapped his fingers on the table. "Besides, it must be awfully boring running this city and dealing with all of the problems that come along with it. So why don't we have some fun, you and I? I can tell you everything I know while we play." He chuckled as if he really was enjoying himself despite the urge to tear the man's heart out. "You can name your prize if you win. What do you say, sound fun?"

"But what do you want if you win?" Rivers leaned forward as well.

"Oh gosh, I don't know." Digby let his eyes wander the room as if he didn't already have something in mind. "All I ask is that you'll consider becoming my ally against the threat that I have seen on the horizon."

Elenore took a sharp breath. "What about my——"

"Oh yes, of course." Digby slapped his forehead as if he'd forgotten about her plight, figuring it was an attitude that would feel relatable to his opponent. "I swear, I'd lose my head if it weren't attached to my shoulders." He gestured to Elenore behind him. "And throw Ms. Sharp's child in if I win as well."

Rivers stared at him for a few seconds before letting out a laugh. "I gotta say, you're an odd guy, but you've got one thing very right. I don't get to have much fun here."

"Perfect," Digby stood up and stared down at the disgusting man. "Let's play."

CHAPTER EIGHT

Digby followed two men in suits, the aces of clubs and spades, as they led him up a stairwell. Rivers walked in front with two more men, the aces of hearts and diamonds. Digby debated simply killing them all before they had a chance to call for help, but he refrained. As much as he disliked this Rivers fellow, he wasn't completely sure he would be able to kill all of his men before one of them called to the rest of the high-cards down stairs. Not to mention he wasn't completely sure how many more men Rivers had.

If the playing card system proved true, then there were at least fifty-two. Alone, Digby wouldn't have been so concerned, but considering he had brought Elenore with him, he wasn't sure he could keep her alive if everything went to hell. He was just glad Alex and Rebecca had a Barrier spell to keep themselves safe.

That being said, it was looking less and less likely that he would be able to find a way to work with Rivers. Some of his men, such as Deuce, seemed open to changing sides, but it was clear the high-cards enjoyed the privilege of their status and he wasn't sure about the rest.

Doesn't look like I can simply cut the head off the snake. Digby grimaced, looking back for a second to catch a hateful glare coming from Elenore. Apparently she didn't appreciate the way he'd acted so casual when discussing the release of her child. He offered her a wink to imply that he had something in mind. As far as that something might be, he was still making things up as he went along.

Rebecca and Alex brought up the rear, each of them looking confident as they walked deeper into the belly of the beast.

Well, at least they trust that I know what I'm doing.

That was when Rivers pulled him out of his thoughts.

"I've been thinking about what I want if I win."

"Name your prize." Digby tried his best to stay friendly despite a growing urge to lunge at the man. "As long as it is within my power, I will make it happen."

Rivers shuffled forward, staring at the ceiling. "I want that woman you brought with you to apologize for taking advantage of me."

"What?" Elenore shrieked, clearly having no intention of apologizing to the man that held her child captive.

"That's it?" Digby didn't give her a chance to argue.

"No." Rivers slowed for a few seconds. "I'd like your loyalty. You might look like a nobody but you have guts. I can appreciate that. So I'd like you to swear fealty to me."

"I can handle that." Digby smirked. "If I lose, that is."

"We'll see. I never lose, you know." Rivers stopped at a door and pushed through into a gaudy room covered in more gold than even Digby could appreciate.

A table covered in green felt sat in the center of the room with several chairs surrounding it. The only other detail in the room was a bar with a selection of bottles sitting behind it.

"This is the high-roller suite. It's where the big boys used to play." Rivers plopped down into a chair and pulled up to the table.

The door of the room slammed closed as soon as Digby and his accomplices were inside. The aces of clubs and spades stood guard while the heart and diamond moved to bracket Rivers where he sat.

Digby sat down without hesitation. Dropping both hands to his sides below the table where Rivers couldn't see, he beckoned to his

Heretics. Rebecca and Alex got the hint, moving to stand behind him to mirror the other side of the table. Elenore simply stepped around to watch from the sidelines as tension filled the room.

"You there, two of clubs. Come over here and deal." Rivers tossed a small box in Deuce's direction, forcing him to lunge forward to catch it as the man's throw hadn't quite had the strength to travel far enough.

Taking his rifle off, Deuce leaned it on the table near Elenore. Digby arched an eyebrow, wondering if he had placed the weapon within her reach on purpose. There was a chance that the man was more willing to change sides than he had thought. Digby filed that little tidbit away in case he lost the game.

"Here we are." Rivers grabbed a stack of poker chips from the side of the table.

Digby hadn't been sure of their purpose the day before, but thanks to his night spent watching the same heist movie over and over, he understood that the chips were meant to be used in place of money during games.

"Hmm." Rivers placed ten of them down in front of Digby "I think this is about what your loyalty is worth." He added one more. "And this is what that woman's apology means to me."

"Alright, and for you, we have your consideration of an alliance." Digby held out a hand toward the other side of the table.

Rivers smirked and placed three stacks of ten in front of himself before adding another five. "And these are for the kid. If you can take everything, then I'll give you what you came for."

"I can't help but feel I'm at a disadvantage." Digby flicked his eyes between his pile of chips and his opponent's.

"Like I said before, I've done very well for myself. Having an advantage comes with the package." Rivers laughed. "If you feel you need more bargaining power, you can throw in something, or someone, else to sweeten the pot."

"Don't worry, Lord Graves. You've got this." She responded in a flattering tone that caused him to double check it was really Rebecca who had just spoken. Even Alex shot her a sideways glance as she slipped her arm around Digby's shoulder, letting her hand slide to the back of his neck, where she tapped the base of his skull with one finger. A second later he felt the familiar sensation of mana moving through her blood.

"Thank you, Becky." Digby glanced to his HUD to where her name was listed.

REBECCA: 279/294

She was fifteen points down. Digby ran a mental inventory of her spells to figure out what she had just cast.

Veritas? Digby smiled.

With the perception spell active, she would be able to tell whether or not Rivers was lying whenever he played a card. As long as Rebecca could figure out a way to let him know the results, all Digby had to do was get him to say something that might indicate the contents of his hand.

"We're gonna keep things simple." Rivers placed a single chip down in front of him. "Give me five."

Digby placed a chip as well, receiving a hand of cards in return.

This isn't so hard. He fanned out what he'd been dealt. *Now how does this game work again?* Digby had watched Mason and the other soldiers play poker once or twice over the last two weeks, but not quite enough to fully grasp the game. Rivers didn't give him time to figure things out.

"Going to start strong." He dropped five of his chips into the center of the table.

"Alright." Digby matched his bet.

"Give me two more." Rivers slid a pair of cards face down to Deuce, who slipped him two in return.

Digby froze for a moment, trying to remember how the game worked without letting on that he'd never actually played before. There seemed to be a middle step where he could trade in the cards that he didn't want before betting again. He stared down at his hand.

All he had was a pair of fives and an ace. At first glance he thought about throwing away the ace, since it was only worth one, however, judging by the fact that the men in suits guarding the room were all marked with an ace, he assumed they were somehow more important and thus, worth holding on to.

Digby placed five chips in the center and asked for a pair the same as Rivers. In response he got a six and another ace. Digby remained calm, assuming the trade had given him something to work with. That was when Rivers pushed nearly a third of his chips to the center of the table.

"Feeling confident, are you?" Digby tried his best to keep his voice even, unsure if he should be concerned or not.

"Oh, I think I'll do very well." Rivers smiled down at his cards.

Rebecca touched her finger to the back of Digby's neck to traced a letter T across his cold skin.

I suppose that means the man is telling the truth.

Digby wasn't completely sure how betting worked, but it made sense that he would have to match the amount with his own chips. Glancing at his pile, he realized that he would have to bet everything he had to stay in the game. Digby clenched his jaw, realizing that Rivers would be able to use his chip advantage to pressure him into submission. It was infuriating.

"Sometimes in this world, you have to take a risk." Digby pushed the rest of his chips into the center and grinned. He wasn't about to let some pompous ass push him around.

"What do you have?" Rivers flipped his cards over showing two pair as well, except with kings and fives.

"Seems luck was on my side." Digby let out an awkward chuckle as he won by a narrow margin. He claimed his winnings, bringing his war chest close to the amount of his enemy's. "Shall we go again?"

A new hand was dealt, leaving Digby with a fairly strong set of cards. He bet accordingly, feeling a little more comfortable now that he wasn't so far behind. His opponent did the same, but kept his bets a little more conservative. With Rebecca's help, they were able to gain ground little by little.

"So tell me, what is this threat that you say is coming?" Rivers placed a few chips.

Digby matched his bet. "Have you heard of an organization called Skyline?"

Rivers arched an eyebrow as he requested another three cards. "I have. They're a private military contractor."

"Well, that's the threat." Digby passed two cards to Deuce. "They are the ones who spread this curse through the world and created the new monsters that your people call shriekers. Though the proper name for them is revenant."

"Why would Skyline want to do that?" Rivers glanced down at his hand.

"Because destroying the world allows them to rebuild it in the image of the organization who pulls their strings." Digby locked eyes with the unpleasant man to let him know he was serious. "Behind Skyline is another organization. I'm still investigating them, but they are building some kind of empire."

"Why should I care what they do?" Rivers showed his hand, winning a small amount of chips.

"Like I said, this empire is growing. And to do that, they need subjects." Digby placed a single chip out to start the next round. "So far they are recruiting everyone they possibly can. The youngest ones are sent to their training facility to be indoctrinated and the rest are sent to a colony that's being built on the other side of this country. They are a threat to Vegas because they will certainly have an interest in the people here and they will not sit by and let you rule the city."

"And like I said." Rivers claimed a new hand. "I have plenty of guns and people to shoot them."

"That won't be enough." Digby shook his head. "Skyline and their parent organization have far more power, and they gain more with each passing day. I intend to fight them when they arrive and, in time, you will be forced to as well, whether you join me or not. What I'm asking of you is to assist me now, so that we might deal a striking blow against this mutual enemy before they become too powerful to be stopped."

"Hmm..." Rivers stared at his hand, trading in three cards. "That's a pretty big request. What sort of weapons and manpower do you have?"

"A fair question." Digby exchanged two cards. "As far as fighters go, I have a small combat team."

"You're not bringing much to the table with that." Rivers sat a little taller, clearly feeling superior.

"True." Digby nodded. "However, I also hold a weapon that will help to even the odds. Without it, there would be nothing capable of standing in the way of Skyline's path." Digby kept his explanation vague, not wanting to tell the man about the Heretic Seed. If only because revealing the existence of magic was sure to make him sound like a madman.

"What kind of weapon are you talking about?" Rivers probed a little deeper.

"That is information that I shall save for when our game here ends." Digby puffed out his chest making it clear that he considered himself an equal.

Of course, that was when Rivers pushed all of his chips into the center of the table. "I'm all in."

Digby hesitated, unsure what to do. Glancing at his hand, he had three of a kind, which was relatively strong as far as he understood it.

"Thinking you have a winning hand over there, do you?" Digby eyed his opponent, hoping he would give an answer that Rebecca could read as either true or false.

"I'm sitting pretty right now." Rivers smiled and leaned back in his seat.

Rebecca traced the letter L along the back of Digby's neck with one finger.

A Lie.

Digby grinned as he added up his chips and compared them with what was in the center of the table. He had been doing well with Rebecca's help, so he had enough to match the bet. Though, it would nearly clean him out and leave him with only a single chip with which to continue on. Tossing the risks aside, Digby pushed his chips in. Considering Rivers had just lied about what was in his hand, moving forward was the only choice. Rivers must have been trying to pressure him into folding.

"Let's see how this plays out, then."

"I respect that. You only live once, so take everything you can." Rivers nodded in approval. "That's what I always say."

"You'd be surprised how many lives I've had." Digby smirked as he dropped his cards to the table and reached for the pile of chips between them.

"Not so fast." Rivers leaned forward and placed his hand on the table. A self-satisfied chortle creeped from his mouth as he revealed a pair of jacks and two tens.

What just happened? Digby froze as his mind struggled to process the turn of events. *How did I lose?* Rebecca's hand tensed on the back of his neck. She was just as confused as he was. *But, he was lying when he said his hand was good. How could it have been the opposite?*

Then, it was obvious. His opponent's hand had changed between his lie and when he revealed his cards. Digby replayed the man's actions in his mind. Rivers had leaned back just after lying. It didn't seem suspicious at the time, like he was just getting comfortable, yet he had dropped his hands down into his lap where they were blocked from view by the table.

You filthy cheat.

Digby had to suppress a cackle. If Rivers wanted to play dirty, he should have chosen his opponent better. At the very least he needed to be less obvious about it. A crooked smile slithered across his face.

Never cheat a cheat, you fool.

"Well done." Digby picked up his last chip and slapped it down at the center of the table. "I suppose you should finish me off then."

"Of course." Rivers matched him and claimed his cards.

Digby did the same, looking down at his hand. It was full of nothing but low cards. Three were in numerical order but the other two were entirely unhelpful. Despite that he pumped his eyebrows and nodded as if he was satisfied with what he got. "Looks like I should be able to turn things around."

"Good luck." Rivers laughed and slid two cards to Deuce for an exchange.

"How many would you like?" Deuce turned to Digby.

"None for me." Digby sat back, making sure Rebecca could see his hand. "I think this will do nicely." He felt her fingers press down on his neck clearly questioning what the hell he was doing.

Glancing back to her, he reached back to place his cold hand on hers and added a request that he hoped she would understand. "Wish me luck."

A smile, followed by the familiar sensation of her moving mana through her blood told him she'd heard him loud and clear.

"Yes, this will do fine." Digby placed his worthless cards down.

Rivers tossed his cards aside the instant he set eyes on the illusionary straight sitting in front of him.

Bravo, Becky. Digby clapped his hands and reached for his chips, replenishing his supply back up to ten. Of course, his cards were still worthless, but thanks to a Waking Dream spell, the faces of two of them had changed values to create a simple numerical straight. Digby let a villainous chuckle slip as he opened the next round.

Take that, you overconfident ass.

The hand that followed went the same as the last, ending with Digby claiming another stack of chips. It was too easy. Even better was the look on Rivers' bloated face. With each subsequent hand, the man turned a darker shade of red until his cheeks puffed up like a corpse that had been left in the water for too long. The chips rolled in, leaving Rivers flabbergasted. Even with his continuous cheating, he couldn't compete against the Heretic Seed's magic.

Cackles snuck out here and there as Digby began to enjoy himself a little too much. Once his dominance was clear, he glanced at his coven's status on his HUD and made a note of his illusionist's remaining mana.

REBECCA: 99/294

I should end this before she's forced to use the rest of her MP.

It wouldn't do if she ended up needing it later on. Digby nodded to himself and pushed all of his chips into the center to force Rivers to go all in. The braggart complied, grumbling as he traded out a pair of cards for his final hand. It wouldn't help. Nothing would.

Digby tossed another worthless hand to the table, letting

Rebecca change it into something sure to win. In this case a pair of eights and two queens.

"Well, thank you for playing, but I suggest you have one of your men bring Ms. Sharp her child." Digby sat back in his chair, catching a hopeful expression on Elenore's face from the corner of his eye before letting his gaze fall back on his opponent.

Rivers glanced back and forth between his hand and the cards on the table, clearly in shock from the fact that he had lost. There was no way, he had something that could win.

"You cheated."

"I'm sorry, what?" Digby cocked his head to the side.

"I don't know how, but…" Rivers set his hand down revealing a queen of hearts that was also present in Digby's winning hand.

Well, damn. Digby clicked his tongue. The one weakness of Rebecca's spell was that there was always a risk of her changing a card's face to something in his opponent's hand. *I have to think fast.*

"Are you sure that duplicate isn't from the box you have hidden under the table?" He covered his crime with an accusation of his own.

"No." Rivers slapped his hand on the felt. "I was dealt that queen at the start."

"Oh, so you admit that you have been switching cards out this entire time, then?" Digby smirked.

Rivers continued to look back and forth between his cards and Digby's as the illusion unraveled, causing the queen in question to melt away to reveal a three that had been there the entire time.

"What just happened?" Rivers jabbed a plump finger down on the card. "How did it change?"

"Let's call it a trick of the trade." Digby, shrugged. "Considering we both cheated, I would call it even and stand by our previous wager."

"Not a chance in hell." Rivers raised his voice. "I never had any intent on handing over the kid from the beginning."

"You bastard." Elenore practically leapt forward, threatening to spark a conflict.

"Hold on." Digby held up a hand to prevent the situation from getting out of control as he attempted to keep the negotiations going. "I have to ask, what good does taking someone's offspring do for you?"

Rivers settled down as a cruel expression settled onto his face. "Payment."

Digby narrowed his eyes. "Payment for what?"

"Simple." Rivers shrugged. "You screwed up worse than you could imagine, Mr. Graves."

"That's Lord Graves to you," Digby corrected through his teeth.

"I don't think so." His voice took on a mocking tone as he spoke. "You talk a big game, but you're a nobody just like I thought. I mean, you walk in here telling me about Autem and how they're going to take over my city, and you don't even know how wrong you are."

"I never said the name Autem." Digby dug his fingernails into the edge of the table.

"You didn't?" Rivers paused looking up and to the side. "I guess not. Whatever, it doesn't matter."

Digby closed his eyes as the pieces began to fall into place. He had messed up, indeed. He had underestimated how depraved the man sitting across the table from him could be. His eyes snapped back open, settling on his enemy.

"Let me guess, shortly after you took over this city, an airship from Autem showed up and offered you a deal?"

Rivers sat back, looking smug as he gestured to himself. "I am a good businessman, and I know a winning trade when I see one. Autem offered to supply my people with whatever I might need to dominate Vegas. I got it all; guns, food, anything I asked for."

"And all they asked in return was for you to send them recruits." Digby eyed the man. "Hence the children that you've been taking."

"You're not so dumb after all." Rivers laughed. "They come by once a week and pick up whoever I can gather. They're building an army, you know. Training them special and everything. That's why they need kids. They want soldiers that they can mold."

"You're a monster." Elenore gasped.

"Please, don't." Deuce stepped in front of her, almost as if he feared for her safety more than his employer's.

"You have no idea what I am." Rivers shook his head so that his jowls swayed back and forth. "I saved this city. If it wasn't for my business sense, all of you would have been eaten by those monsters without me. And Autem isn't bad either. I don't know anything about them helping to spread this plague, but who cares if they did? They're building something better. And when they do, I'll be coming out on top."

"Bah." Digby scoffed.

"Think about it." Rivers leaned forward. "A new empire that actually can keep its people under control."

"Sure, by killing off or exiling anyone that disagrees with them. What do you think will happen to you when they decide you're not useful to them anymore? Do you actually expect them to keep you around when you run out of children to give them?"

"They have guaranteed me a place in the empire once they have enough people. That was part of my deal with them. For now, they need men like me to help them get started. It's no different than investing in a startup. Like I said, I know a good deal when I see one."

"If you seriously believe that, then you're not nearly as competent as you think." Digby struggled to hold in his frustration. The man was clearly a fool, but if there was a chance to get him to understand the situation, he still had to try. Gaining a fighting force of fifty was worth the effort.

"I don't have to sit here and let you talk to me like that." Rivers stood up. "No one can talk to me like that. No one. Especially not some nobody."

"I realize you think you can trust Autem, but they don't have your people's best interests in mind. They will simply give this city an ultimatum. Join them or be executed." Digby tried his best to appeal to whatever humanity the man had, recognizing the irony that he was the only one in the room that wasn't human.

"What do I care about these people? They just need to do what they're told and they won't have anything to worry about. If they don't, then whatever happens, happens. Honestly, I'd be fine with losing some of these ungrateful losers." Rivers almost seemed amused at the idea of letting people that stepped out of line die in the streets. "The empire will be better off without them."

"You really are a monster." Digby shook his head in disbelief.

"I'm a businessman." Rivers placed his thumbs under his lapel and stood tall. "And I'm no more of a monster than you are."

"You have no idea." Digby burst out laughing. "You pathetic fool."

The tension in the room ramped up as Digby let his contempt for the man slip. The four aces in suits reached for the strange guns hanging under their coats as Deuce retreated back to stand beside Eleanor. The woman shook with anger as it became clear that she had followed Digby into a deathtrap.

Rivers gestured to Deuce. "Don't just stand there like a moron. Shoot this asshole."

The conflicted man's hand shook as he did as he was told and pulled a pistol from a holster.

"Oh please." Digby held up both hands to diffuse the situation like he had before. "I just got a little carried away. There's no need to start pointing firearms at—"

The sound of a gunshot was the last thing he heard.

CHAPTER NINE

―――

Alex froze as the scent of gunpowder drifted through the air. Digby's head hung limp over the back of his chair with black goo dripping from a gaping hole in the back of his skull. Of course, a bullet to the brain couldn't kill the necromancer, but it would keep him down for a minute or so.

The zombie must have been kicked back to the imaginary space where the Heretic Seed resided. Alex just hoped he didn't decide to hang out there longer than he had to.

I'm going to have to hold my own until he gets back out here.

Alex glanced to his HUD.

COVEN
DIGBY: 243/253
ALEX: 261/261
REBECCA: 69/294
ASHER: 87/87

He relaxed as soon as he noticed that Digby had already used ten points of mana, meaning he'd already cast a Necrotic Regeneration to repair his liquified gray matter. Alex tensed back up as soon as Rivers turned his attention to him.

"Don't you even think about doing anything stupid."

"I wasn't." Alex held up both hands and glanced around the room.

"God damn it, Graves, I trusted you!" Elenore shouted at Digby's corpse as that Deuce guy tried to hold her back. She flicked her eyes to Becca, who was also trying her best not to look threatening. "Why the hell are you just standing there? Your boss just had his brain sprayed all over the carpet."

"Yeah, he probably should have quit while he was ahead." Becca shrugged matter-of-factly.

Rivers ignored her altogether and gestured to the men in suits around the room. "Get over here and grab these two, we'll hand them over to Autem on their next pickup. That's sure to earn me some capital with them."

"Umm, hey, ah, there's no need to grab anyone." Alex tried to keep himself from being restrained. As much as he didn't want to start a fight, he wasn't about to let someone put him in a more disadvantageous situation. Hurting other people was not something he looked forward to, but if these people were really working with Autem, then they were just as much an enemy as Skyline's mercenaries.

The four men in suits raised the sub-machine guns that they wore slung under the jackets and started moving closer. Alex noted that their weapons were all aimed at him rather than Becca, almost as if they didn't perceive her as a threat.

Hooray for sexism. Alex rolled his eyes at the fact that she was far more likely to Icicle someone in the head than he was. Then again, his other options were limited. They had taken his machete away at the entrance, leaving him with no weapons to enchant. Of his attack spells, Terra Burst would certainly give him some room to work, but it required access to bare earth to cast. That just left Icicle and Fireball. Both would do some damage, but they were also flashy. Using either would almost certainly cause the men in suits to start shooting.

The only question was, would his Barrier spell be able to take that much punishment. Alex brought up his stats and glanced down the list to check something.

Current Level: 20 (2,684 Experience to next level.)

ATTRIBUTES
Constitution: 38
Defense: 33
Strength: 34
Dexterity: 33
Agility: 35
Intelligence: 36
Perception: 33
Will: 51

With his stats where they were, he was technically as strong as a man twice his size without sacrificing speed. That might give him the element of surprise.

Maybe I can get in a lucky punch.

Unfortunately, that was when he realized that all his mental planning had taken too long, leaving everyone in the room staring at him. Then, just as fast, they all turned to Becca as a blue shimmer swept over her entire body.

"What was that?" Rivers took a step back from her.

"What was what?" She played dumb, like she hadn't just cast Barrier.

Of course, Alex knew what it was. He had been avoiding casting the protective spell on himself because it manifested visually. Apparently, Becca wasn't being as conservative with the prospect of being shot at.

"Well, shit." Alex shrugged and cast Barrier. "I guess this is happening."

Without any further hesitation, he spun and punched the man behind him straight in the face. An audible crack struck the air as the suit's head snapped back. A second later, he hit the ground, out cold, just before several bullets from the ace beside him lit up

Alex's Barrier. At least a half dozen shots slammed into his side just below his ribcage. His Barrier held, but the impacts still hurt, like that time he'd done paintball with a few coworkers back in his life before the apocalypse.

Alex turned in the direction the attack had come from while simultaneously reaching for the back of a nearby chair. The suit's eyes darted around, clearly unable to figure out how he was still standing after taking a half dozen rounds from a sub-machine gun. Alex didn't give him time to figure it out before swinging the chair into the man's head. Wood cracked and splintered against his skull, putting him down for the count and leaving Alex standing there with a broken seatback in his hand.

Did I just do that? Alex stared down in disbelief at the two unconscious suits on the floor. His stats had given him more power than he'd realized. *Holy shit, I did that.*

"Don't you dare make another move." Rivers retreated back to a door on the other side of the room while his remaining aces guarded him. "I don't know what sort of body armor you got on, but a bullet to the head will work just as well as it did on him." He pointed to Digby.

Alex hesitated, realizing that both of Rivers' men had their guns aimed at him. If they opened fire at once, it wouldn't matter where they shot him. His Barrier spell was sure to fail. It was only rank D, after all. Even if he recast it, he couldn't take two full magazines and keep breathing.

That was when a sputtering noise came from Digby's chair, causing both men to snap their aim to his corpse as the necromancer twitched.

"What the hell?" All color drained from Rivers' face. Even Elenore and Deuce looked terrified. They all jumped back as Digby's cold dead hand snapped forward to grab the table, his fingers clawing at the felt for a solid grip. Then, with an unnatural twitch, Digby raised his head. Alex watched as the back of his skull reformed to close the gaping hole that had left its contents leaking out. Once it was gone, the dead man spoke.

"Fats no fay to seat a rest." His voice was horribly slurred. Clearly his brain wasn't quite back to normal.

"How?" Elenore backed up until she ran into the bar that sat behind her at the edge of the room. "That's not—"

"Possible." Digby snapped his gaze to her as he finished her sentence, his voice returning to normal. She let out a horrified gasp as her eyes locked with his emerald pupils.

"But I killed you?" Deuce's pistol started to shake.

Digby stretched his neck as if working sensation back into his body. "Sorry, but you can't kill what's already dead, and I've been dead since before everyone in this room was born. So I suggest you lower that gun. It really won't do you much good."

"What—what?" Deuce's aim faltered but kept his weapon pointed in his general direction.

"Took you long enough." Becca folded her arms as if the display had been completely normal to her, which at this point, it was.

"Yeah." Alex gestured to the men lying unconscious on the floor. "I had to start without you."

Digby glanced down at his accomplishment. "Indeed. Well done, lad."

"Shut the fuck up!" Rivers shouted as he took another step back toward the door behind him. "Who are you really?"

"I told you." A smug look stretched across Digby's face. "I am Lord Graves."

"What do you want from me?" Rivers' voice shook.

"I already told you that too." Digby slowly turned to the man, filling his voice with venom. "All I wanted was your cooperation. All I wanted was for you to help me protect this world from those that would grind it under their heel. All I wanted was for you to stand up for your world alongside me." He held out a hand toward Rivers as if the offer was still on the table.

"Get out of my city." He shook his head. "I don't know what you are, and I don't care. And don't even think about hurting me. I'm too important. Vegas can't run without me."

"I suppose that means you aim to decline my benevolent offer, then?" Digby let his outstretched hand fall a few inches.

"You're fucking right I decline." He shoved a hand under his suit jacket to retrieve a small radio. "This is Rivers, all cards report to the high-roller suite. Our guests have outstayed their welcome." He dropped the radio back down. "There's no way you're getting out of here. My people will kill every single one of you. And when they're done, I'll send them to kill the rest of your group. You're an idiot if you think I would ever help you fight."

"Pity." Digby closed his hand and lowered it back down. "Fortunately, I have amended my desires and your cooperation no longer ranks highly among them." He let out an amused chuckle. "No, now I think I prefer a decent meal."

"What are you talking about?" Rivers stepped back again, nearly reaching the door behind him.

"First, I'm going to kill everyone in this room that is pointing a gun at me." Digby flicked his eyes to Deuce, who promptly lowered his gun to his side. "Good boy." He nodded and returned his attention to Rivers. "Then, I'm going to eat you."

"You're insane." He reached back, fumbling for the door knob. "My men will be here in ten seconds."

Digby narrowed his eyes. "Oh, I can do a lot in ten seconds."

The moment the words left his mouth a black spike of blood erupted from the floor, impaling one of the aces and launching his corpse up to the ceiling. Elenore screamed at the sudden attack while the other ace raised his sub-machine gun to spray the room.

Bullets tore through the suite, peppering the walls and shattering bottles behind the bar. A few hit Alex's Barrier before he was able to duck. The spell collapsed as soon as he hit the floor, stopping the rounds just before failing. Rebecca dove for cover as well. They both looked at each other awkwardly as they waited for the barrage to stop.

Digby staggered backward as a few rounds thumped into his bone armor. A couple more went straight through his gut. It wasn't enough to hurt him but it did throw off his focus for a second.

Finally, the bullets stopped.

Alex hopped back up, ready to brawl with whoever was still standing. He swept his eyes around the room. Rivers and his remaining ace were nowhere to be seen. The door on the other side of the room hung open a few inches.

"They made a run for it." Digby started after them.

"Shit, what about the rest of his guys?" Alex turned back to the other side of the room.

That was when the last person they expected to do something brave, took the opportunity for what it was. Reaching for a radio, Deuce thumbed the call button and issued an order. "This is the two of clubs speaking to all low-cards: do not approach the high-roller suite. I repeat: do not approach the high-roller suite. This is the chance we have been waiting for. The coup is on. I repeat: it's happening now." As soon as he was finished, he dropped his radio to the floor and staggered back into the bar, clutching his stomach.

"Shit, he's been shot." Elenore caught him before he fell.

"I'm okay." Deuce coughed. "It doesn't matter what happens to me. The low-cards have been planning a takeover, we just needed an opportunity. I don't know what the hell is going on with you people or how you're still standing after being shot, but make sure Rivers doesn't escape. My men are still outside and the rest of the low cards are on patrol so they won't be able to help, but my announcement will at least cause the high-cards to think before they attack rather than rushing in here. I bought you a minute at best." He turned to Elenore. "Your kid is in one of the rooms upstairs, just make sure you don't get killed before you get to him."

"Well, aren't you the surprise of the day?" Digby gave an approving nod to the dying man.

"Yeah, sure, just live up to your words and keep Vegas free and safe." He coughed again. "The rest is up to you."

"Oh, shut up." Rebecca groaned. "Quit talking all heroic like you're about to die."

"Hey what?" He shrank away as she grabbed at the Velcro straps of his bulletproof vest to see the wound just below it.

"Quit squirming." She tore off his gear and looked him over. "You took two rounds to the gut, but they went straight through. Probably shredded your kidney and intestines."

"Good, there won't be anything to block a spell." Alex pulled out one of the flasks that Digby had looted from the gift shop back at the Never Say Die and cast purify. "Here, drink this, it will help you heal."

"Wait, no. I'm not going to make it. We would need a hospital." Deuce attempted to push him away, but lacked the strength. "There's no way to treat—"

"Shut up." Elenore grabbed his hand. "You just saw what happened. That jerk just got shot in the head and is still talking. And I don't even know how to explain that." She gestured to the suit on the other side of the room, where he still dangled from a blood spike. "Obviously we are out of our depths here."

"Fine, give me the flask." Deuce snatched the container from Alex and tipped it back. "I don't know what a drink is going to…" He trailed off as the minor healing of the purified water went to work.

"Yeah, see. Trust us, we know what we're doing." Alex grabbed his flask back and dumped the remainder on the man's wounds.

"Hey, that's cold." Deuce squealed before wincing in pain.

"Don't be a baby." Becca cast Regeneration, causing both Deuce and Elenore to fall silent as his wounds began to knit themselves together. "Yeah, I'm going to have to explain a few things."

Before she had a chance to say more, a sudden alarm blared through the halls.

"Explanations will have to wait." Digby turned away to face the door. "Our minute is almost up and company is still on the way."

"Plus we have to catch Rivers," Alex added.

"He's making a break for the garage. That's what the siren means. The asshole must have pulled one of the fire alarms on his way. He must have gotten spooked by my announcement and decided to flee. If the high-cards follow his evacuation plan, only a few should show up here. The rest are going to move to cover his escape." Deuce tried to pull himself up. "I can help."

"I think not." Digby eyed the struggling man. "You would only get in the way."

"Fine, but there's sixteen of them plus the last ace. You'll have to fight your way through all of them." Deuce sat back down in one of the chairs that Alex hadn't smashed.

"I'll be fine." Digby turned to Alex. "Think you can stay here and deal with whoever shows up so these people don't end up as my new minions? Rebecca is almost out of mana, so you're all that's left."

"I can do it." Alex nodded, trying to sound confident.

"You might have to do more than knock them out." Digby made a point of holding eye contact.

Alex glanced down at the two men that he'd taken down without killing as he realized what Digby was saying. He had killed before, but that had been back in California after watching Skyline's guardians murder a group of innocent people. This, this was different. These people were survivors just like he had been once. They weren't innocent, not by a long shot. Still, though, they were regular people.

"I can." Alex nodded again.

"Alright. I'll leave the rest to you." Digby made for the door that Rivers had escaped through. "Good luck."

With that, the necromancer slipped out of the room, leaving Alex alone to watch his back. A noticeable weight settled across his shoulders. Digby had never left him in charge of anything before. At least nothing serious. That was when he realized the zombie had stopped calling him 'boy.'

When was it that things changed?

Alex shook off the question and crouched down to the men that he'd knocked out. Unclipping their sub-machine guns from the harness that secured them to their shoulder, he claimed not one but two of the weapons. Sure, it would have been ridiculous for a normal person to attempt to wield both at once, but he was a Heretic, and Heretics were far from normal. He may not have been superhuman, but he probably had enough strength to handle the recoil.

Checking the safeties, Alex stood back up with both guns and checked his mana.

MP: 221/261

Plenty left. He cast Enchant Weapon twice. The high-cards would be there any second and with both of his sub-machine guns powered up, they would be able to shred the door like paper. Hopefully that would help him to get the drop on anyone on the other side. He approached the entrance of the room and held still, waiting and listening to catch a sound that might give away their presence.

That was when he got a brilliant idea.

Well… actually, it wasn't his idea. It was Kevin McCallister's.

Alex shoved one of his guns under his arm to free up a hand and held his palm over the doorknob to cast Heat Object.

"Time to put Home Alone logic to the test." He caught Becca shaking her head at him from behind the bar with the others just as the Heretic Seed notified him of a new rank for his cooking spell.

SPELL RANK INCREASED
Heat Object has advanced from rank C to B. Maximum temperature has increased to from 600 degrees to 1,200 degrees.

Alex reread the message, realizing that the max temp had gone up by double, making him question if the spell was really meant for cooking. He pulled his hand away before the knob started to glow and stepped back to cast Barrier on himself. He glanced at his mana, finding over half remaining.

The door handle shook a second later, followed but a sudden cry of obscenities. Alex's mind went blank. He would have liked to think that he would stay calm and aim carefully, but instead, he fired a wild spread of bullets. The sub-machine gun in his right hand tore through the door and surrounding wall, unleashing a burst of mana-infused rounds. Shouts erupted from the other side followed by a heavy thud.

1 armored human defeated, 110 experience awarded.

Without thinking about anything more, Alex slammed a foot into the door, putting his enhanced strength and adrenaline to the test. The wood cracked and splintered as he crashed forward into the hall outside.

Everything else was a blur.

Alex thrust his left gun at the first human form he saw and pulled the trigger. The man screamed and fired back in the same instant, sending a dozen rounds into the wall and ceiling. The man's shout cut off abruptly as fragments of plaster rained down. The air smelled of a mix of chalk and smoke.

1 armored human defeated, 110 experience awarded.

It happened so fast. The body fell, only to reveal another enemy raising a rifle. Alex pulled the trigger of his other gun, putting the threat down before they had a chance to shoot.

1 armored human defeated, 110 experience awarded.

Another enemy stood behind the last, forcing Alex to adjust his aim. Before he could pull the trigger, impacts lit up his Barrier from behind. Blue light shimmered across his body as he lurched forward. In response, he whipped his left hand around to aim in the direction of the attack. He fired before he even saw how many enemies were behind him. He pulled the trigger of his other gun as well, holding them both in opposite directions to take out the last of the men in front of him. Bullets came from both sides in response, all but one missing. The lone impact struck his shoulder. His Barrier flickered, stopping the round just before failing.

1 armored human defeated, 110 experience awarded.

If Alex had been paying attention to the Heretic Seed's notifications, he would have realized that he had only killed the target in front of him, meaning he'd missed whoever was behind him. A side effect of firing in a direction that he wasn't looking. A bullet in the ass reminded him of the threat, prompting him to spin to meet it as the flow of adrenaline dulled the pain in his rear.

He swept his right gun around to aim both down the hall, finding one enemy remaining. A jack of clubs was pinned to his body armor while a confused expression covered his face. He winced as Alex pulled the triggers of both guns.

Click.

Click?

Alex paused to process the sound as his overworked mind realized he'd emptied both weapons with his last attack. The man before him noticed as well, stepping back and leveling a rifle at him. Alex dropped his guns, letting them clatter to the floor at his feet as he cast Icicle. Moisture condensed into a frozen spike in the air. With a flick of his hand, he launched the shard of ice in the man's direction. It shattered against his rifle harmlessly but managed to throw off his aim as a bullet blew past Alex's ear.

He cast Icicle again, this time sending it into his enemy's chest where it slammed into his body armor and shattered into dozens of glistening fragments. The impact drove him back as Alex stomped forward, casting a third Icicle that hit home, driving itself into the jack of clubs pinned to his gear.

1 armored human defeated, 110 experience awarded.

Alex stood panting before remembering to check the hallway for more enemies. Thankfully, it was empty save for the five bodies on the floor. For a moment, he slapped a hand over his mouth as he struggled not to throw up. The scent of blood made his stomach turn. The feeling subsided after a few deep breaths.

Getting a grip on himself, he turned and headed back into the room where Becca and the others waited.

"You okay?" She rushed out from behind the bar as he approached.

"Yeah, I'll live." He dropped down into a chair. A sudden jolt of pain reminded him of the bullet he'd taken. He winced in pain and leaned to one side to avoid putting weight on the wound.

"Did you get shot in the ass?" Rebecca arched an eyebrow at him.

"A little." He sighed. "Try not to laugh."

"I won't." She leaned on a nearby table and patted one corner. "But I'm going to need you to come over here and bend over. Can't heal you with a bullet still in there. So…" She trailed off and patted the table again.

"Great." Alex sighed again. "Just great."

CHAPTER TEN

"Where are you, breakfast... I mean, Rivers?" Digby called out in his snarkiest tone as he stepped into the hall after leaving Alex to handle things in the high-roller suite. Adding on a thin layer of sarcasm he shouted again. "Sorry, that was just a joke. I'm definitely not planning on eating you."

He was having a little too much fun. Discounting the bullet to the head, things were shaping up rather well. Digby had been worried about going up against a force of fifty men, but with Deuce trading sides and calling off the low-cards, he had cut the opposition down to less than half. The odds were certainly looking up, so much that it was hard not to feel confident. Not only that, but if he played things right, he may have found the allies that he desperately needed.

"I'm coming to get you, Rivers!" he shouted as he rounded the next corner, only to find a hallway of eleven armed men. The burly man from the dining establishment down on the first floor now stood in the front. The king of diamonds. Digby grinned. "It's about time someone tried to stop me."

Debating on casting Emerald Flare to start things, he decided against it. It was best not to irradiate the building for the time being. Not to mention it was a bit too destructive to be an indoor spell. Especially when he was thinking about claiming the hotel as his new palace.

"That's far enough." The king of diamonds pointed his rifle straight at him. "One more step and we fill you with holes."

"Do you really think that will be enough?" Digby narrowed his ·eyes and opened his maw on the floor to call forth his staff.

The group of armed men all stepped back and stared in astonishment as the weapon rose from the shadowy puddle. Even in this new world, it was clear that they had never witnessed magic. Reaching out to wrap his hand around the shaft, Digby cast Forge, causing the necrotic blood that ran down its surface to surge up the weapon to collect around the hollow shape seated at its top where a glossy, black blade formed. Having a little fun with the spell, he added a skull at its base for added style. He checked his mana.

MP: 207/253

"Now, where were we?" Digby took one step forward.

"Let 'im have it." The king of diamonds opened fire, followed by everyone else in that hall.

"Gah!" Digby leapt back and ducked around the corner as bullets shredded the wall, showering him in debris and white dust. "They aren't taking chances, are they?"

Digby clutched his staff close in one hand, realizing that his other arm hung limp with a dozen or so wounds. Looking down he noticed several more holes in his coat.

Good going, Digby. Way to walk out in front of a firing squad, you half-wit. He shook his head at his miscalculation. *I really didn't think they'd start shooting that fast.*

He cast Necrotic Regeneration to handle the damage and waited for the gunfire to stop. They had to reload eventually. Again, he considered hitting them with an Emerald Flare, just to demonstrate who they were dealing with. Then, he got a better idea.

Sure, flare was his most destructive spell, but it wasn't his only powerful ability. No, if he wanted to make an impression, resorting to his mutations would have more impact. Digby let a slow chuckle bubble in his throat as he summoned the necrotic armor of his Temporary Mass.

His spine cracked and popped as each individual vertebra repositioned itself, tearing through the back of his coat. The garment had already been filled with holes, so there was little point to taking it off first. Tendrils of necrotic tissue snaked around his body into a latticework of tendons that carried plates of bone and slabs of reanimated muscle. The macabre armor knit itself together to encase him, leaving an open seam running from his navel all the way up to his neck. A dozen hands formed along the opening, clawing their way across his chest to close the seam on his armor like a zipper. Several more hands reached up to encircle his neck in a collar of outstretched fingers.

Lastly, a necrotic hood slid up the back of his head and over his ears. Four quadrants of bone snapped together over his face to form a deathly mask, replacing his normal vision with a slightly blurred and colorless view of the hallway. The muffled pops of a few more gunshots were all he could hear through the protective layer of flesh and bone.

Strength increased by 11.
Defense increased by 9.
Enhanced attributes will persist until temporary mass is
damaged or until released.

Indeed. For once, Digby agreed with the Seed's commentary. *This should even the odds nicely.*

With his armor formed, he waited, holding his staff like a spear. It looked small in his oversized clawed hands. Actually, not having used the ability before inside, he was now becoming aware just how much it increased his size. Not only was he covered in a thick hide of muscle and bone, he was also over a foot taller.

The gunfire ceased a second later, followed by a gruff voice.

"Go see if we got him."

Digby suppressed a cackle, picturing the looks on their faces when he stepped around the corner. He waited a moment to give the poor unfortunate souls that had been sent to investigate his fate a chance for them to get closer. Then he simply thrust his spear around the corner, feeling the weapon hit something firm. A choking scream followed. Digby took that as his cue.

Stepping back into the hall, he found his spear buried in the chest of a terrified man. He stared down at the wound before raising his eyes to meet Digby's horrific form.

"Sorry about this." He thrust his spear up using every ounce of his armor's enhanced strength to ram his enemy's head through the ceiling. He yanked his weapon back down to tear it free from the corpse, leaving it hanging from the hole above him.

1 armored human defeated, 98 experience awarded.

Two more of Rivers' high-cards stood just behind his first victim, each frozen in terror. Before they could react, Digby simply reached forward to run one of them through, while placing his oversized hand against the head of the other. With a flick of his wrist, he shoved the man's head to the side. His skull slammed into the wall with a crack, leaving a large, bloody dent in the plaster.

2 armored humans defeated, 196 experience awarded.

That was when the remaining high-cards further down the hall opened fire again. Bullets tore through the walls and thumped against Digby's armor as he shielded his face and chest with his arms. A couple points of discomfort told him that a pair of bullets had gotten through, though the fact that everything still function informed him that nothing important had been hit. He let out a wild cackle as they again ran out of ammunition. His voice came out dark and inhuman beneath his mask, causing a wave of sheer terror to sweep through his enemies.

The corpse hanging from the ceiling fell as if to emphasize an unspoken threat. With that, Digby reached out toward the bodies on the floor, getting a message from the Seed.

2 Corpses: Human, 77 MP required to animate.
Animate corpse? Yes/No

Why not?

Both corpses began to twitch, their limbs reaching out to steady themselves as they rose from the floor. Digby felt his Bond of the Dead form between him and his new minions.

2 zombies animated. You have 13 points each to distribute.

Without a thought he tossed five points into intelligence and the rest into strength to enhance their capabilities. The pair of reanimated corpses clawed their way up the wall until they could stand on their own to bracket him on both sides. Their eyes locked on the burly man with the king of diamonds pinned to his chest. Unsettling moans flowed from their mouths.

"Fucking run!" The leader of the high-cards pushed past a few of his comrades before shoving through a door at the end of the hall. The rest of the men followed, all running for their lives. Digby glanced up to a sign hanging by the door labeled stairs.

Hmm, how much do I want to bet that leads to the garage? He gave pursuit, chasing his prey as they fled for the stairwell. His minions staggered forward behind him, clawing at the air with each step.

The high-cards poured into the stairwell. In a panic, they slammed the door, abandoning one of their number that had lagged behind. A ten of spades peaked out from under a strap on his chest armor. Desperate pleas filled the hall as he banged on the door, begging for the others to let him in. When it became obvious that they wouldn't, he pulled a pistol and fired in Digby's direction.

"That really isn't helping." Digby reached out to curl his claws under the man's armor to lift him off the ground.

"Let go of me, you freak!" He flailed and clawed.

"Alright." Digby wound up with every ounce of his necrotic strength as he slammed the man head first into the wall next to the door. His victim cried out, the plaster giving way under the momentum of the impact. The top of his body burst through the wall to terrify the rest of the high-cards hiding in the stairwell. Several muffled shots went off as the men on the other side ended him, clearly firing on reflex. Digby left him in the wall with his legs dangling a foot above the floor.

Another experience message streaked across his vision.

After seeing how easy the wall was to break through, Digby simply punched a fist into its surface and reached for the lock on the door handle on the other side. He tore it open a second later, catching one of the high-cards frozen in fear. Snagging his armor with a claw, Digby hefted him up and tossed him back to his minions in the hall behind him. One word told them what to do.

"Rend."

The rest of the high-cards ran, making a break for the garage on the first floor. Digby opened his maw beneath the feet of the closest one and released enough mana into the gateway to increase its size. His prey cried out as he splashed into the inky pool, only to vanish beneath its surface. The shadowy opening disappeared as well, leaving nothing but a black smear on the landing.

One of the men on the steps below fired, emptying his weapon in Digby's direction. Sparks flew from the metal handrail that spiraled down into the stairway. He shrank away along with his minions to avoid any unnecessary damage. The rest of the men used the opportunity to flee.

Peeking through his oversized claws, Digby focused on a spot on the wall below to open his maw and cast forge. A black spike erupted from the opening to skewer one of the high-cards as they ran. Their legs kicked as their brain struggled to process the fact that it was already too late.

Digby pushed on, descending the stairs to the garage. Passing by the man he had just killed, he reached back and pulled him from the black spike to heft his corpse up onto the railing. Looking down the spiraling stairway, he watched as the men raced for the bottom.

"Let's brighten things up down there." Digby cast Cremation and launched the corpse down the center of the stairwell.

Emerald flames engulfed the body as it fell. He cackled in victory as it landed directly on top of one more of the high-cards to spread the fire to their clothing. Another tried to jump over the flaming mess. Digby cast another Blood Forge in the same instant, causing a jagged blade to burst from the burning corpse.

Two left.

Descending the stairs, Digby found the last of the high-cards trembling at the bottom. The king of diamonds fired another useless burst from his rifle. The bullets thumped into his chest, doing nothing to slow him down. In a display of cowardice and desperation, the burly man shoved his remaining comrade to the floor and ran for the door that led to the garage.

Digby simply stepped over them to leave the meal for his minions. After watching the king of diamonds sacrifice his own man, there was no way he was going to let him escape. Bursting into the garage, he closed in on the burly man as he struggled to run.

"Stay the hell back!" the king of diamonds shouted before pulling the trigger of his gun. It clicked.

"Out of bullets, are you?" Digby kept walking, unwilling to show mercy to the man.

"Shit!" The king of diamonds threw his rifle down and pulled a small pistol. "Why don't you die?" His finger squeezed the trigger.

Digby scoffed at the meager threat that the weapon posed, just as the loudest bang he'd ever heard rocked his surroundings.

What?

Suddenly, the king of diamonds exploded in a burst of blood and gore, his hand landing at Digby's feet still holding the small firearm.

"What!" Digby staggered back in confusion.

That was when he noticed the steady rumbling of an engine coming from the other side of the garage.

During his weeks of watching every zombie movie ever made by mankind, Digby had seen a wide variety of weapons and vehicles, which was how he recognized the source of the rumbling as soon as he saw it.

Apparently, Rivers hadn't been lying when he said he had a tank.

CHAPTER ELEVEN

"You missed!" Digby shouted as he willed the mask of his necrotic armor to retract from his face so he could address the rumbling monstrosity before him. Smoke wafted from the barrel of the enormous cannon pointing at him from the form of the tank that he assumed Rivers was currently hiding inside. He flicked a scrap of the late king of diamonds off his shoulder.

"Sorry, I've never fired this thing before." A voice came from a speaker system mounted on the vehicle. Digby didn't recognize it.

"Don't apologize to him," Rivers shouted over the first voice before issuing a threat. "Hold still out there and he'll take another shot."

"Oh sure, I'll stay right here." Digby pointed at the ground at his feet.

"Really?" the first voice, probably the last remaining ace, asked.

"No! Not really." Digby closed his mask and leapt behind a stone pillar.

The hulking black form of the armored tank rumbled forward, heading toward him from where it started on the other side of the parking garage. Digby had seen a few vehicles like it before in the movies he'd watched, giving him a somewhat limited idea of its capabilities. All he really knew for sure was that it was heavily armored and carried a big gun. Fortunately, Rivers seemed to need time to reload before firing again.

At least I have a moment to think. He glanced at his mana.

MP: 78/253

Damn. If he had more, he might have been able to open his maw wide enough to swallow the entire thing whole. Then all he would have to do was wait for its occupants to suffocate. Unfortunately, with less than a third of his mana remaining, he didn't have many options.

Digby struggled to keep his oversized body hidden behind the pillar. Peeking out from behind cover he found the tank getting closer. It rolled forward on some kind of belt mechanism. *Interesting.* He wondered if he had anything in his arsenal that might be able to disable the vehicle's mobility.

That was when another earth-shattering bang echoed through the garage. The world blurred as the pillar he'd been hiding behind detonated into rubble, throwing him forward and burying him in a shower of debris. The necrotic armor that covered his body snapped and spasmed as it took the brunt of the damage before coming apart at the seams. His Temporary Mass was finished.

Digby flailed and clawed at the ground to pull himself free of the rubble and slabs of dead muscle that held him down. He reached out for his staff with his left hand, unable to feel it nearby. For that matter, he couldn't feel his hand either. A look to the side told him why. His staff was indeed still within his grip, the problem was that his arm was no longer attached to his body.

"Gah!" Digby held up what was left, finding everything from his elbow down missing. "That is less than ideal."

Even worse, the tank was still coming, its treads rumbling closer to where he lay with each second. With a frantic kick, he cleared the debris from his legs. Relief swept over him as he found them both still attached.

"Not so tough now, are you?" Rivers shouted from the tank's

speakers as he barreled forward, practically on top of him. "Try surviving this!"

Digby raised one leg, planting a foot against the vehicles moving tread just long enough to shove himself clear. The tank passed by, crushing his severed arm and staff into oblivion beneath its mass.

Imbued Staff destroyed. Donated mana has been refunded.

Digby watched his maximum mana tick back up thirty points without restoring anything to his available MP.

Well, that doesn't help.

The tank continued on its path, its massive gun rotating back to search for him.

Wait a second. Digby's eyes widened at a sudden realization. The damn thing couldn't shoot him if he stayed close. It would certainly be easier to stay out of the line of fire if he denied Rivers the advantage of being able to fire from range.

"Get back here." Digby shoved himself up with his remaining arm and got to his feet. Running for all he was worth, he darted out of the tank's line of fire and raced around the back faster than the vehicle could adjust its aim. Once he was in position, he grabbed hold of a ridge on the back of the machine and held on, letting the thing drag him behind it. The barrel of its oversized gun rotated back to aim well over his head.

"Not so easy to shoot me now, is it?" Digby opened his maw and cast Forge to send a flood of necrotic blood into the inner workings of the vehicle's belts where it hardened all at once. At rank B, the spell was advanced enough to create a form durable enough to do the job, causing one side of the tank's treads to grind to a halt in seconds. The thing veered off to one side as Digby clung to the back and cackled in victory. "Enjoy going in circles, you bloated scoundrel."

Eventually the tank slowed to a stop, its gun rotating in circles in an attempt to find him within its sights. A minute later that stopped as well, leaving Digby safe, leaning against the back of the vehicle where Rivers couldn't shoot him. Unfortunately, this also left Rivers safe where he was, hiding inside the vehicle where no one could eat him.

"You can't hide in there all day." Digby reached up and tapped his fingers against the side of the tank's gun.

"That's what you think," Rivers responded from inside. "This is my escape plan. It's foolproof. I have a day's worth of food in here and my friends at Autem are due to come by tomorrow. How do you think they'll feel if they find a monster like you trying to kill one of their valued partners?"

"First of all, I doubt Autem values you as much as you think." Digby slipped into a casual tone. "And second, how much of your food do you intend to share with the henchman you have hiding in there with you?" Digby let his question sink in along with the obvious implication. "Actually, now that I think of it, how about I make your last ace an offer? Kill Rivers, and I'll let you walk right out of here."

Digby waited with his ears pricked up. There was only one reasonable response to his offer. A moment of dead silence passed by. Then a muffled bang.

"Good choice, ace." Digby nodded. "As a zombie of my word, you may go free."

"Nice try," Rivers growled through the speaker.

"Oh, you're still alive?" Digby wrapped his knuckles against the tank while trying his best to sound as smug as possible. "I take it from that last gunshot that your henchman might not have been as loyal as you thought. Probably one less occupant in there now. Oh well, at least you've learned how it feels to get your hands dirty. I get the feeling that's not a common occurrence for you."

Rivers didn't answer.

Digby focused on the corpse inside the vehicle, to see if it could be animated. That would certainly be a fitting end for his enemy. To be killed by the henchman that he'd just sacrificed. Unfortunately, it seemed he was either unable to access the corpse within the vehicle's walls, or Rivers had shot the poor man in the head.

Oh well. At least it will be a decent meal.

Digby glanced down at his missing arm, making a note to claim a replacement before eating the deceased ace inside. He shook off the thought and tried again to convince Rivers to exit the vehicle.

"You know, that corpse isn't going to smell great in a day or so. You sure you want to spend that long cooped up with your man as he rots?"

A long pause went by before Rivers answered. "I'll deal with it."

Digby rolled his eyes at the fool's persistence. The bloated braggart was becoming more and more irritating with each passing second. He scratched his chin. There had to be some way to get into the vehicle. He smiled as a new approach became clear.

Focusing on the space just in front of the metal behemoth, he cast Emerald Flare, watching from behind the tank as the spell's sickly energy streaked through the air. Green light converged into a single point just before exploding harmlessly out of range of the tank.

Rivers squealed over the speaker. "What the hell was that?"

Digby smirked. "That was a spell."

"A spell?" The tone of River's voice climbed an octave.

"Yes, as in magic." Digby shook his head in annoyance. "I'm not going to bother explaining everything now. But what I will say is that my spells sometimes carry an additional effect that lingers in the area."

"Additional effect?" Rivers shrieked.

"Yes. In this case, radiation poisoning. You should start to feel it shortly. It will start as a slight feeling of nausea, which will eat away at you little by little until you expire in what can only be described as horrific agony. You should be able to resist the poison for a few minutes but once it sets in, well, there's really only one outcome."

Rivers didn't respond. Of course, there was no way to be sure what the man's constitution value was, but with the radioactive area effect of the Flare spell, it was only a matter of time. Sure enough, a minute later, Rivers shoved open the hatch at the top of the vehicle and tumbled out like a sack of potatoes. He took one look at Digby and started running.

"You just have to make this difficult, don't you?" Digby started after him.

A string of unintelligible words dribbled from the man's mouth as he rushed up the ramp at the center of the parking garage. Clearly his mind had been consumed by panic, otherwise he would have fled the area altogether rather than climbing higher into the structure's upper floors.

He must be retreating to the safety of his palace on instinct.

The fool had probably never done anything for himself, let alone fought for his survival against the dead that now inhabited the world.

"Looks like you've run out of luck." Digby stalked his prey until the cruel but desperate man cornered himself at the top of the structure.

Rivers spun back to face him, thrusting a pistol in his direction. He emptied the weapon into the air around Digby, only striking him on the shoulder with one bullet. When the gun clicked empty, Rivers simply threw it. Digby ducked to the side and thrust his remaining hand out to curl his fingers around his prey's neck.

"Wait, wait!" Rivers tried to break free, nearly falling over the side of the garage in the process.

"Hold still, damn it." Digby held firm.

Rivers let out a blood curdling scream that trailed on for longer than one would have expected. Digby cringed and waited until he was finished.

"Are you through?"

"Please, don't kill me." Rivers clawed at his arm. "I'll leave. I'll just go. You'll never see me again."

"You'd only tell your friends at Autem about me. And I can't have that." Digby began to tip the man back over the edge of the barrier that ran around the top of the garage.

"I won't." Rivers kicked his feet as they left the ground. "I'll do anything you want. Just please don't drop me."

"What?" Digby stopped short before pulling the man away from the edge to safety as if doing exactly what he'd asked. "I'm not going to drop you."

"You're not?" Rivers relaxed a bit.

"Lord, no." Digby chuckled. "That would be a waste."

Before Rivers had a chance to respond. Digby yanked him forward and sank his teeth into his throat. A gurgled cry erupted from the man before trailing off.

It had been quite some time since Digby had last eaten like the zombie he was, and to be honest, he missed it. He may have looked more human now, but the difference was only skin deep. Besides, for Rivers it was really the only option. For a man that had preyed on his fellow people and considered himself the top of the food chain, it was a fitting end.

"Oh no way." A woman's voice came from behind him. "I am not seeing this."

Digby craned his head back, tearing a meaty chunk from his prey in the process before finding Elenore and Deuce gawking in horror. Rebecca and Alex followed close behind.

"It's true, then. You are a zombie." Deuce trembled as he spoke.

"We explained everything," Alex added, making a point of not looking directly at Digby while he chewed. "They're still coming to grips with some of it."

"The mess you left in the hallway downstairs didn't help, by the way." Rebecca glowered at him, unfazed by his table manners. "You realize you left a corpse sticking out of a wall and two of your minions eating down there."

"Oh please, my minions aren't hurting anyone." Digby paused awkwardly. "Well, other than the people they killed."

"Yes, but now that Rivers and his high-cards are gone, what are your orders?" Deuce stepped forward now that Digby wasn't actively eating anyone.

"Orders?" Digby dropped the corpse in his hands. It hit the ground with a wet thud.

"Yes. Your people explained what's happening and what might be coming here. I agree that we can't just sit around and wait." Deuce tensed up as he spoke. "I don't want a war, obviously, but it looks like Rivers was just a middleman for these Autem people, and it doesn't sound like they will stop coming."

"And letting them take our kids is not an option," Elenore added.

Deuce closed his eyes for a second before snapping them back open. "Honestly, I don't know what to think about the fact that you just ate my old boss, but you did help us. And you're clearly capable of getting things done. So, again, what is your plan? I will give you the benefit of the doubt for now."

"And what if I don't stand up to expectations?" Digby eyed the man. "Will you plan another coup?"

"I might. But only if you hurt the people of this city." Deuce stood a little taller, looking less submissive than he did before.

"That's fair enough." Digby brushed a few scraps that remained of his necrotic armor from his shoulder, flicking what looked like a finger in the man's direction. It tumbled to the ground at his feet.

"Yeep!" Deuce jumped back before letting a full-body shudder pass through him.

"That's messed up." Elenore pointed at the finger.

"Sorry, I—" Deuce gagged for a second before getting himself under control. "I wasn't expecting that."

"Better get used to it." Digby gave him a predatory smile.

"Yes." He shook his head. "Anyway, the rest of the low-cards are coming back to base. How do you want to handle the transition of power?"

Digby opened his mouth for a moment before shutting it again. He hadn't intended to become the city's lord when he set out in the morning. No, he was just hoping to negotiate an alliance and maybe free Elenore's child. He certainly wasn't expecting to overthrow anyone. In fact, it would have been better if he could have kept someone else in charge so that he could keep to the shadows until the time came to show himself. He thought back to the movie he watched several times the night before.

What would a criminal mastermind do? He flicked his eyes to Deuce a second later.

"How many people here saw me and my coven enter this morning?"

"Just me and my team guarding the door. You killed everyone

else that laid eyes on you. Why?" His new accomplice eyed him suspiciously.

"And when will the rest of your low-cards be back here?" Digby answered his question with another, just as suspicious as the first.

"Within minutes." Deuce arched an eyebrow.

"Good, good." Digby paced for a moment. "I want you to keep them out of the hallway where I dispatched the high-cards. Just let my minions eat. They won't hurt anyone since they are under my control, but I'd seal off the hallway until we can move them to a better hiding place. Somewhere larger that I can store a horde."

"A horde?" Elenore spoke up.

"Yes, if we are going to fight Autem, we will need to bolster our forces. The dead will fill out our ranks just fine." Digby continued to pace as his plans came together.

"And what do you want to tell the rest of my people?" Deuce stepped forward, ignoring the finger on the ground.

"Nothing." Digby scratched his chin with his remaining hand.

"Pardon?" Deuce furrowed his brow.

"I don't want them to even know I exist for now." He grinned. "Yes, yes, I want you to tell them that you saw an opportunity and that you killed Rivers and his high-cards. Tell them that you're in charge now and explain what you've learned about Autem."

"Me?" Deuce stepped back.

"Indeed." Digby approached the man, forgetting how bad using his necrotic armor made him smell. "I want you to take over as the new leader of Las Vegas. Then I want you to invite every survivor group to this casino where you will share your supplies with them. Give everyone a place here and offer them a chance to help take back their world from Autem. I will send my people here as well. Among them are three soldiers, they will help you get things organized and help train whoever wants to fight."

"What about you?" Deuce screwed up his eyes, clearly confused.

"I will do the hard part." Digby started pacing again. "I have a plan to strike a blow at Autem and to help bolster our strength in the process. Unfortunately, it requires a more nuanced approach, so it's best that I maintain a low profile. I'll keep you informed, though. And I'll give you whatever support you need."

Deuce shook his head. "I don't know if I can—"

"You can." Digby jabbed a finger in his direction. "You cared enough to attempt a coup, after all. Now show your people what sort of leader you can be."

He threw out both his arms. "Sure, but I didn't do anything in the end but get shot and say a few things on the radio."

"Digby is right." Elenore stepped forward. "Deuce, you have been trying your best to protect people without getting yourself killed this whole time. I'm starting to see that now. So yeah, you might not have been the one to kill Rivers, but you've been doing what you could in a shit situation."

Deuce let out a long sigh. "Okay, fine, I'll do what I can."

"Perfect." Digby gave him a wink. "Now, would you mind leaving me to my breakfast?" He gestured to the corpse on the ground. "Unless you would like to watch."

"Oh, Jesus, no." Elenore turned and headed for the stairs. "I'll go get my kid and head back to my group to tell them what's happening. We'll gather our crap and head back here by the afternoon."

"Thank you." Digby said in his sweetest tone to counteract the blood that covered his chin.

"No, thank you." She waved a hand back at him without turning around. "I won't forget what you've done for me here." She shuddered for a second. "Even if I tried, I don't think I could."

"Same." Deuce nodded. "I'll do everything you've asked."

"Good." Digby smiled at the nervous man. "I'll bring my group over this afternoon as well. Just pretend like it's the first time we've met."

"Yes sir," he added, seemingly out of habit, before heading for the stairs.

"Oh, and Deuce?" Digby stopped him.

"Yeah?" He looked back.

"You can leave off the sir. Not really my style." Digby grinned. "No, you may address me as Lord Graves."

CHAPTER TWELVE

Digby stood in front of the mirror back in his room at the Never Say Die and stared down at his hand.

Well… it wasn't his hand.

It was the hand of the ace that Rivers had murdered while hiding in that tank. After having his forearm crushed beyond recognition, Digby had been forced to find a replacement. He was just lucky that the deceased henchman had been the right size. Especially considering that he had to remove the rest of his old arm up to the shoulder joint to find a good place to connect the new limb. He flexed his new fingers.

"Not a bad fit."

The limb tingled as his body adopted it as its own and the Heretic Seed altered the tissue density to match his attributes.

"Thank god for that."

He had been a little worried that the Seed would leave the arm as it was. That would have been a nightmare. He shuddered to think about what he would do if the new limb remained weaker than his old one.

Raising his hand up to his face, he made a fist. The word 'luck' was spelled out across his knuckles in black ink.

"Hopefully that will prove more accurate for me than for this arm's previous owner." He looked over the rest of his new skin, noting over a dozen tattoos that covered his skin like the sleeve of a shirt. Rotating his arm, he smirked at a skull on the back of his hand. "That's appropriate." He snorted a laugh at an image on his wrist of five playing cards fanned out in the grip of a skeleton's fingers. The words 'Dead Man's Hand' were written across a banner that curled around the design. "That is oddly literal."

Digby lowered his arm and pulled on a new shirt. He grabbed another coat from his supply on his way out of the room, making sure to refasten the Goblin King's Pauldron to it before tapping his shoulder to call Asher. The reanimated raven had spent the morning scouting the area while he had been busy overthrowing the city's previous leadership. From what he'd learned from her, the strip was mostly free of monsters, be they zombie or revenant.

"We'll have to travel further in search of new minions. There's bound to be some of the dead lurking further out." He scratched her chin as they reached the main floor of the casino where the rest of his people were waiting. It had seemed prudent to get cleaned up before heading over to meet Deuce.

After packing up the sun goddess statue, the survivors all piled into their vehicles. Digby dropped into the passenger side of a sedan, expecting Alex to take the wheel as he usually did. To his surprise, Mason joined him instead. Rebecca climbed into the back along with Sax and Hawk. Digby craned his head back to look at the group.

"Where's Alex?"

That was when an impractical, two-door car pulled up alongside them with his apprentice at the wheel and Parker in the passenger seat. The sound of an oversized engine rumbled from beneath its hood. Digby arched an eyebrow at the black double stripe that ran down the cherry red paint job.

"Never mind, it seems he has found his own transportation." Digby shrugged.

"Yeah, Parker stumbled onto a Mustang this morning while you guys were out." Hawk settled into his seat in between Mason and Rebecca.

"What do horses have to do with anything?" Digby tilted his head to one side.

"It's the model of car," Mason chimed in as he secured his seatbelt.

"It's pretty cool," Hawk added.

Digby smirked. "I guess I can appreciate that then, nothing wrong with riding in style. Maybe I should look into finding something a bit more eye catching, as well."

Hawk brightened up a bit. "I'll keep an eye out. You should steal yourself a limo, or a Cadillac or something. That seems like your kind of thing."

"I'll leave that up to you then. Let me know if something jumps out at you." Digby glanced back at the boy in the vehicle's mirror. "I'm surprised you're not riding with them."

"Nah. I'm fine riding with you. Plus, their back seat is tiny." Hawk kicked at the back of the center console.

"Suit yourself." Digby chuckled as the car pulled out of the parking lot.

Not long after, they approached the main strip's finest casino where Rivers' reign had ended earlier. He froze as soon as they reached the doors.

"Were you expecting this many people?" Digby's eyes widened as he entered to find nearly three hundred survivors occupying the main floor. The crowd had formed a few lines at the hotel's check in area where several people worked to keep track of them.

"Hey, Graves!" Elenore called from one of the lines while holding a clipboard.

"What the devil is going on here? I had no idea there were this many people here in the city." Digby stopped short, realizing that he hadn't asked to make sure she had been able to reunite with her offspring. "Oh, your child, I trust everything has worked out?"

"Yes. He's upstairs in my suite. I have one of the people from my group with him. He's had a rough day so I thought it would be best to let him take things easy." She glanced at Hawk who stood by Digby's side with his hands in his pockets. "I see you have a child of your own? That's surprising, I didn't take you for the, um, the parental type."

Digby furrowed his brow for a moment as he processed her comment. "Oh lord no, this one is an orphan."

"'Tis true, I am, I am." Hawk swung one arm back and forth as he brought back his atrocious British accent.

"Cut that out, you sound like a peasant." Digby glowered at the boy. "Now go bother Parker and Alex. I have things to do."

"Ugh, fine." Hawk rolled his eyes and wandered off.

"Sorry, the boy is a handful." Digby inclined his head. "But anyway, what is going on here with all these people?"

Elenore shook her head and blinked twice before answering. "Well, you're right, there's a lot more survivors in the city than I thought as well. So we're checking everyone into the guest rooms to try to keep track of them all. Families are getting the larger suites and singles are getting the smaller rooms. There's plenty of space for everyone, though."

"Are you using the hotel's check in system?" Rebecca stood on her toes to look over the crowd at the counter.

Elenore nodded. "Yeah. The internet is mostly dead at this point but the casino's internal network is still functioning, so we're using the room notes to create a profile for everyone. That way we can mark down what their skills are and see what resources we have that can help this settlement grow."

"That will be important in the weeks to come," Rebecca added.

"Especially if we end up having a fight on our hands." Elenore swept her eyes across Digby's group as they filtered into the building. "Speaking of which, you mentioned you have some military personnel."

"Yes." Digby turned to Mason. "Why don't you get checked in and get a lay of the land?"

"On it. I'll get the goddess statute situated once we're all set." He grabbed Sax and made for the shortest line.

"Goddess?" Elenore raised an eyebrow. "Is that a magic thing?"

"Sort of. It has an enchantment that keeps some of the monsters away." Digby shrugged. "It messes up the balance of the ambient mana in the area though. Disrupts my absorption rate too."

"Yeah, I'm sorry I asked." Elenore shook her head, clearly not following the specifics of how magic worked.

"Whatever." Digby ignored her confusion. "Where's Deuce? I should probably discuss some things with him."

"I think I saw him hiding in the shopping center." She rolled her eyes.

"Shopping center?" Digby furrowed his brow before jumping to the more important detail of her answer. "Wait, why is he hiding?"

"Most of the casinos on the strip have a full shopping mall in them somewhere. Just follow the signs. And Deuce is hiding because the crowd spooked him. After explaining the situation to the first few groups, he slipped away. I picked up the slack after that to keep things moving. Guy's lucky I'm here, honestly."

"Indeed." Digby swept his gaze across the area to find a sign. "I will seek him out then."

"We should check you in first." Elenore looked down at her clipboard.

"Probably best that we don't." Digby frowned.

"Yeah, we're going to try to keep a low profile for now," Rebecca added. "Leave Alex out of your records as well."

"Oh, ah, okay." Elenore lowered her clipboard.

"Perfect." Digby spun on his heel and headed off toward the nearest sign that read shopping.

Rebecca followed, casting her cartography spell once they were out of sight to map out the interior of the building. She cast Waking Dream a second later to create an image of the place that floated in the palm of her hand. The only parts of the structure that were beyond her view were the places with locked doors. Navigating the area, they found the man they sought within minutes.

Actually, he was hard to miss.

Deuce was pacing in a frantic loop at the center of the darkened shopping area. He had removed his body armor, probably to appear less threatening when he welcomed the other survivors.

Unfortunately, the shirt he had on underneath was a mess of stains and sweat. He perked up the moment he saw him.

"Oh, thank god. You got to help me here, man." Words flowed from him at a rapid tempo. "There're so many more people than I thought would be showing up. I only ever dealt with the group leaders so I never got a full count. I can't do this. You've got to take over."

"I think not." Digby folded his arms. "You were the one that decided to announce a coup. This is your mess."

Deuce growled at himself. "I know, but this is way too much. I never thought—"

"Too bad. It's too late now." Digby shrugged, refusing to show the man an ounce of pity. If he was going to be a member of his crew, then he was going to have to stand on his own two feet.

Rebecca elbowed him in the side. "But we did say we would support him."

"Oh man, you're right, it is too late." He spiraled further down the rabbit hole. "How did I convince myself that this was a good idea?"

"Okay, calm down." Rebecca stepped in to pull him back up. "Elenore said you used to work security, there's some authority to that. I'm sure you can figure this out."

"Ha!" Deuce let out a sudden mirthless laugh. "Authority? All I did was walk around the casino floor and check ID's. I made minimum wage. I'm no leader, I'm only playing the part while you all make the decisions."

"Not with that attitude, you won't be." Digby grimaced at the man's outburst.

"I know, I know." Deuce's body deflated like an empty sack.

Digby waited for him to settle down, relating to the man a bit more than what made him feel comfortable. Not everyone was cut out to be a leader. He himself had failed more times than he could count and that was just in the last month. The only reason that he had gotten to where he was had been sheer coincidence and improvisation. Well, that and his solid ability to lie and fake his way through everything he'd faced so far.

Honestly, he had a lot more in common with Deuce than he

would have liked to admit. The realization sent him walking deeper into the shopping center.

"Come on, I think you need a lesson in leadership."

Seeking out the most impressive clothing emporium he could find, Digby headed inside without hesitation. If there was one thing that always made him feel better, it was looting. He flicked a switch on the wall in an attempt to turn on the lights only to frown when nothing happened.

"We shut the power off to most of the hotel. Right now, it's only running a couple of the guest floors and parts of the casino." Deuce lowered his head as if apologizing.

"No problem. Just close your eyes for a second." Rebecca cast another Waking Dream.

Digby nodded to Deuce and they both did as they were told. When he opened his eyes again the emporium was bathed in a bright light. He looked up to find a chandelier hanging from the ceiling.

"How did you...?" Deuce stared up at it. "That wasn't there before."

"I'm going to need you to not ask that question." Rebecca held up a finger. "This spell only works if you either believe what you see or if you know that it's not real and accept that it's an image produced by magic. So just accept that there is a chandelier there and move on. Because if your mind tries to reject it, we'll be stuck in the dark again."

He rubbed his palms into his eyes for a moment before shaking off the ideas. "Good god, this stuff is going to take some getting used to."

"True." Rebecca nodded along with his assessment before adding, "On the upside, the spell just ranked up, so that's cool. I can anchor illusions to other people now and let them go regardless of range."

"What do you mean by ranked up?" Deuce held up a hand. "Wait, never mind, I don't want to know."

"Yes, best not to ask too many questions." Digby waved away the conversation and jabbed a finger in his direction. "Now strip."

"What, why?" Deuce took a step back.

Rebecca let out a snort. "Sorry, I'll turn around, if you're uncomfortable."

"No, it's fine, I'm a grown-ass man. But why do I need to strip?"

"Because being a leader is about presenting the right image. You'd be surprised how far you can get with the right outfit. Besides, I shan't have you looking like that if I'm going to lend you my support." Digby wandered over to the shelves and claimed a suit of black fabric. "Here, put this on. You are now the official figurehead of our little crime family."

"Crime?" Deuce's voice went up an octave as he spoke.

"Indeed." Digby headed back to the shelves to see what else the store had. "A wise man once said to me that this world can't be won through heroics. No, it will be underhanded and sneaky acts of questionable morality."

"Who said that?" Deuce pulled off his shirt.

"It doesn't matter. He's dead now, and I never liked him." Digby waved a hand back and forth. "What's important is that he was right. Autem is moving fast and growing. If we want to dent their operation, then we have to hit them anyway we can. Hence, crime."

"Dig wants to infiltrate their base and steal something that might make us more powerful to even the odds," Rebecca added. "He watched a heist film last night and has been on this kick all morning."

"I don't hear you coming up with something better, Becky." He shot her an annoyed look.

"I'm not arguing. Just being honest." She held up both hands. "Given our situation, I agree. It's a high risk, high reward plan. But that sort of thing has worked before, so why stop now?"

"Indeed." Digby grabbed a dress shirt from a table and unfolded it, realizing he could use a wardrobe upgrade as well. "Now, what I need to know, Deuce, is what is the procedure for when Autem's people come by looking for recruits?"

"Umm, they just show up once every week." He changed into a pair of expensive-looking slacks.

"Do they come by land or by air?" Digby held a shirt up to his chest to check the size.

"Air." He zipped up his fly. "They show up in those weird aircrafts to pick up the kids."

"That's how we get in, then." Digby pulled off his shirt, revealing the plates of bone that covered his chest as well as the veins of dark lines that spiderwebbed across his skin from where the Heretic Seed's shard lay buried in his heart. His Sheep's Clothing mutation may have done wonders for his face but the rest of him was still quite monstrous in many ways.

Deuce froze, staring at his chest. "You really are a zombie."

"Yes, and you saw me eat someone this morning, so you really should be past this point by now." Digby pulled on a clean white shirt, allowing himself to indulge in the finer things that life could still offer him.

"Are you going to eat any of the people here?" Deuce eyed him as he buttoned the garment.

"No." Digby made his answer as clear as possible. "I'll always want to, but I won't." He snatched a black tie from a rack and threw it at the man. "Besides, eating the revenants out there provides me with just as many resources as a human. So I'll have plenty of prey to eat without having to hunt the humans under our roof."

"That's… good." Deuce flipped up his collar and went to work tying his tie. "So back to your plan, how will Autem's pick up help you get in their base?"

"Simple; we stow away." Digby pulled a pinstripe vest off a rack and slipped it on. "Rebecca and I will sneak aboard when they land and use her magic to stay hidden."

"Are you insane? I can't keep us concealed for an entire flight. You're bound to do something that disrupts my spell."

"Then we get on the roof?" He tried again.

"There's a camera up there. I can hide us from it, but I don't know how much I want to ride on the outside of a moving aircraft." She held out both hands as if the problem should have been obvious.

"Oh, you'll be fine." Digby checked a mirror to admire his new vest. He unfastened the top button of his shirt collar to match a character from the movie last night. "I've ridden on top of a kestrel before, it's not that bad. We can climb off when we land and sneak off to meet with East…" Digby trailed off, realizing that he probably shouldn't mention Easton's name in front of anyone. "I mean, our contact on the inside."

"Smooth." Rebecca shook her head. "So what you propose is that we sneak into a kestrel that is sure to be guarded, climb on top without being seen, ride on the outside of an aircraft for over two hours, and then sneak around within the heart of our enemy's operation to find our contact. That about sum things up?"

"Yes, yes, it's all very complicated." Digby claimed another ten vests from the rack as well as several shirts, trousers, and shoes. Having a spare outfit was always helpful, considering how often he destroyed them. All he had to do was find a container to keep them dry, then he could store it all in his void to call forth when needed.

Actually, he had a room now, so he could keep his belongings there as well. The thought sent a feeling of comfort through him at the realization that he might have stopped running.

"Are you done shopping?" Rebecca folded her arms and leaned against a table full of shirts.

"I am." Digby spun to face her, gesturing to his new look.

"Good, because your plan has one more flaw. What do you think the team from Autem is going to do when they get here and find Rivers is missing?" She glowered at him. "You know, because you ate him this morning."

Digby scoffed. "I seriously doubt they care if that fool is alive or dead. Deuce here will just have to explain that the territory is under new rule and that he wishes to continue their relationship. They won't even skip a beat. Hell, we could straight up tell them that we murdered Rivers and I doubt they would care. They just want recruits."

"And what happens when we don't give them any recruits?" She poked another hole in his plan.

"We'll just tell them that we don't have any kids at the moment and to check back next week." He shrugged.

"Isn't that a little suspicious?" She didn't let up. "First there's a change in management, and in the same week they don't get the recruits that they came for."

"Well, I'm not going to just hand children over to them. I'm dead, not heartless." Digby slapped a hand down on the table just as a voice came from the entrance of the store where Hawk stood with his hands in his pockets.

"I could go."

"What the devil are you doing here?" Digby stared at the boy. "Didn't I tell you to go bother Alex?"

"Sorry, I was just looking around and heard you talking." Hawk locked eyes with him, looking far more serious than usual. "If you need to give them a kid, I could go."

"Are you insane?" Digby shook his head. "I'm not giving you to Autem."

"I don't mean for keeps." Hawk fidgeted. "Just until you get what you need. Then you can come get me."

"I'm not doing that. You're a wee child. What if something went wrong?" Digby held out a hand toward the boy.

"I'm not a child. And I can help." Hawk pouted.

"That's exactly what a child would say," Digby snapped back.

"He has a point though," Rebecca chimed in. "Lana's brother is going to be there as well, and I assume you intend to break him out while we're there. It won't make much difference if we have to get two kids out instead of one."

"You're not helping." Digby jabbed a finger in Rebecca's direction. "You don't exactly have a good track record when it comes to using children to further your goals. Need I remind you of your lapse in judgment in Seattle?"

"That's… actually fair. I will shut up now." Rebeca closed her mouth.

"But I want to help." Hawk stomped forward, ignoring Digby's protests.

"I know, I know, but I don't want to risk you getting hurt or worse. These people at Autem are dangerous." Digby tried to appeal to the boy's sense of reason without being dismissive. Clearly, he'd had some success with his plan back in California and it was making him a little big for his britches. "There's no negotiation on this, alright? We will do our best with what we have."

A long pause went by, leaving them both staring at each other with narrowed eyes. Eventually Hawk let out a frustrated groan and stormed off back into the shopping center. "Fine."

"That's right. It is fine!" Digby shouted after him on instinct to get the last word.

"I know, I said it was fine already!" Hawk shouted back.

"Good, now go back and stay with Alex," Digby ordered as he disappeared around a corner. "And don't steal anything on your way back."

"Whatever," his voice trailed back.

"Whatever." Digby bobbed his head as he repeated the word in a mocking tone.

"You know he looks up to you, right?" Rebecca pushed off from the table that she'd been leaning on.

"What? No he doesn't." Digby brushed off the idea. "I'm not even human."

She reached up to straighten the collar of his new shirt. "Yes, but you say whatever you want all the time and fight anyone that threatens you or your friends. Obviously, I know that you're only doing all this because Autem has us all backed into a corner, but to an impressionable child, you're kind of cool and a little heroic."

Digby held still to let her fix his shirt. "Aren't you the one accusing me of being a villain all the time?"

"That's only because you keep cackling and calling people fools." She smirked. "Honestly, you could try to be a bit more of a role model."

"Bah, I'm fine the way I am." He shrugged off her words and turned to Deuce, who was just getting the last part of his suit on. "Now, that's more like it. You look like a leader already."

"Thanks." The man gave him an awkward smile.

Digby frowned. "Try not to smile though, it makes you look goofy."

"Oh." His face fell.

"Now, let us be off." Digby grabbed a few more suits and tossed them in a bag before shoving it into Deuce's hands. "There is much to do before Autem arrives and you need some time to get into character."

"Character?" The man held the shopping bags awkwardly.

"Yes." Digby grinned. "You're part of my gang now. It's not enough to look the part. You're going to have to act it too."

CHAPTER THIRTEEN

After giving Deuce a pep-talk and parting ways with Rebecca, Digby went upstairs to claim a room. Unlike in the Never Say Die, he wasn't given a choice. Rather, he was assigned a living space by Elenore, who had tried her best to place him and the rest of his group in the same hall. This left him at the far end in one of the nicer rooms. It was easily larger than any of the places he'd stayed in before and came complete with a view of the strip and a kitchen. Granted, he had no use for the kitchen.

Once he'd settled in and put away his new clothes, the rest of the day passed by in a flash. Digby could hardly believe it.

There was just so much to do.

Thanks to Mason, they had actually gathered a small army, with nearly a hundred survivors signing up to fight Autem. After learning the truth about what they were up against and who had been behind spreading the curse, it hadn't taken much convincing.

The arsenal of weapons that Rivers had accumulated was moved to a more secure area within the casino where Sax set up an armory. That way, the inhabitants of the building could simply stop at one of the counters and check out a rifle if they had a job to do outside their walls.

Sax even organized a team of people to chip away the hardened blood that Digby had used to stop the tank in the parking garage. It would take some time, but eventually, they would get the machine fully functional again. Of course, Digby wasn't sure what he would do with the thing, but he was sure it would come in handy at some point.

As far as food and supplies went, members of the various groups had gathered everything together and created something of a communal dining area within one of the casino's eateries. Alex and Parker volunteered to handle the job of securing more supplies and James began drawing up plans to use the rooftops as gardens. Of course, the revenant nightflyers would present a problem, but as long as they made sure that no one went up to pick vegetables after dark, the creatures shouldn't be an issue.

Thanks to a crash course in acting, which consisted of watching several more heist movies, Deuce had begun to fill out his role. Digby was still making all of the decisions, but still, the man was doing well. Plus, he looked good in a suit.

All in all, things were looking up and the people were in high spirits. Digby would have been tempted to take things easy, but as the sun rose on the next day, the time to relax had officially expired. According to Deuce, Autem was due to land at noon, on top of the parking garage where he had killed Rivers. He made a point to have someone clean the blood off the stone over there. No sense leaving the evidence of his murder spree right out in the open.

It was decided that only he and Rebecca would brave the flight back to Autem's base. He would have brought Alex along as well, but since Mr. Blue Hair had decided to get creative with his appearance the other day, it was pointed out that he would have trouble blending in with the rest of the mercenaries there. With that in mind, he left his room and headed down to the lobby to collect Rebecca so they could get into position.

On his way down the hall, he spotted Lana. She waved immediately before breaking into a jog to catch up. Digby tensed up on reflex, remembering that the last thing he'd said to her was that he'd eaten her father. His first instinct was to duck back into his room and hide until she went away.

Maybe she's not really jogging to you. Maybe she'll just pass right on by and there will be no awkward conversation to be had. He broke into a brisk walk.

"Wait up, Dig!" the young woman called out, making it clear that she wasn't jogging for any other reason. Digby stopped and turned around, not wanting to make the situation worse. No longer dressed in Skyline uniform, she now wore a strange set of matching blue garments. Both her pants and shirt lacked all decorative elements, like they had been made for a purpose other than style. He arched an eyebrow. It didn't look like clothing that one would wear outside of their home.

"That's an interesting outfit." He called attention to it in an attempt to distract her, just in case she aimed to bring up his past sins.

She stopped short and looked down. "Oh yeah, I found some scrubs. I figured if I was setting up a medical facility here, I should look the part."

"Really? And is that something that the doctors of this time wear?" He scratched at his chin.

Her mouth dropped open for a second before answering. "Oh shit, I forgot you're not from here. How old are you again? You never actually told me. I just heard it from Becca the other day. Honestly, a lot of things make sense now that I know that."

"I'm eight hundred...ish." He continued walking. "How is your new calling working out, by the way?"

"I'm doing what I can." She gave a weak nod, making it clear that something was still weighing on her. "We were lucky the hotel already had its own health services department. It's no hospital, but it has some supplies and necessities. Plus, Elenore found a couple nurses and a surgeon in the survivors that arrived. They were glad to have me when I said I wanted to help and they've been teaching me what they know." She let out a sad laugh. "My dad would actually be proud of what I'm doing."

"Ah yes." Digby tensed up. "I'm sure he would."

She sighed. "I'm not mad, you know. That you ate him, I mean. He wouldn't be either. If you hadn't, you wouldn't have been able to help me and my brother back there in Seattle."

"That's… true." Digby waited for a but to follow.

"But, I will say this." She turned to face him and placed a hand on the shoulder of his coat. "I feel guilty that I'm not going with you to Autem's base, but I understand why I would only be in the way of you and Becca. So I just wanted to say, I am counting on you to get my brother back."

"I will certainly do everything I can to bring him home." Digby avoided eye contact to avoid conveying a promise that he feared he might break if he failed.

She squeezed his arm. "Good, and when you find him, for the love of god, don't blurt out that you ate our father. That was messed up when you said it to me, but he's just a kid still and he doesn't need to know the details."

"I see your point." Digby nodded.

"I'm glad we had this talk then." She let go of his arm and gave him a half smile that retained the same apprehension that she carried before. "Good luck."

"Thank you." He shoved his hands in his pockets.

She waved and headed down the hall, leaving him feeling more nervous than before. The pressure certainly couldn't get any higher. He tried his best to shake it off as he headed down to the lobby where he found Alex and Rebecca. His apprentice wished him good luck as well, to which he responded with a snide remark about leaving him and his blue hair off the mission. After annoying his apprentice for a few minutes, Digby wished him luck as well. After all, it would be the first time that he would have to handle things without him.

Once they were ready, he and Rebecca climbed the stairs of the parking structure to where Autem's kestrel was expected to land. An abandoned cargo van sat off to the side, giving them an ideal place to hide. Casting Blood Forge, the same way he had back in the gift shop of the Never Say Die, he shaped a key that would fit the lock and pulled open the door so Rebecca could enter.

He called to Asher before climbing into the vehicle. The deceased raven flapped down to his shoulder without hesitation.

"There you are." He stroked her head. "I'm going away for a

day or two but I shall return with something to make us far more powerful. I trust you can handle things here while I'm gone."

She nodded enthusiastically.

"Excellent, I knew I could rely on you." He picked her up and placed her down on the barrier surrounding the top of the parking structure. "Now, while I'm away, I want you to listen to Alex and help any way you can. Alright?"

She nodded again, this time, with less excitement. He could feel her uncertainty over their bond as she conveyed a few words to explain.

Alex lives. Don't trust.

"Oh, don't be like that." Digby frowned. "He may not be dead like us, but he's still trustworthy. And besides, I bet if you try really hard and do a good job, he might just let you into the jewelry store down in the casino's shopping center."

Asher cocked her head to the side, sending another few words over their bond.

Don't understand. Tell more.

The raven was far smarter than a normal bird, but it had become clear that she had hit her limit before fully reaching a human level of consciousness. Though, none of that really mattered. She seemed content with herself and remained curious, which aided in learning. In time, she would understand more, even if some words were lost on her now.

"I mean that Alex will give you shiny things," Digby explained to help her understand.

Asher responded immediately, flapping her wings and hopping in place.

Shiny!

"Yes, yes, shiny." He scratched her chin. "So be good and help the best you can."

The raven nodded with more enthusiasm before flapping back up and diving back down to the street, clearly in search of Alex in hope of earning her reward.

Digby chuckled to himself as he watched her go. When she was out of sight, he turned and climbed into the abandoned van to hide. Rebecca made sure to leave one door open at the back so they could sneak out quietly without disrupting her concealment spell. The rest of the survivors that now populated the hotel were ordered to stay in their rooms until it was safe to come out. It wouldn't do for Autem's people to find out how organized they had become. Best to keep their inhabitants secret.

Digby laid back on the floor of the van's cargo area. "And now we wait."

"Yeah," Rebecca answered with a quiver in her voice.

"Nervous?" Digby eyed her.

"Kinda." She shrugged. "Actually, more like scared shitless."

"I suppose that's reasonable. I don't exactly want to do this either, but it seems we're backed into a corner." He gave a half-hearted shrug. "If we don't find a way to even things out, we may run out of time."

"I know." She nodded. "It's still terrifying, though. Plus, the idea of being caught after being free for a month feels like throwing myself back in prison."

"Don't worry, we'll have a look around, find a few weaknesses, and get out quick once we have Alvin and the Seed's fragments." Digby tried his best to believe his own words.

"I hope so." She pulled out her smartphone and powered it on. The device had been becoming less and less useful as the days passed. Other than a few messaging systems, the network it required to function was almost nonexistent. Fortunately, it was still able to communicate with Easton, who she had spent the last night and most of the morning writing to in order to get things ready for their arrival. She stared at the screen for a minute before speaking again. "Easton has set up a space where we can stay hidden without anyone stumbling onto us. He was also able to steal some uniforms, but we will have to sneak our way to a maintenance room to get them. He's sent a rough map of the base to help us get there. Once we get changed, we can make for his hiding place."

"Excellent." Digby nodded as the plan started to sound like it might actually work. "Now we just have to make sure no one looks at us long enough for their analyze ability to expose us."

"That might not be so hard, actually." Rebecca lowered her phone.

"Really?" He arched an eyebrow. "How so?"

"I asked Lana about that and the Guardian Core's analyze system is more intrusive. It constantly pops up and fills their vision with information that they don't need or care about. Not only that, but their HUD is always visible, unlike ours that only shows up when we look for it." She glanced to one side, clearly looking at her mana. "I guess having that stuff all over their vision all the time gets annoying and gives people headaches, so most of the guardians just disable their HUD while they're on base."

"Alright then. I suppose this will be easier than we thought." Digby pumped his eyebrows and laid back again.

"I wouldn't say that. They can reactivate it if we do anything suspicious." She narrowed her eyes at him.

"Oh, don't look at me like that." He folded his arms. "I've never done anything suspicious in my life."

"Uh huh." She continued to stare at him for another few seconds before the sound of a kestrel's rotors grew outside. "Shit, that's them." She shoved her phone in her pocket and got ready to move.

Digby shoved forward to peek out the window as an airship came into view. The craft was similar to the ones he'd seen before, but with a few key differences. For starters, it was entirely white rather than black, as if they wanted to announce their presence instead of hide it. As the airship descended, he caught the image of a large crest emblazoned on the bottom.

It looked almost medieval, like something from Digby's time.

A golden shield bracketed by two winged lions lay beneath a crown-like halo. Underneath, a line of nine stars followed the contours of the shield. At its center sat a symbol. Digby mistook it for a cross at first glance, but as the craft grew closer, he saw the difference. A long bar ran down the middle, but instead of two arms, the points of a large X reached out from behind it.

"That kestrel must belong to Autem rather than Skyline." Rebeca peered out the window beside him. "They must be sending out their own personnel instead of relying on Skyline."

"Yes, and I wonder what that crest could possibly represent."

He stared up at the emblem until the airship dropped below the edge of the parking structure. "Wait, what?"

"Shit, it was supposed to land on the roof." Rebecca scrambled to get her radio out. "Deuce, what happened?"

A nervous voice answered. "I don't know, I don't know. I thought they always landed on the roof but I was never actually around when it happened. I just heard it from the high-cards." He paused. "Oh no, I think they're landing on the street. What do I do? What do I do?"

Digby snatched the radio and thumbed the button. "Pull yourself together, man. I shan't have the figurehead of this colony panicking. So calm down and stall them. We'll move and try to make a break for the airship." He didn't wait for a response before tossing the radio aside and leaping from the van. "Come, Becky. We need to get down there now."

Together, they raced down the ramp at the center of the parking structure. Digby skidded to a stop when he reached the second level from the ground as he heard the familiar click-clack of the airship's ramp unlocking just outside. He ducked low and crept his way to the edge of the floor to peeked over the side. The kestrel sat just below. The same crest adorned the roof.

"Think we can jump down?" Digby glanced back to Rebecca.

"No way we could land quiet enough." She crouched beside him.

"Maybe I can lower you down." He leaned forward and tried his best to gauge the distance.

"Shit, duck." Rebecca grabbed his shoulder as a man in white armor exited the craft.

"Good, there's only one—" His face fell as another five men walked down the ramp. Digby focused on the first enemy.

Guardian: Level 27 Holy Knight

"Damn, another one of those bastards." Digby grimaced. He didn't have a good history with the class. "Hope I'm not forced to kill that one too."

"You better not." Rebecca shot him a sharp look. "If any of

them go missing, Henwick will probably wipe Vegas off the map before we have a chance to fight back. Whatever we do, we need these guys to think the people here are cooperating."

"Good point." Digby squinted at the rest of the men.

Guardian: Level 30 Artificer
Guardian: Level 20 Cleric
Guardian: Level 14 Mage
Guardian: Level 22 Rogue
Guardian: Level 13 Fighter

Out of the group, most of them weren't too threatening. Plus, he'd dealt with each of the classes before except for the rogue. Digby stared at the man. "I've never seen that class before."

"Neither have I." Rebecca squinted. "We should be wary of him. We don't know what his class can do, but I bet it's a perception build like mine. Maybe a more combat-focused one."

As she spoke, the man turned toward them as if he had sensed them watching. They both ducked lower until he turned back around.

Digby nodded. "Stay away from the rogue. Noted."

The knight in the lead surveyed the area as if questioning something about their reception. The plan was for Deuce and his men to remain inside and come out when they arrived. It might have seemed suspicious if they had already been standing there like they were waiting.

Deuce appeared seconds later, pushing through the nearest door. To Digby's surprise, he stood tall and appeared somewhat confident. He had been able to pull himself together, after all. Behind him, Elenore followed, wearing armor that had once belonged to one of the high-cards. The only weapon she carried was her revolver. It seemed prudent to carry a gun, but not to be armed to the teeth. That way they showed that they weren't a target to take advantage of without appearing too aggressive. Another one of Deuce's men emerged from the casino behind her, also with a pistol on his hip.

"Hold it right there," the holy knight called out as soon as Deuce came into view. "Where's Rivers?"

The rest of the guardians stood at the ready, but refrained from casting any spells or reaching for their swords.

"Hello!" Deuce called out, sounding friendly. "I apologize for the surprise but we have had a change in management here."

"I asked where Rivers is," the knight repeated.

"Okay, I'm going to be honest here." Deuce held up both hands for a moment to show that he wasn't armed before dropping them back down. "He's dead."

"And how did that happen?" The knight arched an eyebrow.

"That's not important at this point." Deuce kept his voice suspiciously even, making his words sound a little harsh. It was a choice Digby could respect. Aggressive without seeming too dangerous.

Looks like someone is beginning to get in touch with their inner crime boss.

"And what is important?" The knight let out a short laugh.

"What's important is that we know about the relationship your people had with our former boss and we are happy to pick up where he left off. As long as you continue to hold up your end." Deuce stepped forward to negotiate. "And let's be honest here, you've met Rivers. I imagine you would rather work with someone more professional."

Digby smiled at his accomplice's remark. Sure, it was never nice to speak ill of the dead, but Rivers had been exceptionally vile.

"You have a point." The knight walked forward to meet him, apparently in agreement about the change in leadership. The rest of his men remained near the Kestrel.

Move, you idiots. Digby cursed them for not cooperating with his plan to sneak aboard their airship. With the group standing so close, it would be impossible to lower Rebecca down without being noticed.

"So where are our recruits?" The knight asked as soon as he and Deuce approached each other. "You did say you wanted to continue with the deal your predecessor made, right?"

"Yes, of course." Deuce seemed to hold himself together better when under more pressure to do so. "Although, as you can probably imagine, Rivers did a fair amount of damage on his way out. Unfortunately, that left us with little to offer right now. But I can assure you that we will do what we can to meet expectations in the future."

"That's unfortunate." The knight gestured back to the airship resting by the entrance to the garage. "I have a kestrel full of supplies back there, that we were intending on giving your people in exchange for a few healthy recruits." He locked eyes with Deuce. "You sure you don't have anyone young in the age group we need?"

"I can promise that we don't," Deuce replied, a little too fast.

The knight stared at him for a moment before finally relaxing. "I understand why you may want to keep things from us. After what Rivers has probably said, you must think we're kidnapping children to use as soldiers."

"Umm, aren't you?" Deuce ducked his head, letting some of his submissive nature show.

"Not at all." The knight laughed off the question. "With the world the way it is, we need the next generation to be prepared to build a better future. It's true that combat training is a part of that, but there's much more. Everyone we take under our wing is given the tools they need to survive and flourish. They will be safe and well cared for. Honestly, hiding children from us is doing them a disservice."

Deuce hesitated before answering. "I understand and will keep that in mind. However, I was being honest when I said we had no one to offer at the moment."

"I see." The knight glanced back to his men standing by the kestrel. "Go ahead and unload the supplies anyway."

"What?" Deuce's eyes widened as the group of guardians went to work retrieving several crates from their airship and carrying them over to where Deuce and Elenore stood. Setting the supplies down, they returned for more.

"We're not heartless." The knight smiled. "Your people still need supplies and we have plenty."

"But we didn't give you anything." Deuce furrowed his brow.

The man held up a hand. "I know, and that's fine. Think of it as building trust. We at Autem understand that the world has been through something traumatic. Now isn't the time to threaten or fight with each other. That's no way to help the human race to heal."

"Charlatan." Digby sneered at the knight, suppressing the urge to leap down from his hiding place to murder him. "Does he expect anyone to believe any of that?"

"Doesn't matter." Rebecca started to crawl over the railing. "This is our chance; we have to move while the guys down there are focused on unloading the supplies." She swung her leg over the side and held out a hand to him. "Get me as close to the kestrel as possible before letting go."

"Alright." Digby clasped his fingers around her wrist, catching her cringe as his cold dead hand touched hers.

Shaking off her discomfort, Rebecca grabbed hold of his wrist. He braced himself on the railing as she let herself slide down the outer wall toward the craft below. When he'd lowered her as far as possible, he snapped one hand around the railing and crawled over as well to lower her further. Hanging on tight, he planted both feet against the stone and dangled his accomplice until she was nearly level with the airship. He made a point to move carefully to avoid making a sound that might disrupt her concealment spell.

Thank the lord we've both increased our attributes so much. Digby kept his grip firm. Neither of them were supernaturally strong, but they had reached a level on par with the average circus performer. They could probably execute a trapeze performance if push came to shove.

With a gentle swing of his arm, Digby brought her close enough to the kestrel that her momentum could carry her the rest of the way. She dropped down, catching herself so that she landed as quiet as possible. Once she was stable, she flattened herself to the roof.

Perfect. Digby celebrated momentarily before looking for a way to get down as well. That was when one of the guardians stepped out of the kestrel just below him. The rogue.

"What was…?" He trailed off, looking around as if he had heard something but wasn't sure where it had come from.

Digby froze, unable to pull himself back up without making a sound that was sure to blow his cover. Even if the man looked up with suspicion in his mind, it could be enough to unravel Rebecca's spell. *Please don't look up. Please don't look up. Please don't look up. Just go about your business. There's nothing to see here.*

That was when Digby made eye contact with Elenore who happened to be staring at the exact spot where he was hanging. She immediately looked away as if she'd seen him.

Oh no.

Digby snapped his gaze down at Rebecca as she stared up at him, with her eyes bulging in panic as she mouthed something up to him. "The spell failed."

Oh no.

The reality of what had happened hit him like a truck. Elenore must have been wondering where they were or if they had made it onto the airship. With that thought in mind, she'd just happened to look at him by sheer coincidence.

Oh no. Oh no. Oh no.

He stared down at his fellow Heretic with urgency in his eyes, hoping she could read his thoughts.

Damn it, Becky, recast your spell!

She mouthed back a response. "I can't recast, someone knows you're there already. It will only fail again."

Damn it all to hell.

He couldn't hang there forever. His grip may have been strong enough but eventually that knight would finish with Deuce and turn around. From where he stood, Digby had to be in his view. The man would be an imbecile to not notice him.

Jumping wasn't an option either. That would be too loud. As would trying to climb back up. The sound would surely cause the rogue below him to look up. With no other option available, he held his ground and hoped with every necrotic fiber of his being that the rogue would simply go away before it was too late.

The rogue did not oblige.

Instead, the man walked closer to the parking structure's

entrance and stared into the shadows within. It seemed he was dedicated to finding the source of whatever noise had drawn his attention.

Panic surged through Digby's body as his entire plan threatened to come apart at the seams. It would only take a glance for someone to notice him. Then, before he could do anything else, the sound of shouting drew everyone's attention to one of the casinos.

"Hey, what do you think you're—" One of Deuce's men burst through one of the building's side doors, struggling with someone else. Someone much smaller than he was.

No! Digby's entire body tensed.

"Le'me go, you asshole." Hawk fought to wrench his left arm free of the man. In his right, he held several cans of food.

Dropping most of what he carried, he lobbed one item at his captor, forcing him to let go. Once the boy was free, he scrambled to pick up the cans and kept running as if fleeing the scene of a crime. Confusion settled across Digby's mind. Hawk had no reason to steal food, and he certainly didn't have a need to flee. Unless… *no!*

It was an act.

"What is going on?" The knight stepped closer to Deuce. "You said you didn't have any kids in there."

"I um, don't know what's happening either." The look on Deuce's face made it clear he was being honest. He really didn't have a clue what the boy was doing. Or why he would disrupt the plan in such a way.

"Whatever, get him!" The knight thrust a finger in Hawk's direction.

"On it." The rogue standing beneath Digby took off in a sprint, racing after Hawk. He grabbed a can from the supplies they were offloading and launched it at the child's legs. Hawk fell flat on his face twenty feet away.

Digby flicked his eyes back to where the rogue had thrown the can from but found the space empty. The only trace that he had been there was a vague feeling of mana passing through a human's blood echoing through Digby's senses.

Hawk pushed himself up and spun around in search of his attacker. Confusion fell across his face as he swept his eyes over the area. Eventually, he grabbed up the cans he'd dropped and started running again, passing by the supplies that Autem's men had set down. He stopped short as the rogue stepped out from behind the boxes and snagged his collar with one hand.

"Le'me go–hurck!" The boy's escape was stopped in an instant.

How? Digby glanced between where the rogue had been and where he had appeared. There had been enough time for him to have crossed the distance, but Digby hadn't seen him move. He'd just sort of lost track of him. Then, his eyes widened.

He used Conceal.

Rebecca had been right. There must have been some common ground between a rogue and an illusionist, after all. He shook off the thought. It didn't matter now. No, what mattered was that Hawk was in danger.

A string of words spilled from the boy's mouth, all of which were inappropriate for a child. He struggled to break free from the rogue's vice-like grip, but failed entirely and continued to shout regardless.

"I just wanted food. You prick!" He squirmed. "I don't even know you people." The child's lie made clear what Digby suspected. He hadn't been caught by accident. No, it was far worse. He was trying to help. Hawk shouted louder in protest, shooting Digby a meaningful glance as he hung from the front of the parking structure for all to see. Then he repeated the same phrase. "Let go!" Clearly it was meant for Digby as much as it was the child's captor.

God damn it, boy, I told you to stay out of this. Digby did as Hawk said, letting go of the railing and kicking off the wall. He landed with a thud as his pint-sized savior shouted insults at the guardians to cover the noise. Digby nearly kept moving. The need to leap from the kestrel's roof and free the boy screamed at him from within his mind. Clearly, Hawk must have been watching from one of the casino's windows and seen the plight Digby was in, then chose to enact a plan to distract Autem's guardians. It was brilliant and brave.

Digby cursed him for it.

He'd made himself clear, hadn't he? He didn't want Hawk involved. Rebecca grabbed his shoulder and squeezed to stop him from doing anything that might jeopardize their mission. It was too late to stop things now. Digby sank back down and resigned himself to let the child's ill-conceived plan play out. Rebecca cast Conceal to hide them from sight in case someone looked in their direction.

"Hey, that's enough of that." The knight approached Hawk with one hand raised as if he didn't mean any harm. "You're safe."

"Safe my ass, le'me go." Hawk stomped on the rogue's foot.

He grunted in response but refused to release the child. "Quit squirming, would ya?"

"Yes, please do stop that." The knight knelt down, completely ignoring Deuce and Elenore. "I assure you, I won't let anyone hurt you."

"Sure, whatever. Who are you people, anyway?" Hawk settled down, if only by a little.

The knight let out a friendly laugh. "You've got a lot of fight in you. That's good. After everything I'm sure you've been through, being able to hold onto that level of spunk is rare. To answer your question, we're part of an organization called Autem, and our goal is to rebuild the world into a safer place for people to live. I'll be honest, we don't quite have the room or resources yet to help everyone. But we do have the ability to save children like you."

"I'm not a child." Hawk growled back in defiance.

"Of course not." The knight chuckled and gestured to the rogue, telling him to let go of the boy's collar before placing the can back in Hawk's hands. "The nightmare you've been through is over. We're here for you now. There's no need to keep running and no need to steal food to survive. You have my word that we will keep you safe and that you'll never go hungry. Our base isn't far away. We can take you there in just a couple hours. " He rested one hand on Hawk's shoulder. "What do you say?"

Hawk stood still for a long pause, clutching the can to his chest. Digby tensed every muscle in his body, unsure if the knight's lies were working on the boy.

"He's right, kid." The rogue spoke up without looking down at him as if he didn't know how best to appeal to a child but was trying to help regardless.

Hawk looked up at him before returning his attention to the knight. "Are there other kids there?"

"Of course. You'll be able to make lots of friends." The knight smiled and stood back up, keeping his hand on Hawk's shoulder to guide him back to the kestrel. "Come along now, let's get you settled in."

Hawk didn't argue, allowing himself to be led back to the airship.

If Digby didn't know better, he would have thought the boy really did want to go. An uncomfortable twinge of dread took hold in his chest. He did know better, didn't he? Hawk wouldn't really turn his back on them. Digby had only known him for a couple weeks. How could he really be sure?

That was when Hawk passed by underneath. As he walked, he stared straight ahead making sure not to glance up at where he must have assumed Digby was hiding. Then, despite the fact that he wasn't looking at him, he winked.

That tricky little brat.

Digby shook his head as guilt began to bubble through his insides.

I may be a poor role model after all.

CHAPTER FOURTEEN

Digby groaned to himself as he struggled to type using the screen of Rebecca's smart phone. It was easier now that he had a normal right hand, though the device was still a little unresponsive on account of his dead fingers. He made do regardless, typing out a question before handing it to the illusionist laying on the roof of the kestrel beside him.

How much longer are we going to lay up here?

She immediately rolled her head to the side and stared at him as if to say, seriously? Then she typed a question of her own and showed him the screen.

Seriously? It's only been a half hour since we landed on the base.

Digby rolled his eyes and groaned again just as she nudged him in the side to show him the screen again.

And stop groaning, someone will hear you.

She wasn't wrong. There was a pair of guardians below them, performing some various tasks around the kestrels. Despite that, the waiting was killing him. The squad from Autem had taken Hawk to somewhere else on the base just after they'd landed, leaving him concerned with the boy's fate. It was maddening.

He grabbed the phone from her and added another line.

Can't your Conceal hide us while we make a break for it?

She shook her head and typed in an answer.

It's active now, but I don't fully trust it. If there were less people around, I would say yeah. But with so many guardians surrounding us, I feel like someone is going to see through the spell. Not to mention the sound of us dropping from this kestrel might break the concealment anyway. Casting Waking Dream might work if I use it to disguise us as some of Skyline's people, but it won't explain why we're jumping down from the top of a kestrel no matter what we look like. So for now, waiting is our best option.

Digby let out a musty sigh instead and resigned himself to wait atop the airship they rode in on for the guardians below to clear out. He turned his attention to his surroundings to occupy his mind. The base was far larger than he had anticipated. A part of him was still working off the expectations of the world back in his day when things were much smaller. Based on that, he'd expected something the size of the casino back in Vegas, but no, it was so much more.

Leaning his head to one side, the place stretched out all around him. The airfield alone could have fit the entire casino within it. A row of two dozen kestrels ran down one side, each sitting on their own landing space, marked by white lines painted on the pavement. Most of the airships were black, but a few were white with that strange crest on them. Five large hangars stood behind the landing area, with a pair of runways stretching into the distance. An aircraft far larger than any he'd seen sat at the end of one as if waiting to take off.

Beyond the airfield, Digby could see countless buildings. What they were for, he had no idea. Though, from where he lay, he was able to make out the base's main entrance. It was a wide open area with a few guard houses and other buildings. One road stretched out into the seemingly empty desert that the oversized outpost rested on.

Digby swept his eyes across the perimeter, finding a fifteen-foot wall surrounding the entire place. Turrets were mounted along its top at regular intervals. He cringed, realizing how difficult it would be to attack the stronghold. He was just glad they had already found a way in, despite a few hiccups here and there. If he could calm down and be patient, the Seed's fragments would be in his hands soon. Then, all he had to do was learn to use its power. He forced himself to relax. Things might actually work out, after all.

He tensed right back up when the kestrel's engine powered on.

Digby snapped his head to the side catching Rebecca as her eyes bulged.

"Shit shit shit." She braced herself on the roof.

"We have to go now." He sat up and crawled for the rear of the craft.

Rebecca grabbed his leg. "We can't, there's still two guardians down there and my concealment will be useless if they hear something."

"Well, we can't stay here, Becky." He yanked his leg from her grasp. "Lord knows where we'll end up if we stay here. We have to move. The engine will cover the sound of our movement." Digby peered over the side to check for guardians before rolling off, making a point of moving fast so Rebecca wouldn't have time to argue. He just hoped her Conceal spell would hold up. In the end, it was still a roll of the dice.

"Oomph." Digby hit the ground with a hard thud, immediately rolling over to find the kestrel's landing pad free of guardians.

They must have boarded the craft.

He glanced up to make sure Rebecca had followed just as the airship lifted off. A short shriek came from above, just audible over the engines. His fellow Heretic crashed into him an instant later. Before he could complain, he noticed a pair of boots in his peripheral. One of the guardians must have been standing on the other side of the kestrel. With it lifting off, there would be nothing between him and them. Digby followed the boots up as the airship ascended, feeling a wave of relief to find the man facing away from them.

Oh, thank the lord.

"There," Rebecca whispered as she thrust a finger toward a fuel truck sitting off to the side of the landing pad.

Digby wasted no time, rolling the illusionist off of him and scrambling to the vehicle. He dove straight for safety, sliding under the fuel truck. Rebecca rolled underneath as well just as the pair of boots across the landing pad turned around and uttered a single, intrigued syllable.

"Hmm?"

Digby froze as the man started walking toward them. He glanced at Rebecca, trying to ask her with his eyes if the Conceal spell was still active. She shook her head to indicate that it had failed. They both snapped their attention to the boots that were still coming closer. Digby opened his maw on the ground by one of the vehicle's tires to impale the man if he showed any sign of looking under the truck. The idea of killing a guardian in the middle of their base was lunacy, but what choice did he have?

The boots stopped at the side of the truck.

Both Digby and Rebecca held deathly still as he focused on the dark pool of his maw, ready to attack. Then one of the boots vanished. The second followed. The sound of the fuel truck's door closing came next.

"Holy crap that was close." Rebecca lowered her head to the pavement as she relaxed. Digby did the same. Then the truck's engines turned on.

"Oh, come on, really?" Digby flicked his eyes to the enormous wheels that surrounded him to make sure he wasn't in their path. He'd already had a part of him run over recently, and he didn't want to repeat the injury.

"Get close." Rebecca scooted to his side, clearly wanting to avoid being run over as well.

"Wait, no." Digby stared up at the bottom of the truck looking for something to grab on to. Finding nothing secure enough, he reached up and opened his maw to cast Forge. Black blood poured forth, attaching to the metal to form a set of handles before streaming across the surface to create a support that he and Rebecca could hook their feet onto.

"Are you insane?" Rebecca flicked her eyes to him, clearly understanding what he intended to do.

Digby reached up and grabbed hold of his makeshift handle

before hooking his leg up. "It's a fuel truck. It might head back into one of the hangars."

"And that's better?" Rebecca begrudgingly did the same.

"It's better than being left laying out in the open." Digby opened his maw again and forged another blood formation that reached under them both so that they could rest their weight on it.

"Okay, this is happening." Rebecca arched her back so that the blood-forged support could pass underneath her.

The vehicle's brakes hissed a second later as the wheels began to turn. Digby let his weight rest on the Blood Forged shelf beneath him and reached down to grab hold of his coat. It wouldn't do for it to drag on the ground and draw attention to their hiding place.

The truck traveled out to the perimeter of the airfield before taking a right turn. Wherever it was taking them, Digby hoped it was better than where they were. Rebecca would never let him hear the end of it if it wasn't. He relaxed when the vehicle entered a building.

He turned to his accomplice as if everything was going according to plan. "See? Things are looking up."

She responded with a groan.

The truck continued into the back of a large hangar where it slowed to a stop. Digby waited to see a pair of boots get out. As expected, the man dropped down to the floor and walked away, leaving them alone in the back corner of the hangar by a large fuel storage tank. They both shimmied out of the Blood Forged support and rolled out from under the truck.

"See, what did I tell you?" Digby nudged Rebecca.

"Fine, you're a genius." She rolled her eyes. "But you better hope no one looks under this truck and sees your modifications. That would be sure to raise a few eyebrows."

"We shall cross that bridge when we come to it." He crouched down and peeked around the truck.

Rebecca followed behind, only to point past him at a white kestrel sitting over by the hangar's open door. "Isn't that the one we flew in on?"

"Umm, no?" He shrugged.

"Yes it is." she flicked her finger back and forth at a number written on one of the protective guards that surrounded its propellers. "I was staring at the whole flight. It's the same number." She dropped her hand to her side. "We could have just stayed where we were and ended up in the same hangar."

"Well, it worked out in the end, didn't it?" Digby ignored her criticism and leaned around the truck's front.

"Fine, we're safe, that's what matters." She sighed. "Now, we just need to find a way out of here and over to the maintenance room where Easton hid our disguises. We need to be careful, though. We can't afford to kill anyone to cover our tracks. People will start to wonder if someone goes missing."

Almost as soon as her warning left her mouth, Digby heard a boot squeak behind him.

"Hey, how did you get in here?"

Digby spun to find a man in black overalls staring at them. He wore a belt carrying various tools, though a gold band on his finger marked him as a guardian. His mouth hung open as if he was just as surprised to find them as they were at having been discovered. He must have walked around the truck and stumbled upon them.

Trying his best to act like he belonged there, Digby stood tall and approached. "I'm terribly sorry. My friend and I seem to be a little lost. That right, Melissa?" He nodded to Rebecca, making a point of assigning her a fake name just in case.

"Yes, yes." She leaned into his deception, placing a hand on his shoulder. "My husband, George, and I were just rescued by some of your people but got separated from the rest of our group."

"Indeed, indeed." Digby nodded. "Do you think you could point us in the direction of an appropriate area for us? Clearly, we aren't supposed to be here." He hoped that by calling out the obvious his honesty would make him seem less suspicious.

"That's right, you aren't supposed to be here." He reached for a radio clipped to his belt amongst his tools.

"Damn." Digby groaned before opening his maw at the center of his palm and forging a dagger of necrotic blood. He lunged forward just as an Icicle shot past his head to slam into the man's eye.

Guardian, Level 1 Fighter defeated. 48 experience awarded.

Digby let out a surprised, "yeek," and spun back around to see Rebecca with her hand out stretched in the man's direction. "Did you just—"

"I panicked." Her eyes darted around as the body crumpled to the floor.

"Weren't you the one who just said we can't afford to kill anyone?" Digby glowered at her.

"Yeah, but I couldn't let him call anyone. What was I supposed to do?" She glanced down at the blood dagger in Digby's hand. "And don't lecture me, you were just about to stab him too."

"I have no idea what you are referring to." He shoved the dagger into his coat and tried to act innocent, before turning to check the area for anyone else that might be unfortunate enough to stumble upon his murder-happy illusionist. With the truck parked at the back of the hangar next to the fuel storage tank, they were fairly secluded. There were plenty of people over by the aircrafts at the center of the building but not so much where they were. They were just lucky that there was enough background noise from the various vehicles in the area that no one had heard the recent murder. "It seems this poor soul was the only witness, so you can calm your bloodlust for the time being."

"Oh, shut up, we don't have time to banter. We have to hide the body." Rebecca leapt forward and grabbed the corpse's feet only to drop them again a second later. "Wait no, we don't have to hide anything." She glanced at Digby before adding, "You just have to do what you do."

"Don't mind if I do." Digby opened his maw wide enough to swallow the corpse whole and started to roll the man toward it.

"Wait." Rebecca reached out. "We should take his clothes."

"And now you want to rob the man?" Digby shot her an accusatory look before reconsidering. "Actually, that's a good idea, let's loot this corpse."

"Yeah, we can dress you in his coveralls so you don't stand out." She reached down and tugged at the zipper that ran down the man's chest.

Digby crouched down to help, grabbing for the man's hand to remove his guardian ring. "Can't forget this little fella."

"Good thinking." Rebecca slipped the corpse's clothing down over his shoulders.

Digby closed his hand around the ring, getting a message from the Seed in response.

Compatible spell detected, Kinetic Impact.

Choosing not to take the ability for the moment, he slipped the gold band onto his finger to complete his disguise. With the man's clothes and ring, he could pass for a member of Skyline without much trouble. He could always extract Kinetic Impact later.

Rebecca tossed him the man's coveralls while he removed his coat. He made sure to remove the Goblin King's pauldron, hoping to fit it underneath his disguise. He handed her his coat and stepped into the deceased guardian's clothes. Zipping the front, he leaned to the side to check his appearance in the truck's mirror. It was a bit uneven with one shoulder looking larger than the other but it would have to do.

"Quit looking at your reflection and eat this guy already." Rebecca stood back up and grabbed his coat to keep anyone from finding it and wondering who it belonged to. With nowhere to store the garment, she simply tossed it in his void.

"Hey, that was mine." Digby reached up as it sank.

"You have more, it's fine." Rebecca didn't skip a beat, helping to push the dead fighter's body into the pool of darkness. Digby groaned at her but stepped in to help regardless. He checked his mana as soon as the evidence of her murder sank.

MP: 87/157

He winced. His two animated zombies back in Vegas were really killing his maximum value. It didn't leave him with much to work with. Though, he probably still had enough to be able to kill one or two more guardians, provided they were low level or they got caught by surprise. "Should we hunt down another bite to eat, so we can find you something to wear too?"

"No." Rebecca closed her eyes for a moment as mana moved through her blood. "Close your eyes and try not to think too hard about what I look like."

Digby shrugged and did as he was told, opening his eyes back up to find her dressed in a black skyline uniform complete with gold ring. He made a point to mentally accept the spell so he didn't end up messing things up.

She stood up straight like a guardian. "There, that should do it."

"Indeed, now we must get moving. No telling when someone will come looking for…" He looked down at a name patch on his chest before adding, "Gus."

"True." She stepped out into the open and stood still as if making sure that her illusion was really functioning. She let out a satisfied breath when no one turned her way.

"Not bad, Becky." Digby stepped out as well, pulling on Gus's hat and tucking his white hair up underneath to keep it hidden.

Rebecca took the lead, considering her illusionary uniform outranked Digby's stolen maintenance outfit. Hugging the wall of the hangar, they kept their distance from the building's other occupants, eventually reaching a heavy metal security door. It looked like something out of one of the zombie movies he'd seen that took place in space, with an interlocking seam running up the center. Aside from the heavily populated entrance that the kestrels went in and out of, the security door was their best option to get out.

"Damn, there's some kind of scanner." Rebecca stepped up to a panel to the side with a red light on top. "They must log everyone who accesses the door." She glanced back to Digby. "Is there a key card, or an ID cuff on your tool belt?"

He searched Gus's equipment before checking the pockets of his overalls. Turning them inside out, he found nothing except the guardian ring he'd stolen from the man's corpse. On a whim he slipped the gold band on his finger and placed his knuckles to the panel. The light flickered to green.

"That's not a good sign." Rebecca deflated. "It may be more difficult to move around if all the doors require a ring to access."

"Indeed, and I'm willing to bet there's a limit where this level one ring can get us." Digby stepped through the door. "We may need to execute a few more guardians while we're here."

After stepping out into the open, they simply walked like they owned the place as they made their way across the base. The theory that the guardians kept their analyze function deactivated while on the base proved true, as no one seemed to give them a second look. It made sense, considering Skyline had grown significantly in the last couple weeks after recruiting so many survivors of the apocalypse. The new guardians had been willing to sell their loyalty, but it had done nothing to instill a level of discipline. From what he could tell, Skyline had opted for quantity rather than quality when taking on new guardians.

It didn't hurt that no one would suspect that the necromancer that had just declared war on Skyline would be wandering around within the heart of their operation. The only close call they had was a moment where they caught a glimpse of Bancroft walking into one of the buildings near the center of the base. Behind him followed six guardians as if they were his personal guard. Digby focused on the group.

Guardian: Level 30 Holy Knight
Guardian: Level 22 Artificer
Guardian: Level 20 Pyromancer
Guardian: Level 25 Rogue
Guardian: Level 21 Cleric
Guardian: Level 19 Illusionist

Digby nearly hid on instinct but suppressed the urge since it would certainly make him look more suspicious. Instead, he kept his distance and pulled the brim of his hat down. Despite both of them being well-disguised, it still didn't make sense to get any closer. The last thing he wanted was to give Bancroft the satisfaction of catching him. The man wouldn't hesitate to bring down a bolt of lightning to burn him to cinders. Granted, the fact that his enemy hadn't noticed them immediately spoke well of his plan to hide out in the open.

Even better, they were able to gain a bit more information. After getting a good look at the illusionist in the group, they both recognized him as the one they had faced briefly as a projection back in Seattle. They made an additional point to steer clear of him as well, considering that he would have to have a high perception attribute.

Making their way across the rest of the base, they found it populated mostly by Skyline's mercenaries, but as they got closer to one corner, the white uniforms of Autem's guardians became more prevalent. Eventually, they reached a gate where two men stood guard. Rebecca did a quick about face before they got close enough to look suspicious. Digby did the same, not wanting to press their luck. From what they could tell, Autem had claimed that section of the base as their own and weren't letting anyone but their personnel in. Not even Skyline.

Digby leaned to Rebecca. "If the Seed is here, then it's gonna be past that gate. Let us hope Easton has figured out another way in."

She nodded. "True. A security door is one thing, but I'm willing to bet the guards have their analyze ability active and I don't want to get caught passing myself off as a guardian."

"Good point." Digby surveyed the buildings they passed, finding that the vast majority also required a guardian ring to enter.

As much as he hated to admit it, the security set up a cleverly simple solution to a complex problem. With Skyline making use of so many untrained survivors, it made sense to use their rings to keep them organized and in line. If they allowed them more freedom, their men might find a way to misbehave.

With nothing left to do but meet up with Easton, they headed for the spot on his map that he'd marked as safe. Digby couldn't hide his disappointment when they found it nestled into a row of identical structures.

"That's our secure hiding place? It's not even hidden." He stared up at a simple building with a curved roof that reminded him of the cabins back in the campground he'd stayed at in California for a night.

"What did you expect, an underground bunker with a secret door?" Rebecca sauntered up the stairs to the entrance.

"I don't know, but definitely something a little more clandestine." He followed.

Inside, a slender man in a Skyline uniform paced back and forth in the aisle between two rows of beds.

Easton.

His hair was closely cropped and a pair of glasses sat on his nose. He spun toward the door as soon as they entered.

"Why didn't you stay where you were? Did anyone see you? You didn't kill anyone, did you?" His questions ceased the instant he made eye contact with Digby. "Oh lord."

"Indeed, I am Lord Graves." Digby gave the man a smug grin.

Easton staggered for a moment, taking a step back. "Sorry, I just haven't seen you in person since that night you killed my, everyone, in Seattle. It all just sort of came rushing back."

"Ah, yes I would apologize for that, but you know… a zombie's got to eat. Right?" Digby gave him a toothy smile.

"Dig, don't be a creep." Rebecca elbowed him and released her Waking Dream to cancel the illusion she wore as a disguise.

"Good." Easton nodded at her. "You've got an ability that will help us out here."

"Yes, but we should try not to rely too much on illusions. We weren't able to get to the uniforms you hid for us, but if we could get our hands on some more that would help." Rebecca dropped onto one of the beds to sit.

"Damn, I'll have to go get the disguises and drop them by in the morn…" Easton trailed off as his gaze traveled to the name tag on Digby's overalls. "Shit, you've already killed someone, haven't you?"

"It was unavoidable," Rebecca answered first, clearly trying to keep Digby from outing her as the culprit.

He shot her an accusatory look regardless. "As unfortunate as poor Gus's demise was, we were able to use his guardian ring to get us out of the airship hangar."

"Did you use it anywhere else?" Easton eyed him sharply.

"No."

"Good. Don't." Easton closed his eyes and sighed. "I'm sure they've noticed someone is missing by now so that ring's access is burnt. You'll get flagged if you try to use it again."

"Well, then if I have no use for it." Digby closed his hand around the ring and willed the Seed to extract the Kinetic Impact spell. It crumbled to dust a moment later.

Easton stared at the remains of the gold band before shaking his head and continuing. "The quality of Skyline's personnel has gone downhill since they started recruiting regular survivors into their ranks, so they shouldn't raise too many alarms if one guy doesn't show up for his shift." He flicked his eyes to Digby. "Provided they don't find the body. You did hide it somewhere safe, right?"

"I'd say so." Digby patted his stomach, feeling pretty satisfied with himself when Easton shuddered in response.

"Gross, but also, good." He sat down. "We have to be careful. Bancroft has one hell of a vendetta against you. It's to a point that he's managing the search for your people personally, rather than delegating anything to a subordinate. So you have his full and undivided attention. He's even assembled a team of his best guardians to follow leads in order to hunt you down. Judging by how angry he's been, they've found nothing so far."

"That is less than ideal." Digby perked up a second later. "Wait a second. Where does Bancroft sleep?"

Easton folded his arms. "He has a stand-alone apartment near the front of the barracks. It's not too far from here. Why?"

"Because I might pay him a somewhat lethal visit while he sleeps." Digby couldn't help but grin at the thought.

"First of all," Easton held up a finger, "he keeps a guard in front of his door all night. And second, isn't he a much higher level than you?"

"Right, right." Digby lowered his head. "There is a chance that I could drop him into my maw before he wakes up, but the odds still favor him. He might just wake up and slay me on reflex."

"It's probably best that we stick to the plan then." Rebecca leaned back.

"Indeed. But in light of how obsessed Bancroft is with my capture, as well as his close proximity to this very building, couldn't you have found somewhere better to hide us?" Digby gestured to the room around him.

Easton shook his head. "Exposed or not, no one is going to look for you here and no one is assigned to live here. This base has always been larger than needed, considering the amount of people stationed here, so there are plenty of unused barracks. I had always wondered why, until recently."

"Skyline must have intended on recruiting a large amount of people fast and wanted the room to grow prepared in advance. Taking that into account, this whole world domination thing seems more and more like their plan A, rather than a happy accident." He shrugged. "Either way, we still have dozens of empty barracks that have yet to be filled. As long as we don't put a sign out front that says resistance headquarters, no one will have a reason to come knocking. As dumb as it is, this is probably the only place Bancroft and his men won't think to look for you."

"Alright, no obvious signage. Got it." Digby nodded.

"I'd still keep the lights off though," Easton added.

"What about Henwick?" Rebecca chimed in. "It doesn't seem like his identity is known to anyone in Skyline except for Bancroft. So I assume he isn't on base."

"Yes." Digby tensed up. "We shan't want to bump into him while we are here."

"As far as I know, there is no one that fits his description on base." Easton shrugged. "I don't know where he is, but I feel confident that he is not here."

"Good." Digby relaxed.

"Anyway, down to business." Easton clapped his hands together. "As you know, we are running out of time to strike, but if what you say is true and Autem really does have the remains of your Heretic Seed, then that might tip the scales."

"That's the theory." Rebecca took a seat on one of the beds.

Digby did the same. "Now, what can you tell us about the security here?"

"I'll be honest, my information on the parts of the base that Autem controls is limited." Easton deflated. "Over here in Skyline's territory, everything is locked down on account of there being so many new people, but you can get around as long as you have a guardian ring or one of these." He held up his hand to display a metal cuff on his wrist. "However, I can only access a limited number of areas."

"Could you get a guardian ring?" Digby raised his eyebrows hopefully.

"I have been offered, but I've been avoiding taking one since I'm still not sure what sort of effect it might have on me. And as I was getting to, it won't get us in anywhere in Autem's area. Their rings are ranked higher. Plus, they have more security patrols and their personnel are more disciplined. The only upside is that Autem has less people. Most of their forces are stationed at whatever colony they're building on the East Coast. They only have people here to handle the recruitment and training of the children they take in and to man their research and development area."

"R&D?" Rebecca furrowed her brow. "What are they researching?"

"No idea." Easton shrugged.

"My guess is it has something to do with the uncommon zombies and revenants that they have been collecting." Digby grimaced at the thought.

Easton folded his arms. "Well, whatever they're doing, the research buildings are your target. If the Heretic Seed's fragments are anywhere, it's got to be there."

"That brings us back to the question of how we'll slip in." Digby folded his arms just as someone knocked on the door. Both he and Rebecca froze.

"It's okay, that's our newest resistance member and our way into Autem." Easton stood up to answer the door.

"You didn't say anything about another member of this operation." Rebecca stood up.

"Well, he hasn't really been a major part of things so far."

Easton glanced back. "But now that you're both here, he's become a valuable asset."

He pulled open the door to reveal a large man in a Skyline uniform carrying a stack of white containers. He wore no armor and his sleeves were rolled up as if he'd been working hard just before entering. Easton took the containers from him and gave an introduction, "This is Campbell."

"Um… Hi, Campbell." Digby gave him a sarcastic wave.

He waved back. "Hello, fellow resistance member."

"That's subtle." Rebecca buried her face in a hand.

"And what is it you do here at Skyline that makes you a valuable asset to this quest?" Digby didn't get up to greet the man.

"I work in the mess hall." Campbell took the top container from Easton and passed it to Rebecca.

She popped it open, finding a pile of rice and some sort of fried chicken strips. "You're the lunch lady." She flicked her eyes to Easton. "Why did you recruit the lunch lady?"

"I am right here, you know." Campbell frowned before shrugging and handing Digby a container of food, clearly unaware of his obvious dietary restrictions.

"Thank you, my good sir." He passed the container to Easton. "Unfortunately, I'm on a strict diet."

"Suit yourself." Campbell shrugged and took the remaining two containers for himself before sitting on one of the beds opposite them.

Easton claimed a strip of fried chicken and sat down. "To answer your question, Campbell is valuable because he can get you both into Autem's part of the base, including the high security building."

"How is he going to do that?" Rebecca looked to him.

Campbell chomped down on a piece of chicken. "You see, Autem's people over there have some pretty impressive facilities, but one thing they don't have is their own mess hall. Now, some of their people just come over here to eat, but the higher ups usually request meals to be delivered to them. They also have a whole set up brought out there to feed the new recruits that they're training."

"And that's your job," Digby assumed.

"I head over there at lunch and dinner with a cart full of food so they don't have to walk their asses all the way over to the mess. And if there's one advantage to the job, it's that they don't even remember my name, let alone give me a second look. Those Autem guys have a real superiority complex going on, and it gives them a false sense of security. If you can squeeze close together, I can fit you both in my cart; they practically never search it when I go through the gates."

"Practically never?" Digby arched an eyebrow.

"Well, yeah, there's a couple guards that still take a look but we should be able to avoid them." He shrugged as if it would be easy.

"That's a step in the right direction." Digby nodded. "What sort of security is in there?"

Campbell let out an awkward laugh. "The research facility has the same ring scanners. My ID cuff won't get us in, but there's a guard in the entryway that will scan his ring to let me in. From there, we just have to walk through a big door and find somewhere to let you out of my cart. After that, you'll be free to explore most of the building. If I take you at dinner time, you'll have all night to do what you need to. I can pick you back up in the morning and get you out of there."

"That doesn't sound so bad." Digby started to relax. "If all we have to is get past one guard, we might even be able to forgo the deception and simply kill them. I would have expected more security based on what Lana said."

"There is if you include the turrets and stuff?" Campbell continued to eat as if he hadn't just said something important.

"I'm sorry, but what was that about turrets?" Digby stared at the large man.

"Nothing major, but the entrance of the building is protected by two auto turrets and there's some weird panels on the wall. I assume they're some kind of weapon but honestly, your guess is as good as mine. The guard will shut them off when I go through so we should be fine."

"Oh joy." Digby rolled his eyes. "Is that all?"

"Um, no, actually." Campbell looked up from his food. "I've

been through most of the building, but there's one place that I've never gone near."

"Of course there is." Digby beckoned with a finger to draw out more information.

"There's an elevator on the first floor, which is also guarded by another locked door and a woman who sits at a desk nearby. She always comes out to get her food so I've never gone any further than that. I've only seen this elevator through the window in the wall." He furrowed his brow. "The weird part is that I've been on the other floors and, as far as I can tell, that elevator doesn't go anywhere. My only guess is that it goes to a sub-level or something."

"That vibes with our theory that the Seed's fragments are here." Rebecca nodded. "If it goes down, then that would certainly be a good place for a secure vault."

"The other weird thing about that elevator is the doors are gold."

"I don't like the sound of that." Rebecca put her food down. "Plus, if that woman is guarding that elevator, she might be a high-level guardian."

"We'll have to figure out a way to get past her, or find a time when she's away from her post." Digby scratched at his chin before letting out a sigh. "This may be harder than the movies made it out to be."

"Everything always is," Rebecca added.

Digby turned to stare off in the direction of Autem's area of the base. "I just hope Hawk can stay safe until we're ready to move."

CHAPTER FIFTEEN

Alex buried his head in his hands as he sat on the bed of his overly fancy hotel room. He hadn't been able to relax since the visit from Autem's men the day before. How could he?

What am I going to do?

Digby was gone. Becca was gone. Even Hawk had been taken away.

After losing his family like everyone else in the apocalypse, they had been a source of comfort. Surrogates for the people he'd lost. He'd been an only child before, but Becca was like an older sister. Supportive but quick to call him out whenever he did something dumb. Hawk was the bratty brother. Good for a laugh, always in trouble, but fun to play games with. Then there was Digby. He was the weird uncle. Always had a story to tell, though you had to wonder if he was telling the truth. He was the uncle that would let you stay up late and eat candy for dinner when they babysat.

They were all gone. They were behind enemy lines where one failed move could get them killed. They were his family, and they might not come home. He didn't want to lose them.

Choking down his fears, Alex glanced to the circle floating at the edge of his vision to open his status.

STATUS
Name: Alex Sanders
Race: Human
Heretic Class: Artificer
Mana: 261 / 261
Mana Composition: Balanced
Current Level: 20 (2,024 Experience to next level.)

ATTRIBUTES
Constitution: 38
Defense: 33
Strength: 34
Dexterity: 33
Agility: 35
Intelligence: 36
Perception: 33
Will: 51

At least he'd come a long way in the few short weeks that they had been together. He swiped the display away when a knock sounded from his door.

"Hey," Parker called out from the other side. "You in there?"

Her voice sounded apprehensive. She probably felt the same as he did. Actually, if it wasn't for her, he would be far worse off. Fitting into his surrogate family, she was the cousin that got caught sneaking beers on Thanksgiving. She was kind of a mess, but a reliable partner in crime.

Pulling the door open, he found her standing there in a leather jacket. It was covered in zippers and decorative elements that screamed fashion. She carried a second one draped over her arm.

"I got you something." She pushed it into his hands. "I figured you could use a new jacket to cheer you up. I know I did."

He held the garment up, finding an elaborate design of rhine-stones on the back featuring a skeletal hand wearing a massive, skull shaped ring. Sparkling roses filled the background. He nearly choked when he saw the price tag hanging from one sleeve. It was worth seven thousand dollars.

"I realize they're a little douchey, but I thought they seemed like something Dig would appreciate." She spun around and hooked a thumb to her back where the same over the top design sparkled. "Plus, we already did weird stuff with our hair, so why be subtle now?"

"Good point." He pulled the jacket on over his Hawaiian shirt and zipped it up. To his surprise, it fit like a second skin, to the point where it actually accented his frame in a way that really worked for him. Apparently there was a reason for the insane price tag. As far as apocalypse wear went, he could do a lot worse.

"So, um, what's up?" He scratched at the back of his neck.

"I need to get my mind off things, so I thought I might try to get a new forge built." She hesitated for a second, letting her hands rest on the handles of her daggers that were sheathed at her sides. "You maybe want to help?"

"Oh yeah, I actually had some ideas about it." Alex grabbed his machete from a hook on the wall meant for a bathrobe and headed into the hall.

"Really?"

He nodded, letting himself indulge in the distraction. "I have a spell called Heat Object. I learned it originally from cooking but I've ranked it up a couple times and the maximum temperature has doubled each time."

"Umm… okay?" She strolled along to match his pace.

"When I first discovered the spell, it could heat things to three hundred degrees," Alex explained.

"I get it. If you can rank it up four times, you'll be able to heat things to forty-eight-hundred degrees. Which is plenty to run a forge." She took his explanation right out of his mouth.

Alex glanced at her with his jaw hanging open, unsure how she put it all together so fast. She didn't exactly seem like the type to be great at math, what with the frequent napping and such. Then again, he thought back to the board games he and Hawk had played with her over the last week and a half. She had beaten him almost every time. Maybe there was more going on in there than he realized.

"A magic-based forge would be cool. We wouldn't need fuel,

and it would make building the thing way easier. Just need some material to heat up that won't melt at that temperature." She shoved her hands in her jacket pockets.

"That's what I'm thinking." Alex reached the stairwell that led to the main floor of the casino, running into Mason as he rounded the corner.

"Either of you seen Sax?" The soldier slowed as he ascended the steps.

"He said he was going to inventory the ammo." Parker pointed back down the stairs. "My guess, he's in the armory."

"Probably should have checked there first." Mason turned around to walk with them down the stairs as an awkward silence engulfed the stairwell.

Alex couldn't help but feel like a third wheel. Mason and Parker were both around his age, but considering they were both in the military together, he felt like they were on a different level than he was. He had known a few other ex-military guys back at his old job. They always seemed to find an instant bond between them, built by mutual experiences that he didn't share. It had always made him feel unwelcome.

They were good people, but he always got the sense that they didn't see him as an equal. Though, that may just have been his perception of things. Either way, it was a feeling that he wasn't sure how to shake even now. Parker may have been a friend, but there was still a distance that he couldn't quite cross to stand alongside her and the other soldiers.

"I'm glad I ran into you, Alex." Mason broke the silence as they reached the landing on the main floor. "With Dig and Becca away, we still have a ton to do back here. I want to have a meeting with all of us together, Deuce and Elenore too."

"Oh sure, I'll catch up with you later then." Alex slowed to a stop, not wanting to hold them up. "Parker and I can do the forge stuff when you're done."

"Huh?" She furrowed her brow.

Mason stared at him as well, looking equally confused. "You do realize that when I say, 'all of us together,' that includes you."

"Me?" Alex pointed to himself.

"Yes, I mean you." Mason slapped a hand against his thigh. "You're one of only three people in the world that hold the power to fight these guardians on equal ground. Not to mention you've fought Skyline longer than the rest of us. Actually, now that I think about it, I was only in the army for eight months before all of this happened, so I'm pretty sure you have more combat experience."

"Wait, what?" Alex dropped his hand to his side. "I just kind of figured I would get in the way."

Parker snapped her eyes to him. "Why would you think that? We need you. I would be a zombie or something by now if you hadn't Cleansed me back in California." She raised her arms in front of her and pretended to try to bite Mason before continuing. "Not to mention your magic has been the only thing that has let the rest of us humans stand up against all the freakin' monsters out there. If I didn't have these enchanted daggers, I'd be nothing more than a delicious snack."

Alex opened his mouth to respond but found the words missing. He hadn't actually considered that he had a role to play without Digby around. He was always willing to help but other than his magic, he wasn't much more than the necromancer's assistant.

That was when a memory from the day before flashed through his mind. The scent of gunpowder climbed up his nose as the weight of two sub-machine guns filled his hands. It was only yesterday that he had fought his way through the high-cards that were protecting Rivers. He had killed them. No, that wasn't right. He had fought to protect his coven, as well as two new allies that had already proved valuable.

A small part of him wanted to stand tall and accept the responsibility that Mason's words implied. The rest of him felt too weak to carry the weight of it all.

How did I not realize?

There was so much at stake. He hadn't really stopped to think about it. He had just followed Digby and Becca, swinging a machete like a child playing with a toy sword.

"Whoa…" Heat swept across his forehead as his knees began to buckle.

"Shit, are you okay?" Parked rushed out to slip under his arm for support.

"Sorry." Alex didn't know what to say other than to apologize. "I think a lot of stuff just sank in." He took a few deep breaths. "Holy crap, I'm in so far over my head."

"Join the club." Parker snorted, though her voice trembled a little.

"The whole world is drowning right now," Mason added as he rested a hand on his shoulder. "Unfortunately, we're all it's got left."

Alex nodded, getting a hold of himself. Parker stayed close even after his knees stopped shaking as if she needed just as much support. She kept her sense of humor, but he could feel her hands tremble. Having worked through some things, he was able to at least give the appearance of being able to keep his shit together as they continued on their way.

They found Sax where they expected, taking an inventory of the weapons and ammunition that had been left behind by Rivers and his high-cards. The soldier had taken over one of the exchange counters where the casino's employees would have handed out poker chips and paid out winnings. The secure area worked well to store the arsenal that they had inherited. Mason called Deuce and Elenore over a minute later.

With everyone together, they ran down a list of priorities, at the top was moving the two zombies that Digby had left in one of the hallways upstairs. They couldn't keep the area sealed off forever, and people would probably notice the smell eventually.

Alex volunteered to take care of the issue. With his purification magic, he was the only responsible choice. It was unlikely that one of Digby's minions would bite him, but if they did, he could at least Cleanse the wound. Parker raised her hand to go with him.

As for Sax's weapons inventory, they had enough firepower to arm every man woman and child that currently resided in their settlement twice over, and even more ammunition. Not that they actually would arm the children, obviously, but at least there was plenty to work with. It was a good thing too, since there was plenty of interest amongst the survivors they had taken in the day before in fighting back against Skyline and whatever empire Autem was building. Once the people had been informed that their enemy's plan involved taking their family members, even the people who had no one left to lose were willing to sign up. Surprisingly, the end of the world seemed to bring out the good in people just as much as it did the bad.

Fortunately, Mason and the others weren't the only ones in the group with military experience. There were a few National Guardsmen and Air Force members. It wasn't much, but they were at least able to help organize the people and no one put up a fight when Mason took charge. All in all, they had around seventy-five fighters available. Well, almost. Most of them needed training first.

It was decided that, for now, it would be best to keep the existence of magic and the Heretic Seed a secret from most of the casino's inhabitants until there was a way to bestow it upon others. Keeping them in the dark would hurt their amateur army's ability to fight against whatever opposition their adversaries put up, but with nothing but ordinary firearms, there wasn't much hope of winning anyway. Against guardians that could sling spells and cast Barriers around themselves while wielding enchanted swords, their chances were bleak. At least, they were until Digby and Rebecca returned with the Seed's fragments.

With their limitations understood, they agreed that their newly recruited troops would be best suited in dealing with the revenants that wandered into the city. If Digby's plan was successful, that might change, but in the meantime, it made more sense to play it safe. There was no sense in getting everyone killed the minute they finally made some progress.

The forge was further down on the list of priorities, but thanks to Deuce and Elanor's familiarity with the area, they were able to take over some of the preparations. After giving them a list of materials, Alex was free to deal with Digby's minions waiting upstairs.

"That should wrap things up." Mason clapped his hands together.

Deuce raised his hand. "Actually, there is one more thing that

I'm not sure what to do about. Well, actually, it's less of a thing and more of a who."

"Did we forget something?" Alex leaned on a desk in the back of the armory.

"I would say so." Elenore stepped forward. "Remember the two aces you knocked out?"

"Oh shit." Alex slapped a hand over his mouth, realizing that everyone had run off after Digby to make sure he wasn't in danger without restraining either of the goons he'd punched out.

"It's fine." Deuce held up a hand. "I had my guys come and take care of them before they woke up."

Alex let out a relieved sigh at the fact that they hadn't escaped. Then he sucked it back in. "Wait, when you say you took care of them, do you mean…?"

"God no, we didn't kill them." Deuce threw both hands out at his sides. "I mean, I know they would have deserved it, but we had already won."

"Yeah, we aren't really big on doing our own executions," Elenore added.

"I get that." Alex nodded. "I don't want to kill anyone we don't have to either."

"Where are they?" Mason scratched at his beard.

"We have them locked up on the floor above the rest of the guest rooms with a guard outside. No one but us knows they're there. So, do we wait for Digby to come back and, you know…" Deuce trailed off.

"What, eat them?" Alex stared at the man with his head cocked to one side.

"Well, I don't know what to do with them." Deuce shrugged.

"That would be the same as executing them," Mason argued.

"Yeah, let's not serve them up as dinner quite yet," Parker added.

"Maybe if we treat them real nice, they will cooperate and join our people," Alex offered.

"Sure they will." Elenore folded her arms. "So far we've gotten nothing but curse words from them. Plus, I'm not so sure I want to work with the guys that protected the man that tried to steal my kid."

"That's a reasonable concern." Mason let out a sigh.

"Can we see how things turn out over the next couple days?" Alex held out a hand toward Elenore and Deuce. "They might come around. And to be honest, we need all the help we can get."

"Maybe." Elenore grumbled something under her breath that Alex couldn't make out.

"Okay." Mason clapped his hands together again. "Let's go get things done then."

Parker hopped down from the table where she'd been sitting before making her way to the door to the casino's weapon storage. She glanced back to Alex before leaving the room. "I'm gonna grab a few guns? You want anything?"

"No thanks, I'm more dangerous with a blade at this point." Alex shrugged. "Besides, we just have to move Digby's zombies. They shouldn't give us any trouble as long as they've had plenty to eat. And I should be able to get Asher to help."

"Suit yourself. I'm still going to grab a shotgun just in case. I'm probably delicious, so I'm not taking any chances." She let out an awkward laugh combined with a snort on the way out.

From there, Alex headed for the hallway to find Digby's stray minions. He found them sitting right where they had been, though from the look of things, they had eaten everything that remained of the high-cards. After being left alone with the corpses, all that was left were a few large bones.

Neither of the monsters had obtained a mutation, which was odd since he was pretty sure they had both eaten plenty of bone to form claws. That was when he remembered that, as their master, Digby could choose the path they were on. It made him wonder what the necromancer had in mind.

"Oh well, I'll find out eventually." He beckoned to the zombies, hoping Digby had given them a command to listen to him. "Come on, you two, we have to get out of here."

Both minions immediately pushed themselves up and stood at the ready. Alex gave them an approving eyebrow pump as he realized how normal interacting with the dead had become. There was a part of him that felt like he was simply greeting a new coworker.

"Right this way." He headed for the garage, turning to add, "Be careful on the stairs, though. I know you both might still be a little unsteady." His deceased coworkers nodded as if they appreciated the warning. They both used the railing on the way down.

Reaching the bottom, Alex radioed Deuce to move any of his people from the garage that weren't aware of the dead's cooperative nature. Once the coast was clear, he headed out and called for Asher. Hopefully, she was close enough to hear him. The zombified raven swooped in a moment later as if she'd been waiting there. His whole body tensed when she flapped up to his shoulder.

"Ah, hey there, Asher. How are you?" Obviously, Digby had ordered her to help him but he'd never been under the impression that she liked him. "Wish I was able to hear you like Dig is."

The deceased bird cocked her head to one side before awkwardly opening her beak. "HELLP!"

"What!" Alex nearly fell over as the raven cawed at full volume in a manner that sounded like the word help.

"HELLP HELLP HELLP!" Asher continued to shout the poorly formed word in his ear.

"Help what?" He winced as he waited for the auditory assault to end.

"I... HELLP... ALLLEXX."

"Oh, I get it." He relaxed. "Digby asked you to help me."

Asher nodded. "I HELLP. ALLEX, GIVVE."

"I give?" That was the first he'd heard of payment. "What do you want?"

The raven glanced from side to side as if trying to maintain an element of secrecy, prompting Alex to lean his head to her expecting a whisper. Of course, that was when she shouted, "SHINNY!"

"Okay, I suppose I should have expected that." He rubbed his ear. She was a bird after all, she didn't really have the internal structure to speak in normal human tones. Still, it was a surprise that she could speak considering he'd never heard her before.

I guess she never really had to since she can speak directly to Digby across their bond. Despite the volume and mispronunciation, it was helpful that they could communicate.

Their conversation was interrupted when Parker drove down the ramp in the cargo van that had been left on the top level. She leaned out the window as the vehicle rolled to a stop in front of him and his zombie coworkers.

"Get in losers, we're going exploring."

"LOSSER!" Asher shouted in response, looking pleased with herself.

Parker's eyes widened. "That's new."

"Yeah, it's also loud." Alex held a wince, worried that the raven might have something else to add. Fortunately, she didn't.

The zombies entered the van without any trouble, and Parker moved to the passenger seat so she could put her feet up. Alex climbed in behind the wheel. As soon as their deceased passengers in back sat down, they pulled out of the garage to head for the other end of the strip. If they could find a way to gather a new horde, then they were going to need somewhere big enough to house it so that it couldn't be seen from the air. It also made sense to put some distance between their new home and the dead. Alex may have gotten used to working with the deceased, but the rest of the survivors would probably be uncomfortable with a horde next door.

Alex leaned forward on the wheel as they pulled up to a building shaped like a massive pyramid. At first glance it looked like a prime candidate, but as he looked closer, he saw a reason for concern.

The area was quiet, just like the rest of the strip. What drew his attention, however, was a truck. Just a lone pickup. The odd part was that it was parked with its front bumper placed up against a pair of double doors.

"That's weird." Parker leaned against the window.

"Yeah, are you thinking what I am?" He stopped the van a dozen feet away.

She nodded. "Either that truck is keeping something in or trying to keep something out."

Alex glanced back at the zombies in the back, wondering if

they would be able to help if they found something dangerous. Of course, they didn't have to investigate, but if they ignored it, they might end up regretting it later. He popped the door open.

"We'll just peek in through a window." He stepped out and carefully approached the truck.

The doors it was holding shut were barricaded with some metal plating that had been welded to cover most of the glass, but there were slivers that he might be able to get a look through. Crawling up onto the truck, he slid down the hood.

"CAERRFULL!" Asher cawed from the van.

Alex cringed and glanced back. Parker held a finger over her mouth to tell the bird to hush. Asher ducked her head as if she understood.

After waiting half a minute to make sure nothing had heard them, Alex leaned closer to a small section of windows that was still visible. Inside, he saw nothing but shadows. He kept looking, waiting for his eyes to adjust.

Then he saw a familiar shape.

"Oh no." Alex pulled away from the window. "We have to go."

CHAPTER SIXTEEN

Hawk ran with everything he had as the steady slap of feet hitting the ground behind him chased him forward. His lungs ached and his legs burned.

Faster!

He had to run faster.

He had to succeed.

With his eyes locked on a white, painted line in front of him, he pushed himself to his limits.

"Good hustle, Hawk." A man in a weird lab coat clapped as he passed the finish line. He glanced down at a tablet computer to enter some data.

Hawk slowed to a stop, bent over gasping for air. A quarter-mile athletic track surrounded him. Ten other kids of varying ages crossed the line behind him, each having run a mile.

"I won." He panted. "I actually won."

Of course, it wasn't actually a race, but he was glad to have come in first even if it didn't matter.

After arriving the previous day, Hawk had been taken to one of Skyline's barracks where he'd been fed and allowed to spend the night. He had even been given a clean set of clothes. Nothing fancy, just a pair of athletic pants and a plain t-shirt. They smelled better than what he'd been wearing though. His evaluation had been scheduled for first thing in the morning. If he passed, he would be allowed to join Autem's guardians.

He had to pass.

Considering he had thrown himself into danger after being told to do the exact opposite, he didn't want to blow his chance to gain information. That was what Dig would have done. The necromancer would never have hid in the casino if there was an advantage to be gained. True, Digby had been the one to order him to stay out of things, but Hawk had promptly ignored him. The zombie wouldn't have let anyone tell him what to do. So why should Hawk?

As far as what joining the guardians meant, he wasn't exactly sure since the soldiers running his evaluation seemed to be keeping things vague. Though, Hawk understood some of what they were trying to do based on things he'd overheard Dig and the others talk about. He was just lucky that the magic zombie had a tendency to shout half of what he said.

Back in California, he'd seen some of Skyline's guardians in action and they used the same magic as Dig. Hawk couldn't deny that a part of him really wanted that power. With it, he wouldn't have to be protected. With magic of his own, he might actually be able to help. He hoped he could learn more about where the power came from as well.

Catching his breath, he stood upright, making a point of holding his head high. If he was going to claim the power that Digby had, then he was going to have to pass this test.

The other kids didn't have the same determination, each still struggling to deal with what the world had become. Hawk could relate. Things had been hard for the last month. If it hadn't been for Digby, his Heretics, and the protection they provided, he would have been in worse shape. His life wasn't at all what someone might call stable, but he'd come a long way in the last couple weeks. Learning things from Digby and playing board games with Parker and Alex gave him a kind of anchor that helped him to push through the horrors that he'd witnessed.

Hawk made a point to limit his interactions with the other

kids, not wanting to say anything that he shouldn't. Digby would be pissed if he ever let something about Vegas or their heist slip. The other kids seem to be fine with his choice, having little interest in others beyond their own safety. They all seemed to think that monsters would burst through the walls and attack at any second.

Hawk swept his eyes across the base, feeling a combination of anxiety and calm. It was true that everyone around him was an enemy, but as long as he could keep acting his part, he was safer than he had been even in Vegas. Plus, the barracks that he'd spent the night in had been comfortable. The food in the mess hall was good too. Well, not that good. Then again, no one had to risk their lives to find more, and there wasn't a limit to how much he could have.

Thinking about it, Autem's people kind of had it made, as long as you could overlook their plan for world domination.

"Come on in!" The man with the clipboard called out while beckoning to all the kids. "Time to head back inside for the rest of your evaluation."

Hawk followed back into a building nearby where he and the rest of the kids were seated in a waiting room that reminded him of a doctor's office.

So far, his morning had reminded him of gym class. Before running a mile, they walked balance beams, touched their toes, did sit ups, lifted weights, and tossed balls around. The base even had a batting cage. Obviously, Hawk had never liked gym class but there was something to be said for doing something so mundane.

One by one, the other kids were called in before it was his turn. After an hour of waiting, a woman dressed in white scrubs came out to get him. Following her, he entered a small room with a bench seat, where he was asked to sit. He did as he was told, trying his best to be cooperative as she gave him a pretty standard physical.

The only weird part was when she took several vials of blood. He wasn't sure what she could have possibly needed it all for. If he didn't know better, he'd think she was keeping a pet revenant in the back and needed to feed it. He hoped that wasn't the case. Either way, when she was finished, she brought him to another room and shut the door.

Hawk stood awkwardly, not sure what to do now that he had been left alone.

The room was entirely white with no windows. Looking up, the ceiling was high despite the overall space being relatively small, just large enough to house a table at its center. A chair sat on either side. Each piece of furniture was made of stainless steel. Strangely, the room was lit by a row of strip lights that ran vertically in the corners of the space. It reminded him of a set from a science fiction show.

Hawk debated sitting down, but instead opted to walk around the table a few times. The room was uncomfortably quiet, as if it had been soundproofed or something. At least, walking around created a little noise and made him feel less nervous. With nothing to do, Hawk bent down to look under the table, finding nothing. After that, he proceeded to knock on the walls to see what they were made of.

That was when a robotic voice came from overhead.

"Book, clock, computer, September, manager, horse."

Hawk flicked his eyes up, finding a black dome mounted to the ceiling. It was obviously a camera. "What?"

"Book, clock, computer, September, manager, horse."

"Um, okay." He dropped his eyes back down, not sure how else to respond.

A new voice followed, this time sounding more natural. "What were you doing to the wall?"

"Um, nothing."

"It didn't look like nothing." The voice chuckled, sounding a little girlish.

"Okay, I guess I wasn't doing nothing." Hawk decided to be honest. Before the apocalypse, he got in trouble enough to know that it was best to tell the truth as much as possible. The thing about lying was that it always made it harder to keep a story straight. It was best to save his lies for when he really needed them. "I wanted to know what the walls were made of."

"What made you wonder?" the voice asked without offering a reason for the question.

"It's too quiet in here for the walls to be made of anything normal." Hawk remained honest.

"Good observation." The voice paused. "Why did you look under the table?"

Hawk furrowed his brow. He had done that a couple minutes before the voice had started talking to him. Had they been watching then?

They must have.

He answered with a shrug. "I was bored and curious, I guess."

"Curiosity. A good trait when applied in the right direction, though it can also be a bad trait if it leads you astray." The voice sounded amused.

"Umm, okay." Hawk didn't know what to say to that.

"I have your name listed here as Hawk. Is that right?"

"Yeah?" he answered, his voice climbing up a bit at the end like a question. Obviously, Hawk wasn't his real name, but it was the name he'd decided on when he lost the need for his old one.

"No last name?"

"No, just ah, Hawk." He shrugged.

"Are you sure your name isn't Marcus Calder?"

Hawk froze at the mention of his real name. No, not his real name, but his original name, the one he had been born with. The one he never wanted to be called again. "How did you—"

"You were microchipped when you entered the California foster system."

Hawk immediately looked at his wrists and arms for any indication that something had been implanted.

Nothing stuck out.

"It's behind your ear."

Hawk rubbed at his ears. He found something the size of a grain of rice and felt a little angry that something like that had been done without his consent. It was true that he had been in foster care. His real parents hadn't been financially stable or ready for the responsibility that having him meant.

"It's actually quite fortunate for you that the C.F.S. took the precaution to have you chipped. It made things much easier for us to track down your information."

"How much do you know?" Hawk asked, afraid that there might be something that might betray a half-truth or two that he might have told them already.

"Nothing too detailed. We know your medical history and school records. It seems that your grades were never particularly good, but your teachers thought you were capable of more. A text-book case of not being challenged academically. With more attention, you may have fared better, but considering that you spent your life being moved between various foster homes, it was unlikely that you would amount to much."

"You're wrong." Hawk raised his hand to the camera. "Not about amounting to much. That's probably a good guess. But I was adopted eventually." It wasn't an important detail of his life, but he didn't want it erased.

"Ah yes, it does say that. How long did you live with your adoptive parents?" The voice started to sound bored.

"Almost two years. They fostered me for a while and decided to keep me a few months ago. I didn't call them mom and dad or anything, but they were nice to me." A quiver snuck into his voice, catching him off guard.

"What happened to them?" The voice sounded interested again.

"They died…" Hawk trailed off before adding, "I think."

"You think?"

Hawk thought back to the night that the world ended. "I didn't see it happen. I woke up when the window in their room broke. At least that's what I think the sound was. I thought we were getting robbed, so I got up and hid behind my bedroom door."

"You didn't go try to help?"

"No." He winced, still wishing he had. It was one of the reasons he'd run out of the casino the day before, when it looked like Dig and Becca might get caught. He didn't want to lose anyone else.

"Were you scared?"

"No. But I'm not stupid. I'm a kid. I thought I'd be in the way if I went in there." He clenched his jaw. He wasn't going to make that mistake again. "After a few minutes, the sounds coming from their room changed. I could hear movement, but nothing like a struggle or anything."

"What did you do?" The voice asked before he had a chance to think.

"I knocked on their door eventually, but no one answered. Whatever was in there started scratching at the door. I almost opened it but I heard screaming from the house next door before I could. That was when I realized something was happening. I went to the window and saw a pair of zombies eating someone."

"You didn't try to help them?"

"It was too late." Hawk shook his head. "I grabbed a baseball bat and hid in my closet until morning. Some of the neighbors tried to get away the next day, loading up their cars and making a run for it. Most made it, but a few didn't. The zombies followed the people that left. So most of them left my street. I stayed where I was and kept quiet. I didn't know what else to do. Part of me was still hoping Maria and Jose…" He hesitated before adding, "Those were their names, my parents, I mean. I think I was hoping they would somehow come out of their room and be okay. I hoped that help would come and we could all get away."

"That didn't happen though."

"No, but whatever was in there kept scratching." Hawk shrugged. "I went to the living room to get Maria's laptop. I found out what was happening and that it wasn't just my town."

"Did you stay there after you learned that help wasn't coming?"

"I thought about it. The few zombies outside didn't seem to know I was there, and I had enough food in the house for a week or two." Hawk sat down in one of the chairs at the table. "I probably would have stayed if I hadn't noticed that the scratching at Maria and Jose's door was getting louder. Whatever was on the other side was going to claw its way through eventually. I couldn't stay. I loaded a backpack with whatever food I could. I didn't know much about what else I would need. In the end, I got my bike from the garage and took my chances."

"And you got away?"

"Yeah, the zombies were slow and they weren't able to block the street or anything." He slouched back in his chair.

"Where did you go?"

"I'd seen enough movies to know I needed to get away from town. I figured there would be less zombies if there were less people around to be turned." Hawk nodded at his thought process.

"Good thinking, that probably saved your life."

"I got pretty far too," Hawk added, letting a hint of pride enter his voice.

"How did you avoid the revenants once they started showing up?" The voice sounded a little smug.

Hawk opened his mouth to speak, nearly giving himself away. The only reason he knew what a revenant was because he'd heard Dig and the others use that word. He covered by doing his best to sound confused. "The what?"

"Revenants." The voice sounded bored again. "That is what those other monsters are called. How did you avoid them for this long?"

Again, Hawk opened his mouth only to close it again. So far, he had been able to tell the truth, but he was going to have to start lying if he was to keep his cover secret. That was when he remembered something else.

They can detect lies.

He froze. Becca had a spell that could tell if people were lying. He'd seen her use it on Digby to annoy him. Actually, he was pretty sure he'd heard her mention that her drone's camera could do the same. He looked back up to the black dome on the ceiling.

"I avoided the monsters by staying away from the people." He kept his statements vague. "Eventually, I made it to a campground where I met an old woman. She died though." That much was true. "After that, I found out that the new monsters didn't attack during the day. Kept moving after that." He took a slow breath to stay calm, hoping that the voice wouldn't question him any further. If they did, it wouldn't be long before he had to tell a real lie. He breathed a sigh of relief when the voice changed the subject.

"How many children were in the group that ran the track with you earlier this morning?"

"Ten?" he answered, not entirely sure if he had been right.

"What were their names?"

Hawk furrowed his brow. "I don't know."

"You don't remember any?"

"I didn't ask." Hawk shrugged.

"Have you killed anyone in the last month?"

"What?" He shrieked his answer by accident.

"Did you have to kill anyone while trying to survive in the last month?" The voice spoke the question in monotone, as if it wasn't a big deal.

"No," he answered back without hesitation.

"Would you have if put in a situation where your life depended on taking another's?"

"I don't know," Hawk answered honestly, surprised that his answer hadn't been a straight no.

"Have you stolen anything to survive?" The voice questioned his morals again.

He tilted his head back and forth. "I don't think you could find anyone now that hasn't looted anything to survive."

"That's understandable." The voice sounded amused at his answer. "I have one last question."

"And?"

"What were the words that the automated voice listed before I started speaking to you?"

Hawk squinted up at the camera. "What?"

"What were the words that the automated voice listed?"

"I can't remember that," Hawk argued with the disembodied voice.

"Try." It sounded annoyed.

Hawk lowered his gaze and stared at the wall while he attempted to remember. He opened his mouth a moment later. "Book, computer, September, manager, horse."

A long pause went by before the voice responded, "You left out clock."

"Is that bad?" He cringed.

"According to our estimates based on your physical and mental evaluation, your attributes are as follows. Constitution: fifteen, defense: nine, strength: ten, dexterity: seventeen, agility: fifteen, intelligence: eighteen, perception: seventeen, will: sixteen."

Hawk listened as the voice listed off his stats like a video game. He hadn't gotten to play a lot of them, other than a few mobile games. He raised his head up to the camera above.

"Does that mean I passed?"

CHAPTER SEVENTEEN

"Holy fucking shit, we are going to die!" Parker shouted as she dove back into the van that Alex had parked outside the suspicious casino at the end of the strip. "How many did you say were in there?"

"I don't know, I don't know." Alex's heart raced as climbed behind the wheel and turned the key, still struggling to process what he had just seen.

From what he could see through the window, the entire casino was filled wall to wall with revenants. There were so many that they had formed a pile of pale, writhing bodies. More were packed into the walkways above to the point that a few of the balconies had collapsed under the weight.

It was horrifying.

Alex hadn't been able to get any kind of count, but based on the overall size of the hive, there must have been tens of thousands.

"Drive drive drive." Parker slapped the dash repeatedly.

"DRIVVE!" Asher squawked from the back of his seat.

Alex yanked down on the gearshift but stopped just before stepping on the gas. "Wait a second."

"What?" Parker gripped the handle of the door tight.

Alex put the van back in park and sat back. "Why are we worried? It's day time. The revenants inside aren't going anywhere right now. We could open the doors and ask them to lunch and they would probably stay right where they are. Not to mention they didn't break out last night or the night before, so I'm pretty sure they're trapped in there."

"That's not the only place they're trapped." Parker pointed to another nearby casino that had a truck parked against its doors.

Alex eyed the second prison. "That's not great."

"I guess we know why there are so few revs wandering around the strip. They're all in there." Parker started to relax.

"But how did they get there?" Alex tapped on the steering wheel.

"No idea, but I bet I know who can tell us." She released her grip on the handle above the door.

"You're right. I think we need to pay a visit to the two aces we're keeping captive. My guess is Rivers had something to do with this. We need to know more about what happened here before figuring out what we're going to do about it."

With the situation understood, Alex unloaded Digby's minions and told them to stand outside the hive for now. After that, they made it back home in fifteen minutes, wasting no time. He got a few odd looks as he passed through the casino from some of the other survivors due to the white raven perched on his shoulder. She looked alive enough for no one to suspect that she was dead, but still it was a strange sight. He was just glad she decided to stay quiet. It wasn't long before Alex was climbing the stairs toward the rooms where they were keeping Rivers' aces.

Both of the captured henchmen were held on the fifth floor of the hotel with two of Deuce's men guarding their doors. To his surprise, the guards stepped aside as soon as he got there, practically saluting as they did.

That's going to take some getting used to.

He suppressed the urge to turn around and find Mason. If he was going to act as Digby's proxy while the necromancer was away, then he was going to need to accomplish things on his own. That being said, he had no idea how to interrogate a potentially hostile prisoner.

He turned to Parker before entering. "You want to do good cop, bad cop?"

"Sure." She shrugged. "I don't have any better ideas."

"Okay then, here goes nothing." Alex turned the doorknob and headed in, stepping aside to let Parker enter before closing the door.

A man sat in a chair by the window. The last time Alex had seen him had been when he'd punched the guy's lights out. The man's eyes widened the moment he saw him. Clearly he remembered him too.

"What do you want?" The prisoner sat up straight.

"To talk." Parker sat down on the bed.

Alex decided to stay quiet and follow her lead, realizing that they hadn't actually discussed who was the bad cop and who was the good cop. Though, considering he'd already knocked the guy out once, it made sense for him to be the intimidating one. He decided to lean against the wall to keep his presence imposing. The fact that Asher was still perched on his shoulder helped sell the image.

The ace spoke before giving them a chance to ask questions. "Is it true you're guy that killed Rivers?"

"Yes." Alex nodded, without offering more.

"That's right." Parker gave him a sympathetic smile, revealing herself as the good cop. "Rivers has been taken care of, so you don't have to worry about following any orders that he may have issued. You can talk to us freely."

Alex couldn't help but notice that her speech had slipped into something more appropriate for a soldier, as if she was falling back on her military experience.

He opened his mouth to say something intimidating, but closed it just as fast when he found the words missing. The ace simply looked at him expectantly before turning back to Parker.

Being the bad cop is going to be harder than I thought.

Running through his abilities in his head, Alex wondered if any would be useful for interrogation. For a moment he considered his Heat Object spell. With that he could simply make himself a hot poker to prod the man for information. He dismissed the idea as soon as he had it, finding that the concept of torture turned his stomach. Apocalypse or not, there were some lines that people just shouldn't cross.

As it was, the man didn't even know magic was a thing since Alex had knocked him out before Digby had started throwing spells around the other day. Trying to explain it now would almost surely be met with skepticism. Thinking back, the only spell that the man had actually witnessed was a Barrier, which wasn't visually impressive enough to be convincing.

Parker continued the conversation when he failed to say anything. "We just made a trip down to the other end of the strip."

The ace's eyes widened at the mention of the place. "I don't know what you're talking about."

"Really? 'Cause your reaction says otherwise," Alex chimed in, trying to get into character.

"You don't have anything to worry about." Parker leaned forward and placed a hand on his knee. "Rivers isn't here anymore. We just want to know how he was able to gather the monsters and how secure those buildings are."

"Bullshit." He slapped her hand away. "I saw what you guys did to the rest of the high-cards. Deuce's guys brought us into that hallway where you massacred them. They had to turn around and take us out the other way when they saw the zombies. There were more of our men dead out that way too. If you expect me to believe you're not going to kill me, you have another thing coming. So no, I'm not telling you shit. I'm dead the moment I do. I understand that much. As far as I'm concerned, if you want information from me, you need to let me go first." He punctuated his statement by spitting on Parker's pant leg.

She flinched, before glancing down a thick glob of saliva. "Blah, gross. Who the hell spits on people?"

The prisoner simply smirked, clearly proud of himself for getting a rise out of her.

"Ok fine, that's the way it is, then." Parker got up and headed to the nightstand to search one of the drawers.

"What are you looking for?" Alex stepped away from the wall just as Parker pulled out a phone book.

She shouted, mid-throw, "This!"

"The fuck?" The ace ducked as the phonebook flew over his head slammed into the wall behind him.

Asher let out a surprised caw in Alex's ear.

"Shit, Parker, we're not here to beat information out of him," he shrieked as they swapped roles without warning.

"Then he should start talking instead of spitting on people who are just trying to help him." She went back to the drawer, pulling out a bible and winding up.

The man fell back in his chair only to duck behind it. "You're both insane. I'm not saying anything until you let me go."

"Why are you being so difficult?" Parker spiked the Bible into the floor and growled in frustration, resembling herself a little more.

"Because I'm not an idiot, you idiot." He continued to duck.

"How about we come back later?" Alex tried to diffuse the situation.

"Yeah, you do that. I'll be right here when you're ready to let me go." The ace gloated, having succeeded in getting them both flustered enough to make mistakes.

"Oh, will you shut up?" Alex groaned, wishing he'd come up with a better comeback.

With their failure complete, both he and Parker headed back out into the hall.

"That could have gone better." Alex sighed as soon as the door was closed.

Parker stomped back and forth while releasing a steady stream of obscenities before punching a wall. "Ow! God damn it."

Alex couldn't help but smirk. "You okay there?"

"That guy is an asshole." She shook her hand out to sooth her injured knuckles before calming down and letting out an awkward laugh. "Well, damn, I really messed that up now, didn't I?"

"A little." Alex held up his hand with two fingers close together. "But I wasn't that helpful either."

"Sorry I lost it in there." Parker blew out a sigh. "Getting spit on is kinda a thing for me."

"Yikes." Alex cringed. "Didn't need to know that."

Her eyes immediately widened as she realized how her words had come out. "Gross, not like that." She leaned her head to one side. "Though, not judging anyone that's into it." She shook her head. "But it's a thing from a long time ago. Just a jerk back in high school. Used to spit on people and it really bothered me. He was a creep."

"I guess that explains why you threw a phonebook in there." Alex arched an eyebrow at her now that she had relaxed.

"I wasn't going to hit him." She pouted with her arms folded. "I'm not a monster. I know enough to understand that beating answers out of people has a crappy success rate."

"Ah, yeah." Alex nodded, feeling worse about having thought of threatening the ace in there with a hot poker. "Well, any ideas?"

"Sorry, fresh out." Parker gave an exaggerated shrug. "You could try your hand at the ace in the other room. At least we haven't embarrassed ourselves in front of him."

"True." Alex tapped at his chin as he ran through his spells a second time in hope of coming up with an idea. Eventually he let out a sigh as everything kept coming back to horrific acts of torture that would probably fail. Accepting that his magic wouldn't help, he had another thought: what would Digby and Becca do? He dropped his hand to his side a second later. "If my spells don't help, what about some else's?"

"What?" Parker cocked her head to one side.

"Come on, I have a plan." Alex smiled and started down the back down the hall toward the parking garage. "I'll explain on the way."

Taking the Mustang instead of the van, Alex made a quick trip back to the Never Say Die where they had spent their first night in Vegas. He gave Parker a brief rundown of what he was thinking as he drove. She responded with a laugh snort followed by an enthusiastic thumbs up. He hopped out of the car as soon as they reached the level of the garage where they had left the kestrel.

It was true that his magic wasn't able to solve the current problem, but Digby had left behind a few minions that could help. His zombies were obviously too dumb to be of any use, but there was a certain dude-bro skeleton that might be able to lend them a bony hand. It wasn't long before he found the infernal spirit he was looking for. Parker waited in the car with Asher.

Tavern remained standing guard just as they had been ordered to when they had arrived. Though from the look of it, the animated skeleton had spent most of their time playing tic tac toe with themselves. One of their bony fingers had been ground down to a nub, clearly having been used to scratch in the few hundred games that covered the pavement. Alex wondered how a game like that would go considering the spirit inside the skeleton was made up of the lingering fragments of multiple consciousnesses.

Could they actually play a real game against themselves? He shook off the question.

"Hey Tavern." Alex waved to the skeleton. "I have a job for you. Just need you to come with me for a bit."

"Nah, bruh." They glanced around. "Don't see the boss 'round. We'll hang here."

"Ah…" Alex trailed off realizing that he didn't actually have any control over the skeleton. Unlike Asher, Digby hadn't given Tavern any orders to listen to him while he was out. He decided to take a different approach. "There's a minibar full of shooters in it for you."

"'Kay, bro. We're all yours." The skeleton walked toward him.

"Good, but hang on a sec." Alex held up a hand to stop them and ran into the kestrel to grab a duffle bag that had been stored under the seats. He emptied it out and tossed it to the skeleton's feet. "We have to do this all secret like."

"Gotcha, on the DL then." Tavern simply leaned forward and collapsed into the duffle so most of their bones landed inside.

"That was surprisingly easy." Alex tossed any loose bones into the duffle and zipped it up before heading back to the casino to enact his plan.

Once they got back, he stopped by Sax to pick up a few guns and radioed for Mason and Deuce to meet him outside the ace's room. To his surprise, Mason seemed to jump at the chance to help. The soldier had plenty to do of his own, but he didn't seem to mind taking on more. Alex assumed he was just trying to keep his thoughts off of the fact that Becca was on a mission behind enemy lines. They had a phone capable of messaging her, but still, he assumed it was little comfort in the current situation.

From Deuce, they were able to find out a little about the ace that they had not tried to interrogate yet. Apparently, the man had been a cop back before the world ended. It wasn't much, but it was something to get them started. After some more planning, they sent the guards upstairs on break and gathered the few men that Deuce had that already knew about magic. Anyone not in the know would only complicate things.

Without Becca's illusions, Alex needed the details to be right, so they waited until the sun set to make their move. He hoped the darkness would help sell what he had in mind. If Alex had learned anything from his time as Digby's apprentice, it was that force usually meant nothing. No, winning was all about only showing your opponent the cards you wanted them to see and keeping them off balance. Not to mention that, in Vegas, smoke and mirrors was a way of life.

After moving the less cooperative ace that they had spoken to earlier to another floor and giving some of the survivors a heads up to expect some noise, Alex dumped the duffel bag of bones on the carpet. The pile laid still until he tossed the bag aside and dropped a tiny vodka from one of the mini bars into the pile.

Deuce and his men all jumped as several fingerbones snapped together to wrap themselves around the bottle. Mason and Parker didn't bat an eye as Tavern reassembled their frame piece by piece to rise from the carpet while simultaneously pouring vodka into their jaws. The skeleton dropped the bottle to the floor the instant it was empty.

"Is that normal?" Deuce pointed to Tavern as the liquid ran down their ribcage.

"Pretty much." Parker shrugged before clapping her hands like the set manager of a movie production. "Everyone ready?"

Asher nodded from a perch on her shoulder.

"Okay." Alex took his place at the center of the group. "Commencing Operation Spooky Scary Skeleton."

Silence answered him from everyone in the hallway as Mason and Deuce stared at him, clearly unamused. "Seriously?"

Parker laughed. Though, Alex wasn't sure if it was a pity laugh meant to make him feel better or just an awkward one to fill the silence.

"Whatever." Alex deflated. "Just do the thing."

Mason didn't argue as he raised his radio and thumbed the button. "Cut the power to the floor."

"On it," Sax answered from the other end just before every light in the hall shut off at once.

Alex immediately pulled a small flashlight from a pocket and raised a hand like a conductor. He let the darkness engulf them for a long moment before turning it on. That was when he heard movement in the ace's room. He just hoped this one would be more cooperative than the last.

"Here goes nothing." Alex took a deep breath before pointing to Parker, who quietly walked to the far end of the hall before letting out a scream that would make Jamie Lee Curtis proud.

From inside the ace's room, a voice called out, "Hello? What's going on?"

Alex responded by pointing to Asher. The deceased raven took flight and flapped down the length of the hall. A menacing caw echoed through the space in her wake. Alex nodded at the effect of Asher's cries. It set the stage well.

Next, he pointed to Mason, who shouted, "Where is it?"

From beside him, Deuce added, "I don't know."

As soon as the hall grew quiet again, Parker raised a shotgun, took aim at a wall, and pulled the trigger. The blast shattered the silence. She pumped it and fried another shell. The scenario might have been more believable if she had used a rifle, but they didn't have any blanks and the bullets could potentially ricochet. It was safer to use a shotgun that would just demolish one wall. Without Becca's ventriloquism, it was the best option.

One of Deuce's men screamed next, making sure to trail off with a horrible gurgle.

Deuce ran the length of the hall, hitting the floor hard with each step before stopping at the end and yelling. "It went that way!"

Another of his men cried out, this time, leaping against the wall in front of the ace's room with a loud thud.

Finally, Alex pointed to Tavern. "You're up."

The skeleton gave a casual salute and marched toward the door. Alex lent a hand by casting Icicle a dozen times, driving each frozen spike into the wood around the lock to weaken it. He could hear the ace inside shriek as the door splintered apart. Tavern wrenched the knob from the resulting mess. Alex tossed a Fireball behind them, setting the carpet alight to give the skeleton the right backdrop for their entrance.

Obviously setting a fire was a little risky, but they had made sure to have a few buckets of water ready to put it out when they were done.

Another shotgun blast rocked the hall as Parker emptied her weapon into the wall. She tossed the weapon to Mason as he took a position just outside the ace's door near the flaming carpet. One of Deuce's men let out blood curdling death scream for good measure.

The ace cried out in terror as Tavern tore the door open and stepped inside the room to display their form in all their bony glory. The fire really did add a nice touch as the skeleton opened their jaws to shout. "Heeeerrreee's Johnny, bro."

Alex would have preferred that they not add the bro in there, but it was good enough.

A series of panicked shouts came from the ace as Tavern stalked in to block any path the man might use for escape, giving him a crash course in the reality of magic. That was when the ace started shouting for help.

Alex nodded to Mason and hooked a thumb at the door just before rushing into the scene himself. Mason followed, panting as if he'd been running for his life. Inside, the ace scrambled across the floor with Tavern standing over him, snapping their jaws open and shut. The hard clack of teeth against teeth sent a chill down Alex's spine as he pulled a flask from a pouch. Tavern made a point of slowing their attack to give him time to get in position and splash the contents of the container on their back. The skeleton lurched to the side the instant the liquid touched their bones.

"We burrrrrn!" Tavern flailed and slammed into a lamp as the water sizzled against their cursed frame. Alex flung more water at them, the skeleton crashing into a table in panic.

Of course, it wasn't technically necessary to purify the water in the flask, but Parker had convinced him that the performance needed a little extra sizzle. The spell couldn't actually kill Tavern, but it still caused some discomfort. Though, Alex had once witnessed the skeleton down a bottle of purified wine despite the burning sensation, so he wasn't that worried about it.

Tavern continued to flail even after the flask had run out of water, forcing Alex to clear his throat to tell the skeleton that they might be dragging their performance out a little too long. With that, they let out one last howl and collapsed into a pile of bones as if vanquished.

That was when Mason stepped toward the ace to take over the scene. "Get up!"

"What was that thing?" The ace shoved himself up, glancing back to the pile of bones.

"We don't know, but there are more of them." Mason pumped the shotgun to eject the last spent shell and shoved it into the man's hands. "Right now, we need every man that we can get."

Deuce rushed into the room next before the ace had time to check if the weapon still had any ammo in it. "Did you get it?"

Alex grunted and pointed to the pile of bones where Tavern had collapsed.

"Thank god." Deuce relaxed.

"What was in that flask?" the ace asked.

"Holy water." Alex shoved the container back in his pouch.

Mason growled. "Yeah, I know how that sounds, but I'm not

arguing with results." He flicked his eyes to Deuce. "What about the rest of those things?"

Deuce shook his head as if he was having trouble believing the situation. "They just killed the others and left."

"What do you mean they left?" Mason argued.

Alex hoped the ace would follow their conversation and put together the implications of their made-up scenario.

"I mean they left," Deuce insisted. "One of those skeletons shouted something about freeing the others and they all just made a break for it. They were heading for the other end of the strip."

Mason pulled a handful of shotgun shells from his pocket as if he intended to give them to their prisoner. "Deuce said you used to be a cop, right?"

"Yeah." The man sounded unsure.

"Okay, we have bigger problems than whatever disagreement we had going before." Mason stepped toward the window. "We have to go after those things. It's dark out, but there's no monsters on the strip other than those flying ones. We'll load up and try to catch up to the rest of the skeletons before they free whatever the hell they were talking about."

The ace's eyes widened. "Wait, no. We need to run."

"What?" Alex arched an eyebrow.

"If there are more of those things heading for the other side of the strip, then we have to get out of here." He seemed genuinely scared.

"Why, what's at the other end of the strip?" Alex asked as if it was the first he'd heard of anything.

"Shriekers. Thousands of them. All trapped in some of the buildings." The ace glanced back and forth. "If they get out at night, they'll kill all of us."

Mason stepped in and grabbed the man by his shoulder. "What do you mean there's thousands of them trapped in the buildings? How did they get there?"

The ace fell silent for a second.

"We don't have time for this." Mason shook the man a little. "Just tell me what you know before we all end up dead."

"Rivers made us do it!" he shrieked. "He made us lure the

shriekers into the casinos and seal them up. They've been there all month. They can't get out on their own, but if something helped from the outside then we'll be overrun."

"Good god." Mason let go as if he was done asking the important questions. Then he added, "How the hell did you lure them all in the first place?"

The ace grimaced and stared at floor. "It was Rivers. He made us do it."

"Made you do what?" Mason asked in an almost casual tone that made Alex glad he had picked him for the role.

"We used people." A remorseful tone flooded his voice. "Rivers had us tie them up and hang them over the casino floors. They cried for help but that only brought more monsters until they piled together high enough to reach them."

Alex's stomach churned at the thought.

"That's horrible." Mason shook his head in disbelief.

Alex pushed past the confession and focused on confirming what was most important. "You're sure those, umm, shriekers, can't get out on their own?"

The ace nodded. "We couldn't fight that many, so we made sure of it."

That was when Mason blew out a long sigh. "Think that's enough?"

"Yeah." Alex nodded. "I think we've learned more than we ever wanted to know."

"What?" Confusion fell across the ace's face.

Mason immediately snatched the empty shotgun from his hands. "Give me that and sit in the corner."

"What's going on?" The man glanced between them. "What about that thing that was—"

"You can get up now, Tavern." Alex tossed another bottle of vodka in the direction of the pile of bones.

The ace jumped backward as the skeleton reassembled themself and downed the bottle.

"Thanks for your help." Alex nodded to the bony minion as the ace stared in horror.

"No prob, brah." Tavern tossed the empty bottle over their shoulder and held out a skeletal fist.

Alex shrugged and bumped his knuckles against theirs before turning back to the ace. "Welp, I guess that answers that."

"No it doesn't. Somebody tell me what is happening." The man thrust a finger at Tavern. "And tell me what that thing is?"

"That's an animated skeleton." Parker entered the room, passing a bag of tiny bottles to the infernal spirit. "Magic is real. Try to keep up."

Asher flapped in to land on the bed, adding a loud caw that resembled the word, "MAGIC!"

The ace dropped into a chair, clearly having trouble processing what had just happened.

"We might want to let him, umm, marinate on all this." Alex gestured to the door. "And we have what we need."

Leaving the man to work through the existential crisis that they might have caused, the group headed back out into the hall just as one of Deuce's men doused the fire on the carpet with a bucket of water.

"What do we do with them, now?" Parker asked as they moved the confused ace to a different room with a functioning door.

"I don't know." Alex shook his head. "What they did is pretty bad, but they were acting on Rivers' orders, so I don't know how guilty that makes them."

"For now, we can keep holding them, until we figure something out." Mason shoved his hands in his pockets.

"True, and at least we know that we're not in any real danger right now," Alex added. "Actually, we might be able to make use of those revenants that they trapped."

"How so?" Mason arched an eyebrow.

"Food for a horde." Alex held up a hand as if it was obvious. "We have Digby's two zombie minions. My guess is that they're on the path of the brute since they haven't mutated yet, and that had the highest resources demand that I know of. Those revenants would go a long way. Especially if we can find more zombies to add to the horde."

"I'm a little horrified that you thought of that so fast." Mason eyed him. "But yeah, that would give us a leg up if we are going to try to put up a fight."

"Sorry." Alex shrugged. "I think being the apprentice to an undead necromancer is starting to rub off on me."

"Don't worry about it," Parker added as she tore open a bag of expensive macadamia nuts from one of the nearby minibars with her teeth. "The dead gotta eat too."

Alex nodded and clicked his tongue at Asher to get her attention. "Can I send you on a mission?"

The raven flapped up to his shoulder and nodded.

"Okay, when we get outside, I need you to head out into the surrounding city and gather any zombies that you find. There may not be any on the strip, but there might be some further out. Lead any you find back to the buildings at the other end of the strip where we found all those revenants. We'll set up a food line of some kind to get everyone you find mutating. Think you can keep them in line once they do?"

She nodded again.

"Thank you." He smiled at her.

"SHINNY!" She flapped her wings in his face.

"Yes, you can take your pick of every jewelry store on the strip." He gave her a friendly pat on her side the way he'd seen Digby do it.

Alex turned back to Parker and Mason. "Now we just need a way to drag those revenants out of there."

Parker's eyes lit up. "I saw a jeep in the garage the other day when I was car shopping. There was a winch on the front. Could work something out with that. Maybe harpoon them with a crossbow or something. Kinda like fishing, but with rev's."

"Gross. But yes, that would work." Alex nodded in approval.

"I'll get some people on it." Mason turned toward the exit at the end of the hallway.

"Oh, you don't have to now, it's already dark." Alex started after him.

"Yeah, but it will give me something to do." Mason looked back. "Can't exactly relax until I know Becca's on her way back anyway."

Alex stopped in his tracks, realizing how distracted he'd been by everything happening in Vegas. His worries were still there in the back of his mind, but he hadn't thought about them for a few hours. The sudden reminder brought it all back at once.

"I hope they're okay too," Parker added from beside him, as if sensing his fears.

"I know." Alex sighed. "Let's just make sure they come back to some good news."

CHAPTER EIGHTEEN

"Get your elbow out of my face, Becky," Digby growled at his accomplice as she jabbed him for the seventh time.

"You get your elbow out of my face first," she growled back as they lay in the cramped space underneath Campbell's dinner cart.

"I would move my elbow if I could, but my left arm had to be dislocated, if you remember. I had to pop the thing out from the socket to save space for your delicate body." He stopped complaining when the cart they rode in came to an abrupt stop.

"Would you both stop fighting?" A foot kicked one of the sliding doors that hid the shelf that they laid on. "We're approaching the gate to Autem's area, and I'd prefer that you not argue while I sneak you in. We still have a ways to go before I can let you out."

Digby rolled his eyes but refrained from any further comments. Rebecca did the same.

"That's better." Campbell began pushing his cart again.

The space was cramped with only the shelf on the bottom open to fit its uncomfortable passengers. The layer above them was full of more of those white containers of individual meals. Campbell wasn't able to make two trips to complete his deliveries and it would have raised suspicion if he had left anyone's order behind.

Digby tried to reposition his leg to give Rebecca more room, but the pants of the uniform that Easton had been able to steal restricted his flexibility. They were a bit too small. He would have complained but Easton hadn't found a lot of options. The fact that they were able to get uniforms at all was enough.

To keep himself occupied, he brought up his spells in the Heretic Seed's HUD and searched for the new one he'd gained the night before. Falling in line with the rest of the spells that he'd extracted from the rings he'd stolen, Kinetic Impact wasn't going to function with his pure mana balance, which was why he'd forced it to evolve while waiting for Campbell to arrive that morning. The result was worth a second look.

Kinetic Impact has evolved into Five Fingers of Death
FIVE FINGERS OF DEATH
Description: Create a field of mana around the fingers of one hand, capable of boring through the armor and flesh of your enemies. Through prolonged contact with the internal structures of an enemy's body, this spell is capable of bestowing an additional curse effect.
Rank: D
MP Cost: 100 (-50% due to mana purity)
Range: Touch
Additional Effect: Curse, Death's Embrace
Contact Requirement for Curse: 30 seconds
Death's Embrace: This curse manifests by creating a state of undeath within a target, capable of reanimating your enemy into a loyal zombie minion. Once animated, a zombie minion will seek to consume the flesh of their species and may pass along their cursed status to another creature.
Limitations: Due to lethality, a minion animated through the use of this spell will have all attributes reduced to 0.
Oh boy, more incapable minions.

Digby stared at the text.

This is it. This must be the spell that created the original zombies that passed the curse along to me all those centuries ago.

There was something satisfying about gaining the spell that had started it all. Until now, the only method he had to create a permanent loyal minion was through his Animate Zombie, which required him to sacrifice MP from his maximum mana pool to build a bond. In a way, this new spell was weaker, since it didn't seem to allow him to distribute any points to a minion, but at the same time, it wouldn't require the same mana sacrifice. His minions may be stupid and weak, but there was no limit to how many he could create, other than his MP's absorption rate and he could speed that up by burying himself and meditation. Stupid or not, a horde of a few thousand was powerful in its own right, especially if he could get a few to mutate.

The possibilities were practically endless. All it would take was time.

His thoughts were interrupted as the cart he rode in slowed to a stop. Outside, Campbell's voice could be heard talking to the two guards that manned the entry gate of Autem's section of the base. He just hoped they wouldn't feel the need to look underneath. The cart started moving again ten seconds later.

Guess not. Digby pumped his eye brows in satisfaction, glad that neither of the guards felt like being thorough. Campbell had passed through that gate every day since Autem had arrived on the base. Surely that had gained him an element of trust.

The cart rolled on.

Digby nudged the door closest to his face, causing it to slip open an inch so he could peek out. He hoped he might catch a glimpse of Hawk or any of the other children that had been taken in by Henwick's empire. At the very least, he would have liked to witness the conditions the boy was being subjected to. He nudged the door closed when he saw nothing.

Hang in there, Hawk. I'll come and get you as soon as I have the Seed. Digby let his head rest against the cool metal of the cart's bottom shelf. It wasn't long before the cart slowed to a stop again. He felt Rebecca tense up against his back. A second later, he sensed mana flowing through her blood.

What the hell is she casting?

Before he had time to think about it, the sound of a heavy

security door tore his attention away. The loud hissing of the door came again as the cart progressed. A heavy click-clack told him that it had locked behind them.

"Hold up." An unfamiliar voice came from outside. It must have been the guard that they needed to deactivate the security systems in the entryway so Campbell could smuggle them through.

"Sure," their newest accomplice replied in a casual tone, handling his end of the infiltration well. "I got a couple extra meals in here if you want one. I think they're ziti."

"No, can't eat while on duty." The guard's tone was much less casual.

"I get that." Campbell continued to shoot the breeze. "Skyline's like that too, the higher ups don't let us take it easy either."

"It's not like that at all. It's important to remain vigilant now more than ever." The guard's voice came closer. His footsteps grew louder as well.

Damn it, Campbell, get moving already! Digby screamed internally.

"Is that cart bigger than the one you usually bring?" The guard's footsteps stopped just outside where Digby lay.

"Ah…" Campbell hesitated. "Yeah, it might be. I just took whichever was free."

The guard let a long pause go by before speaking again. "You load it yourself?"

"Yes sir." Campbell let a professional tone slip into his voice as if making an attempt to appear compliant.

"I'm going to take a look just in case." The guard's boots squeaked on the floor as he moved outside.

"Wait," Campbell blurted out. "The cart is insulated to keep everything warm. So I try to keep it closed unless I'm getting someone's order."

Digby cringed at how suspicious his explanation sounded.

Campbell kept trying. "Sorry, not trying to be weird about it. But with the way everyone talks about Autem back in the rest of Skyline, I didn't want to mess up anyone's food. Some of us are afraid that you guys might not need us once you grow into a larger force, so I just want to do the best I can. I mean, I don't even have a ring, so I just want to make sure I bring some value to things."

"How come you haven't taken a ring?" The sound of the guard's movements paused.

"I'm not a combatant, just a guy that slings slop in the mess. Not sure how much of a future there is for me with that resume."

Digby felt for the man, starting to understand why he had decided to help Easton's resistance. As strange as it was, there was more opportunity in Vegas than there was with Skyline. From what Digby was starting to understand, if a recruit wasn't brought into Autem's fold, their usefulness had its limit.

"Sorry to hear that. But I still have to check this out." The guard's boot squeaked against the floor as if pivoting to one side. Then the door of the cart slid open.

Out of options, Digby simply lay there looking dumb as the guard pulled open the door and looked straight at him from only a foot or two away. He nearly cast Forge right there to impale the man with a spike of blood, but Rebecca yanked on his uniform as if telling him to hold back.

The guard stared straight at him for a moment before sweeping his gaze along the rest of the cart. A second later, he slid the door shut and walked around to check the other side, this time taking a long look at Rebecca.

Digby relaxed. Clearly the spell she had cast had been Waking Dream. By his guess, the guard had seen nothing but a shelf full of lunch containers. Not a necromancer and his accomplice crammed into the narrow space.

"Looks good." The guard stood back up. "Smells a little off though."

Campbell chuckled. "Hey, it's a mess hall, not a five-star restaurant."

"Point taken." The guard let a laugh slip out. "If you're serious about finding a more valuable position, I can't open any doors in Autem, but I can put in a good word with Commander Bancroft. He comes through here a couple times a day, and I'm sure he'd be glad to have a hard worker move up the ranks over on his side of things."

"Thanks. That would really help." Campbell's tone sounded a little brighter. Digby hoped the man was faking it rather than having second thoughts. The last thing he needed was his loyalty shifting at an inopportune moment.

The cart moved on, rolling over Digby's concerns about Campbell's loyalties. From there, the man pushed their hiding place through the building to make his deliveries. As he made his way through the facility's floors, he interacted with several of Autem's members while making a point to state where they were out loud as they passed by. Data storage, security, admin, guardian registration, and several rooms for research and development. There was a lot of ground to cover. Digby noticed Rebecca struggling to make a list on her phone in the cramped space.

Finally, the cart came to a stop.

Campbell slid open the door a second later. "Okay, this is where you get off."

Digby cast a Necrotic Regeneration as he flopped out onto the floor at the end of an empty hallway. His dislocated joints emitted several loud pops as they pulled themselves back into place. Campbell cringed at the sound.

Strangely, the hallway looked less like a modern building and more like something out of a zombie movie. Everything looked reinforced, like some kind of bunker. Rebecca rolled out the other side of the cart, having just as much trouble standing up on account of her legs falling asleep.

Campbell tried his best to help her. "Easy there, miss."

"I got it." She reached for the cart for support.

"Just shake it out." Campbell jogged in place to demonstrate before checking behind him to make sure they were still alone. "Okay, we're on the third floor right now. There are cameras covering most of the halls but this one spot doesn't have one." He hooked a thumb back over his shoulder. "Once you turn the corner into the next hall, security will see everything you do. So try not to act suspicious and don't kill anyone."

"You hear that? No murder." Digby glowered at Rebecca, enjoying the fact that, for once, he could criticize her instead of the other way around.

"That last one wasn't my fault. He snuck up on us." She shrugged.

Campbell shook his head, pushing past the subject for the sake of time. "It's dinner time now, so other than the personnel that I just delivered food to, the place should be empty. On top of that, most of their staff has headed back to their bunks, so you should have all night to do what you came here for. There will still be security guards walking the halls though, so be careful moving around. I will be back in the morning to deliver breakfast and to pick you both up. Just don't get discovered, I'll meet you right here in the morning."

"Thank you." Digby surprised himself. Expressing gratitude wasn't really something he was comfortable with, yet it seemed like the right thing to do. Campbell was taking a risk to help them. A risk that could easily cost him his life.

"You're welcome." He returned to his food cart and began pushing it away. "Just make sure you get what you need so we don't have to do this again tomorrow." He vanished around the corner a moment later.

Rebecca cast Conceal to hide from the cameras. "Shall we get going?"

"Indeed." Digby straightened the Autem uniform he wore and pulled down on the rim of his hat, just in case her spell failed.

From there, they headed down the hall, making sure to keep their distance from anyone that was out and about. Campbell had been right about the guards. A pair of Autem's guardians patrolled each floor continuously, checking each and every room as they did. It took them around fifteen minutes to complete their route. A quick analyze marked them both as level twenty knights.

Rebecca let out a silent sigh of relief when they both failed to notice their presence with her Conceal spell active. Digby understood how she felt. One wrong move could easily give them away. They would have to be extremely careful. Their only saving grace was that the spell's duration left plenty of time for Rebecca to absorb enough mana to cast it again.

The first stop they made was the network administration department. It was close and seemed like a good place to get their bearings. As they approached, a narrow window ran along the hallway's wall, though the glass was treated in a way to make everything on the other side appear blurry. They both stepped closer to see if they could make out a shadow or something moving inside, only to find the frosted glass impossible to see through. The only detail they could make out was that the lights were on inside.

Then, suddenly, the light went out.

The heavy metal door to the room hissed open a second later. A woman stepped out, wearing an Autem uniform that matched the stolen garments that Rebecca wore. She didn't seem to notice them as she headed down the hallway for the exit. Rebecca gestured with her head to follow as she slipped inside. Digby darted in behind her just as it closed behind him.

Inside, the room was empty except for a row of six computer terminals. Similar to the rest of the place, they looked a bit more advanced than any of Rebecca's laptops.

She leapt to one of the stations that still had a light shining on its front and punched a button on the screen. The display came to life, showing that weird emblem that Autem had chosen to represent itself.

"Shit." Rebecca slapped the keyboard as if it might run away.

"What?" Digby's eyes darted around in search of the problem.

"This station is on a timer like the drone console that I used back in Seattle." She let out a relieved sigh a second later before pointing to a corner of the display where a countdown was visible. "On the system I used, I had to input something every five minutes. If I let it remain inactive for too long it would lock me out automatically. It was a way of protecting information so that no one could forget to log out or something." She pointed to a panel that had been built into the desk that matched the ones that granted access to the doors. "If we had gotten in here a few seconds later, we wouldn't be able to access anything without a guardian ring or an ID cuff."

"Oh." Digby's eyes widened as he read the countdown, its numbers ticking down with only forty seconds remaining.

"Oh is right." She tapped another key causing the timer to go back up to sixty. "This system seems to have its countdown set at one minute. Hopefully that means I can access some good information. We have about ten minutes before the guards come back and check this room. Keep an eye out while I find out what I can."

"Alright, but I'm not sure how much I can see." Digby headed toward the narrow window that ran along the wall.

"Just look for shadows. I'll see if there's any mention of the Heretic Seed's location." She plugged a small device into one of the stations and started typing while Digby squinted at the glass. A minute passed by before she came up with something. "Does the name Babel mean anything to you?"

"You mean, biblically?" Digby tilted his head to the side, recalling what little he knew of religious fables. If he remembered right, Babel was a tower that mankind tried to build to get closer to god. It hadn't worked out too well for them.

"I don't think it's meant biblically." She stared at the screen. "There isn't anything that says exactly where the Seed is being kept, but there is a mention of transporting potential dangerous items and specimens to a place called Babel. Based on this, though, I think it's fair to assume that's where the Seed is. What's weird is that this place sounds like some sort of facility, rather than just a storage vault. Some of the information is a little contradictory. An elevator is mentioned though. Maybe there's another facility beneath this building, instead of just a vault like we were thinking."

"Damn, I was hoping to be able to get in and get out of there easily, but it sounds a bit more complicated." Digby furrowed his brow, before remembering that the Seed wasn't their only objective. "Is there any record of what they intend to do with Hawk?"

"Let me see." She mumbled to herself as she searched, repeating the word 'recruits,' until hitting a key especially hard. "Found it. They have a whole file on him. He's listed as having passed their assessment. His likely class is fighter with a concentration on rogue."

"That must be a possible path that lies beyond fighter," Digby added. "One of the men that was with the squad that picked him up was a rogue."

"Maybe it's a rare class." She started typing again without spending too much time in his file. "Actually, if they have information on him, then they must have a file on us." She fell silent while she worked. "Yes, I found myself."

"What's it say?" Digby arched an eyebrow.

She let out a laugh before answering. "They don't know anything about me." She laughed again and clapped her hands. "Not a damn thing."

"What?" Digby turned away from the window.

"All it says is that I'm assumed alive." She furrowed her brow. "They must not have seen me during the fight in California. I never actually showed myself. The only reason they have to assume I'm still alive is that someone flew a kestrel and I'm the only likely suspect." She turned to him with a smile on her face. "Do you know what that means?"

Digby shook his head.

"It means they don't know we have an illusionist on our side. I was hoping they might not have figured it out but, shit Dig, they don't know anything. I'm just a big question mark. They don't even have a current photo other than screen grabs of the feed from my apartment. The one they have set as the main image is from years ago." She started typing again. "There's a file on you too."

"Oh yeah?" Digby's ears pricked up, though he pretended not to care what it said.

"Oh wow. They want you dead bad." She smirked.

"Lovely." He rolled his eyes.

"Like, real bad," she added.

"That's not helpful." He glowered at her.

"Sorry, but yeah, they want you destroyed ASAP." She let out a quiet whistle. "There's even orders to have you dismembered and to have the pieces sent to that Babel place."

"Hmm." Digby scratched his chin. "If it wasn't for that dismemberment part, I would say getting captured might be an easy way in to find the Seed."

"True, we could pull a whole Chewbacca thing." She nodded.

"I don't know who that is," Digby growled back. "But regardless, allowing myself to be dismembered is probably a bigger risk than I want to take."

"I get that." She smirked. "We'll reserve that for if we get desperate."

"Indeed—wait, no." He stumbled on his words as he realized what he was agreeing with. He would have argued, but before he had the chance, he caught a shadow moving outside the window out of the corner of his eye. "Damn, the guards are coming."

He jumped back to stay close to Rebecca as she cast Conceal again. She tapped a button on the console's screen to turn the display off before flicking her vision to the door. A solid ten seconds went by, making Digby question if the shadow he'd seen had been real or a figment of his imagination. He started to relax, only to tense back up when the door finally slid open.

A pair of men wearing Autem's emblem walked in without a word. They both took a quick look around the room while Digby and Rebecca froze in place, hidden in plain sight by her magic. He couldn't help but notice she was holding her breath. A sudden flash of dread swept across her face as her eyes flicked to the computer in front of her. At first, Digby didn't know why, then the same feeling of dread hit him too.

The console was still on a timer, just like it had been when they had come in. He did the math in his head, assuming they had a little over thirty seconds before the system locked them out. There was sure to be more valuable information within Autem's network and they couldn't let the opportunity slip by. He snapped his vision back to her, realizing she was standing further from the console than he was.

The guard stopped at the other end of the room while the other waited in the dead center of the space. Digby cursed them for being so thorough as the chance of them finishing their security sweep and leaving before the computer locked them out grew smaller and smaller.

Damn it, I have to do something.

Rebecca gave him a nod as if coming to the same conclusion. Digby made his move, creeping toward the console. The guard in the middle of the room stood dangerously close to his target. Digby struggled to balance his movements. Too fast and he would break the spell. Too slow and he wouldn't reach the terminal in time.

Digby was glad he didn't need to breathe, finding it easier to keep calm without inhaling. Making a bit of progress, he froze when the guard in the center of the room looked straight at him. He squinted at the guard's eyes, trying to figure out what they were focused on. The man glanced away a second later, allowing him to creep closer, nearly within reach.

Digby didn't know a lot about computers, so there was always a chance that whatever key he chose to hit might make some sort of chime or sound. He hoped that wasn't the case as he reached out a finger and pressed a button at the edge of the keyboard bearing an arrow that pointed down. He winced, expecting the system to let out a telltale alert, only to relax when none came.

The guards grouped up shortly after, making their way back to the door. Rebecca let out a long sigh as soon as the door closed behind them. Digby stepped out of the way as she jumped back into the station's chair and reinserted her small storage device.

"I'm not wasting any more time here. I'm going to copy every-thing I can and go over it later." She highlighted the files that Autem had on herself, Digby, and Alex. After that, she found several files that were labeled with a long line of numbers.

"What are those?" Digby tapped a finger on the desk.

"They're a log of kestrel flight paths." She dragged the file to a different icon. "I don't expect that Autem would have a complete list of their facilities available on any system, but with these we can at least see where they are flying to. They are bound to have more installations than just this base, and I should be able to get an idea of how many and where they are by going over their kestrel activ-ity. Figuring that out would be a high tactical advantage for when the time to attack comes. Not to mention they may be making trips to other settlements the same way they have been back in Vegas. Who knows, they might have more arrangements out there like the one they had with Rivers."

"I hope not, otherwise we might have to pay them a visit when things settle out." Digby smiled, proud of his fellow Heretic and the fact that their mission had already borne fruit. The information was valuable, indeed.

After getting what she could, Rebecca pocketed their spoils and let the console lock itself down as if they'd never been there. Unfortunately, with the door locked and without a ring to open it, they were forced to wait for the guards to return so that they could slip out while they were walking into the room.

Digby found it odd that they searched the room in its entirety every half hour, despite having done so already. If it were him, he would have merely glanced. Hell, he probably wouldn't even do it. He'd just lie and tell his superior that he had. Actually, that would probably get him in trouble. He shook off the question. Clearly, Autem's soldiers were more dedicated to their duty than he would have been. As it was, they were more disciplined than Skyline's people as well.

I guess that's the difference between hired goons and a force of real soldiers that believe in their cause. Now, if Digby could find out more about what their actual goal was, that would be helpful.

Digby pondered the subject as they made their way down the hall, following the guards at a medium distance. He would have liked to stay further away from them, but the need to slip through the doors before they closed, required them to stay close.

Next, the guards entered the research and development area through another heavy door that led to a new hallway. Digby and Rebecca followed, finding themselves staring at a wall of more heavy doors. The R&D facility must have needed more space than just one room. Fortunately, it was only the main door to the area that required a ring to get through.

They headed into the first room they came across.

"Jackpot." Digby snapped his fingers as he found several glass boxes, each containing a guardian ring. He beckoned to Rebecca. "Help me do some looting, these may come in handy."

"Wait!" She leapt forward to block his path. "It looks like they're doing some kind of maintenance or connecting their system to the rings."

"And?" Digby arched an eyebrow.

"I'm pretty sure they'll notice if any are missing."

"True." He glanced at the rings, then back to her. "But with one of these, we might be able to get into the rest of the doors that have a lock protecting it. Without one, we'll be stuck waiting for those guards to make their rounds. And getting so close is risky."

She looked back at the rings and tilted her head to the side. "Okay, that's true, but we can't just take one…" She trailed off. "Actually, we can. We just need to make sure to come back here and put it back when we're done."

"That works for me." Digby stepped past her only to have her cut him off again. "What now?"

"Let me do it." She spun to approach the nearest case. "This place looks like a laboratory so there might be some sort of security in place. My perception is much higher than yours, so I should check to make sure there isn't anything that looks out of place."

"That's fair." Digby stepped aside to give her space.

Rebecca nodded before taking a pass around the case. She nodded again a moment later before reaching out to open the lid on top. Digby couldn't help but notice her wince as she did, like she hadn't been completely sure that the coast was clear. She let out a calm breath when nothing happened and snatched the ring up.

"You might have a career as a cat burglar in your future." Digby gave her a wink.

"I'll keep that in mind if this whole Heretic thing doesn't pan out." She tossed him the ring.

He caught it and headed out into the hall. "Always good to keep your options open."

From there, they searched the rest of the laboratories. Unfortunately, most didn't have much to discover. It wasn't until they reached the last room at the end that they found something interesting. Well… maybe interesting wasn't the right word.

"I don't like the looks of that." Rebecca approached a wall of small metal doors.

"What is it?" Digby followed behind out of curiosity.

"Some sort of morgue." She pulled open a door revealing a metal slab that pulled out like a drawer. "Yup, knew I wasn't going to like it." She covered her nose as she stepped away from the locker's contents.

A man's corpse lay on the slab with the top of his skull missing. His brain was absent as well. Pulling the drawer out further, Digby found that his heart had been cut out too. Rebecca checked the next door, finding a corpse in the same condition.

"Well, that confirms our theory about how they hijacked my curse." Digby shoved one of the bodies back into its locker. "They are clearly feeding a zombie to enhance their intelligence. That fits with the assumption that Henwick has made his own necromancer. They're probably a zombie master by now."

"I hope that doesn't end up biting us in the ass." Rebecca closed the locker she had opened.

"Literally." Digby chuckled. "If they really have an undead necromancer somewhere, they might very well bite you in the ass, indeed."

She groaned at the obvious joke.

With nothing left to discover there, Rebecca refreshed their Conceal spell and they headed back out into the hall. Taking a left at the end, Digby nearly froze when he saw what was around the corner.

Another heavy door barred entry to a room at the far end with a vertical window running down one side. Unlike the other panes of glass in the building, this one was not treated to block the interior of the room from sight. Through the window, Digby saw a woman. He leaned to the side, catching the edge of a gold door.

Remembering that Rebecca's spell was in place, he relaxed. He might have been able to see the woman, but she couldn't see him. Her hair was styled differently from anyone that he'd met since being thawed out in the modern world. It was strange and curled in a way that looked stiff. It definitely wasn't a style well suited for battle. For that matter, she wasn't wearing a uniform either. Just a simple yellow dress with a sweater tied around her shoulders.

Rebecca shuddered. "That's one hell of a Stepford wife."

"What's that now?" Digby arched an eyebrow.

"Sorry, you haven't seen that movie." Rebecca paused. "I mean she looks like she comes from the fifties."

"That was a common style back then?" He stared through the window at her hair and outfit.

"She must be the woman that guards the elevator that Campbell told us about." Digby scratched his chin. "We'll have to find somewhere to hide until she leaves. With a little luck, she'll take a break and we can check out whatever structure they have below. Might even be able to recover the Seed's fragments." He started to feel hopeful.

Of course, that was when the woman looked up from her desk to lock eyes with him.

Digby nearly leapt to the side out of view, but remembered they were still safe with Rebecca's spell active. Then, the woman smiled.

Rebecca gasped. "Shit, my spell just failed."

"What?" Digby snapped his eyes to his accomplice.

"We're not hidden." Rebecca froze in place. "She sees us."

"Alright, alright." Digby forced himself to remain where he was to avoid looking suspicious. "Remember what Campbell said, there are new faces here all the time. As long as we act like we belong, she has no reason to investigate."

Rebecca gasped again. "Oh god, I analyzed her."

Digby fought the urge to turn his head and stare. Instead, he only moved enough to focus on the woman with his peripheral.

Guardian, Level 40 Seer, Friendly.

Panic alarms went off in Digby's head. Whatever a Seer was, it must have had a perception attribute high enough to see through Rebecca's magic as if it wasn't there. Their disguises had kept them from registering as hostile, but there was no telling how long that would last. Before he could process the implication of the woman's class and level, she stood up from her desk.

"We have to move."

Rebecca nodded and headed for the nearest door. Digby forced himself not to run to maintain their appearance of innocence. Keeping an eye on the end of the hall, he placed the ring he'd borrowed against the door's panel and stepped inside a darkened laboratory. With his eye on the open door, he waited for it to close automatically like the others in the building. The sound of the heavy security door down the hall hissing open sent another jolt of terror down his spine. The slow click-clack of high heels followed, just as the entrance to the room he was in finally slid shut.

Digby stood in the dark, stalk still, watching the door. There was nothing stopping the woman from following them. He gave thanks to the fact that his heart didn't beat. Surely it would have leapt from his chest.

A moment of silence went by.

Then another.

Finally, he relaxed as it became clear that the seer wasn't following them. She must not have thought they were suspicious after all. The fact that she had gotten up from her desk must have been a coincidence.

Digby took a step back away from the door, only to run into Rebecca.

"Watch where you're standing, Becky." He turned to find her staring in the shadows of the laboratory, her body shaking. "What is the problem?"

Digby reached for the light so he could see whatever her heightened perception had shown her in the dark. The room lit up as soon as he flicked the switch.

He immediately wished he hadn't.

CHAPTER NINETEEN

Digby recoiled as the laboratory's lighting clicked on. The dull orange eyes of five revenants stared straight at him from the other side of the room where they stood. His first response was to open his maw to Forge himself a weapon. Rebecca put the impulse to rest as she held up a hand.

"Wait. They aren't attacking." She crept forward.

"Careful." Digby reached out to stop her. "We don't have Alex here to Cleanse the curse. If you get bit, it's over."

She stopped and looked back. "Maybe you should take the lead."

"Why not? Can't get any more cursed than I already am." He stepped forward, watching the creatures for any sign of aggression. That was when he noticed a row of small, metallic rods floating in the air between them. At first he thought he might be imagining them but as he stepped closer, he found that they were actually levitating.

"Okay, that's weird." Rebecca inched closer while staying behind him.

"Indeed." Dig raised a hand in front of one of the revenants and waved it in the air. The creature didn't react.

"I don't think it cares about us." Rebecca did the same. "They aren't even staring at anything in particular, they're just looking at the wall over there. It's like they're in some sort of standby mode."

"Maybe it has something to do with these." Digby reached out to poke one of the metallic rods.

The reaction was instant.

A sudden screech came from the closest revenant as the metallic object wavered in the air. Both he and Rebecca jumped backward. The rod's movement stabilized and returned to its starting position. The revenant's behavior did the same, its sudden outburst fading until it was standing still again.

"It's some sort of ward." Digby stared at the metal rods, remembering how they had found a few buildings back in California that held a similar enchantment. The rods were only a few inches long and covered with engraved runes. "Didn't Lana say something about Autem having some way of warding that they hadn't shared with Skyline?"

"This must be what she was talking about." Rebecca turned to look through a number of compartmentalized drawers that held more of the warding rods, stored in bundles of four. She immediately shoved a few into her pocket.

"I thought we couldn't steal anything." Digby gave her a sideways look.

"It looks like they have plenty of these stored up and might not notice a few are missing right away. At least, I think it's worth the risk. Just think about how much this kind of tech could help the people out there in the world."

"Provided we can figure out how it works." Digby grabbed one of the bundles and pocketed it as well. "I'll have Alex take a look when we get back. Maybe he'll be able to make sense of one of these things with his artificer class."

With that, they headed back to the door, hoping that the coast would be clear. Peeking out, Digby tried his best to check if the seer was back at her desk without looking suspicious. The door at the end of the hall was closed just as it had been before. He furrowed his brow when he saw her empty chair through the window, unsure if that was a good or bad thing. With her away from her desk, he had no idea where she was. The thought made him feel like she might sneak up behind them at any moment. Then again, this might be the opportunity they were waiting for, giving them a shot at getting into that elevator she guarded.

He snapped his attention back to his accomplice. "Are you thinking what I'm thinking?"

She nodded. "We need to get in there."

Digby grinned back. "Indeed."

Rebecca glanced back and forth. "Okay, I'll keep an eye out."

Digby wasted no time, sauntering down the hall to place the guardian ring he borrowed against the locking panel. His shoulders sank as a red light flashed above the metal plate. *Well, that's disappointing.* Digby spun on his heel and headed back to Rebecca.

"No luck?" She met him halfway.

"Not so much." He held up the ring. "This thing must not rank high enough to grant access."

Rebecca sighed. "We might need to identify someone with access and take them out. That seer might be a good target since we know they have access. Attacking a level forty is a little risky, but we might be able to make it if we throw everything we have at her and catch her by surprise. We'll just have to make sure we get the Seed and get out of here before anyone realizes she's missing."

"Still a little blood thirsty, I see?" Digby gave her a sideways glance.

"Oh, like you weren't thinking it." She shrugged.

"Good to know I'm rubbing off on you." He chuckled.

"Don't remind me." She shuddered as they headed to take a left back down the hallway they had come from. Digby followed only to run into her back for the second time that night. He suppressed a complaint when he saw the reason.

The seer was standing directly in their path. A friendly smile hung on her face and a polished wooden box sat in her hands.

Digby's eyes widened. He would have been ecstatic to have his prey walk right up to him, but the fact that a familiar man stood behind her sent a surge of panic through every necrotic cell in his brain.

Bancroft.

What the hell is he doing here? Digby would have tried to hide his face but it was already too late. Skyline's commander was already looking straight at him. It was over. Everything they had worked for was about to go up in smoke, or at least, it was until the seer spoke.

"Oh good. I saw you both head into your lab and was worried you might miss tonight's ceremony. Working late is all well and good, but the Nine would notice if any of our people skipped a service." Her voice was sweet and kind, with a hint of judgment.

"Yes, if I have to go, so does everyone else," Bancroft added.

"Oh, don't be like that, Charles." The seer nudged him playfully.

Oh... My... Lord... Digby fought back a villainous grin that threatened to slither its way across his face. Bancroft didn't recognize him. His Sheep's Clothing mutation had actually worked. Not only that, but the man didn't even suspect that he didn't belong in the building.

He glanced to Rebecca, who was making a point of keeping her head low so that the brim of her hat covered at least some of her face.

Bancroft was sure to have seen her file, right?

Maybe. Then again, if they weren't aware that she had become a Heretic, they may not have spent much time focusing on her. Couple that with the fact that her file's primary image was a few years old, it became possible that Bancroft couldn't recognize her either.

"We..." Digby started to speak but quickly restarted, this time making a point to try to mask his accent. If there was one thing that Bancroft might be able to recognize, it was his voice. Especially after the way Digby had taunted the man. "Yes ma'am, we were just checking up on something."

"Those dreadful creatures no doubt." The seer frowned.

"Yes, the revenants in there are securely warded, but it never hurts to double check before leaving for the night," Rebecca chimed in.

"That is a comfort, considering my desk is only down the hall from here." The seer glanced to the door of the laboratory, letting a sneer sneak onto her face for an instant. "I just wish the warding could do something about the odor. I swear I can smell them from out here in the hall, even with the door closed. My sympathies certainly go out to you for having to work with those foul things."

"Yes, but it is a sacrifice that must be made if Autem is to secure a foothold in this world." Digby tried to imitate the level of enthusiasm that the guard at the entrance had earlier to push past the subject. Though, for once he was glad to have the revenants around to take the blame for any unfortunate odors. Especially when he was pretty sure that the smell she was complaining about had more to do with his zombified condition.

"Sorry for making you worry. We're both new to this facility and still acclimating to things on the base." Rebecca stepped in to explain away the fact that they hadn't been met before. She kept one hand hidden, clearly trying to keep anyone from noticing that she wasn't wearing a guardian ring.

"That's understandable. I'm Kristen." She inclined her head to them both, unable to shake their hands on account of the box in her arms. "And you must already know Charles, here."

"Yes, now can we go?" Bancroft barely looked at them as if they weren't worth remembering.

"Fine, if you won't stop your grumbling." She let out a feminine chuckle and gestured with her head for Digby and Rebecca to follow as she turned around. "Come on, you can ride with us."

"Umm…" Digby nearly panicked.

They had hit a stroke of luck in that neither this seer or Bancroft had analyzed them or realized that they didn't belong there, but they couldn't just leave. Not without investigating further. They still hadn't gained access to that golden elevator. They still needed to find the Seed.

"Nonsense, we wouldn't want to hold you up." He tried to decline her offer gracefully.

"It's no trouble. Plus it's already so late, you'll never make it to the cathedral if you walk." She patted a hand on the lid of the polished box she held. "You'll be sure to be on time if you ride with us. They can't start the ceremony until we arrive, after all."

Digby glanced to Rebecca, getting no help as neither of them could think of a way out of the situation. Not with Bancroft looming over them. The only thing maintaining their cover was the fact that no one had thought to analyze them. If they continued to protest, they might push their luck too far. The problem left them with little choice.

"In that case, we would appreciate the assistance." He gave up and resigned himself to going with the flow. They would have to find a way back into the building the following day. Perhaps they might find another way to access that elevator by then.

"Come along then." Kristen turned cheerfully. "Don't want to be any later than we have to be. After everything the Nine have done for us, they deserve at least an attempt at punctuality from their followers."

Digby waited for Bancroft to turn and head for the exit before taking a place at the back of the group. Rebecca walked at his side. Catching her face in his peripheral, he could relate to the terror in her eyes. She looked like she wanted to run for her life.

Not only that, but Digby didn't like the sound of this ceremony they were walking into. For that matter, he didn't like the religious nature of this seer's words, either. At least, not in the context that the seer had used them. There was something off about it.

What was that other thing she said? Something about the Nine?

The way the seer had spoken made it sound like she was referring to some sort of deity. Digby grimaced. Whoever or whatever the Nine were, he already knew he didn't like them.

Following the seer and Bancroft from the facility, Digby cringed as they passed the entry way that Campbell had snuck them through earlier, making a note of the size of the two turrets that were mounted on either side of the walls. They had gone through so much just to get in that it was almost painful. Their mission had borne fruit, but still, they hadn't gotten everything they needed.

That was when he remembered he was still wearing the ring they had borrowed. The one that they had planned to put back so that no one would notice it was gone. He shook off the concern. It was too late now. All he could do was hope that the theft wouldn't come back to haunt them.

Bancroft climbed into a small vehicle that was waiting just outside. Digby wasn't sure if he would call it a car or not. It had a roof but no doors, almost as if it was built to traverse the base rather than the outside world. Another one of Autem's men sat at the wheel.

The seer slid in next to Bancroft and placed the wooden box she carried on her lap while holding it carefully. She almost seemed to be treating the container with respect. Digby couldn't help but wonder what might be inside.

The vehicle sped off once he and Rebecca took a seat in the back. It only took around five minutes for them to reach their destination. Digby arched an eyebrow at the building they pulled up to.

A structure, about the size of a small cottage, sat in an open area of the base. From the seer's words, he had been expecting a grand cathedral, but with the size of it, he couldn't see how it could fit any more than a handful of people.

The exterior was covered by ornate stonework like a mausoleum, complete with statues lining the walls of the structure. Digby counted four meticulously carved human figures on both sides, making eight in total. A golden circle was embedded in the stone behind them as if meant to suggest a halo. Looking up, he noticed one more statute standing at the apex of the roof holding up another of those cross-like emblems that was plastered all over Autem's side of the base. A pair of angel wings stretched out from the figure's back. Including the statue on top, there were nine in total.

That can't be a coincidence.

Bancroft headed for the door without waiting for anyone. Digby got the feeling that the man had no interest in being there. Almost like he didn't want to sit through the ceremony that was about to take place within. Digby could relate, but seeing as the seer stepped aside as if to let him and Rebecca enter first, it didn't look like he had a choice.

Not wanting to raise suspicions, he headed inside. A streak of fear passed through him when he saw what awaited them. The interior of the building was bare save for more intricate carvings adorning the walls, and a stairway that led down.

I do not like the look of that.

His original observation had been correct. There was certainly no way to fit more than a handful people in the building itself, but he couldn't be sure about whatever room lay below. Digby cursed himself for not realizing the possibility that the tiny structure was merely an entrance to something bigger.

With every fiber of his deceased body, he wanted to run. It was too late for that. He pushed onward, stepping down to another large security door which Bancroft promptly opened. Again, the impulse to flee climbed back up his spine as the cathedral's true interior came into view.

It was huge.

Even worse, it was full.

Row after row of pews filled the floor below, with an aisle in the middle that led to a large stage. Guardians packed the space from wall to wall. Digby tried to count them but lost track after a few dozen. A rough estimate found that there were over a thousand enemies in the room. He focused on a few.

Guardian: Level 32 Holy Knight
Guardian: Level 3 Mage
Guardian: Level 7 Enchanter
Guardian: Level 38 Artificer
Guardian: Level 27 Pyromancer

He stopped checking after the first few. He didn't need to know any more. It didn't really matter. If he or Rebecca did anything to blow their cover, there was no way they would escape. There was little chance of anyone recognizing him, but still, the odds of Autem's soldiers having their HUDs active were high. If any of them looked at him too hard, it would be all over.

With no way out, Digby resigned himself to follow along and blend in. The seer nodded and headed for a large stage at the front of the room, leaving him and Rebecca to find a seat. He took a right at the bottom of the stairs and headed toward the back to find a spot. From there he watched as the seer stepped up onto the stage and placed the box she carried on an altar that sat in the middle.

Before he had time to take in the rest of his surroundings, the lights within the cathedral dimmed. A bit of tension melted away from his shoulders as the low lighting would serve to ensure no one would analyze him.

Shortly after, the curtain at the back of the stage opened to reveal a black wall that flickered to life, displaying the same golden emblem. A man in a white coat appeared on the oversized screen from the bottom as if walking up a set of stairs behind the display to take the stage. Digby didn't recognize him, but he was clearly important.

"Thank you all for joining us. We have been blessed with the arrival of a new dole of guardians that will shape our world for years to come. As the sun sets on the corruption of the old, these young guardians may help guide our growing flock in this new dawn under the light of the Nine and will of the One." The man paused only to have every guardian in the room respond in unison.

"May the will guide them."

Digby nearly choked in surprise, not expecting the sudden response. Rebecca wasn't any more prepared, but covered by opening her mouth to act like she was speaking along with the crowd.

The entire thing felt strange, like a church service but somehow wrong. There was mention of the One, but he had no idea if they meant it as in god, or something else entirely. He had never been religious, so either way, he was pretty sure he didn't like what was happening here.

The room went silent so the man on the screen could continue. "Again, I thank you all for being here, as well as for your service to the will. I shall now hand this ceremony over to Bishop Harker."

A second man in a similar outfit ascended the stage, this time within the actual room they were in rather than appearing on a screen.

"Thank you, Chancellor Serrano." Bishop Harker bowed to the man on the screen.

Chancellor Serrano? Digby's ears pricked up, remembering that Lana had mentioned the man as being the one in charge of

Autem. Henwick's name didn't seem to be known to anyone within Skyline, except for Bancroft.

This chancellor fellow must be somewhat of a figurehead that takes the spotlight while Henwick runs things from the shadows. Digby couldn't help but wonder if the man was better or worse than the hunter he'd known all those centuries ago. Probably just as bad, if he had to guess. He shook his head. It seemed he was gaining more enemies by the minute.

The bishop took his place behind the altar and opened the box that the seer had placed there. Then, he gestured to the side of the room where a group of six boys and girls stood. Some may have been in their mid-teens while a few were quite young. A bright gold guardian ring sat on each of their right hands.

The sight of them was enough to turn his stomach despite the fact that he couldn't actually be sick anymore. He knew that his enemies had a penchant for using children and raising them to serve their interests, but seeing it from so close up horrified him. His disgust twisted and flipped into hope at the realization that Hawk might be among them.

He wasn't.

Though, he did recognize one of their number.

Alvin.

Lana's little brother. The brother she was desperate to rescue.

Digby had only known the boy for a couple hours back in Seattle, during which he had barely said a word. Focusing on the child, the Heretic Seed told him what he feared.

Guardian: Level 8 Mage

Damn. The boy had been accepted into their little cult. Digby just hoped he hadn't been one of them long enough to start believing in whatever fairy tales Autem had been telling him. The group of children all saluted by placing a closed fist across their chest. The image made Digby wince. Even Rebecca looked uncomfortable.

That was when things got worse.

Another six youths stood and made their way to the stage.

Digby's eyes bulged when he saw Hawk bringing up the rear. They merged into the first group of children and paired off, spreading out across the stage. Digby couldn't help but notice that each pairing contained a boy and girl of similar ages. Alvin stood next to a girl in her teens and Hawk was placed beside a girl that looked a little younger.

The Bishop took things from there.

"Tonight, I welcome you six to an ancient calling. For nearly a millennium, the guardians have stood before the chaos of the world to protect and guide humanity to true prosperity. Through the light of the Nine, you will be bound to their guidance in following the will of the One. Do you submit to his will?"

The group of children all answered in the affirmative, each nodding their heads in unison. It pained Digby to see Hawk following along. At the very least he wanted the boy to rebel, despite knowing full well that he didn't have a choice in the matter.

The Bishop proceeded to reach into the box on the altar to retrieve a small velvet pouch. Dumping it into his palm, a child-sized guardian ring tumbled out. He walked across the stage and handed it to the first of the young guardians. After that he proceeded to do the same for the others, handing the last ring in the box to the girl standing beside Hawk.

The Bishop returned to the center of the stage. "With this ring, I bind your will to his and bestow upon you the blessing of the Nine."

With that, each of the young guardians turned to their partners and slipped the ring on to their finger. Digby's jaw tightened. The ceremony reminded him of some sort of twisted wedding. If he hadn't been a corpse, he was sure that his blood would have boiled in his veins.

The child pairings separated and formed one line as the Bishop continued to spew nonsense for another twenty minutes. After that, the ceremony ended and the congregation of guardians exited the cathedral the way they had come in. Digby and Rebecca filtered into the crowd and made their escape, not wanting to run into that seer again.

Back above ground, they made for the gate that led to Skyline's side of the base. Without Campbell's dinner cart, there was no way to get back into the secure building that they had been sneaking around in, no matter how much they needed to. They would have to retreat and try again the next day. With the aid of a Waking Dream spell and a few well-timed Ventriloquisms, they managed enough of a distraction to slip past the gate's guards to make it back to the barracks on Skylines side of the base where they could hide.

Digby grumbled the whole way back.

After witnessing everything in the cathedral, his resolve had become firm. Autem, Skyline, and Henwick all needed to be stopped. There would be no running away.

One way or another, he was going to put an end to them.

CHAPTER TWENTY

Hawk yawned in his bunk as a light flickered to life above him to remind him that he was still being held within Autem's training facility. He assumed it was morning, but there was no way to be sure since there were no windows in the room. Unlike the rest of the survivors on the base, the kids that passed their assessments were housed in a separated area and divided up to keep the girls and boys apart.

The room he was in consisted of a long space with cubby-like bunks lining the walls. Every surface was white with gold accents here and there. More of those black camera domes were embedded in the ceiling. Hawk had been assigned to a bunk the night before after that weird-ass ring ceremony. Most of the beds in the room were filled by other kids that had been through the same tests he'd been given. None of them were very talkative. Instead, they just followed the instructions of the people in white that ordered them around.

He wasn't sure where Digby and Becca were hiding, but he hoped he could find a way to sneak off and find them. From the look of things, that was going to be difficult. Especially since he had no idea how he would even get out of the building or where to go from there.

Hawk stared down at the gold ring on his finger. He'd seen the ring that Skyline had given Lana before Digby destroyed it. Hers had been a simple gold band. His, however, was different, like the rest of the guardians in Autem, whose rings were shaped to bear that weird emblem. It made the stupid piece of jewelry look chunky and ridiculous on a child's finger.

It wasn't all bad though.

———

NAME: Marcus Calder
GUARDIAN CLASS: Fighter
LEVEL: 1
MANA: 122/122
CONSTITUTION: 15
DEFENSE: 9
STRENGTH: 10
DEXTERITY: 17
AGILITY: 15
INTELLIGENCE: 18
PERCEPTION: 17
WILL: 16

SPELLS:
HUSH: Create a field of mana capable of absorbing the sound of your movements.
BARRIER: Create a layer of mana around yourself or a target to absorb any incoming attack.

———

Wow. Hawk stared at the display hovering in the air. *I have magic.*

It was just like a game.

Granted, it was nothing like Digby's magic and he didn't have anything he could use to attack with, but it was still pretty cool. Just the fact that he could produce a Barrier that could potentially take a bullet was amazing. It made him feel like a superhero.

Then again, he wasn't a fan of that ceremony from the night before. It felt like church, and church was weird. Even stranger was the way the people in Autem spoke. It was like they actually believed all that stuff.

Whatever. Hawk shook off his worries. If these people wanted to worship some kind of god or angel, it didn't matter to him, not so long as he got some magic out of the deal. Though he could have done without the display that took up the edges of his vision. He rubbed at his temples as he began to feel a headache coming on. The blinking colon between the letters MP and his mana value was not helping the situation. A list of information ran down the other side that included a log of every spell he cast and how much experience he had to gain to reach the next level. The shitty readout was even there when he closed his eyes.

He wished the ugly display would just go away.

To his surprise, it did exactly that.

What? His entire body tensed as if he's just spilled a drink on a keyboard that might kill someone's laptop. He blew out a sigh of relief when a line streaked across his vision.

REESTABLISHING...

A few seconds later, his same irritating display returned. Apparently, the Guardian Core's readout could be deactivated. He willed it to go away again, hoping his headache would fade before he had to turn his HUD back on.

Sliding to the side, he touched his feet down on the cold tile floor. A row of drawers were set into the wall next to his bunk. They were filled with everything he needed. A simple uniform sat in the top drawer. It had that freaky symbol on the shoulder the same as his ring. A pair of boots peeked out from under his bed. He changed out of the pjs that he'd been given the night before and into the uniform. It was stiff and scratchy and the collar was tighter than he was used to.

He glanced up at the cameras in the ceiling.

Hope you got an eyeful, ya creeps.

There was something messed up about the place. It seemed

like everywhere he went, he was being watched. No one else seemed to care. Maybe that was the norm for Autem's people. A chime announced the arrival of a man in the same uniform as the other adults. The man simply clapped his hands and the boys in the room formed a line.

Hawk hesitated, unsure what to do. He was the only new kid in the room, and the others seemed to already have an idea of what to do. Without a better option, he shrugged and followed the others. The man at the door nodded like he had done the right thing. He wondered how many other rooms like this there were.

How many kids do they have here? That would probably be something good to find out. There were only a handful at the ceremony the night before, but he hadn't been given the opportunity to find anything out. The only contact he'd had with the kids that had already received their rings had been on stage when that girl slipped a ring on his finger. The skin of his neck prickled, remembering the moment. It wasn't exactly how he imagined holding a girl's hand for the first time would be.

Following the rest of the boys down the hall, he counted twelve from his room. They joined together with another three groups of around the same number, all boys. The man in the lead brought them into a cafeteria where they met up with the girls. Granted, they were still kept separate, as his group was told where to sit and to wait for their turn to get breakfast.

Hawk took the moment to look over the room. He recognized some of the other kids from his assessment group. They were easy to spot from the awkward way that they sat or tried to make conversation with the children around them. From the looks of it, the rest of the kids were pretty quiet, mostly focusing on their breakfast and watching the line while they waited for their turn.

There was something off about the other kids. They ranged from fifteen or so to as young as eight. Hawk couldn't help but notice how quiet and well behaved they were. It was like they had accepted Autem's routines completely and ignored any impulse that might cause them to step out of line.

Hawk shrugged. It wasn't like he had much interest in getting to know any of the other kids anyway. If things worked out, he would be on his way back to Vegas soon. Then again, there was one other boy that he'd been trying to keep an eye out for.

Alvin.

Hawk hadn't talked to Lana much, but he knew the situation. Dig had helped them back in Seattle where everything started but Skyline had taken them in. From what his sister had said, Alvin had passed his assessment and had become a guardian just as Hawk had. If he could find him and think of a way to get close to him, he might be able to learn something more.

Sweeping his eyes across the tables, Hawk tried to narrow down the possibilities. The only things he knew were that Alvin was a couple years older than him and that he was black, like his sister. Out of the three dozen or so boys in the room, only six were black and only two were the right age. He kind of wished he'd paid more attention to the details.

Before he was able to figure anything out, his table was called up to get their breakfast. Hawk hopped up with enthusiasm. He wasn't going to turn down a free meal. Despite his interest in food, he made sure to be the last in line so that he could look over the room while he waited. He hoped he might be able to overhear Alvin's name if he listened carefully. Unfortunately, the fact that the other kids didn't do much talking made the effort pointless.

That was when he got a brilliant idea and willed the Guardian Core's display to come back. As annoying as it was, it might actually come in handy. Sweeping his vision across the room he focused on the first of the two boys.

Guardian: Level 2 Mage

He shifted his gaze to the other.

Guardian: Level 8 Mage

Hawk considered his findings. If Alvin had been taken in by Autem back when the apocalypse started, then he would have had more time to level up. If that was true then the level eight had to be him. Hawk stared at the boy.

Hello Alvin.

The breakfast line moved forward before he had a chance to investigate further. Hawk followed in to grab a tray, immediately disappointed by his options. The cafeteria wasn't fully stocked like the one back in Vegas, or the one on Skyline's side of the base where he'd been his first night. Actually, it wasn't really a cafeteria at all. Sure, it was a large room with tables set up, but from what he could see, there was no kitchen. Instead, a long cart holding tubs of eggs and other breakfast staples sat in the corner next to a counter stacked with trays and silverware.

It looked like the food was prepared somewhere else and wheeled into the training facility. Hawk grimaced, wondering how long the eggs had been sitting there. There was a little steam rising off the tray of the kid in front of him, so the food had to be at least somewhat warm.

A large man in a Skyline uniform stood behind a cart, dishing out servings to each of the kids in line. Hawk couldn't help but notice he wasn't dressed like a member of Autem.

I guess the cook staff isn't important enough.

The second thing he noticed was that the man wasn't wearing a guardian ring.

Yup, definitely not an important guy.

Fortunately, the man seemed friendly. He gave each kid a smile as he shoved a biscuit on top of their plates. It was kind of a relief to see someone normal. Hawk was beginning to think everyone on the base had been turned into mindless drones.

Stepping to the side, Hawk held his tray out. The man started to scoop eggs from the tub in front of him but stopped after looking at his face. That was when he did something strange, reaching for a mostly empty tub of eggs beside the full one that he had been serving the other kids from. Hawk watched as the big guy reached to the back of the tray and scooped up a large portion of eggs. He even placed his other hand on top to make sure none of them fell from his spatula.

The portion hit his tray in a congealed mass of cold eggs that held a rectangular shape like a brick. He wondered what had made the guy switch tubs when there were better portions in the other one. Hawk wished he was back at the casino where the breakfasts were full of cinnamon rolls and bacon. There was a little more rationing but at least the food was warm. Despite that, he didn't complain. He doubted it would get him very far. In the end, food was food.

That was when the big guy serving breakfast smiled and said something weird. "Dig in to that."

"Ah, okay." Hawk stared down at the block of cold eggs.

"I mean it. Dig... in." The man winked as he said the word dig.

"Sure, I will." Hawk wasn't sure what to say or why the man was being so weird about things.

"Good, just make sure to Dig in carefully." The big guy placed a biscuit on top.

Hawk didn't say anything else, opting to let the awkward moment pass. He stepped to the side and grabbed a carton of milk from a counter and headed back to the tables. He stopped half way there and made for the table that Alvin was sitting at. There was a spot open across from him and now was as good a time as any to make an introduction.

"Mind if I sit?" Hawk dropped his tray down without waiting for anyone to respond.

No one objected.

Then again, none of the kids were very welcoming either. Alvin barely looked up from his food. The kid was a little taller than himself and looked to be in better shape.

"Sorry, I'm new. How long have you guys been here?" Hawk made a point of staring at him.

Alvin didn't answer.

"So, level eight, huh? That's impressive." He grabbed his biscuit and took a bite while continuing to speak with his mouth full. "I analyzed you. Pretty cool that we can do that."

Alvin looked up at the mention of his level. "I received my ring a month ago after being rescued from Seattle. My training has helped me to increase my level in a safe environment."

"That's good, I hope I can do that too." Hawk tried to sound positive about his prospects in Autem. "Wasn't Seattle where all this started?"

"It was," Alvin responded matter-of-factly. Hawk found the kid's answer strange. Everything he said had a robotic feel to it. He wasn't sure what that meant.

"Were they able to rescue anyone else back in Seattle?" Hawk finished off his biscuit as he tried to get more information.

Alvin frowned for an instant. "Only my sister survived."

"You're lucky. I wish I had someone who made it." Hawk let himself be honest for a moment before asking another question. "Where is she now? Did Autem take her in too?"

"They did but she didn't pass the assessment, so she joined Skyline. I should get to see her soon, but I know she has been busy over there, since Skyline is handling most of the rescue operations." Alvin sounded sad.

A dull ache echoed through Hawk's chest. Autem was lying to the kid. They hadn't even told him that his sister had left. It made sense. They probably didn't want to disrupt his training. The thought of it made Hawk mad. He debated on if it would be smart to tell Alvin the truth. After all, if someone ever lied to him about something like that, he would never forgive them. If the kid knew the facts, then they would at least have a reason to work together.

That was when a group of armed Autem soldiers entered the room wearing full body armor. A squad of Skyline's mercenaries followed as a man in a black coat walked in front of them. Hawk recognized him from back when Dig had made everyone hide in the empty pool back in California. That man in the coat had stared right at them while Becca hid them under an illusion of water.

What was his name?

Hawk furrowed his brow.

Bancroft, that was it.

He froze the moment he remembered that the guy was in charge of all of Skyline.

Why is he here?

He watched as the group walked across the cafeteria to the lunch cart where the soldiers surrounded the large but friendly man that had served Hawk a brick of cold eggs. He tried his best to hear what they were saying, but wasn't able to catch much. A moment later, the big guy set down his spatula and left his cart to follow the group. His face looked worried as they passed.

Hawk held his breath. He'd gotten in trouble enough times to recognize the expression of someone who knew they'd been caught doing something they shouldn't. That was when he remembered the weird stuff the guy had said while serving him. He'd kept telling him to dig in. Hawk shook his head a second later when the obvious message dawned on him.

Dig… as in Digby.

He poked at the brick of cold eggs on his tray, feeling something hard within the shape with his fork. He glanced around at the boys sitting at his table. Alvin and the others were watching Bancroft. Hawk took advantage of the distraction to scrape away some of the eggs and grab the object underneath. He shoved it in his pocket without even looking at it.

Slipping his hand in to feel around, he grimaced as he realized how much egg he'd just shoved in there. After feeling around, he found the familiar shape of a small smartphone.

Digby had smuggled in a way to talk.

Hawk hid a smile. The zombie really had everything covered. His urge to smile faded a second later. Dig may have gone too far. Clearly Bancroft was on to him, judging on how they came to get the big guy that had snuck him the phone. He just hoped nothing would lead to him.

With no way to change anything, he decided to refocus his attention on Alvin. "You must miss her."

"What?" Alvin looked back to him, clearly forgetting what they had been talking about after watching Bancroft arrest the cafeteria worker.

"Your sister," Hawk added. "I'd want to see my family if they were still alive and this close."

"Yeah." Alvin dropped his eyes down to his tray. "I know she's working hard, but I can't wait to see her."

"How come you don't sneak over and try to find her?" Hawk forced a friendly laugh. "I mean, that's what I would do."

Alvin stopped eating abruptly as if he hadn't thought of doing that. "I don't want to get in trouble."

"I get that." Hawk nodded. "Still though, probably worth it. What's the worst they can do, yell at you?"

"Maybe." Alvin seemed to be thinking about it.

Hawk smiled. It wouldn't be long, now. All he had to do was make sure he was a bad influence on the kid and wait for Digby to come get him. He glanced back to the door where Bancroft had just exited with his prisoner.

I just hope Digby comes for us soon.

CHAPTER TWENTY-ONE

Digby stared at the ceiling of Skyline's unused barracks, fantasizing about sneaking in to Bancroft's bunk to murder him in his sleep. He suppressed the urge, waiting in hope that Campbell might be able to sneak him back into Autem's secure facility later that day. Rebecca lay face down on one of the beds at the other side of the room, drooling all over her pillow. Her quiet snoring filled the silence. She awoke with a start when the door flew open. Digby jumped as well, not expecting visitors so soon.

"What the hell did you two do!" Easton scurried into the room, slamming the door behind him and darting to the window to peek out.

"What happened?" Rebecca nearly fell out of bed before wiping her face on her shoulder.

Digby leapt up. "Yes, what's the meaning of—"

"The base is being locked down and Autem has requested a full-scale search." Easton spun back around.

"Why the hell would they do that?" Digby scoffed.

"You tell me." Easton locked eyes with him.

Digby looked away. "I assure you, I have no idea what—"

"Really?" Easton cut him off again and gestured to his hand. "So that isn't a stolen Guardian ring on your finger then?"

"Ahh…" Digby shoved his hand behind his back.

"I figured as much." Easton slapped a hand to his head.

"What is it that actually happened?" Rebecca approached the distressed communications specialist. "Maybe we can salvage things."

"It's bad." Easton dropped into the nearest bunk and deflated. "The mechanic you killed yesterday has been reported missing. If that had been it, then they would have assumed he deserted or something, but this morning, they found a ring that had access to most of the base missing, as well as some other sensitive equipment."

"Sensitive equipment?" Digby furrowed his brow. "We didn't take any equipment."

"Shit." Rebecca shoved a hand in their pocket. "The warding rods." She pulled out a bundle of the metallic objects they'd taken the night before. "I didn't think they would notice if I only took a few."

"They might not have, but with the missing mechanic and the ring, Autem did an inventory and checked their security recordings." Easton looked up at them. "Do you want to guess what they saw on the tapes?"

"Us?" Digby pointed to himself.

"Yes, both of you." Easton shook his head.

"Crap." Rebecca slapped a hand to her head. "The camera was able to see us after my spell failed."

"You think?" Easton gave her a harsh look. "They're circulating your pictures throughout the base now. They figured out who Becca was pretty fast, but haven't confirmed your identity, Dig. Apparently, they haven't figured out that you can change your face."

"That's not good." Rebecca's eyes widened. "Do they know I'm a Heretic?"

"There's nothing about it in their notice, so probably not. But you've definitely pissed some people off." He stood pack up and paced by the door. "Bancroft is absolutely bullshit about it. So is one of the higher-ups in Autem."

"Probably, Kristen, that seer." Digby frowned. "If our pictures are being sent around, both she and Bancroft must have realized by now that we literally snuck by under their noses without them noticing."

"You what?" Easton stopped pacing.

"We sort of ran into Bancroft and a woman that the Heretic Seed labeled as a seer." Rebecca chimed in. "My Conceal spell didn't work on her so we had to take a different approach."

"Yes, it seems that their people have so many faces going in and out, they weren't suspicious of us," Digby added. "It probably didn't hurt that it was pretty much unthinkable that we would have the gall to sneak into the heart of their operation. They even gave us a ride to their subterranean cathedral. That's why we had to steal this ring." He held up his hand. "We intended to put it back, but after getting caught, we had to leave and watch some disgusting guardian initiation ceremony."

"Ceremony?" Easton arched an eyebrow.

"Indeed. It was a perverse display of some twisted form of worship. I'm not religious and even I felt it was blasphemous." Digby stood up, unable to remain seated as his memory of the night agitated him.

"Okay, yeah, I get that. They do seem sort of cultish." Easton shook his head. "But whatever, that doesn't matter. Right now, we need to get you both out of here."

"Absolutely not." Digby swiped a hand through the air. "I'm not going anywhere without Hawk and Alvin. Not to mention we still have to retrieve the fragments of the Heretic Seed. We just need a little more time. If Campbell can get us in there again, we can—"

"No, you can't." Easton slapped the back of one hand to the palm of his other. "Once they realized you'd penetrated their security, it didn't take long to figure out how you got in. Bancroft went to arrest Campbell personally. Things have only been lax here because Autem and Skyline thought they couldn't be touched. But now that you have slipped in here and caused havoc for an entire night, they aren't about to let things slide anymore. As we speak, they have dozens of squads searching this entire base with orders to destroy you on sight. It's only a matter of time before they come to search the barracks. I'm just glad I was able to get here to warn you before they did."

Digby stomped a foot. "And I already said, I am not leaving before I get what I came for."

"You don't have a choice." Easton brushed his words aside. "You have to use whatever illusion spell you can and get out of the base anyway you can. It's a twenty mile walk through the desert before you reach a rest stop. You should be able to salvage a car there or get your people to come get you. Make sure you take some water. It gets hot out there."

Digby marched forward. "Look here, I said I'm not—"

He shut his mouth at the sound of voices outside.

"Crap, they're here." Easton ran to the window.

Digby followed, peeking out behind the man to see two of Skyline's guardians, armed with swords and pistols, walking straight toward his hiding place.

Guardian: Level 12 Mage
Guardian: Level 13 Knight

"Blast." He pulled away from the window. The pair would be there in less than a minute. "Quick, Becky, Conceal us."

"Wait." Easton snapped his attention back to Digby. "They aren't checking any of the other bunks."

"Crap, they must have spotted you on your way here and decided to see what you were up to." Rebecca joined them at the window. "Either that, or they are on their way somewhere else and just happen to be passing by."

Glancing back out, Digby watched as the pair slowed as they approached the bunk house. They looked to each other, then back at the door of the building. A second later, the fighter snapped his sword from the magnetic sheath on his back. That settled it; they definitely intended on entering.

"Hurry up and Conceal us." Digby stepped away from the door.

"Shit, I can't." Rebecca flicked her eyes to Easton. "At least, not all of us."

"What?" Easton's voice climbed an octave.

"If they saw you come in here, then it's likely they won't believe that you simply vanished." Rebecca spoke faster as time ran out. "If they doubt what they're seeing just even a little, it will cause the spell to unravel."

Easton stepped back, clearly afraid of what that meant.

"Relax." Digby grabbed him by the shoulder of his uniform and shoved him toward one of the beds. "We can still use the spell if Rebecca only casts it on the two of us. All you have to do is give them a plausible reason for why you have snuck off to this bunk. They won't suspect you as long as you aren't seen with us."

"What do I do then?" Easton's eyes darted around the room as the sound of footsteps climbed the stairs just outside the door.

Digby pushed him down into the bed. "I already told you, relax." He'd watched Parker sneak away to nap enough times to know that slacking off was as believable as anything else.

The moment Easton's head hit the pillow, Rebecca retreated to the corner of the building's interior to the right of the door and cast Conceal. Digby followed, making sure he wasn't standing in a position where the guardians might bump into him. As long as Easton could keep calm and sell a performance, the guardians might leave. All they needed was a little more time to figure out a new plan.

The door flew open, tearing Digby away from his thoughts. The knight rushed in first with his sword drawn while the mage slipped in behind him. Easton sat up with a rather embarrassing shriek.

"State your name and designation." The knight stood with their sword pointed in his direction.

"Trent Easton, Communications Specialist." He scrambled to get out of the bed.

"What are you doing here?" the mage demanded from behind the knight.

"I, ah, oh shit, I'm sorry." Easton lowered his head in a submissive manner. "This bunkhouse has been empty for weeks and no one checks it, so I sneak out here to sleep."

"What?" The knight arched an eyebrow.

"I know I shouldn't have, but this place is stressful and…" He shook his head. "Please don't exile me, I'll do whatever it takes to—"

"Shut up." The knight let his sword fall a few inches. "That's really it, you're just a slacker? You have nothing to do with the security breach?"

"Security breach?" Easton played dumb.

"Yes. Bancroft is ready to start taking heads. Notices were sent out first thing this morning to alert everyone. That's why we're doing a full-scale sweep of the base." The knight dropped his sword a couple more inches.

"I didn't even know about the breach." Easton started to relax. "Is there a chance that you could maybe let it slide that I was here, since you have your hands full searching for the thieves?"

Finally, the knight sighed and reached back to put his sword in its sheath, clearly deciding that Easton wasn't a threat. The mage behind him stepped forward and whispered in his partner's ear a second later. Digby crept forward to eavesdrop.

"He just said thieves, but we didn't say if anything was taken."

The knight froze with hand still on the grip of his sword.

Damn. Digby cringed as Easton's credibility crumbled. He glanced at Rebecca, who nodded back. The time for talking had passed. All that was left was force.

The knight drew his weapon again. "Where are they?"

"What?" Easton raised his hands in defense. "I just told you I have no idea what—"

Digby lunged forward while the attention of both guardians was on their suspect. He cast Five Fingers of Death before the mage realized he was there. It was about time he tested the spell.

Rebecca took the fighter, occupying him with a Waking Dream of a revenant that leapt for his throat. Digby kept his attention on the mage, hoping to snuff out the threat before they had a chance to heal themselves or the knight. Speed was everything.

Letting the violent mana of Five Fingers of Death bore into the mage's back, Digby drove his fingertips into his prey, the man's flesh giving way like a piece of rotting fruit. The mage started to scream, but Digby slapped his other hand over his mouth. In desperation, his victim cast a healing spell. Digby felt it surge through their body with his blood sense.

"Oh no you don't." Digby pushed harder, burying his fingers in the mage's back deep enough to grab hold of a few ribs. The man's mana flowed around his hand, mixing with the power of his spell.

Rebecca kept her illusion going as long as she could, but after a swipe of the knight's sword, he figured out it wasn't real. The spell collapsed the instant his doubt became too strong. He leapt back and cast Barrier, sending a ripple of blue energy across his skin. Then he reached for a radio on his belt.

"Don't let him call for help." Digby held firm on the mage's ribcage to make sure the curse could take root.

"I'm on it." Rebecca simply unleashed a barrage of Icicles just as he opened his mouth to speak.

"This is—" His call for help was interrupted under assault.

Digby watched her mana fall with each shard of ice. They shattered on impact, causing the knight's Barrier to shimmer. The man tried to swat them away with his sword, but only managed to deflect one of the frozen spikes before another punched through his Barrier. Rebecca didn't stop, sending one after another into the man's body until his fate was sealed.

He hit the floor with a heavy thud as the mage in Digby's grasp finally succumbed to the additional effect of Five Fingers of Death. Death's Embrace claimed the man shortly after, leaving a new minion standing in his place.

Guardian, Level 12 Mage defeated. 1,148 experience awarded.
Guardian, Level 13 Knight defeated. 1,248 experience awarded.

Everyone in the bunkhouse held still, clearly waiting to see if anyone had heard the struggle. The surrounding barracks may have been empty but the fight hadn't been quiet.

After thirty seconds of nothing, Digby relaxed and pulled his hand free. He tensed right back up when he glanced at his HUD to see how much mana Rebecca had remaining.

Rebecca MP: 53/303

After casting so many Icicles to break through the knight's Barrier, she only had enough left for one more illusion. Digby glanced at the door. The knight hadn't been able to call for help or say where he was, but he had been able to get two words out before being killed. Surely, the communication had been enough to raise the suspicions of the other guardians. They may not have known where to search exactly, but he was positive they would know enough to narrow it down.

Damn it! Digby cursed the situation.

They couldn't stay. Hawk would have to hang in there for another day or two while he came up with a plan B. Thinking fast, he rushed to the knight's body and cast Talking Corpse. He gave the spell a few seconds to take effect before asking his first question. "How much time do we have before your friends find us?"

The knight's voice came out raspy and filled with darkness. "Around ten minutes."

Digby tensed, hoping they would have more time. "Alright, what is the fastest route off this base that will steer us clear of the squads that are searching for us?"

"Exit and go right. Head straight for the back of the base and scale the perimeter wall."

"Does the wall have any security measures?" He asked a follow up question.

"There are cameras mounted on the top of the wall, facing the surrounding desert to detect approaching enemies. Any movement will be reported, along with images."

"Shit." Rebecca rubbed at her temples. "Conceal won't be stable enough to get us to the wall with so many people looking for us, but if I use Waking Dream to disguise us, we'll show up on the cameras once we get to the other side. They'll know how we got out and what direction we went. I don't have the mana for both and we can't wait here for me to absorb it."

Digby grabbed the knight's collar. "Are there any blind spots?"

"Yes. If you go over the wall in the exact center between two cameras, there will be a five-foot blind spot. The camera will not be able to see you as long as you stand flat against the wall."

"Alright." Digby turned to Rebecca. "We'll use Waking Dream to get us there, then go over the wall and hide in the blind spot. Once we're on the other side, we can wait for a few minutes until your mana replenishes enough to use Conceal again. That'll get us past the cameras from there."

Rebecca shook her head. "What if someone sees us go over the wall?"

"We'll just have to make sure they don't look that way." Digby turned back to the corpse below him. "Can you give my minion an order for me if I'm not around?"

The knight answered with a simple, "No."

"Right, right, you can only answer questions." Digby scratched at his chin for a second as he considered the limitations of his Talking Corpse spell. A moment later, he snapped his fingers and rummaged through the pouches of the corpse's armor. Finding a grenade, he rushed to the mage that he'd taken as a minion a minute ago. He checked their pouches as well to procure a second explosive. "Someone remove that corpse's boot laces."

Both Easton and Rebecca jumped on the task, handing the strings up to him. With one, he tied the two grenades together and fastened them to his minion's chest armor. He looped the other lace through both metal rings attached to them so they could be triggered at the same time.

Unfortunately, since he'd used his Five Fingers of Death spell to raise the zombie rather than Animate Corpse, his minion lacked the bond points that he would normally be able to distribute to increase their intelligence or dexterity. With that knowledge, he needed to make sure the task he gave them was simple and easy to perform.

He headed back to the knight's corpse and pulled off their chest armor, including the magnetic sheath that was attached to the back. He slipped it on and picked up their sword, figuring the weapon to be worth stealing. At the very least, Mason might appreciate the upgrade. Before placing the blade back in its sheath, he put it to use, severing the knight's head from their corpse with a couple hard chops. The Talking Corpse spell created sound using magic, so it wasn't like the head needed to remain attached to the knight's body.

Easton gagged.

Digby ignored his reaction and tucked the head under his minions' right arm. "Hold onto this, will you?"

The zombie curled their hand under the base of the bloody neck hole. Once it looked like his minion would be able to carry the head without dropping it, he grabbed their left hand and tied the boot lace that hung from the grenade pins around their wrist. "Alright now, hold your arms just like this."

The zombie obeyed without a problem, despite having an intelligence attribute of zero. Digby glanced down to address the severed head under their arm. "Alright, I know you can only answer questions, so here's one with a lengthy answer. What are the last fifty movies that you saw?"

The head began listing titles.

"Why did you ask that?" Rebecca stared at the knight's face.

"I just needed the thing to keep talking for a bit." Digby slapped a hand to his minion's shoulder. "Alright, here's your orders. I want you to go outside and walk that way." He pointed in the opposite direction from where they intended to go. "Keep walking until this head stops talking, then pull your arm down. Got it?"

The zombie let out a moan that carried a feeling of understanding before heading for the door. Easton grabbed the handle and held it open.

"Alright, that should give us about a minute before they blow themselves up." He turned to the others. "Easton, you stay here until you hear the blast, then slip out. Rebecca, make us look like the two guardians that we just killed."

She nodded and cast Waking Dream.

"Let's go." Digby gave Easton a final nod and pushed through the door.

Once outside, they ducked behind a bunkhouse and walked

between the rows to stay out of sight. The fact that the buildings were unused acted as a double-edged sword. There were few guardians around for them to run into, but that only made himself and Rebecca stand out more, even with the illusion spell disguising their appearance.

Digby's lone minion walked off in the opposite direction. The sound of movie titles being listed trailed off into the distance as they fled the scene. It wasn't long before they reached the wall. The barrier was a least fifteen feet high with thicker portions spaced out every fifteen feet. Sweeping his gaze across the top, Digby recognized the cameras. He followed the wall to a point exactly in the center between them. If the knight's severed head was correct, then that was where they needed to climb.

Digby let out a nervous laugh, realizing there was no ladder or hand holds in sight. "Hope your agility is high enough to scale that."

Rebecca took one look at the barrier. "Should be. I'm not exactly superhuman, but I'm well above average. With a running start, I think I can make it."

"Oh yes, me too." Digby nodded as if trying to convince himself as much as he was his accomplice. He would have used his forge spell to launch himself up and over but it was sure to leave enough crystalized blood behind to give away their exit point. With their need to return for Hawk, Alvin, and the Seed, he didn't want them increasing security along the rear parameter. Not if he wanted to get back in.

Rebecca got into position about twenty feet away from the wall's blind spot and scanned the area before. "We definitely have guardians in line of sight. Two directly behind us and another three by a building fifty feet away. Analyze marks them all as over level twenty. I give it about thirty seconds before they start to question why we're standing here doing nothing."

"Wait for the distraction." Digby resisted the urge to run for the wall. "Just pretend we're two innocent mercenaries. Well, as innocent as Skyline's sellswords get, at least."

That was when a loud boom echoed from a few hundred feet away.

Common Zombie, lost.

"Now." Digby dashed for the center of the wall. Kicking off with everything he had, he leapt nearly seven feet in the air to plant a foot halfway up the surface. His momentum carried him a couple steps further before he ran out.

Oh no! He slapped his fingertips down on the edge of the wall, just barely enough to find purchase. His boots found traction as he hoisted himself up. Swinging a leg over, Digby rolled his weight and dropped his foot down the other side to straddle the wall. He threw a hand down toward his accomplice to help her make the climb.

Rebecca hit the wall right behind him, running straight up the vertical surface without even needing help. She did have seven more points in agility than he did, after all. The illusionist's eyes widened as she simply rushed all the way to the top as if she was just as surprised by her physical prowess as Digby was. Blowing straight past him, she flailed her arms to find her balance as she came to a stop standing at the top.

They both turned around taking a last look at the base before dropping down on the other side. Digby landed with a thud, standing back up to flatten himself against the center of the wall.

Rebecca landed beside him. "Do you think anyone saw us?"

"We'll know in a minute or so." Digby leaned his head to one side, assuming that Skyline's guardians would be on them by then if their distraction had failed.

They both remained still for a few minutes, until it became clear that no one was in pursuit. "I think we're in the clear."

After waiting another minute for Rebecca's mana to replenish enough to cast Conceal, they stepped away from the wall. She shook her head and stared out into the surrounding desert. "Easton said there was a rest stop a little over twenty miles away."

Digby stepped forward before turning back to her. "We better start walking."

CHAPTER TWENTY-TWO

The twenty-mile journey through the desert was long.

After sprinting out of the base's camera range, Digby activated the necrotic armor of his Temporary Mass mutation. At first Rebecca questioned the need for it, but she figured it out quickly when he picked her up in a princess carry. The illusionist was level twenty-one and in good physical condition for a human, but a death march through the desert under the hot sun was still a significant test of constitution, especially with the lone water bottle that they had been able to take with them. It didn't make sense for her to overexert herself when he could travel the distance without getting tired.

The armor helped to keep his speed up while carrying the added weight of his fellow Heretic. He didn't smell great, especially to Rebecca's oversensitive nose, but she didn't argue with the result. Thanks to her Cartography spell and his undead endurance, they made the trek to the road and subsequent rest stop in just under five hours. Digby had to reform his necrotic armor halfway there after it fell apart under the strain of the continuous running. It failed a second time just as they reached the rest stop. Fortunately, the armor was no longer needed.

The place was nothing special, just a patch of pavement in the expanse of sun-drenched sand and rock. It offered a gas station and a few eateries to replenish the road's weary travelers. A group of twenty revenants huddled together in the shade of an overhang, while a single set of uneven footprints led off into the desert, painting a picture of the events that must have transpired there.

Most likely, in the first few days of the apocalypse, either a zombie or someone who'd been bitten had passed on the curse to the people that were taking refuge there. Everyone must have turned revenant at night and gotten trapped under the overhang when they were unable to leave with the sunlight beating down on the land in all directions. The zombie who started things off must have wandered off and left them behind.

No matter, the creatures would make a fine meal.

Digby approached the group of revenants as Rebecca headed into the gas station in search of food and water. Executing the weakened creatures would have been easy, yet, he stopped and checked his HUD.

MP: 156/156

"I wonder?"

Five Fingers of Death would take a third of his mana, but he felt the need to try it. The revenants were already cursed despite the fact they were still alive, so killing them with the spell should result in nothing but a corpse. Then again, if the added effect of Death's Embrace was able to somehow reapply the original curse, it might overwrite the hijacked version that Henwick had added into the mix.

Zombies were few and far between due to the fact that the revenants were more efficient killers and had a higher conversion rate. It was a situation that made forming a horde difficult. Though, if Death's Embrace was capable of replacing the curse, he might just be able to fill out his ranks.

There was only one way to be sure.

"Excuse me." Digby grabbed at the tattered garments that one of the revenants wore and dragged them, kicking and screaming, into the sunlight. The rest of the creatures reached out after him but failed to give chase, opting to remain in the shade. Digby threw his victim down and drove his fingers into them as soon as he'd gained enough distance. The revenant clawed at his arm but was too weak in the light to put up a real fight. "Easy now. Let's see if you have a future on the winning team."

He waited until he could feel his spell mingling with the creature's mana system before pulling his hand free.

1 dormant revenant defeated.

As the body lay still, he frowned at the lack of experience he received on account of his level.

"What are you doing?" Rebecca wandered out of the gas station chewing on some sort of protein bar and sipping a bottle of something blue.

"Wait." Digby held up a finger just as the revenant began to twitch.

"Oh wow." She dribbled her drink down her front. "That spell can reinfect revenants with the original curse."

"It seems so." Digby grinned as a new member of his horde staggered to its feet.

1 zombie revenant animated.
1 trait present.
NIGHT STALKER
As a zombie created from the corpse of a deceased
revenant, this minion will retain a portion of its attributes
associated with physical capabilities. Attributes will revert to
that of a normal zombie during daylight hours.
+8 Strength, +8 Defense, +4 Dexterity, +8 Agility, +5 Will.

Not bad.

The zombie had one of the traits that belonged to the last revenant he'd animated back in California. Sure, it had lost the ability to heal and it could only access its strength at night, but that was better than nothing. He glanced to his HUD as his new minion appeared on the list.

1 Zombie Revenant, 1 Skeleton, 2 Destroyers.

"What?" He shrieked as he read the list again, at a loss for words.

Other than his newest minion, all he had was Tavern and the two zombies he'd animated back in Vegas. He'd left Asher and Alex in charge so he hadn't really looked at his minion count since he left. He had set them both onto the path of the brute on account of his need for some quick muscle. Sure, he'd hoped that Alex and Asher would be able to procure enough food to get them to mutate, but he never expected anything more. Now though, it was clear that his apprentice and his feathered friend had been busy. They must have stumbled upon enough revenants for his minions to reach the mutation tier above brute.

A momentary jolt of fear streaked through his mind that the monsters might hurt someone in his absence, since Asher would have no power over another rare zombie. Then he remembered that he had animated the zombies personally. The fact that his mana still flowed through their systems would have maintained their complete loyalty.

Still, it was a bit of a shock.

He just couldn't believe Alex and Asher had been able to find enough food to make that much progress. Clearly, things had been eventful back in Vegas in his absence. He shoved the subject aside to be dealt with when he returned and opted to fill out his ranks a bit more.

Dragging another revenant into the sunlight, he cast Five Fingers of Death again to let Death's Embrace do its work. Once his new minion was on its feet, he used what was left of his mana to cast Burial. With the day flooding the world with life essence, his absorption rate was nearly nonexistent. Fortunately, the same wasn't true beneath the earth. Despite this tactic, his absorption rate was still slow.

That's irritating.

He opened his maw and cast Blood Forge to dig himself free of his grave. Once he was back on the surface, two more revenants joined the side of the dead. He buried himself again and repeated the process until he had another ten minions. The rest of the revenants were claimed by his maw since it didn't seem wise to remain there for too long and the effort of converting the creatures into viable members of his horde was time consuming. When he was done, he checked his void resources.

AVAILABLE RESOURCES
Sinew: 31
Flesh: 15
Bone: 28
Viscera: 15
Heart: 33
Mind: 27

He still had a way to go before he could take any of the mutations available in the Path of the Emissary that he'd discover a few days prior. For that matter, he hadn't leveled up in a while either, since killing guardians on the base was frowned upon. Hopefully something might change when he made it back to the casino.

The thought reminded him that they needed to get moving.

Once he and Rebecca had gathered everything they wanted to take from the rest stop's facilities, they loaded it all into the cargo compartment of a large truck. They might have taken something smaller, but with his new minions coming along, they needed the passenger room. Finishing up, Rebecca struggled to figure out the steering mechanism for a few minutes before pulling the vehicle onto the road.

The view from his window held nothing but desert until, finally, he saw casinos on the horizon.

CHAPTER TWENTY-THREE

"Alright, where's Alex?" Digby dropped out of the cargo truck that he and Rebecca had traveled back to Vegas in.

"Who are you?" A man that Digby didn't recognize stopped him at the door, holding a rifle while a second stood guard at his side.

He deflated, realizing that a side effect of trying to keep himself out of the spotlight was that the majority of the people at the casino wouldn't recognize him. It probably didn't help that his necrotic armor had made him smell so bad that Rebecca had needed to drive with the windows of the truck open.

I suppose I can't just declare myself lord and boss people around now, can I? Digby shook off the thought and tried again. "Excuse me, sir. I am an acquaintance of your leader, Deuce, and I need to discuss a number of things with him."

One of the men gagged as he got close while the other covered his nose.

"Yes, I smell terrible. Let's all call attention to it." Digby threw up his hands. That was when Mason appeared in the door, rushing out to meet him.

"You're back, did you get what we—" He skidded to a stop and pulled his shirt up over his nose. "Woah, man, you reek."

"Tell me about it, I was just stuck in a truck with him for several hours." Rebecca stepped forward to greet the soldier.

"You don't smell great either." Mason kept her at arm's length.

"Good lord, people, there are more important things at stake than how we smell." Digby pouted and tapped a foot.

"Okay, sure, let's get somewhere that we can talk freely." Mason beckoned for him to come inside and told the two guards by the door it was alright. "I'll get Alex and Parker on the horn. They should be able to wrap up what they're doing and get back in about an hour. That's, um, plenty for a shower. I'll gather everyone together in the high-roller suite."

"Where is Alex?" Digby arched an eyebrow as he followed him through the door. "Also, what is a zombie destroyer?"

"Oh, that." Mason let out an awkward laugh before shaking his head. "I should probably let Alex explain it when he gets back. He took a little trip to the other end of the strip to deal with something."

"Fine, then. I will meet you in an hour after I have bathed, if that will satisfy you people." Digby rolled his eyes, annoyed that everyone was so focused on his hygiene. They never said a word about it back when he looked like a corpse. It was as if regaining his human appearance had somehow placed a higher expectation upon him.

Mason cringed as he turned his attention to Rebecca. "You might want to go shower as well."

"Oh really?" She squinted at him for a moment before letting out a sigh. "You're probably right. Plus I have a USB drive full of stolen intel to look over. I should at least read though some of it before we meet."

"Before you go." Mason stopped her. "I did a little looting in the shopping center and found something you might like, so I left it in your room."

"Oh really?" she repeated, this time with a mischievous grin and a wink. "Is it something for later?"

"No, it's nothing weird. Get your mind out of the gutter." He shook his head at her.

"Ah, something practical then." She sounded disappointed as she shrugged and headed off toward her room.

Digby started for his as well before stopping to remove the sword and Skyline armor he'd stolen from the base. He dropped the chest protector to his feet and shoved the sword into Mason's arm. A bit of necrotic tissue leftover from his armor dangled from its hilt. "Here, I thought you could use an upgrade."

"Thanks." Mason's face soured. "I'll go wash this."

"You do that." Digby laughed as he walked off. "And have someone move my truck. The cargo in the back might need to eat something soon."

Climbing the stairs, he found Lana leaning against the wall as if waiting for him. She must have seen him arrive and headed up to catch him before he got busy with something.

"You didn't find him?" She stepped closer, making no mention of how he smelled. "Alvin, I mean."

"I did, but I wasn't able to get him or Hawk out before having to flee." Digby grimaced, still irritated that he hadn't been able to achieve more.

"Damn it." She deflated.

"I'm sorry." Digby dropped his eyes to the floor.

She let out a sigh. "You don't have to apologize. I lived at the base for weeks and couldn't find a way to get to him. I know what you were up against."

Digby raised his head and looked her in the eyes. "I have no intent of letting things lie. We're meeting in an hour upstairs to discuss how to proceed. Why don't you join us? It can't hurt to have an ex-guardian present."

"I will." She sounded sad. Digby didn't blame her. He wasn't feeling good about the outcome either.

Leaving Lana behind, Digby made his way back to his room, peeled off the uniform he'd stolen and stepped into the shower to wash away the day's grime. Once he was clean again, he threw on a new shirt and vest and headed for the high-roller suite early. He found Parker sleeping with her head face down on the poker table when he arrived. There were packs of cards sitting nearby, with a mess of poker chips scattered across the felt.

"Busy day?" Digby slapped the felt next to her head to wake her up.

"Hey what yeah!" Her head shot up the instant he hit the table. There was a playing card stuck to her forehead. After gasping a few lungfuls of air, she settled down and waved. "Oh hi, Dig."

"Hi." He waved back and sat down across the table. "How's the forge?"

"Good." She nodded with enthusiasm. "We have a new method of heating so we don't need fuel."

"Really?" Digby arched an eyebrow.

She nodded again. "Alex got his Heat Object spell ranked up while you were gone, so we are using magic now. All we had to do was set up a space that can withstand the temperature. We haven't made anything yet, but we should have a new staff for you real soon."

"That would certainly be helpful." Digby leaned back in his chair as Mason walked into the room, carrying a shopping bag in one hand and his new sword in the other.

"When you're done with Dig's staff, think you could try to make a copy of this?" The soldier set the sword down on the table. It had been cleaned thoroughly.

She picked it up and pulled the blade from its sheath. "I can try."

Sax, Deuce, and Elenore filtered in after that to catch him up on the casino's situation. Their combat force was small but coming along. They weren't in any way ready to make a move against their enemies, but the volunteers were at least starting to get organized to a point where they understood a chain of command.

His accomplices had divided up their roles to get everything done. Mason was in charge of bringing up their newly minted armed forces while Deuce and Elenore had focused on keeping their new home stable and protected. Fortunately, the people had been fairly cooperative and willing to work together to survive. It didn't hurt that they now had enough to eat and a safe place to sleep.

They still sent out patrols to deal with threats on the strip, but other than the occasional lightwalker, they didn't have too much to deal with. That was when Alex pushed through the door.

Asher darted in behind him.

The deceased raven made straight for the table, landing in front of Digby with an excited caw. She hopped from side to side and flapped her wings to get his attention. A thought traveled across their bond.

Returned, returned.

"Aww, I missed you too." He picked her up and placed her on his shoulder where she could nuzzle against his cheek. "Have you been good while I was gone?"

"She has been extremely helpful, actually." Alex pulled up a chair without hesitation. "Though she could probably do less shouting."

"Shouting?" Digby arched an eyebrow.

"Yes, apparently she talks when you aren't around to translate for her." Alex nodded. "She has no control over volume though."

"Well, that is impressive." Digby scratched at the bird's side as he let Alex continue.

Alex leaned forward, seeming more confident than he'd been when Digby had left. It made him look like he belonged at the table with the rest of their group's leaders. "Asher has been sweeping the city surrounding the strip and compelling every zombie roaming around to converge at one of the hotels on the other end of the strip. The dead were spread pretty thin, but thanks to her they have come back together to form a modest horde."

"How many teeth?" Digby grabbed a poker chip from the table and turned it over in his hand.

"We have well over two hundred and growing." Alex draped one arm over the back of his chair. "Plus, Parker and I found a massive hive of revenants down the street."

"A hive?" Digby's eyes widened, concerned that the situation might become dangerous.

"It's nothing to worry about." The artificer shook his head. "Apparently Rivers had his high-cards tie up a bunch of innocent people in there to lure the creatures in before welding the place shut. They're trapped in there now, and haven't been able to get out. I've got a team using crossbows and ropes to harpoon the revenants and drag them out a few at a time during the day. Your minions have been eating nonstop." He pumped his eyebrows. "They're getting big. I even got a level out of it. The dormant revenants aren't worth much XP, but there are plenty in there to make some progress."

"So that's how I ended up with two destroyers listed on my HUD?" Digby relaxed again.

"Yup." Alex held his hands out wide to indicate some sort of scale. "You will need to come see, because saying they're huge really doesn't describe it well enough. The only downside is that neither of the destroyers have much intelligence. They seem to have lost whatever bond points you put into their mental stats when they mutated. I'm just glad that they are under your control, or else I would probably be dead. But on the upside, they're big enough to take down even a rare revenant."

"Well, now you have me excited." Digby smiled. "Oh, and I have a few new minions in the truck I left outside. I discovered a new spell that lets me animate corpses as long as I'm the one that kills them. It even works on revenants, despite them being cursed already. I can't distribute bond points but they are able to retain some of their attributes at night and I don't have to sacrifice any mana. We'll have to take my new minions to your little feeding zone as well, since they will remain completely under my control after they mutate. They're not real bright, but it will be good to get some extra muscle."

"I can do that." Alex nodded. "Can a couple become leaders? Asher could use some help keeping the horde in line. I've kind of been bitten a few times today while trying to get the rest of the horde secured in one of the other casinos."

"Yes, that would be wise." Digby considered the problem. "I'll try to get my minions to fill the roles we need. I'd say one leader for every hundred commons would keep the horde well under control. Beyond that, I could also use some devourers, and I'd love to find out what tier comes after lurker at some point."

"I'm kind of curious too." Alex nodded.

"Same," Parker added.

Lana entered the room just as they finished discussing resources. She kept to the side of the room and settled down on one of the stools by the bar. That was when Digby noticed Rebecca was late.

Now where the hell is my tardy illusionist? He watched the door while the rest of the group talked about various tasks that didn't concern him. Rebecca poked her head in a few minutes later. She didn't say anything or give a reason why she was late, but Digby couldn't help but notice that she was avoiding eye contact with everyone.

Another detail he noticed was a change in clothing. Up until now, she had mostly worn a pair of denim trousers and complained about being uncomfortable, but now, she'd changed into some sort of tights.

Mason leaned over the back of his chair to talk to her. "So, how do you like them?"

Rebecca took a moment to respond before bringing her attention to him. "What?"

"The leggings, are they good or are they not your style?" He fidgeted a little in his seat.

"Oh, ah, yeah." She dropped her eyes down to her knees. "They're good."

"Um, okay." Mason turned back around, clearly expecting a more enthusiastic response for his thoughtfulness.

Digby arched an eyebrow at the woman, wondering what might have happened between now and an hour ago. Eventually, he put the question aside and stood to address the room.

"Alright, now that everyone is here. We need to discuss what the hell we're going to do next. Rebecca and I were able to make it inside Autem's secure facility, but we were forced to flee before we were able to spring Hawk and Alvin. Not only that, but we were unable to find the Heretic Seed's fragments."

"Can we sneak you guys back in?" Alex raised his hand.

"Not likely." Digby shook his head. "We may have exposed a few of the holes in their security and how lax some of their forces have become." Digby gestured to the poker chips that were strewn all over the table as a representation of their forces. Then he collected them up into several neat and organized stacks. He placed one more in the center to signify Bancroft. "No, our friend the commander will have shored things up by the time we make it back there. The guardians will be more vigilant. Hell, the only reason we were able to move around under their noses was that it was unthinkable that we might be there."

"Were you able to find anything useful out while you were inside, like where the Seed might be?" Alex chimed in.

"Or a weak point that we could exploit to get back in?" Mason added.

"I should let our expert field that one." Digby gestured to Rebecca, hoping she had found something more in the information she was able to steal off Autem's computers. He remained silent as he waited for her to take over. After a few seconds of silence from the woman, he snapped his fingers in her direction. "Becky, we are waiting."

She shook her head in surprise. "Sorry, what was—"

"Tell the people what we've found out." Digby swept a hand through the air in frustration.

"Oh, yeah." She nodded as if lost in her own world before coming back to reality. "The Seed is being kept in a facility that Autem calls Babel. From what I can tell, it is some sort of secure area where they keep dangerous items. The location, however, is a little vague. It's mentioned a few times in their communications, some of which make it sound like a separate facility, but the flight logs don't line up to back that up. I think it's definitely on part of the base."

"Maybe they just don't let many people in." Parker slouched in her chair.

"That's a possibility, and if we allow ourselves to operate under that assumption, then there is a strong possibility that we found the entrance."

"The golden elevator," Digby chimed in, getting several puzzled looks in return. He tapped a finger on the table and turned back to Rebecca. "Can you use Waking Dream to show everyone your map of the base?"

She stood from her chair and cast the spell, filling the table with a three-dimensional map of their target.

"Woah." Deuce took a step away from the table.

"That's new." Elenore did the same.

"You get used to it." Parker yawned.

"Indeed." Digby stood up so he could direct the planning. "The elevator we need to get to is here." He stabbed a finger down into the image of Autem's secure facility. "However, to get there, we have to get through multiple locked doors. The first is protected by a guard as well as auto turrets and temperature sensors. We managed to sneak past this barrier by hiding in a dinner cart, but that is no longer an option, so we'll need to find another way."

"What about the other two doors?" Alex stood up to peer over the illusionary map.

"The second door is easier, we just need a guardian ring that holds a high enough level of clearance." Digby pulled the ring he'd accidentally stolen from his pocket. "We used this one when we were in there last time, but my guess is that its access has been revoked."

"And what about the third door?" Alex piled another question on.

"That's the worst of them." Digby shook his head. "We never made it past that one. And the only person we know for certain has access is level forty and a class we haven't seen before."

"What class?" Alex raised his head from the map.

"She's a seer." Rebecca rejoined the conversation. "We don't know what she can do, but her perception is high enough to see through my illusion spells." She sighed. "And that isn't even the worst of it."

"What do you mean?" Digby raised an eyebrow.

"Easton messaged us while we were on our way back here. Both Skyline and Autem have drastically increased security. There's more guards and checkpoints all over."

"I figured as much. Even if we can get back in, we won't be able to move around like before." Digby stared down at the map and scratched at his chin.

Rebecca pulled an ace of spades from a deck of cards on the

table and placed it down at the back of the base. "I could still Conceal a small team and slip over here, through the wall's blind spot, but we'll be sitting ducks once we're inside. There's a limit to how many people I can conceal our group from and the security will be on high alert, which will make Waking Dream less reliable."

"On top of that, we'd have taken out some of Autem's personnel so we can use their rings to get through the gates that stand in the way of this elevator." Mason rubbed a hand on his forehead. "All while remaining undetected."

"Plus, we don't know what kind of security will be waiting for us on whatever floor that elevator lets us off at." Alex stared back down, looking stressed.

"Indeed. It certainly seems to be a bit of a challenge. Not to mention we will need to acquire Hawk and Alvin before we're even able to make a run at the elevator." Digby sat down too, feeling the pressure of the situation as it added up.

For a moment, he started to feel like the whole endeavor may have been a mistake. A swell of dread rolled through his chest, reminding him that he had been the one to give the people around them hope. He swallowed it back down, chasing off the usual doubts that had always held him back.

Two weeks ago, he would have shut himself in his room and wallowed in self-pity. He would let everyone down, that was the pattern that had plagued him for his entire life. Things were different now. No one expected much from him back then, but now, well, people believed in him. Even Rufus, that decrepit zombie master back in California, had told him that he was what the world needed. Granted, the old fool had also called him sneaky and underhanded. Digby assumed he meant it as a compliment.

That being said, the situation was still quite bleak. Even the glamorous thieves from the heist film Digby had watched would have struggled to come up with an elegant solution to the obstacles laying in their way.

That was when a crooked grin crept onto his face.

"Security doors, guards, Autem, Skyline." He listed off every-thing before slapping his hand down on the table. "What does all that matter?"

"Umm, kind of a lot." Alex eyed him sideways.

"But do they, though?" Digby tilted his head from side to side. "I'll remind you that the only reason we were able to walk amongst them for as long as we did was because they thought they were untouchable and had let their guard down."

"What's your point?" Rebecca stared at him blankly. "We just kicked the hornets' nest and now they're better protected than ever."

"Exactly, which means that they're back to thinking they're safe and that we won't be able to sneak back in under their nose."

"So?" She cocked her head to one side.

"So why bother?" Digby held out both arms. "You see, they are expecting us to try to slip past their security again. And they have set up obstacles to catch us. So why should we walk into their trap? Why should we play by the rules when we can just as easily cheat?"

"I'm sorry, what?" Alex failed to follow his line of thought.

"I say we abandon the stealth approach." Digby raked a hand through the illusionary map on the table. "I say we go to war."

Rebecca nearly choked. "With what army?"

"The horde." Digby smiled.

Mason's mouth dropped open. "The horde is only a couple hundred."

"Indeed. But with my new spell, I can change that. We'll have to play catch up a little, but if I can convert the revenants from that hive Alex found into the dead, we could bolster our forces enough to rival Skyline in under a week." He picked up two decks of playing cards and bent them with his fingers so that they flew into the air to land all over the table, surrounding the stacks of poker chips he'd placed earlier. "Once the odds are in our favor, we can march the horde right down their throat. Might even be able to win if we can add some uncommon zombies into the mix."

"They would get mowed down before they can get close." Mason held up both hands empty as if he had just stated the obvious. "The destroyers will probably make it but there's only so much damage they can do."

"What if we sent in the kestrel first?" Alex pointed to the front gate in Rebecca's illusion. "The aircraft's weapons could take out some of their defenses."

"It would get shot down," Rebecca added.

"So fly it by remote," Parker chimed in. "We could load it with the explosives Rivers has been hoarding, too."

Rebecca tilted her head back and forth. "The internet is becoming really unreliable. So flying it by remote could fail."

"I say that's still worth the risk." Digby snapped his fingers.

"We could load the destroyers into a couple trucks too. Then we can get your zombies to drive and ram them right through the gates." Parker let out a laugh. "That would surprise the hell out of Bancroft."

"I'd say so." Digby laughed along with her. "And while he's scrambling to get the situation under control, we hit this Autem's facility and reclaim Hawk and Alvin."

"What if the horde isn't enough?" Mason stroked his beard. "I mean, we've seen what Bancroft can do with a couple hundred guardians."

"Then we steal a kestrel from their airfield and run for the hills." Digby cackled. "At the very least, we might cripple Skyline to a point where it will be more trouble than it's worth for Henwick to rebuild his army of hired goons. And without Skyline to do the grunt work, it will set Autem back weeks. By the time they get back on track, we should be able to figure out the secrets of the Heretic Seed. With that, I hope to gain the power to create more magic users to join our ranks. We could actually have a viable army built up in no time."

"That actually could set us up." Mason dropped his hand from his beard.

"Indeed." Digby let a smug tone enter into his voice. "I don't like the idea of sacrificing my minions, but with the Seed's fragment and Hawk and Alvin on the line, I won't hesitate. Especially if there's a chance to bring victory a little closer within reach."

"He's right." Lana backed him up. "And I'm not just saying that because I want my brother back. There's plenty of risk involved, but it might be worth it if we can get that kind of advantage."

"Exactly." Digby shrugged. "Besides, we don't really have a choice."

"When have we ever?" Alex stood up to stand beside him.

"That is also true." Digby turned to Rebecca, expecting a sarcastic but supportive comment. The illusionist, however, remained silent staring at the floor again.

No matter.

Clearly something was preventing her from taking her usual place as his voice of reason, but he decided not to pry. Besides, they had preparations to make, and the sooner they got started, the sooner they got the job done. For once, the fact that he didn't need sleep would prove to be valuable.

From here on out, every second needed to count.

With everyone in agreement, they broke off to get to work.

Digby grinned as he flicked one of the stacks of poker chips so that they toppled over onto the others. The piles fell across the table in an avalanche that left them dispersed amongst the cards that littered the felt. It would all come down to a gamble.

He snatched one chip from the center.

Now let's see who has the better hand.

CHAPTER TWENTY-FOUR

Becca snapped her laptop shut as soon as Digby was finished speaking and made for the door.

She had to get out of there.

More talking wasn't something she could bear.

It wasn't that she didn't care.

The zombie's plan was important, but she just couldn't focus. Not after what she'd found in the files that she'd stolen from Autem's network.

She needed to be alone.

Running to her room, she darted inside and collapsed against the door. Tears welled up as she clutched her laptop to her chest.

"Stop that."

She blinked to regain control before setting her computer down in her lap and opening the file that Autem had compiled on her. According to them, she was a mediocre drone operator with a problem following Skyline's orders. There were numerous notations stating that she seemed to think she was smarter than those who were in charge. She had been successfully desensitized to the violence and suffering of others, but her defiant nature made her nearly unusable.

None of that was new. Her failures had already been laid bare back in Seattle when Skyline had thrown her away. No, that information was not news, or at least, it wasn't anything that would make her run from the others and hide in her room.

Her chest ached as she clicked on a folder labeled 'unapproved communications.' A massive list of scanned images filled the screen.

Letters.

Each image was of a handwritten letter from her parents.

Her family.

The people that had sold her into Skyline's service. The people that she had forgotten years ago when their letters stopped coming. The people that had abandoned her. The people that had surely died only a month ago with the rest of the world.

"It was a lie."

She scrambled to her dresser and pulled out the one letter that she'd kept. Back in Seattle, she'd stored the notes her parents wrote in a shoe box and shoved it under her bed. A part of her had wanted to leave them all behind, still hurt by the belief that they had forgotten her. She still wasn't sure why she'd saved one. It wasn't like she intended to read it again. Despite that, she'd grabbed one at random and stuffed it in a bag with the rest of her worldly possessions.

Pulling the letter out, she read the date.

September.

It was one of the last letters that Skyline had passed on to her before claiming that they had stopped coming. Rebecca tossed it aside, clicked an image file dated December, a few months after her parents had supposedly stopped writing.

———

Dear Becca,

We set up the Christmas tree today and I found the ornament you made back in kindergarten. I know it's just craft paper and toothpicks, but we put it in a prominent place so it would stand out. I know you're probably having your own holiday

activities with your classmates at Skyline, but we wanted you to know that we were thinking of you.

You always loved the holidays. Your father and I were just reminiscing about the time you went downstairs at four in the morning one Christmas to open all the presents by yourself. You just had to know what was inside. You even opened the ones that didn't have your name on them. I know we made you sit in a corner afterward, but thinking back it was still cute. You could never resist investigating something once you got it in your mind that you wanted to know.

We've been trying to arrange a visit to see you, but Skyline said that you'll be busy with training until the beginning of next year. We'll check back with them then. The holidays will feel a little empty without you, but we know you're learning important things and that a future at Skyline is a great opportunity. So we're doing our best to keep a place for you here at home so you can visit when you have the time.

Also, I'd love it if you could maybe send us a letter back, just to let us know you're happy and doing okay.

Love,
Mom

———

Rebecca read that last line over.

"But I did write… I wrote letters almost every day."

She clenched her jaw tight. Skyline hadn't delivered her letters either. Her parents must have thought she stopped writing too. Her eyes welled up again as she clicked on another image dated a couple months later.

———

Dear Becca,

I'm so sorry that we weren't able to work out a visit. We had a date set up but Skyline had to cancel at the last minute. They've been a little difficult to communicate with lately. Honestly, we're getting a little frustrated. When we entered you into their training program, there was supposed to be a visitation schedule set up. Your father and I keep trying to get a new date in place, but they don't seem to be making it a priority. We know that this program is good for your future, especially considering how bad the employment situation has been these last few years, but still, we've been starting to worry if this was the right choice.

We're not mad that you haven't written back, we know you're busy. Though, we'd love nothing more than to hear from you. We'll keep trying to get a date set up in Skyline's schedule. Hopefully they will have an opening. We love you so much and we can't wait to see you. I hope we can make that happen soon.

———

Becca stabbed the touch pad of her laptop with a finger to close the image. She had never heard anything about scheduled days being canceled. Skyline must have been stringing her parents along to keep them from making things difficult. They never had any intent of letting them see her.

She moved the cursor over another image file and tapped the touch pad to open it. This one was from her father.

———

Becca,

I'm so sorry. We both are.

It has become clear that Skyline is being intentionally difficult when communicating and scheduling with us. We're starting to suspect that they aren't even delivering our letters. We fear they might be doing the same to you. We haven't received anything from you for months and, despite how busy Skyline says you are, we find it hard to believe that the same girl that stayed up past her bedtime every night pleading for me to read to her would forget about us so easily.

I know my daughter, and that just isn't her.

I've been trying to push for more information and communication, but Skyline has been blocking every effort. At this point, we don't see any other option but to pursue legal action against them. As much as it pained us, we have decided to dip into the money that Skyline gave us when we signed the agreement on your training. We originally planned to keep it all in an account for your future but with our income being what it is, we can't afford the legal fees that are starting to pile up.

We just hope you'll forgive us when we're able to get you back home where you belong. I know it's unlikely that you'll even receive this letter, but I'm writing it anyway. At the very least, whatever analyst Skyline has screening them will see the pain that they are causing our family.

Despite everything, we both hope and pray that you're doing well. We love you and always will, no matter what stands between us.

Love,
Your Mom and Dad

———

Rebecca let a tear fall. They hadn't sold her off like she thought. They didn't even spend the money they'd been paid until they had tried to get her back. She'd thought the worst of them and didn't even know.

She spent the next hour going through each letter, piecing together a heartbreaking story of how her parents struggled to win against the monster that was Skyline. It had taken them months to find a lawyer that was even willing to take the case after hearing what they were up against. They weren't even part of a reputable firm. Just an ambulance chaser that found something sympathetic in her parent's story.

Anger flared with each letter she read. Skyline had effortlessly blocked every case they raised. Her father had even tried to get the media involved.

Following the documents within her personal file, Rebecca found a mountain of legal information and internal communication from Skyline's side of each case. They had so many people in their pockets that her parents never stood a chance. Between members of the courts, politicians, and media outlets, they held enough sway to keep her parents in check.

Eventually, Skyline put an end to it all by signing a kill order on their lawyer. His death was ruled an accident but she had the documents that proved that it wasn't.

The letters from her parents took a turn after that. They were still loving and kind, but it was clear that the fight had been beaten out of them. By the end of it, they had spent twice the amount that they were paid by Skyline and were left with nothing to show for it.

Feeling like someone had driven a stake through her heart, she read over a short letter that summed things up.

———

Becca,

I'm so sorry. We both are.

Your mother and I believed everything that Skyline had told us. We never thought they would do this. They just told us how much potential you had and we signed you away like idiots. The knowledge of what we've done haunts us. We can only hope that someday you might forgive us.

––––––

Rebeca closed the file, unable to read the rest. It hurt too much to finish. She skipped a couple years ahead in the hope that her parents had found some sort of peace or closure.

To her surprise, they actually had, sort of.

Reading further she found that, in losing her, they had sought to help others. It wasn't true closure, but they had at least found a way to cope. They had moved away from Vegas and found new jobs. Her mother had started work as an adoption counselor working in the California foster system. Her father had taken a job as a nurse.

Eventually, their letters began to feel a little more upbeat. It wasn't that they had forgotten the pain of losing her, but more, that they had found a way to fill the hole in their lives. They even started fostering kids themselves.

To her surprise, a part of her was actually happy for them. She scrolled all the way down to the bottom of the folder's image files and clicked on one of the most recent scans. It was dated three months ago.

––––––

Hi Becca,

It has been a little while since we've written last. We hope you're doing well. We're still doing the best we can. You probably won't get to read this but we wanted to update you on some exciting news.

You're getting a brother.

Your mother is having the adoption paperwork finalized this week. We hope that you will get to meet him. He's really bright and funny. He reminds us of you in a way, though, he's also a smartass and a klepto, so there are some differences. He's getting better though, and he's settling in well. We hope you get to meet him someday.

Obviously we can never replace you, but sometimes a kid comes through the system here that needs a home and a second chance. The best we can do is try to give him what we weren't able to give you.

Your mom and I wish you all the love in the world. And we can't wait for the day that we get to see you again. Skyline can't lock you away from the world forever.

Love,
Your family

————

Tears ran down Rebecca's cheeks as she read over that last part. They had hope until the very end. They had even found a kind of happiness.

"I have a brother."

She smiled on reflex, catching herself off guard. She wasn't prepared for how happy the news made her.

Then her stomach turned.

The last letter in the folder had been written just a few months before the world ended. Rebecca covered her mouth, feeling a wave of nausea sweep through her. It didn't matter if her parents found closure or if she forgave them.

It was already too late.

They were probably dead.

She struggled to hold back tears. It was almost worse than believing they had sold her off and forgotten about her.

"I had a brother."

She gasped through her fingers. He might not have been related by blood, but still, she felt as if something had been taken from her. It was like Skyline had stolen her family all over again.

A knock at the door pulled her out of the despair that had begun to set in. She buried her face in the crook of her elbow to dry her eyes. The last thing she needed was Digby or someone barging into her room right now. She couldn't bear a conversation. Not while she had so much to sort out in her head.

Mason's voice followed. "Hey Becca, you in there?"

A part of her wanted to stay silent, not wanting to talk about what she'd learned. She wasn't ready to open up like that. Mason had probably lost family as well but they hadn't talked about it. Seeking physical comfort was one thing, but sharing her pain was another.

He knocked again when she failed to answer. "Hello? I was pretty sure I saw you come up here."

She bit down on her lip. He wasn't going away. After a third knock, she pushed aside her laptop and composed herself the best she could. Once she was ready, answered the door.

"Oh, you are here." Mason stood in the hallway with a bag in his hands. "You ducked out of things downstairs pretty fast, so I thought I'd come up and check on you."

"I'm fine, no need to be checked on." She held the door halfway open and stood in the way so that he wouldn't get the idea that he should come in.

"Sure, sure." He scratched at the back of his neck with one hand before raising the bag he carried in the other. "I thought about what you said earlier and made a trip down to the shopping center. I…" He glanced around for a second. "I picked you up something a little less practical. If you know what I mean."

Becca frowned. He'd picked the worst possible moment to do something cute, leaving her trapped and unsure how to respond. "Listen, I'm kind of busy, but I'll see you tomorrow."

"You okay?" He reached out to stop her from closing the door.

"I'm fine." She nodded, trying to hide behind a false smile.

"Umm. Okay." Mason hesitated, clearly seeing through her. "If there's anything you want to talk about, I'm here for you."

"I didn't ask you to be," she snapped without meaning to.

Mason's face fell along with his tone. "Okay then, I can take a hint."

"You don't have to be like that. I just want a night to myself." Becca tried to make herself clear without getting into things. "It's not like we're serious or anything."

"Ah, okay." Mason set the bag he'd brought with him down at her feet. The hurt on his face was evident. "I, umm, must have misread some things. I don't want to pressure you, so I'll leave this here. We probably moved a little fast anyway. I can give you some space."

His words cut like a knife, making her feel worse. Despite that, all she did was nod and let him go without saying anything else. That seemed to be the easiest option to put an end to the conversation without having to dig any deeper.

Becca reached down and dragged the shopping bag that he'd left into her room. She closed the door as soon as she could and slid down the other side, leaning her back against it.

Looking inside the bag, she found a bottle of wine, a block of cheese and a package of fancy smoked sausage. Underneath was a sexy yet tasteful bra and panty set.

The bag's contents would've made for a romantic evening. She sighed, wishing she had been in the mood for it. Wishing that she hadn't pushed him away.

Becca stared up at the ceiling, alone with the thoughts.

"Why am I like this?"

CHAPTER TWENTY-FIVE

Hawk snuck down the hall of Autem's training facility. There wasn't an actual need to sneak since he was only on his way to the bathroom, but according to his class information it was probable that he would become a rogue when he reached level fifteen. As such, stealth had become a top priority. Especially considering he wasn't sure how long he was going to be there.

Evil or not, Autem had given him something, and he was going to get the most out of it while he had the chance.

After receiving a message on the phone that had been smuggled to him, worry started to set in. Becca and Digby had been forced to leave without him, leaving him stuck waiting for them to find another way to come get him. With that in mind, he'd focused on being a model recruit so that no one would suspect he was up to no good.

Training had been simple so far, which made sense. They were kids, after all. It wasn't like Autem was going to throw them at a swarm of revenants to either die or gain levels. Mostly he'd only been subjected to a tour of the facility. There was a combat room where they held controlled exercises with monsters, but he was a way off from being sent in to one of those. Instead, he and the newer guardians sat through classes to explain how their abilities worked and what Autem stood for.

Despite reminding him of school, Hawk was actually interested in the subject matter. Learning about magic was certainly more fun than algebra or whatever shit they had tried to teach him before. It was like he'd been sent off to Hogwarts. Well… if Hogwarts was a military organization that trained young wizards to help dominate the world for generations to come in the service of some sort of religious-based empire.

That was the part that he didn't care for. As much as he liked having magic, Autem's goal was clear. The empire was meant to be a place populated by people that believed all the same things and would follow the rules without question. They didn't say it in those exact words, but Hawk had listened to enough adults talk to read between the lines. Not only that, but the way they spoke about outsiders rubbed him the wrong way.

They almost seemed to look down on them.

Even Skyline.

The long and short of it was, if you weren't a follower of Autem, then you weren't worthy of having a place in the world that they were creating. It was like everyone else was somehow unclean.

Religious stuff had always bothered him, and the people at Autem weren't the first to try to shove their beliefs down his throat. Hawk had been in plenty of foster homes that tried to make a good church-goer out of him. Honestly, it felt like they cared more about bringing in new members than actually helping kids. Some of them were downright cruel about it.

It wasn't like every church person he'd met was bad or anything. It just seemed like religion could hurt just as much as it could help. Still though, he had a hard time trusting anyone that put some god or whatever ahead of the people in their lives.

Autem, however, was on a whole new level.

The basic stuff was similar to what he'd learned during his time in various foster homes. Autem believed in heaven and hell, and a god that ruled over everything. Sin was bad, and serving the will of that god was good.

The part that got weird was The Nine.

Believing in some guy in the sky that sent you to hell was one thing, but The Nine was something else. Unlike the religions that Hawk understood, Autem went further than just believing and having faith. They actually claimed it was real. That it was all a fact.

According to the instructor of one of his classes, Nine angels appeared to Autem's founders to tell them that humanity was in need of guidance. That people couldn't be trusted to choose the right path. They had too many differences and believed so many different things that there was no way they would survive if left alone. Someone had to keep them in line.

That was Autem at its core.

They were an organization dedicated to saving humanity from itself by any means necessary. Even worse, the majority of the kids in the training facility had swallowed everything without argument. Some of them had even turned their backs on their own families.

Hawk shrugged it all off.

It was all so stupid. Especially considering that Autem had been the ones that had spread Digby's curse through the world. They were a bunch of hypocrites just like most of the adults he'd known. You don't save humanity by killing most of the world's population.

Hawk wished he was back in Vegas, which was why he was currently sneaking to the bathroom.

Classes were done and the recruits had all been sent back to their bunks for the night. Hawk had stuffed his phone into his pocket and headed to the bathroom to check if Dig had sent him a message. He reached for the device as soon as he made it inside, only to hide it back in his pocket when he saw that the bathroom was occupied by a boy he knew.

Alvin stood by the sink.

"Ah, hey man." Hawk tried to act friendly.

Alvin responded with a nod. The older boy was pretty quiet most of the time, but he didn't seem like a bad kid. It was just hard to figure out where he stood.

Hawk ducked into one of the stalls before the moment got

awkward. Checking his phone, he frowned when he saw his inbox was empty. He'd really been hoping to hear from Digby. He let out a sigh just as a new message popped onto the screen. A smile filled his face for a second before flipping over when he saw that it wasn't from Dig. Instead, it was signed by Lana. All it said was three words.

Is Alvin okay?

Hawk took a breath and decided to go out on a limb. Slowly, he stepped back out of the stall and checked to make sure there was no one else there. "Hey Alvin?"

"Yes?" He looked back over his shoulder from where he stood at the sink.

"What if you could see your sister sooner rather than later?" Hawk held the phone in his hands without trying to hide it.

Alvin looked down at the device then back to his face. "What's that?"

"It's a phone." He shook his head. "But that doesn't matter. What does is I've met your sister and I know she wants to see you."

"She can see me when our schedules match up. She's not that far away." He sounded calm but the sad look in his eyes told Hawk to push harder.

"She's not on the base." Hawk shook his head again. "She deserted and she's working with some people to come rescue you. She sent me a message asking if you were okay."

Alvin furrowed his brow. "What do you mean? Autem told me—"

"They lied." Hawk stepped closer.

"Why would she leave? We're safe here." Alvin took a step away. "What we're doing is important."

"No, it isn't." Hawk pushed further. "Autem is the reason the world ended. I don't know everything, but they aren't the good guys. Your sister wouldn't have left if they were." He shoved the phone into Alvin's hands. "Talk to her and find out for yourself. She just messaged me to ask if you were okay, so I'm willing to bet that she'll write back fast."

Alvin stared down at the screen of the device, his eyes darting back and forth as if reading his sister's question over and over again. He started typing a second later.

Hawk let out a relieved sigh when he saw the boy's face soften. It was like a month's worth of loneliness had just melted away.

"Here, take it in the stall so no one sees." Hawk stepped aside. "Talk to her as long as you want and pass the phone back to me tomorrow. Just don't let anyone see it."

Alvin nodded, looking shocked. Then, he stepped into the stall and closed the door.

Hawk leaned to the door. "My friends are going to come for us, and if we work together, we can get out of here. You'll get to see your sister once we're out."

"Okay," Alvin said quietly from inside.

Hawk could hear him tapping away at the phone's touch screen. The sound made him feel a little better. He may not have gotten a message from Dig, but it made him feel warmer knowing that Alvin would get to talk to Lana after being separated for so long. He may not have had much of a family, but he knew how important it could be.

———

Alvin listened as Hawk exited the bathroom. Then, he looked back down at the screen in his hands.

He deleted the message he'd been typing before entering a simple, I'm okay, and hitting send. He didn't know what else to write. Words had never come easily for him.

Plus, he already knew that his sister wasn't on the base anymore. He'd been told that she defected earlier that day. It had been just after breakfast, when that man that served the food had been arrested. After heading out for his first class, Alvin had been pulled aside by one of his instructors and led to one of the assessment rooms.

A man in a long black coat waited for him inside. The conversation that had followed had been upsetting, but also, informative.

Autem and Skyline shared an enemy, and Lana had chosen the wrong side.

After everything the empire had done for him and his sister, she had simply walked away. Not only had she abandoned him, but she had abandoned the future that he wanted to protect. He couldn't understand why she would do that. It was a world where no one had to be afraid.

Alvin hoped it wasn't too late to bring her back and make her understand.

With a heavy sigh, he exited the stall and headed to the mirror that hung above the sink. Placing his fingers against its reflective surface, he cast Mirror Link. An image of an office filled the glass. The same man in the black coat sat at a desk.

"Mr. Bancroft?" Alvin tried to calm his nerves.

"Yes, my boy?" The man looked up from his desk.

"You were right." Alvin frowned. "They are planning something."

Bancroft smiled. "Good. I knew I could count on you. Thank you for trusting me."

Alvin stood at attention and nodded. "What are your orders, sir?"

CHAPTER TWENTY-SIX

Hawk awoke to the sound of boots running past his bunk.

What's happening?

The lights in the room came on all at once a second later, nearly blinding him. The digital clock above the door read a little after midnight.

The hell?

Hawk rolled out of bed and reached for his boots. Was this it? Were Dig and the others here to break him out? He sat still and listened, half expecting to hear an explosion nearby or the screams of a few guardians that stood in the way.

All he heard was the footsteps of the other boys.

That was when one of Autem's instructors clapped their hands near the entrance of the room. "Everyone stay calm, everything is alright. We're just moving you all to a new training facility. There's no need to take anything with you, new uniforms will be provided when you arrive."

Hawk jumped forward past a few other kids to where the instructor could see him. There wasn't time to wait around, he needed info. "Where are we going?"

The instructor smiled a little too wide. "You're very lucky.

You're going to get to ride on a plane that will take you to the Empire's capital on the other side of the country."

"What? Why?" Hawk stared up at them.

"Because this facility was never meant to be a permanent place for you. Due to some recent events, the Empire's colony is a safer place for you all to continue your training." They knelt down. "As one of our most important guardians, it will be up to you to help guide the people of the world down the right path. So we want to make sure you all have everything you need. Plus the capital will be much more comfortable for you."

"Will we get to have your own rooms there?" one of the other boys interrupted.

"Of course." The instructor stood back up. "There's much more space there, and more people. It will be wonderful to be surrounded by members of Autem with none of the riffraff we have here."

Hawk wasn't sure what to make of it. Sure, he'd heard that there was some sort of city being built over on the East Coast, and it made sense to eventually send their new recruits there. He just didn't think he'd be shipped out so soon. He also didn't expect to be traveling in the middle of the night.

His breath froze in his throat as his mind jumped from one assumption to another.

Shit.

If he got sent all the way to Autem's colony, how would Dig get to him? He might get stuck playing soldier for Autem forever. He slapped his pocket on instinct to make sure he had the phone that had been smuggled in to him, only to remember he'd loaned it to Alvin.

Crap.

He had to get a message to Vegas somehow. There was always a chance that the friend that Dig had been talking to, that Easton guy, might have already told him what was happening, but Hawk wasn't willing to take that chance.

Falling in line with the other boys, he exited the room with his group, hoping to meet up with Alvin once they were outside. To his horror, they didn't stop in the hallway. Instead, he was led outside to where a row of golf carts were waiting. The instructor in the front directed them to climb on board. Hawk did as he was told, unable to argue.

The cart sped off as soon as he and a few other kids were in their seats. There was no sign of Digby or anyone coming to the rescue. He watched as the buildings flew by in the light of the base's lamp posts. The place grew brighter as they grew closer to the airfield. Panic began to settle in as Hawk realized he might not have a way out.

He blew out a sigh of relief as the cart slowed to a stop.

Alvin was there, walking in the middle of a group of kids the same size as his own. He tensed back up when he saw the enormous plane that they were heading toward. It was all black like the aircrafts that Skyline used.

His instructor told his group to join with the others as soon as the cart stopped. He leapt from his seat to run to Alvin, shoving his way past the other boys until he could elbow Alvin in the side.

"Do you still have it?"

Alvin nodded and shoved the phone into his hand.

Hawk stuffed the device into his pocket. "Did you send a message that we're being shipped out?"

"I did, but I don't know if anyone has received it yet. My sister might be asleep."

Hawk hoped that wasn't the case. If so, no one was coming for them. The only ray of hope was the fact that Digby didn't sleep and might still be watching for a message.

With nothing else to do, Hawk followed along with the rest of his group as they boarded the plane through a ramp on the back. Once inside, it was unlike any aircraft he'd been on. The entrance he boarded through was some kind of cargo hold, large enough to store a tank or other heavy vehicles. An armored vehicle was strapped down to the center. On the far wall there was a door that led to a second cargo compartment. At a glance, it was the same as the first until Hawk noticed a seam on the floor. Fear bubbled in his stomach as he realized it was a massive gate. It was probably there so they could drop supplies from the air.

Hawk felt a little better when his group was led into the next compartment that resembled a more traditional passenger plane. He didn't want to ride in a part of the aircraft that could potentially drop him to his death if someone pulled the wrong lever. The rest of the kids climbed into rows of seats and filled the cabin as Hawk pushed into one of the ones closest to the right wall. Alvin dropped into the seat beside him.

Unlike the previous areas, the ceiling was low as if there was another area above the passenger compartment. Looking toward the front, Hawk noticed a ladder going up.

The instructor that had led his group to the plane walked down the aisle toward the back to make sure everyone had secured their seatbelts. Hawk's forehead started to sweat when they continued on to leave the plane entirely, like they had no intent on going with them. As soon as they were gone, a team of armored guardians dressed in Autem's body armor entered. The sight of them sent a nervous shudder down Hawk's spine. They were the same men that had picked him up in Vegas.

The Guardian Core listed off their information.

Guardian: Level 27 Holy Knight
Guardian: Level 30 Artificer
Guardian: Level 20 Cleric
Guardian: Level 14 Mage
Guardian: Level 22 Rogue
Guardian: Level 13 Fighter

Crap. They were sending in the big guns.

It was almost like they expected some kind of attack. Hawk ducked back into his seat as another two squads boarded the plane. Unlike the first group, they consisted of less powerful guardians, all below level five. A party of them took up a position at the rear of the cabin to guard the door, while the rest headed for the ladder at the front. They vanished into the compartment above.

It wasn't long before the plane was ready to take off.

Hawk pulled the phone out of his pocket while the other kids were distracted by the sound of the aircraft rattling as it left the ground. He relaxed, if only a little, when he saw a message on the screen. It was short, but it got to the point.

I'm coming to get you.

Alvin's message must have gotten through.

He stuffed the device back in his pocket before anyone noticed. The plane climbed higher, leaving him unsure of how Digby would reach him. The only thing he could think of was the kestrel. He wasn't sure how far the base was from Vegas, but it hadn't taken that long for him to reach it when he'd flown from there before.

Maybe an hour?

Hawk tried to estimate how long it had taken for the kids to be loaded up and hoped that Dig would make it in time. The other kids remained quiet as the plane leveled off. He wished they would at least talk or something like normal children, but it seemed like they were all more concerned with behaving.

Hawk stared at the seat in front of him for what seemed like forever, only glancing to his side to check on Alvin. The older boy was just as reserved as usual.

After a half hour, the dread began to set in again. Surely Digby would have reached him by now. Questions started running through his head.

What if he wasn't able to catch up?

What if Hawk would never see the zombie again?

What if the home he'd found in Vegas was gone?

He shook his head. No! It wouldn't come to that. He'd find his way back, even if he had to run away and brave the monster-infested world on his own. The last couple weeks had been one of the few times in his life that he felt like he had somewhere to call home. There was no way he was giving that up without a fight.

Granted, Autem was offering him the same, a place to call home. Provided he was willing to join them for real. As the minutes passed and it became less likely that help was coming, he tried to convince himself that it wouldn't be that bad. He forced the thought out of his head, hating himself for even having it.

That was when the squad of high-level guardians slid down the ladder. Hawk watched nervously from his seat as they ran down the aisle and passed through the door at the back into the compartment in the rear. The door at the back slide closed behind them.

The low-level guardians dropped down as well to fill the aisle between the children. They headed for the door at the rear as well. Several drew pistols while others reached for the swords on their backs.

Something was coming.

The cabin fell silent for a solid minute before the sound of gunfire erupted from above. Each shot was somehow loud and muffled at the same time, like it was coming from a larger than normal weapon that was mounted on the outside of the aircraft.

The children in the cabin tensed up.

Hawk did the same.

Something was definitely coming.

CHAPTER TWENTY-SEVEN

Digby braced against the side of the cockpit door of the stolen kestrel as it flew straight for the aircraft carrying Hawk and Alvin. White-hot lead exploded through the front, showering the cockpit in fragments of broken glass. Bullets tore through the cushion of the pilot's seat before hitting the metal wall behind it with a hard thump. Digby ducked as the head of a zombie behind him burst, covering the small horde waiting in the passenger compartment in necrotic gray matter.

"Hold on!" Rebecca shouted from the speaker embedded in the ceiling as the kestrel lurched to the side. It was a good thing she had stayed behind. She would have been killed if she'd been sitting at the helm.

"I am hanging on!" Digby clung to the side of the door with all his strength as the plane ahead of them filled his view.

"We're gonna die, man." Tavern downed a tiny bottle of vodka, spilling it all over the passenger seat.

"You're already dead," Digby snapped at his skeletal minion as the kestrel lurched to the other side.

According to Rebecca, the airship was a Pelican dropship, a craft capable of transporting tanks and other vehicles into war zones.

Right now, it was carrying children.

"Faster!" He stabilized himself and reached for his new staff.

The weapon was the newest creation of Alex and Parker's mana-powered forge. Digby had even helped by Forging the shape of the item from blood for them to create a mold. He'd kept the design similar to his old staff, but added a bit of flair. The hollow diamond still sat at the top, with a blood forged blade already formed around the shape, while a decorative skull adorned the fitting where it connected to a wooden pole. Its looks didn't actually matter, but the design helped him feel like the Lord of Death he claimed to be. More important was the fact that the staff reduced the cost of his spells by twenty percent, saving him MP when he needed it most. Digby glanced at his HUD.

MP: 176/176

Now that he had been able to retrieve his coat and its pauldron of the Goblin King, his maximum mana had gone back up to where it belonged. Though, he still needed every point of MP he could get, thanks to the two zombie destroyers back in Vegas that were still holding some of his mana to keep their systems active. Fortunately, he'd had a little time to work on his horde before receiving a message from Easton about Hawk and Alvin. He glanced over his list of minions, willing the Seed's display to remove any creature that weren't actually present on the kestrel. Only three entries remained.

Minions: 1 Skeleton, 8 Zombie Revenants, 2 Nightflyers.

The third entry had been an unexpected development of his new ability to reactivate the curse within the revenants. At first, when he'd converted the creatures at the rest stop earlier, they had been normal zombie revenants. After feeding them, though, they began to mutate along a new path unavailable to his non-revenant zombies. The result had given him something new to work with.

The nightflyers might have been dead, but the zombies had

regained the attributes needed to fly, making them especially useful now. Digby just hoped they would be enough.

Glancing back at his minions, he wished he'd been able to fit a few more. A destroyer would certainly tip the odds in his favor. Unfortunately, with the kestrel's limited space he'd only been able to take ten, including two winged, zombie revenants.

There was a limit to how powerful the strange zombies could get, considering he couldn't give them any bond points, but still they were better than nothing. He was just glad the sun had set so they could access a portion of the attributes they possessed before he killed them. He still didn't understand exactly how their muta-tion path worked, but there would be time to figure it out later.

Another barrage of bullets tore through the night sky, nearly bursting through one of the kestrel's propellers.

"We have to board them!" Digby shoved his way through his modest horde to the ramp at the back, hoping he could make it to the plane before the kestrel got shot down.

"I'll get you as close as I can," Rebecca shouted from the speaker as the craft tipped forward.

Digby adjusted his balance and hit the ramp's open button. The plane came into view just below. He turned to his nightflyers. "Get down there and find something to hang on to. And be ready to catch me if I fall."

The two winged minions did as they were told, though he wasn't sure how much of his orders they understood. Their loyalty might have been absolute, but they were still as dumb as rocks. As soon as the creatures hit the plane, they tucked their wings close to their backs and clawed their way across the roof.

"You're next." Digby called Tavern to the ramp. "Get your-selves secure and be ready to help the rest of the horde."

The skeleton saluted and poured another tiny bottle of vodka down their nonexistent throat before jumping. They landed in a clatter of bones that fell apart on impact. If not for the magic holding the skeleton together, they might not have made it, yet Tavern's hand pulled back together to reform around a handhold built into the craft's roof. A bony thumbs up followed.

In fear of dropping his staff, Digby stored the item in his void.

Then, without hesitation, he jumped after his minions, aiming for the gun mounted near the back that was firing at the kestrel. He hit the metal plating with a heavy thud, before rolling backward into the rotating gun. He grabbed on for dear life as the wind whipped through his coat. The turret he clung to fired a second later, sending streaks of glowing lead into the clouds.

Rebecca pulled the kestrel to one side to dodge as one of the circular guards that surrounded the front left propeller shattered. Digby acted fast, throwing the length of his coat around the mounted gun he clung to, to blind the weapon.

"Can't shoot what you can't see." He pulled tight. Surely there was some sort of camera device in there somewhere. With a little luck, the fabric would hinder their ability to target the kestrel. Once he was finished, he shouted up to his remaining minions, "Get down here and try not to fall off."

One by one, his zombie revenants dropped from the kestrel. The first two simply bounced off the surface of the plane.

"Damn." Digby debated telling his nightflyers to rescue them but feared that they would never catch up to the plane using their wings. His two fallen minions hit the ground as another four made it safely to the plane with a little help from Tavern.

2 Zombie Revenants lost.

"Two out of ten isn't bad." Digby held firm to the mounted gun just as it opened fire again. "Hey, stop that!"

Firing blind, the gun cut a swath through the sky, this time, cleaving through the propellers of the kestrel. One of the two undead revenants on board leapt as the side of the craft exploded. It hit the plane and tumbled to the side where the hand of one of his other minions snapped out to catch it.

The kestrel flipped end over end, flinging his final minion from the fiery wreckage.

1 Zombie Revenant lost.

"Blast!" Digby lamented the loss of the aircraft even more than his fallen minion. He had worked hard to get that kestrel. Plus they needed it for the attack they had planned. Nevertheless, Hawk and Alvin were the priority right now.

Gritting his teeth, he pushed on as the wind threatened to tear his face off. He wished he'd at least thought to wear a pair of goggles. With a thought, he activated his Temporary Mass mutation to call forth his necrotic armor. He was going to need every advantage he could get.

Holding on became a simple task the moment the suit of muscle slithered around his body. Digby leveraged it for all it was worth, yanking on the mounted gun as it let off another torrent of lead.

"Do you even lift?" Tavern slammed their skeletal body against the barrel of the weapon to help from the other side.

"Shut up and push, you fool." Digby braced his foot and pulled with everything he had until a high-pitched grinding came from the rotation mechanism. With a loud clank, the resistance fell away, causing the gun to lose control of its rotation. It fired one last blast of fire and smoke.

"Balls." Tavern started sliding from the plane as Digby realized the skeleton was missing an arm. The gun must have taken it clean off.

"Get back here." He caught his minion by the rib cage as they passed by.

"Thanks, boss." Tavern found a grip with their remaining arm.

With the gun taken care of, Digby searched for anything he could hold on to, finding a row of handles near the tail of the aircraft that ran down the side. He assumed there would be a hatch down there that he might use to gain entry. To reach it, he simply let go and allowed the wind to push him back to where he could grab hold of one of the handles. Once he was secure, he opened his armor's mask and issued an order to his surviving minions.

"Work together and get back here. Form an undead human chain if you have to." Digby closed his mask again as the undead revenants listened. It seemed the natural instinct to move as a horde was working to his advantage.

That just left one problem.

How do I get in?

Digby stared at the door from where he clung to the side of the aircraft. There seemed to be a movable plate on the surface. The word 'lift' was written across the bottom.

Well, that makes sense.

Slipping one of his armored claws into a slot on one end of the panel, he hesitated before pulling it up. A small, oblong window sat just beneath with the word 'pressurized' written below the glass. Ultimately, there was nothing to indicate danger, but his above average intelligence ran through the possibilities of what it meant.

Why would someone need to know about pressure while on the outside of the craft? He looked up to Tavern as the skeleton crawled closer. "Should I be worried about this?"

"Heh, yup." The infernal spirit nodded their skull.

"I see." Digby erred on the side of caution, moving out of the way to let one of his minions pull the panel open.

"That's it. Pull like your life depends on it."

The undead revenant stopped and stared at him, clearly not understanding the expression. Digby rolled his eyes.

"Just pull, you idiot."

His minion struggled a bit, still lacking the strength to move the mechanism easily while also holding on to the plane. Eventually, it succeeded, making use of the revenant's lingering attributes.

Digby expected there to be a lever or something beneath the panel but was caught off guard when he realized the panel itself was the lever. A strange clicking noise came from the door as soon as his minion raised the panel halfway. Then, the entire door burst from the side of the aircraft, taking the undead revenant with it.

1 Zombie Revenant lost.

"Shame to lose another, but it's a good thing I didn't do that myself." Digby ordered his minions to move into position and wait just outside the hatch before swinging his armored body inside.

"What the fuck is that?" a guardian shouted the moment he

tumbled into the rear cargo compartment and ducked behind a large armored vehicle that was strapped to the floor.

"Your doom." Digby stood as he called his staff from his maw and whipped it to the side to throw off the necrotic blood that covered its surface. Black fluid spattered the wall as twelve guardians surrounded him, each dressed in the armor of Skyline's sellswords. The now familiar sensation of pistol fire thumped into his body, only dealing damage to his armor. A dozen impacts sparked across the hood of the vehicle he stood behind.

Next came a barrage of Fireballs and Icicles. Digby simply raised his staff and cast Absorb to suck in the energy of every attack for a full ten seconds. A surge of power poured into his mana system for later. His MP dropped to one thirty three remaining.

Digby swept his gaze across the cabin, finding all twelve members of the group to be below level five.

"Rend!" He rushed the closest squad as his three undead revenants climbed in through the open door to add to the chaos. Tavern spilled in last, clattering to the floor before reforming into a one-armed skeleton and letting out a war cry of, "Get fucked!"

A guardian screamed only to be cut off as Digby plowed into them, claws first. A second took the blood forged blade of his staff in the throat.

Guardian: Level 3 Fighter defeated. 248 experience awarded.
Guardian: Level 4 mage defeated. 348 experience awarded.

The cabin erupted into another volley of spells, though Digby didn't dare cast another Absorb for fear of wasting the mana. Instead, he took five Icicles in the back that drove through his armor of deceased flesh. Two pierced his lower back underneath while the rest were stopped by the plates of bone that protected the Heretic Seed's shard. A Fireball exploded against his wrist as he blocked, setting the forearm of his armor alight.

A screech echoed through the cabin as one of his revenants lunged over him to rip into an unfortunate enchanter. Another two hundred and forty eight experience rolled in. Digby ignored the fire climbing up his arm and grabbed a man by his neck to throw him from the plane.

Guardian: Level 3 Fighter defeated. 248 experience awarded.

Another two fell beneath his minions.

Guardian: Level 2 Mage defeated. 148 experience awarded.
Guardian: Level 3 Enchanter defeated. 248 experience awarded.
You have reached level 27. 6,748 experience to next level.
You have one attribute point to allocate.

He dropped his additional point into intelligence and snapped his claws around the wrist of a man attempting to throw a Fireball at close range. Bones cracked in the guardian's arm as Digby leveraged every point of strength that his temporary mass granted. The orb of fire fell backward from the man's hand and ruptured on the floor below him to engulf his feet. Digby simply let go as the man flailed and ran across the cargo hold to put out the fire. One of his minions pounced on him before he got far.

1 Zombie Revenant lost.

Digby flicked his head around to catch a fighter standing over one of his minions. His body shimmered with the glow of a Barrier as he pulled his fist from the creature's crushed skull. Digby responded in an instant, swiping his staff in the man's direction. The edge of his blood forged blade scraped across the layer of mana protecting him.

"Nice try!" The man spat in his direction.

Digby answered the fighter's taunt by placing a foot firmly against his chest and shoving him out the door with a near effortless push. "See how that Barrier holds up when you hit the ground."

Before he could turn back to the remaining enemies, a loud bang went off directly behind him. A field of stars filled his vision as he staggered and fell to one knee. The bone of his armor's mask took the impact, but just barely. With a pivot, he caught a glimpse of a shadow on the wall of a man with a pistol pointing down at him. The guardian must have run out of mana and rushed him. From the feel of the hit, the bullet had come from mere inches away. He couldn't take another at that range.

Without further thought, Digby opened his maw on his back and impaled the threat with a spike of black blood. His mana dropped to one seventeen as a scream came from behind him. Digby ran a count of his enemies in his head. There were three left. He was almost done. Then again, he couldn't be sure if there were more in the next compartment.

Digby turned to find the final three guardians backed into a corner by his minions. The shimmer of a Barrier spell swept over one while a Fireball formed in another's hand. The one in the middle reloaded a pistol.

"Hold." Digby called off his undead revenants before willing his armor's mask to retract so he could address the guardians. "I'm going to guess from the color of your uniforms that you're some of Skyline's sellswords, and not members of Autem. So I'll offer you a deal. Tell me what is waiting in the next compartment, and I will let you live as long as you stop fighting right now. No sense dying for someone else's cause, am I right?" He hoped that their mercenary nature would trump whatever sense of duty they might have.

"Deal." The mage holding the Fireball immediately tossed it out the open door of the plane and gestured to the front of the compartment. "There's six more guardians waiting behind that door. All Autem's guys."

"Only six?" Digby arched an eyebrow.

"They're high level," the fighter added while the third sellsword holstered their pistol.

"Alright, then. That was easy." Digby gestured for his minions to stand down.

"Killing for money is one thing." The mage shook his head.

"Dying for money is something else entirely." The fighter headed for the vehicle in the middle of the cargo area and unstrapped it from the floor.

"We'll take our chances on our own." The mage ran to the rear of the craft and pulled a lever.

Digby stepped aside as a ramp similar to the one at the back of a kestrel opened. The surviving guardians climbed into the vehicle and closed the doors. Watching in confusion, they simply backed the heavy vehicle out of the plane.

"Umm, alright?" He stepped to the ramp and stared down as some sort of fabric was released from the roof to slow their descent. He furrowed his brow as the Heretic Seed answered the question in his mind.

Parachute, Common, Safety Apparatus.

"I wish I'd had one of those the last time I had to jump from an aircraft." Digby swept his gaze across the cabin behind him to see if there were other parachutes stored somewhere. Having one of them would be a far cry better than hoping his nightflyers would catch him before he ended up a splatter on the earth's surface. Coming up empty, he determined that if there were more parachutes on the plane, then they were stored someplace else.

"I don't suppose the other guardians would stand by and let me search the craft." Digby backed away from the ramp and turned his attention to the door at the front of the cabin. "No, I suppose they wouldn't."

Peeling off a bit of charred flesh from the forearm of his armor, his wrist was left looking frail. He flexed his hand, finding it hard to move and lacking some of the strength that the mutation provided. Wincing, he closed his mask back over his face, hoping that his temporary mass would hold out for another fight.

He slapped the button beside the door.

There wasn't time to waste.

CHAPTER TWENTY-EIGHT

"What's this now?"

Digby stepped into the next compartment of the aircraft he'd boarded with his remaining two undead revenants. They chittered behind him in anticipation as he entered an empty cabin.

"No one's home." Tavern shrugged with the one arm that they still had.

"I find that hard to believe." Digby focused on the next door at the other end of the space, hoping that Hawk and Alvin were safe and waiting on the other side.

Before he could take another step, a loud, mechanical sound came from below him.

"What the hell?" Digby leapt to the side as the floor split open beneath his feet.

"Doh-no!" Tavern scrambled to the other side, their skeletal feet click-clacking against the floor as the angle changed. An instant later, the infernal spirit vanished into the clouds below, flailing with their remaining arm. If it hadn't been for his above average agility, Digby would have followed. Instead, he'd leapt to one side to land on the edge of the opening.

The Seed informed him when his minion hit the ground.

1 Skeleton lost.

He was just lucky that his remaining two revenants were still standing near the door they had entered through rather than on top of the opening. As it was, the entire floor of the cabin had dropped out from below them, leaving only a narrow ridge on the sides and a few feet at the front and back to stand on. Digby struggled to maintain his footing at the edge of the trap door. His necrotic armor just took up too much of the available space. Choosing to lose the defense in favor of not plummeting to earth, he released his Temporary Mass to make room.

Slabs of dead muscle unraveled and slipped away from his body while his mask of bone crumbled. Seconds later, he stood trapped against the wall with his staff held close beside him. In anger, he shouted at the empty space, "Alright, alright, who's behind this?"

"That would be me." A man in Autem's white armor walked through the door at the front, stopping a foot from the opening in the floor.

Digby narrowed his eyes. The guardian was the same holy knight that had come to Vegas to collect children. The one that had taken Hawk. Another five guardians followed him out. They were also part of the same squad that he'd encountered before.

Guardian: Level 27 Holy Knight
Guardian: Level 30 Artificer
Guardian: Level 20 Cleric
Guardian: Level 14 Mage
Guardian: Level 22 Rogue
Guardian: Level 13 Fighter

Digby grimaced as he read off their classes and levels from his HUD. With only two minions, there wasn't much hope. That was when he remembered his nightflyers that were still clinging to the outside of the craft. If he could get them into position, he might have a shot. Unfortunately, that would take time.

"Don't even think about attacking me," Digby shouted in his most commanding tone, despite being cornered.

"You're not exactly in a position to be making demands." The knight gestured to the open trap door that threatened to claim him.

"Neither are you." Digby forced a grin to detract from the fact that he could slip and fall to his death at any moment.

"Really? And why is that?" The knight folded his arms as if he had nothing to worry about.

"Because when I boarded this aircraft, I absorbed the attack spells of each of the low-level men you sacrificed to slow me down. That power is flowing through my mana system just waiting to be added to whatever I decide to cast. It's easily enough to cause catastrophic damage to this aircraft and send us all plummeting back to earth."

The knight stared at him, clearly debating internally if Digby was bluffing or not. He took the moment to call to his nightflyers in hopes that they might be able to make their way toward the opening in the bottom of the plane. He inched a little closer to the front of the cabin while he was at it. If all else failed, he wanted to be in range of his enemies.

"And might I add," Digby kept talking to buy time, "that was mighty cold of you lot to send a dozen of Skyline's sellswords after me before challenging me yourselves. I knew Autem looked down on others, but I was surprised to see you sacrifice your own allies so easily just to slow me down."

A flash of cruelty showed on the knight's face. "Skyline's forces are made up of scoundrels and mercenaries. They serve only themselves."

"And you serve, what?" Digby laughed and slid a little closer to the squad of guardians. "The Nine?"

The knight's eyes widened at the mention of Autem's fictitious deities.

Digby tried to keep him talking the only way he knew how, by throwing out insults. "That's right, I know all about your little made up religion."

"I assure you, the Nine are very real." The knight frowned at him. "The world will come to realize that soon."

"Oh, I bet." Digby rolled his eyes and probed for information while scooting a few more inches toward the man. "And I bet the world will come to realize who was really behind its demise."

"The world will understand in time." The knight held out a hand as light began to gather in his palm. "But you won't be around to see it."

"Wait wait wait!" Digby waved his staff in the air whilst keeping his balance. "I can still blow this airship to hell."

"Go ahead." The knight pressed the glowing energy in his hand into his chest.

"I'll do it, I swear." Digby inched closer, catching a glimpse of something pale clinging to the bottom of the airship just beneath his enemies' feet.

"I don't think you will." The knight reached for his sword and stepped closer to the edge as the men around him fanned out across the front of the cabin. "You see, Bancroft has shared some information with us. It seems that you have a history with a boy named Alvin. Why do you think we decided to move him?"

Digby frowned as he ran through the facts in his mind. It wasn't that hard to figure out that he might have an interest in rescuing the boy. All Bancroft would have needed to do was look back over whatever records they had of the events that transpired in Seattle. "It's a trap then."

"Of course." The knight laughed. "What better way to draw you out than to dangle some bait in front of your nose. We even got to shoot down that kestrel you stole."

"You got me, I guess. I've fallen for your trap and now I'm at your mercy." Digby blew out a musty sigh before adding a shrug. "Might as well spring a trap of my own then." He immediately opened his maw on the front wall of the cabin and cast Forge to send a post of blood flying at the knight's back before he had the chance to issue an order.

The man let out an embarrassing, "ompf," as his body fell forward through the opening in the floor.

Most of the other guardians leapt away from the edge to keep him from repeating the same tactic. The artificer, apparently feeling brave, stepped forward and fired off an enchanted crossbow bolt. Digby slapped it out of the air with the black blade at the head of his staff. The arrow detonated at the other side of the cabin in a sudden burst of heat and power.

"Now!" Digby shouted as the artificer's crossbow automatically drew back its string to fire another shot.

The guardian leveled his weapon at him just as a pale arm reached up from the opening below to grip one of the straps on his leg. With a solid yank, the nightflyer clinging to the bottom of the craft pulled the unsuspecting man forward to his doom. He let out a terrified scream as his aim faltered, firing another bolt in panic before disappearing into the gloom below. The projectile veered off target, hitting one of the undead revenants that was still waiting at the other side of the cabin. The creature's flesh bubbled and swelled before detonating in a cloud of gore and viscera that painted the wall.

A string of messages flashed across his HUD.

1 Zombie Revenant lost.
Guardian: Level 27 Holy Knight defeated. 2,646 experience awarded.

A few seconds later, another message came in.

Guardian: Level 30 Artificer defeated. 2,946 experience awarded.

Digby smirked, assuming his enemy had hit the ground. Things were actually working out. He slid himself along the wall of the space to reach the guardians on the other side.

"Close the floor!" the cleric of the group shouted as the other nightflyer swiped at his leg. He cast a healing spell on the creature to drive it back. The revenant screeched as if it had been burnt before shrinking back to where it clung to the outside of the craft.

The sides of the enormous trap door began to close, the half nearest Digby's feet raising back up, while the other side ground to stop at an angle. An open space around three feet wide ran down the length of the cabin. The artificer's enchanted bolt must have caused some damage to the mechanism.

No matter, Digby finally had space to work with. Stalking toward his prey, the remaining three guardians stepped backward. That was when an obvious question streaked through his mind.

Wasn't there one more?

He did the math. The squad had been made up of six. With the knight and the artificer dead, that should have left four. Digby didn't need to analyze the group to know which one was missing.

The rogue.

He'd seen the guardian display the same Conceal spell that Rebecca had gotten so much use out of. The rogue must have used it while Digby was distracted by the exploding bolts. He reacted as soon as the realization sunk in, taking a guess at where the threat might be and leveraging every point of agility he had. Sweeping his staff's bladed tip through the air behind him, he aimed for the height of an average man's neck.

A spray of crimson burst into the air in the wake of his weapon's edge. The image of the rogue clutching his throat melted into existence. Without hesitation, the cleric at the other side of the cabin cast a heal to save his squad-mate.

"Oh no you don't." Digby snapped his focus back to his one remaining minion. "Rend!"

The undead revenant leapt for the rogue, still covered in the necrotic blood of Digby's other minion that had exploded a moment before. The creature fell upon the guardian with its jaws open wide.

"No." The mage at the front of the cabin acted fast, casting a volley of Icicles that slammed into both his minion and the rogue. "It's still dark, we can't let anyone turn."

Interesting. Digby nodded to himself, remembering how dangerous the curse was at night. Unfortunately, the result of the cleric's quick thinking negated whatever experience Digby would have received by stealing the kill. It didn't matter, there were still more enemies to deal with.

"Die, you monster!" The fighter stepped forward and swiped

his sword down in an arc to block his path. Digby sensed mana moving through his body.

There was no way to be sure but the spell had to be Kinetic Impact, it was the only thing that made sense for the man to cast. Digby dropped to one knee to shift his weight and block with his staff. The blade of black blood on the end shattered under the power of the spell but the fighter's sword stopped when it hit the metal diamond within. The clang of steel hitting steel rang through his ears.

There wasn't time to be careful.

Digby returned the spell in kind, casting its death-based cousin, Five Fingers of Death, as he shoved his free hand up into the fighter's abdomen. His mana dropped to just sixty-one remaining as the shimmer of a Barrier spell lit up his enemy's form. It winked out a second later. Digby could feel the power behind his attack drain away at the same time, as if the two opposing forces had canceled each other out.

Blast! He had wasted forty points of mana.

The fighter smirked, clearly understanding what had happened as well. Digby didn't give him time to gloat. Instead, he lunged forward and sunk his teeth into the man's neck deep enough to pass the curse. He shoved the man away and leapt back just as the cleric hit him with a heal spell that sent a wave of pain through his body that knocked him down.

The fighter clutched a hand over the bite wound and spun to make eye contact with the mage behind him as his skin began to grow pale. "Wait, no, I can resist it."

The mage's eyes widened, clearly debating on what to do. The fighter's ears began to reform into the pointed features of a revenant, making the choice clear. There was nothing that could be done. Henwick's modified response to the curse was too strong at night.

"The kids!" the fighter shouted in a slurred voice. "There must be an enchanter among them." He scrambled toward the door at the front of the cabin, slapping a bloody hand against the button. His voice shifted into a horrific screech as the door slid open, revealing a plane full of startled children.

"Stay away from them." Digby got himself back up as the heal spell that had hit him faded. He immediately opened his maw on the floor and drove a blood spike up through the newly turned revenant. The fighter's pale corpse flailed before going limp and sliding down the spike halfway to dangle in the doorway.

Messages flashed across Digby's vision.

Guardian: Level 13 Fighter defeated. 1,264 experience awarded.
You have reached level 28. 6,522 experience to next level.
You have one attribute point to allocate.

Digby dropped his extra point into intelligence while the cleric sneered in his direction, as if disgusted by the way the fighter had died.

"Damn you."

Another heal spell followed, lighting up Digby's rarely used pain receptors. Falling back, he tried to cast a spell but found it hard to focus with the life magic bringing his mana system to a halt. That was when the mage joined in, flinging a surge of electricity from his hand. Digby hadn't seen that spell before.

"Yeep!" Digby choked out a random syllable as his mind slowed to a crawl.

What's… happening…

He struggled to understand the spell's damage. Other than a burn, it didn't seem to be physically harming him. The spell faded, running its course. Digby started to stand, only to be hit with another heal followed by another bolt of electricity that sent him crumbling back down with his head hanging in the open space on the floor.

How… do I fight this?

Each thought flowed through his mind like mud. It was as if the spell was slowly cooking his necrotic gray matter from the inside out. He had to repair the damage but the cleric's healing magic kept his mana system in disarray. In desperation, he threw his staff at the man, disrupting his casting long enough to get off a spell.

As his mana system flowed back into place, Digby felt the stored energy that he'd absorbed earlier. With his overcooked gray matter misfiring, he grabbed onto the power and attached it to a Necrotic Regeneration spell without thinking of what it might do.

The result was instant.

All thought became clear as the fog of his melting brain was erased. It was as if the added power had supercharged his body's regenerative process to bring him back to top shape in an instant. Digby immediately became aware he was dangling on the edge of the opening in the floor and pulled himself up.

The mage hit him with another bolt of electricity, but his body dulled it back down to nothing as the damage was repaired faster than it could be caused. The cleric got back into position and raised a hand in his direction. Digby cast Absorb as another healing spell flowed into the purple vortex that extended from his palm. Instead of disrupting his system, the life magic was converted into something usable and funneled away for later. Another bolt from the mage joined it.

"That was a mistake." Digby grinned like a villain as he opened his maw and cast Decay, hoping that adding the absorbed power altered the spell to get it past their defenses. White hot electricity hit them, exploding from his hand in a funnel of death that arced from one guardian to the other. The stored healing energy hit next in a wave of inverted power that amplified the effect of his Decay spell that degenerated the flesh around each impact. Smoke wafted from their wounds as Digby charged.

Both enemies cast a heal on themselves as they struggled to remain standing. It didn't matter, they had been thrown off guard long enough for Digby to grab hold of their armor and shove them through the opening in the floor.

Guardian: Level 14 Mage defeated. 1,344 Experience awarded.
Guardian: Level 20 Cleric defeated. 1,944 Experience awarded.

Not bad. Digby swept his gaze across the cabin, finding his staff on the floor, teetering at the edge of the opening. He leapt over the gap and scooped it up before it fell. Then he glanced at his HUD.

MP: 16/198

He cringed at how close he'd come to running out. Not only that, but he'd lost all of his minions, save for his nightflyers clinging to the outside of the airship. Calling them inside through the opening, he picked a few bits of necrotic flesh from his shoulder from what remained his armor. It was bad enough he smelled like death, but it seemed best to avoid frightening the children on the airship any more than he already had. Once he was mostly clean, he straightened his tattered coat and headed into the cabin ahead.

"Please remain calm, I'm here to help." He dropped the end of his staff down to draw the attention of each of the young faces seated in the compartment. Not that it was necessary. Every eye was already focused on him and the impaled fighter that hung in the doorway. He scanned the space, finding Hawk and Alvin sitting to one side. He resisted the urge to speak to them directly, unsure how much he could trust the rest of the orphans. Instead, he addressed them all. "Autem will not be able to lie to you anymore. We just need to take over the cockpit and—"

"You killed them." A voice from the front of the cabin stopped him in his tracks. It was an older boy, around the same age as Alvin. He stood from his seat and blocked the aisle. "You killed the guardians."

"I did what I had to do." Digby stood tall. "There is no shame in fighting to protect others."

"We don't need protection." The boy clenched his fists at his sides.

Digby took a step back at a loss for what to do. "You don't know what you're talking about." He shook his head. "I know Autem has been filling your heads with lies, but I need you to understand."

"You don't understand! Autem is our home. We belong there." The boy swept a hand through the air in defiance. "And you aren't taking us anywhere."

Several of the other children nodded.

Digby narrowed his eyes. "Get out of my way, boy."

"No." The child's eyes burned with resentment.

Digby leaned forward on his staff, trying to reign in his aggressive nature before he resorted to insults or threats. A more nurturing approach might serve better to win the child over. "What about your families, don't you want to see them again?"

"Autem is our family."

The boy's answer cut like a knife. "You're wrong. For some of you, there are people out there that love you. You belong with them. All I ask is that you give me the chance to bring you back. I just need to get to the pilot's compartment and switch the control of this craft over to my accomplice."

The boy didn't wait for him to say anything else before raising a hand in front of him and moving mana through his blood. Embers swirled through the air, collecting into a sphere in the palm off his hand.

"Hey, now." Digby froze. "There's no need for that. I don't want anyone to get hurt."

"You won't take us." The boy stared up at him as the Fireball in his hand reflected in his eyes.

Then, he threw it.

Digby winced and threw out his arms to make sure to block the spell from hitting any of the children that surrounded him. He could always repair the damage to himself later. It didn't take long for him to realize the attack had never been meant for him.

No. It was so much worse.

Fire filled the center of the aisle near the front of the cabin, surrounding the boy's feet. The child gritted his teeth as the flames climbed up his legs. It was clear he was struggling not to scream.

"You fool!"

Digby threw caution aside and rushed forward. There was still a chance to save him. The boy formed another Fireball before he could traverse the space. Digby watched in horror as the child dropped to his knees and crushed the Fireball in his hand so that it burst in his face. He reached his limit after that. The scream that followed would haunt Digby for the rest of his days.

Skidding to a stop, he struggled to think of something as the child flailed in the fire. Never before had he cursed his deathly mana more. Healing others was beyond his reach. With no way to help, he did the only thing he could.

He watched.

Reaching out toward the body, he etched the image into his mind. The boy was gone. Stolen by Autem's lies.

"Why?" Digby's voice cracked. He would have been sick if he had been able. It was too much to bear. That was when another boy, even younger than the first stepped into the aisle to block his path.

"Leave." His hand shook as he held it out in front of himself. "You won't take us."

"How could you all be so blind?" He swept his eyes around the compartment in horror as the majority of the children began to stand at their seats as if taking a stand against him.

"Leave," the boy in the aisle repeated, his voice shaking with a mix of determination and fear.

"You don't have to do this." Digby threw out a hand to the child. "You don't have to—"

The boy cut him off without a word as he raised a hand to cast a spell.

"Don't." Digby shrank away in surrender. He couldn't stop him. "You win. I'll go. Just don't do any—"

The child kept their hand raised as if ready to cast at any second. "Then go."

"Fine." Digby took one last glance at the charred corpse that lay on the floor and backed away with his hands up. "I will leave this airship and all who wish to remain aboard. But if there were one or two among you that wished to be free of Autem, I can see you safely back to where you belong." He turned and stared at Hawk, hoping he would get his meaning.

"Me." Hawk threw a hand up. "Take me."

"Very well." Digby tried his best to pretend like he didn't already know the boy.

Alvin said nothing as he stared at the corpse on the floor. Eventually Hawk elbowed him in the side and he raised his hand as well.

"Come with me, then." Digby nodded and stepped aside so that they could pass by before looking back at the boy standing in the aisle. "I shan't forget this. What Autem has done here is unforgivable. One day, I hope you will see that too."

With that, he turned away from the horror and heartache that his enemies had created and tried his best to put on a strong front for the two youths that he was able to help.

"Be careful. The floor in here is a bit treacherous." He followed Hawk and Alvin into the previous cabin. Both boys had clearly realized the danger already as they stood with their back pressed against the wall to put as much distance between themselves and the open floor as possible.

"How do we…" Hawk glanced back to Digby. "Get out?"

"Do you trust me?"

"Yeah, sure, I guess." Hawk avoided eye contact.

"Good." Digby answered the question by calling to his night-flyers. Alvin jumped with wide eyes as a pale hand reached forth from the gap and pulled its fearsome owner into view. The undead revenant crouched once inside and unfurled the leathery wings that protruded from its back.

"Oh jeez." Hawk gulped. "That's our ride, isn't it?"

"Indeed." Digby stepped forward as his other nightflyer crawled into the cabin. "I'd hang on tight if I were you."

"Okay." Hawk blew out a nervous sigh and stepped forward to the first of the creatures while Digby gave it commands.

"And no biting." He held a finger in one of the nightflyer's faces as it wrapped its arms around Hawk's back to lift the boy.

Hawk responded by wrapping his legs around the creature's waist and holding on securely to its neck. "Shit, this thing reeks."

"It's the reanimated corpse of a monster, did you expect it to smell of roses?" Digby snapped at the boy before turning to Alvin. "Your sister can't wait to see you. And I am glad to see you again as well. I'm sorry I haven't been able to reach you sooner."

Alvin dropped his eyes to the floor and nodded. "Where will we go?"

"You'll see." Digby smiled down at him and stepped aside so his minion could pick the boy up. For a moment, Alvin panicked as the nightflyer began to wrap its arms around him. Digby placed a hand on his shoulder, forgetting for a moment that he was just as dead as the monster beside him. "Don't worry. I won't let anything happen to you."

"How will you get down?" Hawk glanced around the cabin, clearly realizing that there were only two minions capable of flight.

"Yes, well." Digby checked his mana, finding that he'd absorbed just enough for a single spell after the fight with the guardians. "I have a plan. Sort of."

Glossing over the point, he reached for the lever he'd seen one of the guardians pull earlier when they tried to close the opening in the floor. The mechanism emitted a horrible grinding but opened regardless.

"I'll see you both on the ground." Digby nodded to the boys before giving the order for his minions to dive. Hawk let out a wild shout as his nightflyer dropped into the night. Alvin simply closed his eyes, clearly waiting for it to be over.

Once they were out safely, Digby stepped to the edge.

"No sense hesitating."

With that, he stepped forward into the empty air.

CHAPTER TWENTY-NINE

Regret filled every necrotic cell in Digby's body as his instincts rebelled against his mind.

Did I seriously just jump from an aircraft?

Am I insane?

The wind whipped by as the plane above soared away from him. The sun was just beginning to rise on the horizon, filling the desert below with a soft pink glow.

"Gah!" Digby began to panic as he plummeted to the earth.

With a significant effort, he reminded himself that his intelligence was high enough for him to understand the basics of how a kestrel worked. Hoping he was right, he wrapped his body around his staff as if it could somehow fly like a witches broom. That was obviously out of the question, but if he understood the concepts of flight correctly, then his staff could slow his descent. He just needed to catch the wind.

Digby thought back to the parachute that he had witnessed earlier. Then he considered the function of the propellers that kept the kestrels afloat. Next, he considered how much necrotic blood he would need to use to form something suitable. Then he imagined a leaf, floating on the wind. Last, he estimated how much the blood would weigh. He glanced down at the desert below, realizing how little time he had left to think.

Finally, he opened his maw at the end of his staff and cast Forge. Black blood flowed out from the metal diamond above him, branching out in four directions. Making a full parachute to slow his descent would be too heavy. Instead, Digby had chosen a more complex shape that would serve to slow him just enough to keep him from being splattered into an unrecognizable mess. He would probably still break his legs, but he could deal with that later.

Bracing his body against his staff, the formation of blood spread out to solidify into an organic shape that resembled four leaves not unlike a kestrel's propellers.

"Yes!"

Digby stared up at his accomplishment as he began to rotate. The world spun faster and faster but his velocity began to slow.

"Now that's using your intelligence, Digby."

He congratulated himself just as he started to get dizzy. He'd written off the worry earlier due to the fact that he couldn't get motion sickness on account of his being dead. Though, as he was finding out, the disorientation was still problematic.

"Wait, no. This is bad."

His legs slipped from the staff, leaving him hanging on with both hands as he spiraled toward the ground. The change in positioning threw off the balance of his creation as it wobbled in an uncontrolled circle. A partial thought to activate his Temporary Mass bubbled to the surface of his disoriented brain. At least then he might have some protection when he hit the ground. The idea flew out of his head a second later as he remembered how much the extra muscle weighed.

"No no no no no!" He spiraled down like a leaf on the wind, unable to control his descent. Glancing down, he watched in horror as a brownish blur rushed toward him. He held on to his staff for dear life and did the only thing he could.

He closed his eyes and hoped for the best.

Then, he hit the ground.

———

"Not good." Digby struggled to lift his head as the sound of ocean waves surrounded him. The gentle rocking of a boat lulled him into nothingness.

Everything was blurry.

An all-consuming fog.

Salt bit at his tongue and water sloshed around his face. Yet, the grit of sand crunched between his teeth. It was dry as bone, and hot as hell.

"No! You shouldn't be here."

A familiar voice reached through the fog that fell across his mind. It sounded like his own.

The Seed.

A second voice joined it.

"Oh man, Dig, you gotta wake up."

Hawk?

A third came next.

"Is he okay?"

Alvin.

Finally, Rebecca's voice added. "He looks like crap."

Digby's mind bent around that last statement. How was the illusionist there?

The Seed tried again. "Listen to me. You can't be here. You shouldn't be here. Your brain is still intact but you have no mana and your system is unraveling. You have to stabilize it."

"You have to get up." Hawk's voice came from someplace else.

"You have to help us," Alvin added.

Everything grew quiet.

The Seed pushed him away with a whisper. "You have to eat."

The world snapped back into existence around him. Digby tried to speak but a throat full of sand hindered his words. He yanked his head from the ground and coughed the debris from his vocal cords.

"What happened?"

Digby could tell something was wrong before either of the boys standing over him could answer. Everything felt off. With a glance, he found both legs, twisted and bent. His left arm was just as bad. His back lacked the proper connections to control his lower half. The only thing he could move was his right arm and his head.

His staff lay nearby. The formation of blood he'd created to break his fall had shattered, leaving behind a jagged club at the end. He must have hit the ground harder than intended. Sweeping his eyes across the scene he found nothing but dry clay and sand as far as the eye could see. The sun beat down on him from above, threatening to turn his deceased flesh into leather.

They were stranded in the desert.

"Hang in there, Dig, we're coming to get you." Rebecca knelt beside him. "We just have to find you first."

"But you already have." He stared up at her in confusion.

"No, we haven't. I'm only projecting to you. I'm not really here, and I don't actually know where this is beyond the fact that it's in the middle of the desert. Asher can sense you though, so she's leading the way. It's going to take some time to get to you, but we're coming."

"Well, hurry up then." Digby dropped his head back down. "We'll wait right here."

"No, you won't. Skyline has certainly sent out a fleet of kestrels to find you. The desert is big and they should only have a rough idea of where you jumped out. Plus, they don't have a zombie raven that can track you, so we should get to you first. Right now, you need to find somewhere to hide in case they happen to fly overhead." Her voice faded as her body burst into a cloud of glowing particles.

"Can you get up?" Hawk came to his aid next.

"Yes, I'm alright." Digby forced himself to remain calm. "Everything will be fine. I just need to regenerate my…" His words trailed off when he saw his HUD.

MP: 1/198

What?

How could I be so low?

From the position of the sun in the sky, at least some time passed. How could he have failed to absorb any mana?

Unless… No.

There was no death essence to absorb.

Digby's mind raced. That was impossible. He was in the desert for crying out loud. The place held nothing but death. For a moment a glimmer of hope, reminded him that he had a ritual to complete that required a place such as this. He willed the Seed to show him the description.

UNQUENCHABLE THIRST
Description: Gain a better understanding of your mana
system by depriving yourself of death essence.
Materials Requirement: 1 additional participant.
Environmental Requirement: Ritual must be carried out at a
location completely lacking in death essence.
Rewards: A better understanding of your mana system and
the discovery of a new spell.

A new spell would certainly help, but he shoved the thought away as soon as he had it. There were more important things to tend to at the moment and now was not the time to grasp at power.

He turned his attention to Hawk and Alvin. His two undead revenants stood behind them looking frail. The sunlight must have been taking as much of a toll on the creatures as it was on his mana absorption.

"You there," he addressed one of his minions. "Come here and extend your wings to give these boys some shade. Surely you can manage that."

The nightflyer shuffled over and did as it was instructed, stretching its wings out so that they blocked out the sun. Digby felt around with his only functioning limb and tried to hold himself up. Repairing his body would be impossible until they found some-where with a bit of death essence available. It would have to wait.

Right now, they had to move.

"Alright, you there," he called to his other minion. "Come here and pick me up."

The creature staggered over and attempted to secure a hand

around him. It was like trying to lift an uncooperative child. Digby was, quite literally, dead weight. After a minute of struggling, he fell back to the sand.

"Alright, new plan, drag me." He thrust out his hand so his minion could grab on. The result was underwhelming and slow, but he was at least able to make some progress. He glanced back at the tracks in the sand, finding he'd only moved five feet.

That was when Hawk grabbed onto his arm to help speed things up. Digby swatted him away.

"No, no, that won't do. You'll exhaust your strength within the hour if you take on that sort of burden. I'm no survivalist, but I know enough to understand that you living humans need water." He made a show of glancing around. "Unless you have a canteen or two that I don't know about, you both are going to have to conserve your energy."

"Can I heal you?" Alvin held out his hand. "I have a Regeneration spell."

"Good lord, no." Digby recoiled from the boy, afraid he might cast the spell anyway. "I'm undead, healing magic doesn't have the same effect on me as it does on you humans." Digby glanced at the ring on Hawk's finger. "Actually, you both should avoid casting anything with those rings. I'm still not sure how much information Autem can get from them."

"What can we do then?" Hawk's tone fell, sounding defeated.

Digby struggled to think of a way out of the situation just as the Heretic Seed made things much worse.

WARNING: Your mana systems require at least a small amount of mana to remain stable. If your MP remains low, your mana system will become increasingly unstable. If this issue is not resolved, your mana system may begin to unravel or collapse entirely. In the event of a total collapse, your current existence will cease.

WARNING: Due to a lack of death essence in the ambient mana that surrounds you, there is no source available to absorb MP.

Get up, you fool, before it's too late! You're dying!

Digby froze as the horror of what he had just read set in.

He was dying. After eight hundred years, he was dying!

There was no way to know how much time he had. The Seed was right, he had to find somewhere to replenish his mana. He had to do something.

Digby clawed at the ground with his fingers. There would be death essence further down where the sun's light couldn't reach. Frantically, he dug his fingernails into the dry clay of the desert. He could barely make a dent with just his hand.

"What's wrong?" Hawk leaned closer.

"I need mana." Digby continued to dig. "There should be some I can absorb underground."

"Okay." Hawk started digging too. "How deep?"

"Six feet." Digby hesitated, realizing how much time it would take to get down that far.

Hawk jumped up and ran for Digby's staff. The formation of blood on the end was mostly broken but it served as a better shovel than his hands. Alvin knelt down to help as well. Though, even with that, the goal was distant. Not to mention the boys might exhaust themselves in the process. Digby's insides twisted in knots, worried that he might endanger their survival by letting them help.

Another message from the Seed drove a final nail in the idea's coffin.

WARNING: Continuing to starve yourself of mana may result in the activation of your RAVENOUS status, as a trace amount of mana may be gained through the consumption of live flesh.
Eat, you half-wit!

What? Digby stopped digging and looked up at the boys who were struggling to save him. "Stop."

"No way, we can do this." Hawk continued to dig.

"I said stop." Digby slapped the staff out of his hands.

"What the hell?" Hawk jumped back.

"You need to run." Digby swatted at him again despite the hurt on the boy's face.

"What?" Hawk hesitated.

"Get away from me." Digby gritted his teeth as his void began to howl with hunger. "I don't know how long I can hold myself back."

"Hold back from what?" Hawk's voice wavered.

"From eating you, damn it." Digby's voice shifted to a wild snarl as the Seed sent him the message that he feared most.

Racial Trait, Ravenous, active. While active, all physical limitations will be ignored.

WARNING: Ravenous zombies will be unable to perform any action other than the direct pursuit of food until satiated. This may result in self-destructive behavior.

WARNING: Ignoring physical limitations for prolonged periods of time may result in catastrophic damage.

Digby watched in horror as his hand moved independent of his will, reaching for whichever of the boys happened to be closest. They both leapt back out of reach. The torment continued as his hand slammed down into the ground to drag his broken body toward them.

"Hey, cut it out!" Hawk jumped away again.

Digby clawed toward him, ignoring his body's limitations. It was as if his attributes had suddenly doubled. If it wasn't for the damage he'd sustained, he would have torn them both apart in seconds. He was just lucky his minions hadn't decided to join in. Instead, they simply stood by and did nothing without an order. His hand snapped forward again, this time nearly throwing his body up like a fish out of water. It was uncoordinated and ridiculous but it wasn't slow.

Again, his body lurched forward in the boy's direction. *I'm sorry, I can't...*

"Stop it! Please." Hawk shouted. "Why are you doing this?"

Digby's chest ached as he launched himself closer, losing a few fingernails in the process. He wanted so badly to answer. It wasn't him. It was the curse.

No, it was his true nature.

"Shit, we have to dig the hole." Hawk tried to step around him to reach the area they had been working on.

Digby snarled and swiped at his leg, unable to stop himself. There was nothing the boy could do. With nowhere safe to dig, all chances of burying him deep enough to absorb any mana went up in smoke.

Damn it, no! Digby failed to hold himself back, forcing the boys to strafe around him to stay out of his reach. It was torture. The knowledge that he would cease to exist threatened to devour him as he tried his hardest not to do the same to the children.

How could it end like this? After everything I've been through, how could it all end here?

Digby spewed every hateful thought he could at the curse and what it had turned him into. He was a monster. He was a broken thing that should never have returned from the grave. His death-dependent mana balance was an affront to nature.

As everything went wrong, Hawk and Alvin jogged in a circle around him while his useless minions stood by doing nothing. Eventually, after several minutes of panic, hate, and self-loathing, his thoughts finally calmed.

It helped that the boys proved to be agile enough to dodge his ravenous attacks without worry. Not to mention that continuously surpassing his physical limitations had begun to damage his one functioning limb. His swipes started to slow and he couldn't propel himself nearly as far as before. He was pretty sure a couple of his fingers were broken too.

The knowledge that he might not actually kill the boys gave him some solace. If hurting them had been his last memory before vanishing into oblivion, it would have been too much to bear. With a little luck, Rebecca and Alex would find the boys before they died of dehydration.

Unfortunately, the more he thought about them, the more he wanted to eat them. He just couldn't stop the thought from flowing through his ravenous mind. The mana that could save him was right there for the taking. He could sense it pumping through their blood, and he was so very thirsty.

Stop that! He shoved the thought away, struggling to distract himself. If only he hadn't been in such a state, with the ambient mana matching the requirements of his ritual, he could have gained a new spell if he'd had all his facilities intact. Though, it was strange that the desert would have no death essence available.

Strange, indeed.

Digby remembered the first time he'd cast burial on himself and discovered that there was a higher balance of death essence six feet under. It had surprised him at first but began to make sense after he had been surrounded by it.

Everything dies, and the dead become one with the earth. Then, from the soil, springs new life and the means to keep living.

No, that was wrong.

Life didn't come from the earth. The soil only held the potential for life. It was the light that held the other side of the equation. Without life and death working together, nothing could flourish or thrive. The desert was a clear example. It had too much of one and not enough of the other. With a limited number of plants and animals becoming a part of the land through death, there wasn't much potential for the light to give life to.

Death was necessary.

Death was inevitable.

Well… Almost inevitable.

Digby had escaped it. He dwelled on the thought. Should he exist? He hadn't evaded death on purpose, but if the world needed balance to thrive, then was his existence wrong? Could he be a thumb on the scales, disrupting the equilibrium of everything?

Maybe. The apocalypse wouldn't have happened if he had expired centuries ago like he was supposed to.

No. That was wrong.

Henwick would still exist whether Digby had remained frozen in the arctic or not. If it wasn't the curse, the man would have found another way to achieve his goals. The world would have suffered either way. Henwick would have made sure of it.

So what is my place?

Digby continued to pursue Hawk and Alvin, slowing as he pondered the question. Imbalance was wrong. His mana purity was unnatural. Yet, that was the aberration that had granted him power, and that power… was necessary. It was the only thing that might put an end to Henwick's ambitions. The contradiction seemed to define him.

My existence is wrong… yet I am needed.

The moment the thought passed through his mind, something inside him shifted, as if his mana system had somehow changed. The shard of the Heretic Seed seemed to resonate in tune with the difference. A message ran across his vision a second later.

RITUAL COMPLETE

By depriving yourself of death essence for an extended period of time and allowing your mana system to approach collapse, you have achieved a better understanding of your mana system and your place in the world.

You have discovered the spell, Leach.

LEACH

Description: Drain mana from a willing participant or minion.

Rank: D

Cost: Variable

Range: 10ft (+50% due to mana purity)

Limitations: Mana gained by Leach is determined by how much mana is used to cast it, in a 2 to 1 ratio (+100% due to mana purity) You may not Leach more mana from a target than it currently has. The amount you may Leach will be further limited by your inability to take in any essence other than death.

Do it! Do it now!

Good lord, that's it. I'm saved!

Digby did the math. A two to one ratio meant that he would gain twice the amount of mana he used to cast the spell. The extra hundred percent from his mana purity essentially changed that to a three to one ratio. He checked his HUD.

MP: 1/198

He stared at his single point of mana. Using it would bring him up to three points. With that he could cast it again, and get nine more. Another use would get him what he needed to repair his body. He immediately focused on Hawk, knowing the boy would have a relatively even mana balance with enough death essence present to get him back on his feet.

He stopped himself before casting.

Hawk was an ally, but considering that Digby had recently tried to eat him, it was likely the boy would resist any spell he tried to cast. If he attempted the spell and it proved unsuccessful, he would lose the lone point of mana he had left. That was a risk he couldn't take. Instead, he shifted his focus to one of his nightflyers. Though, he had no idea how much mana they might have, since he'd created them through Five Fingers of Death and not Animate Zombie. All he knew was that it couldn't be much considering how low their intelligence was. At the very least, they had to have something flowing in their mana system. Plus, they were dead, so he knew their balance would be fully compatible with his own.

Spending his single point of mana, he cast the spell and stared at his HUD, watching as a faint trickle of essence traced through the air, barely even visible.

MP: 0/198

Panic surged through Digby's mind just before the value updated.

MP: 3/198

He cast the spell again.

MP: 9/198

One more use brought him up to twenty four. His brain stumbled on the value, running the math again. It didn't add up. It should have got him to three more points. The reason for the discrepancy became obvious when his minion fell face first into the desert ground.

I must have Leached the creature dry.

It was unfortunate but at least he knew where the limit was. Both Hawk and Alvin stared at the nightflyer that had just reverted back to a mere corpse with confused expressions on their faces. Fortunately, a new message passed through Digby's vision, bringing a bit of good news.

Mana system stabilized.
You are no longer Ravenous.

Digby felt his body relax, finally putting an end to his merciless pursuit of prey. "Oh, thank the lord."

Hawk stood out of arm's reach, holding the staff out to poke Digby in the shoulder. "Are you, you again?"

"Yes, it's me." Digby cast Necrotic Regeneration to snap his numerous bones and joints back into place. "I apologize. I went a little ravenous there."

"And you're okay now?" Alvin peeked over Hawk's shoulder, clearly still keeping his distance. The boy winced as Digby's fingers popped into place.

"I am now." Digby raised his head and nodded. "My mana system nearly collapsed and it sent my more primitive instincts into action. Fortunately, I was able to get back in control."

"What happened to your minion?" Hawk hooked a thumb at the nightflyer's corpse.

"I had to Leach away the unfortunate creature's mana to satiate my body's thirst. It seems I took everything it had." Digby cast another Necrotic Regeneration as the first one began to run out of power. "Now, get over here and help me up."

Hawk took a step forward, hesitating just before holding out his hand. "Oh, yeah, you kind of don't smell great."

"Oh shut it," he snapped back without meaning to after the ordeal he'd been through. "I covered my body with necrotic muscle to help save you, so I don't want to hear any complaints. I don't like smelling like death any more than you do. And I will add that I wouldn't have needed to come rescue you if you hadn't run out and gotten yourself taken by Autem."

"Alright, fine." Hawk let out a sigh that seemed to flow from his entire body before doing as he was told. He gagged once as he did. "I wouldn't have needed to get myself captured if you weren't hanging out in the open where everyone could see you, by the way. Also, getting taken in by Autem wasn't all bad. I'm a guardian now. So I have magic."

"Yes, and you better not use it for anything." Digby staggered to his feet. "I don't want Autem or Skyline finding us because you couldn't help yourself."

Hawk responded by repeating him in a mocking tone.

Digby narrowed his eyes at the boy. "Whatever, now come along, we have a lot of ground to cover. It's a miracle a kestrel hasn't spotted us already."

With that, he ordered his last minion to provide shade for the boys and they began walking. All he could do was hope that Asher could lead the others to him before someone from Skyline or Autem found him. Granted, the desert was a big place and it would take significant effort for his enemies to search it all. Hopefully luck was on their side.

Digby considered the uses of his new spell as they walked. As long as he didn't go overboard and drain too much from his minions, he would be able to access a much larger amount of mana. In a roundabout way, it would also increase his mana absorption.

One of the many tradeoffs for the power that a pure mana balance granted him was a slower absorption rate during the day. Oftentimes, the speed at which he took in essence fell far below his fellow Heretics, but as long as his minions could absorb mana at a similar rate, it would give him access to a much larger pool. If that was the case, then he could essentially increase his absorption rate with any minion he added.

The possibilities ran through his mind.

With access to so much more mana, it didn't really matter how low his maximum value was anymore. He could sacrifice more of it to animate minions that he shared a bond with. He would run out more often, but he could always drain some more from the surrounding dead. Hell, Asher and Tavern had close to one hundred MP each. That was enough to cast a number of his more powerful spells.

Digby made a point to do some experimenting once they made it back to Vegas. He set the subject aside when they came to a rock formation that could hide them until dark if necessary. Plus, the boys were looking rather tired. It wouldn't do to keep them walking until they passed out. Even worse, they didn't have any water.

After checking the area for snakes and other threats, both Hawk and Alvin collapsed in the shade of a rock that over hung some of the others. Digby sat down as well and ordered his remaining minion to join them. The creature staggered into the shade and dropped to its knees, clearly not faring well under the sun. With a little luck, Asher would be along with the others in tow.

Sure enough, an hour later an excited caw came from the other side of the rock. Digby's body felt lighter as soon as he heard it.

"Aren't you a sight for sore eyes." He rushed out from under the rock.

Asher flew straight into him, her wings flapping with excitement. She cawed and alternated between landing on his shoulder and flying around him. Digby picked up a relieved feeling over their bond, followed by a few words.

Was worried.

Feared lost.

Never leave.

The raven seemed to have become a little more talkative in his absence. Digby nuzzled her beak and patted her side. "I know, I know. I shan't leave you alone again."

"Thank god you made it." Rebecca stepped into view from behind the rock.

"Yes, we managed, it seems." Digby stroked Asher's feathers as she settled down.

"I was worried." She blew out a sigh of relief. "I tried to help search with a drone so I could look for you from the sky, but the internet failed. The satellites are still good, but the infrastructure is not what it once was."

"Pity." Digby frowned, still not entirely understanding how the internet worked or how the satellites fit into the equation. "Now, where is the rest of your rescue party? Surely you must not be alone." He poked at her shoulder in an accusatory manner as his finger passed through her.

"Yeah, I'm still in Vegas." Her image flicked as he touched her. "I've been using Asher as an origin point for my projection. But yes, Mason is on his way here in a jeep. Asher was riding with him until she started shouting we were close and took off."

"I see." Digby nodded, a little sad that he hadn't heard his minion speak yet.

Mason showed up soon after with several canteens of water. Alvin and Hawk drank them down in record time as soon as they climbed into the vehicle. Digby couldn't help but feel proud of the boys. They had done well. Much better than the rest of the children that Autem had taken in.

Once the boys were taken care of, he ordered his remaining nightflyer into the back of the jeep without wasting time. It wouldn't do to stick around long enough for Bancroft's search teams to find him. It was a miracle they hadn't already. Much to Mason's displeasure, Digby dropped into the passenger seat beside him. The soldier rolled down all the windows as soon as he got in. Digby ignored the implied insult and relaxed.

He was just glad to be heading home.

CHAPTER THIRTY

The ride back to Vegas took some time, but was blissfully uneventful. Digby took the moment to get caught up on his horde's progress from while he had been away for the night. Mason was well informed on the subject. Unfortunately, with Asher heading off to find him, they had been forced to halt much of their efforts since she wasn't around to keep the dead in line.

One of the downsides of using his Fingers of Death spell to reanimate the revenants was they were still on a mutation path that he was unfamiliar with. They had gained a few leaders within the zombie horde that Asher had gathered, but none of them were loyal to Digby. With that, they had simply locked up the casino that the horde was stored in so they could wait until Asher returned.

He would have liked to get a report from Rebecca, but she had promptly vanished as soon as Mason had arrived. The fact that the information network she'd been using had failed her didn't bode well. Then again, it was better that it failed now and not when they executed their plan to attack the base. Not that it mattered anymore, considering the kestrel they'd stolen had been reduced to scrap already.

The loss would set them back.

Without the kestrel to initiate the assault, he would need many more zombies in his horde to make up for the difference. He just hoped his new spells would be able to help him reach his goals. He frowned for a moment before letting his worry go. He may not have won the war, but the night had been a victory nonetheless.

Digby glanced back at the boys in the seat behind him. They had done well, but he would still need to confiscate their Guardian rings. All it would take was a stray thought to accidentally cast a spell and there was no way to know what Autem would find out from that. He would have taken both of the boys' rings already, but they had fallen asleep almost immediately after the jeep had reached the road. He decided to let them sleep.

They'd had a rough night after all.

Hawk slumped on Alvin's shoulder with his mouth wide open. The sight sent a wave of relief across Digby's mind. The young boy had kept up a brave front, but Digby had caught a few fearful expressions here and there. He was tough, but watching a child close to his age set themselves on fire to avoid rescue clearly had him shaken. Digby couldn't blame him. After watching that boy die like that, he had a renewed sense of disgust for Henwick and his organization's influence.

Compared to Autem, Skyline didn't actually seem so wicked. They might be mercenaries, but at least they weren't brainwashing children. He chewed on the thought. No doubt Bancroft and his forces would find themselves on the wrong side of things eventually. Once Autem grew strong enough, they would have no use for hired goons.

In the end, Skyline would probably fall just like the rest of Henwick's victims. If it weren't for the organization's mercenary nature, he might have considered making an appeal to Bancroft to choose a different side. He brushed the thought away as soon as he had it. It was unlikely that Skyline's Commander would see his side of things. Bancroft didn't seem the type to bite the hand that fed him.

After a few hours on the road, they pulled up to the casino that he'd claimed as his territory. Digby roused the sleeping boys in the back.

"Wake up, you lazy children."

Hawk responded with a lengthy yawn before staggering out of the vehicle. The exhausted boy looked dead on his feet. Alvin followed without saying a word. Digby wasn't sure if that was a good thing or not. The child had never been talkative, but still, he would have liked to know if he was at least grateful for being rescued. After all, he was about to be reunited with his sister. The thought sent an odd warmth through his deceased heart. Digby walked a little faster, wanting to see the moment that the two siblings found each other.

Alex and Parker came out to meet him so they could take his remaining nightflyer back to where the horde was stored. It still wasn't common knowledge around the casino that Digby was dead, so getting the zombified revenant out of sight was prudent. Beyond the few people that were in the know, there was no way to tell how the survivors would respond to the knowledge that a deceased necromancer was secretly calling the shots for the territory.

Digby pulled his staff from the jeep and handed it to Parker. The head of the item was still encased in a jagged form of blood that would need to be chipped off. With a nod, she headed inside with the staff. Once she was gone, Digby turned his attention to Hawk and Alvin. Now was as good a time as ever to confiscate their rings. Before he could open his mouth, Lana burst from the doors of the casino.

The young woman sprinted to her brother, practically plowing into him as she threw her arms around him. Neither of them said a word for a long moment. Instead, they just held each other tight. Digby watched as Alvin buried his face in his sister's shoulder. The sight made him smile. After all the horror and pain that the world has gone through in the last month, it was good to finally have some hope.

Eventually, Alvin began to pull away but Lana only pulled him closer. "I'm so sorry, I left you."

"It's okay." Alvin nodded.

"I'm so sorry it took me so long to get you. I tried to see you back when I was on the base, but they just told me no. I tried to find a way to get you out of there, but I just couldn't do it alone. I wasn't strong enough."

"It's okay." The boy repeated. "I know."

She let go only to place a hand on his shoulders as she looked him in the eyes. "Are you okay? Did they do anything to you?"

"I'm fine." He nodded and looked down at the ring on his finger. "They made me a guardian and helped me gain some levels."

"They didn't make you do anything dangerous, did they?" Her face grew serious.

He shook his head. "Not really. They had me kill some of those monsters. But there was always someone there to help if things got to be too much for me. I'm stronger now, though."

She hugged him again. "You're safe now, that's all that matters. Digby has made a home for us here and he's trying to put a stop to everything Autem is doing."

Digby staggered a moment, feeling the crushing weight of her words.

"I, um…" Before he could say anything else, Lana released her brother and rushed to throw her arms around him. "Hey, what do you think you're doing?"

"Shut up, Dig. I'm hugging you." She didn't let go. "You saved him. Thank you."

"Alright, alright, I accept your gratitude." He tried to pry her hands off of him. "You can let go now. I don't smell particularly good."

"I don't care." She squeezed him one more time before letting go and crouched down to Hawk who was standing off to the side. "I owe you thanks as well."

"Damn right." Hawk pressed a thumb into his chest as if he'd been waiting for someone to acknowledge him. "I did a lot back there. I jumped out of a plane and everything."

"So humble." Digby rubbed at the bridge of his nose.

"Plus, I have magic now, just like Dig." Hawk displayed the ring on his finger.

"I should say not." Digby held out his hand. "Give it here."

"What?" Hawk pulled his hand away.

"As much as I'm sure you enjoy having magic, I can't allow children to wield such a thing. Not if it might reveal information to our enemies." Digby snapped his hand open and closed expectantly.

"I won't use it." Hawk clasped his other hand over his ring.

"I'm afraid I can't take your word. I know first-hand how easy it is to cast a spell even when you don't intend to. All it takes is a stray thought. Not to mention those rings seem to have a side effect that alters your behavior."

"It does?" Hawk looked down at his finger.

"He's right." Lana placed a hand on his shoulder. "I couldn't wait to get rid of my ring. I saw too many people change after becoming a guardian. It was like they'd lost a piece of themselves."

"Indeed." Digby frowned. "I shudder to think of that happening to you."

"I don't feel any different." Hawk glanced back and forth between him and Lana. "And Alvin doesn't seem too far gone."

Digby rolled his eyes. "Yes, and it's a miracle that it hasn't taken a toll on him yet."

"I can handle it." Hawk shook his head. "And you can trust me."

"Sorry, but that's not a chance I'm willing to take." Digby softened his words with a smile while trying to remain firm.

"Fine, I'll take it off." Hawk groaned and yanked off his ring, before shoving it into his pocket.

"Nice try." Digby snapped his fingers to indicate that they weren't finished. "It's for your own good, so give it up."

"No way, what if something happens and I need magic?" Hawk folded his arms.

"You don't need magic as long as I'm here." Digby wasn't willing to compromise on the issue.

Hawk scoffed. "And what about when you're not here? Half the time you run off to do random ass stuff. Not to mention, you went through all that trouble to get me a phone back there in the base but never sent me more than a couple words."

Digby's mouth fell open, not expecting the sudden attack. "I assure you, the things I do are important. They only seem random because I can't go around explaining every little thing to everyone." He hesitated before arguing the boy's other point. "And no, I didn't have time to message you. I was busy growing my horde so that we might stand a chance against our enemies."

At least that was what he told himself.

Of course, he could have made time. A more honest answer would be that Digby didn't know what a child would want to hear. It wasn't like he'd forgotten about the boy. He just wasn't good at comforting others. Fortunately, the conversation was interrupted by the last person he expected.

"You can take mine." Alvin stepped forward to place his guardian ring in Digby's hand. The boy turned to Hawk. "We shouldn't keep them."

Hawk's mouth fell open, clearly not expecting Alvin to give up his magic so easily. He stewed for a moment before finally slapping his ring into Digby's hand. "Whatever, just take the stupid thing."

"Oh, come now, don't be like that." Digby closed his fingers around both rings.

Hawk simply spun on his heel and stormed off into the casino. "No one has ever trusted me with anything, why should you be any different?"

"Wait just a damn—" Digby started to follow him, but Lana held out a hand to stop him.

"Yelling at him will only make it worse." She lowered her arm. "He's still a kid, and it doesn't take an expert to see he looks up to you. He's bound to feel betrayed if you take his magic away." She reached down and took her brother's hand. "He doesn't know the toll that power could have taken yet, but he'll understand eventually."

Digby growled for a second before forcing himself to relax. She was right. Hawk was still a child and needed a gentler approach. Yelling would only serve to make things worse. Finally, he forced out a musty sigh.

How have things gotten so complicated?

Deciding to give Hawk some time, Digby bid Lana and Alvin farewell for now and headed off to his room to wash off the grime before anyone else complained about how he smelled. He could really use a change of clothes too.

It had been a long day.

———

Alvin watched the zombie shove his way through the door of the casino. It was weird. He hardly recognized the dead man. The last time he'd seen Digby, he was missing his nose and was dressed in a leather duster and SWAT armor. Now, he looked like a gambler. Especially with the tattoos that covered one hand. Alvin couldn't help but wonder how he'd gotten them.

"You want to see our room?" Lana interrupted his train of thought.

He smiled and nodded, realizing how much he'd missed her. After everything that had happened, he was glad she was safe and happy. The smile on her face when she looked at him reminded him of his mom. His heart ached at the thought.

Mom was gone... probably.

Autem had looked for her but found nothing back at home. She'd either left or been eaten. Either way, she was gone. Alvin held his sister's hand, despite knowing he was too old to cling to her. Still, she was all he had left.

From there, Lana took him into the casino to help him settle in. On the way, she told him all about the room that they would be sharing. He couldn't help but notice how cheerful she sounded. He dragged his feet on the way through the building, trying to take in as much information as he could. He'd even stopped walking at one point to stare a strange statue that had been set up promi-nently. It looked like something out of a mummy movie. Even weirder was that it was made from stone while everything else in the casino was gold. A sign, written in messy handwriting, hung from a velvet rope that surrounded it, the words, 'no touchy,' making it clear that the statue was important.

"That's the sun goddess." Lana looked down at him, clear noticing his interest. "She keeps us safe." She tugged on his hand to get him moving again. "Come on. I'll give you a tour later, let's get settled in first. We have plenty of time after all."

Alvin nodded and followed along, shrugging off his need to investigate the statue further. The knowledge that it was of some sort of goddess was enough for now. It was definitely important, but there were other things that mattered more, like where all the zombies were. Surely a necromancer would have surrounded themselves with the dead. That was what made Digby so dangerous to Autem. There must have been a horde hidden somewhere. Unfortunately, Lana dragged him upstairs before he could find out more.

The room where he was meant to stay had a second bed that was reserved for him. They hadn't shared a room since they were kids. She apologized for it being cramped and assured him that they would find something more spacious when they could.

Once he was situated, someone knocked on the door. It was the same woman that had taken Digby's staff. She looked to be a couple years older than his sister. Maybe twenty one. Alvin listened closely to catch her name.

Parker.

"Hi there, umm, champ." The woman leaned down awkwardly, like she didn't know how to act with people younger than herself and handed his sister a bag of clothes. "I didn't know what you would like so I just grabbed some stuff from the shopping center." She chuckled to herself. "Anything's better than that Autem stuff."

Alvin thanked her politely and headed into the bathroom to wash off the dirt and sand that had accumulated during his time in the desert.

He flipped on the light and turned on the shower, taking a moment to judge how loud the water was. He flicked on the ventilation fan as well, then reached into his pocket to pull out his guardian ring. It was true that he had given one to Digby, but that one wasn't his. No, it was just one that Bancroft had given him as a precaution.

Autem didn't always speak highly of Skyline, but they were still allies and Bancroft certainly had a level of authority. Not to mention his predictions had been accurate so far.

Digby had indeed come for him, just like he'd said.

The Commander had connected his sister to Digby after she deserted his forces. He'd traced back where Skyline had picked her up and concluded that she was still alive, assuming that Digby had gone out of his way to secure her survival. It only made sense that Digby would try to get him out too.

All Bancroft had to do was provide an opportunity and the zombie would come along to pick him up. It was certainly the easiest way to find out where the necromancer was hiding. Alvin could appreciate the simplicity. Of course, it would have been better if the guardians on the plane had been able to capture the necromancer, but since the opportunity had passed, it was Alvin's turn to do his part.

Looking down at his ring, he slipped it onto his finger. Autem was right. Digby was an abomination. His existence went against the will of the One. Alvin didn't need to see any more to understand that, not after the zombie had tried to eat Hawk and him just a few hours earlier. The look in the dead man's eye during that moment told him everything. The necromancer's humanity had faded too far to even be called a man.

Lana would understand eventually. She just needed to accept Autem. Then, she could go live at the colony where she was safe. She just needed guidance.

Placing his hand to the bathroom mirror, he opened a link to Bancroft's office. The commander looked up as soon as the image filled the glass.

"I take it you've made it back to where Graves is hiding."

Alvin nodded. "He's in Vegas."

CHAPTER THIRTY-ONE

Easton struggled to act natural, sitting at his station in the base's comms room. His console sat at the end of a row of similar terminals. Usually no one even looked at him. He just stayed quiet and did his job while also undermining the security of Skyline's operations. Ever since the world ended, there had been a clear feeling of superiority among most of his fellow mercenaries. It got worse as they all gained rings and magic. Many of them had entered the organization at a young age and felt they had little to fear from the monsters outside their walls. Fortunately, their attitude made Easton's work easy. Betrayal was not something Skyline expected. Especially not from someone who was powerless.

At least, that was before things had changed.

Damn it, Dig. He cursed the necromancer. Easton had worked hard to make preparations and find weak points in the base's security. Now, it was all for nothing. The base had been locked down, and his one ally within Skyline had been captured.

Even worse, Bancroft was on the warpath. The fact that Digby had breached their walls was another black mark on the man's reputation. If he failed to bring in Graves before Autem grew any stronger, it was almost certain that they would relieve him of his command. Not even his most loyal guardians could stop that.

On top of that, the commander had completely compartmentalized the hunt for Graves to a point where Easton couldn't find out anything. He had been taking charge of the effort personally already, but now it seemed like he had tightened his grip on the chain of information.

I knew I shouldn't have alerted Digby that Autem was moving Alvin.

Honestly, it was obvious that someone leaked the information. He might as well have worn a sign around his neck saying, 'hey, I'm a spy.' Then again, what could he do? What kind of person would he be if he just wrote off the kid as an acceptable loss?

Easton deleted everything he thought might be incriminating from his system. It was only a matter of time before the trail led back to him. He just hoped Graves would be able to pull off the attack that he was planning. Easton would have to follow in Lana's footsteps. His only chance at survival was to slip away in the chaos and try to meet up with Rebecca.

That was when two members of Bancroft's top squad entered the room. Every muscle in Easton's body tensed up the moment he saw them. His heart leapt into his throat when they looked in his direction.

Shit, this is it. I'm dead.

"Specialist Easton?" One of the men approached.

"Yes?" Easton relaxed a hair when he noticed that they didn't have their hands near their weapon. Then again, he was one of the only people on base that wasn't a guardian. The fact that these guys didn't think they needed weapons to deal with him might also mean that they were far more powerful than a regular human.

"Come with us, please."

"Is there a problem?" Easton tried to read the guy's expressions.

"Not that we are aware of, but the commander wants to see you." The two men stood waiting for him to comply.

Shit. Easton debated making a run for it but abandoned the thought as soon as he had it. There was no way he'd make it. Instead, he stood and followed them from the room. The next thing he knew, he was standing in a conference room down the hall looking Bancroft in the face.

"How come you haven't taken a guardian ring?" The commander sat at the end of a long table like a king at a banquet.

Easton struggled to answer, not expecting the question. He almost would have been more comfortable with an accusation. At least he expected that. "I'm a communication's specialist. Taking a ring wasn't something that was needed to fulfill my job."

"That's true, but it says here in your file that you've been offered a ring twice and turned it down." Bancroft moved some papers around on the table in front of him. "You do realize that taking one would increase your chances of survival and open up new doors for you in terms of advancement in Skyline."

"I do, but I am good at my assigned role." He did his best to get out of the question without offering too many details.

Bancroft nodded and looked down at his papers. "You were in Seattle, is that right?"

"Yes, sir." Easton stood at attention, worried what the question meant.

"Not many survived that night." Bancroft sifted through his pile of papers. "How did you make it out?"

"I was assigned there to operate communications, so when things went south, I was ordered to perform the duties that were less combat oriented. The rest was mostly luck. Only myself and a few others survived." Easton left out the part where Rebecca had warned him to run.

"Ah, yes." Bancroft flipped over a piece of paper. "There were a few other survivors besides yourself. Now that I think about it, there was also a drone operator that survived as well, though she has since deserted."

"I..." Easton hesitated, realizing that he had never been informed of Rebecca's survival through Skyline. The only way he would have known she was alive would be if he was in contact with her. "I wasn't aware Crow's Nest was still alive."

"Crow's Nest?" Bancroft arched an eyebrow before glancing down at his papers. "Oh yes, that was her call sign."

"Sorry, I never caught her real name in the few conversations we had. As I understand, she was not a high-ranking operator." Easton tried his best to sound indifferent.

"Yes, Ms. Alvarez was not good at following orders it seems." Bancroft flicked his eyes up to him. "You haven't had any contact with her after that night, have you?"

"Pardon?" Easton played dumb.

"Has Ms. Alverez contacted you?" Bancroft repeated the question so there was no room for misinterpretation.

"Why would she?" Eason kept the act going.

"I'm following up on a few things, and the only way I can make sense of things is that she must have contact with someone within the base. We had another deserter a week ago during the fight in California. It was a new recruit that had also had contact with this drone operator from Seattle. Clearly, there was a line of communication open for them to organize through. It's also clear that Alvarez and Graves were the two individuals that breached our security here on the base recently, and that someone within our walls helped them. Just last night, they attacked a transport to extract the brother of one of their accomplices. Taking all that into account, there must be someone here on the base that's helping them."

"But you found the culprit, didn't you? He was someone from the mess hall, right?" Easton held his ground and threw Campbell under the bus since he had already been caught.

"Yes, we suspect that the necromancer was smuggled into Autem's R&D in a meal delivery cart. However, there was no previous connection between the zombie and the meal cart's organizer. So I'm still looking around for a leak."

"And that brought you to me." Easton said the words he knew were coming to try to get ahead of it. "You suspect I might have helped them because I was involved with Crow's Nest during the Seattle incident."

"That is the meat of it, yes." Bancroft smiled as if he was glad things had been understood.

"Well, I hate to disappoint, but I haven't been in contact with her." Easton tried his best to sound innocent.

Bancroft's face fell into a severe frown. "Do you remember a man named Clint Howland?"

"Who?" Easton furrowed his brow.

"Mr. Howland was one of the few survivors that escaped Seattle with you."

"Oh, I apologize. Yes, I do remember him." Easton struggled to recall if he had seen the man since that night.

"He's dead." Bancroft said matter-of-factly. "Or undead I think."

Easton flinched. "I'm sorry to hear that."

"I sent him to be debriefed by one of Autem's heads before they took over part of the base here." Bancroft paused before adding, "They killed him."

Easton's eyes widened. "Why are you telling me this?"

"I'm telling you this because I want you to understand your position." Bancroft placed his hands on the table and stood up. "Clint was killed because it was convenient for Autem. He was killed because no one cared if he lived or died. The same is true for you."

Easton opened his mouth to speak but Bancroft held up a hand to stop him.

"My point is that you might be innocent." He shrugged. "I don't have any evidence to know either way. Unfortunately, the Autem Empire holds the chain attached to Skyline's collar, and I cannot go back to them empty-handed. I need to at least show that I'm making some progress. So, you see, it doesn't matter that I don't know if you're guilty for sure. Your time here is finished regardless."

"Wait, I—"

"Don't bother trying to defend yourself. The fact is that the old world is gone and the Autem Empire does things differently. There's no such thing as a fair trial unless they consider you one of their own." Bancroft finished the conversation with all the emotion of a business deal before gesturing to his men at the door. "If you're not with Autem, then you simply aren't worth the time or consideration."

Easton shook off the mental shock of what was happening and held his ground. If his time had come, then that was that. There was nothing stopping him from speaking his piece.

"I understand." He stared daggers at Bancroft. "Autem is a

plague, worse than the curse that ended the world. It's a throwback to a time when all mankind understood was conquest and indoctrination." The men behind him grabbed his arms and shoved them behind his back, but he didn't let it stop him. "Are you sure you're on the right side? When history looks back on this moment, will you be able to say you were in the right? Do you even know what right is?"

Bancroft sighed, looking sad for just a moment. "It's not about being right. In the end, it's about power. And you just don't have it."

"Neither do you." Easton breathed his words through his teeth before being dragged from the room.

The next few minutes were a blur that landed him in the brig. Easton was half expecting to be taken behind a building and shot. He wasn't sure if he should have been relieved or worried. Clearly Bancroft still had plans for him. Otherwise, there would be no reason to keep him alive.

He shoved his face against the tiny slot in the door, struggling to see whatever he could.

Campbell stared out from the cell across from his.

"They got you too, huh?"

CHAPTER THIRTY-TWO

Digby pulled on a new vest from the collection he looted from the shopping center. It was good to be clean again after tearing through those men on the airship to rescue the boys and clawing his way through the desert. He checked his reflection in the mirror as he buttoned it up, noting how close he came to passing for human.

Staring at his image, he couldn't help but feel conflicted. He hadn't been feeling very human of late. Considering he'd been killing and devouring his way through the world, that wasn't a surprise.

Maybe I should make more of an effort to be a part of things here.

With that in mind, he headed downstairs to have dinner with the others instead. Well, not really. It wasn't like he could actually eat with the humans. At least, he doubted they would appreciate it. He just figured spending a little time being normal might help him to feel more like them. After witnessing what his enemies had turned children into, a little humanity was just what he needed.

Fortunately, Vegas had plenty to go around.

Deuce had organized one of the casinos eateries into a one stop banquet hall for everyone. There was some rationing, but it would be months before they ran out. By then, they would either have things figured out, or they'd be dead. Either way, keeping everyone fed and giving them a place to eat together was best for morale.

Despite the pressure of their situation, the survivors actually seemed to be having a good time. A wave of dread reminded him that he and his horde were the only thing standing between them and Autem's conquest. A part of him wanted to turn right around and head straight to the other side of the strip to help Asher with the horde. Unfortunately, the sun had just begun to set. If he were to go there now, the revenant hive would tear him apart the instant he showed any sign of aggression. They might not have an interest in hurting him by default, but that was sure to change if he tried to hit them with his Five Fingers of Death.

He pushed the concern out of his mind for now and continued toward the congregation of humans. The horde would have to wait until the morning when things could be dealt with safely.

Dropping into a seat at the end of a table, he regretted his decision immediately. To his left sat Rebecca, chewing on a bit of bread from the buffet while actively avoiding eye contact with Mason. The soldier sat to his right, pushing a pea around on his plate without saying a word. The tension in the air was palpable.

Maybe I should have picked a different table.

Digby debated on pretending like he'd forgotten something and making his escape. Then, he thought better of it. He'd argued with Rebecca enough to understand her more than he used to. She was a good person, if a little detached. Quick to anger when offended, but slow to reach out when in need of support. Judging by the couple's silence, he got a pretty good idea of the problem.

"Why don't you just apologize already?" Digby leaned on one elbow and stared at Rebecca.

She dropped the piece of bread she was eating back into her plate. "What?"

Digby shrugged. "Let me guess, you two had an argument. Probably due to a miscommunication that hasn't been cleared up, and now you both are having trouble moving past it because no one has apologized."

"Stay out of it, Dig." Rebecca rolled her eyes, before tearing off a large bite of her roll. A silence more awkward than any that had come before settled across the table while she chewed. Eventually, she swallowed and blew out a long sigh before looking to Mason. "Sorry for pushing you away the other night."

A noticeable amount of tension melted away from his shoulders. "It's okay, I wasn't mad. Just a little hurt."

"I figured." She raised her eyes up to look at him. "I had just found out some personal stuff in Autem's files. I wasn't ready to talk about it." She glanced around the table. "I'm still not ready, so you know…"

"Say no more." Mason speared the lone pea that he'd been pushing around. "I get it. I understand that we aren't so close for me to expect you to confide everything with me. I'll admit that I wouldn't mind being closer, but if that's not what you're looking for, I'm okay with that."

"Thank you." She relaxed. "Interacting with people is still sort of new to me, and I'm still crap at it."

Digby slapped a hand down on the table making them both jump. "There, isn't that better?"

"Oh, shut up. You didn't help." She rolled her eyes again. "I would have apologized eventually."

"Sure you would have." Digby gave her his most irritating grin.

"Nobody likes a smug zombie, Dig." Mason folded his arms.

"But smug is my usual attitude." Digby feigned injury, only to let out a laugh at the fact that he might have actually helped the stubborn couple. He may have been more human than he thought. The moment was interrupted by a tray being dropped to the table as Hawk sat down beside Mason. Parker and Alex sat down on Rebecca's side.

"The forge is officially up and running." The pink-haired soldier shoved a fork full of food in her mouth mid-sentence.

"And the horde is growing," Alex added. "I just got back from checking on the progress. Asher is really kicking ass with her search for zombies. Honestly, I've never seen her so dedicated to something. It kinda seems like she knows how important it is. She's heading out to do another sweep of the surrounding city now. The rest of your minions are feeding right on schedule too. If we can keep this pace up for a week or so, we might actually be in good shape to attack."

"That's excellent news. The more minions I can get, the better. And I intend to start converting revenants into zombies first thing in the morning. We will be victorious yet." Digby leaned back in his chair, glad that things were working out for once. It didn't take much to bring him back down.

"Must be nice having minions that do whatever you say." Hawk sawed away at a piece of meat on his plate with as much aggression as he could muster.

"You have something to say, lad?" Digby narrowed his eyes at the boy, expecting another outburst.

"No. Just thinking out loud." He contradicted his denial by stabbing a bit of food with his fork like it had wronged him.

"Let me guess, this is because I took your ring?" Digby assumed the obvious, annoyed that the child was still having trouble understanding the situation.

"Shit yeah it is." Hawk slapped his fork down, drawing the attention of some of the people at the other tables. "I did good back at the base, and you don't even trust me."

"Trust has nothing to do with it. That ring is a hazard." Digby tried to reason with him while keeping his voice down to avoid making a scene that might paint him in a bad light to the other survivors.

"Then give it back." Hawk held out his hand. "I earned that ring, and I want to get stronger."

"I see that, but you don't understand what that magic might do to you or what risks come along with it." Digby shook his head.

"I'm fine with the risk."

"I'm not," Digby answered matter-of-factly.

"You just don't want anyone else having magic," Hawk snapped back.

The accusation grated on Digby like the buzz of an insect in his ear. He had been called out on his selfishness plenty of times, but for once, he was pretty sure that his shortcomings had nothing to do with his decision. The fact he was acting out of genuine concern for the boy made the venom in Hawk's words all the more irritating.

Digby leaned forward. "Now you listen here, child, I shan't have you throwing accusations at me just because you're mad. I understand that having power taken away just as soon as you've obtained it is frustrating, but you are failing to understand the situation. I didn't rescue you just to lose you to the temptation of power that ring offers. Besides, even if I were to give it back, you are too young. The battlefield is no place for children."

"I didn't see Autem having trouble trusting kids even younger than me with magic." Hawk stared straight at him.

"And you think they are better than I because of it?" Digby scoffed with indignation. "You have the gall to even think that after what you witnessed on that aircraft. Autem has corrupted the young in their care." The memory of that child's burning corpse flashed through his mind to push him over the edge. "They have twisted and betrayed the role of a caretaker into something perverse and manipulative."

"Yeah, and so did most of the foster houses that I was sent to." Hawk stared daggers at him.

"I don't know what that means," Digby spat back before pulling Hawk's ring from his pocket. "But this thing here is a symbol of corruption. Now, if I could find a way to bestow upon you the same power as a Heretic, then I would gladly trust you with it. But this ring has no place in this world, let alone on your finger." Unable to suppress his irritation with the argument, Digby opened his maw and dropped the ring in to remove the temptation once and for all.

Hawk's eyes widened as the golden ring sunk into the necrotic blood of his void. Digby snapped the gateway shut the instant it was gone. He'd had a good mind to extract a spell from it to see to it that it was destroyed for good, but the look on Hawk's face told him that would be going too far. For a second, it looked like the child might explode. Then, he calmed down and stood up. "Whatever, I don't even care anymore."

With that, the boy stormed off for the second time that day.

Digby immediately slumped back in his chair and crossed his

arms as the rest of the table stared at him. "What are you all looking at?"

Everyone's eyes drifted back to their food.

Digby forced out a long, musty sigh. "I knew there was a reason I didn't like kids."

CHAPTER THIRTY-THREE

"Shit, shit, shit." Sax rushed through the casino with a couple of Deuce's men in tow as he reached Digby's table in the dining area.

"What the hell is the matter?" Digby stood up, still annoyed by the argument he'd had with Hawk.

Sax hunched over the table to catch his breath. "There's a kestrel heading straight for us. They'll be on the ground in under a minute."

"What?" Everyone else at the table stood up in unison.

"It's flying low over the strip now," Sax added.

"Damn!" Digby spun, realizing the casino's two hundred or so inhabitants that Autem didn't know about were all right there in the dining area. "Everyone has to hide, quickly, lest we get ourselves caught in a lie that exposes our entire plan." He grabbed at Sax's shoulder. "Find Deuce and get him down here. I need him to play his part."

"What about everyone here?" Alex stepped to his side. "Is there time to get them up to their rooms?"

"No," Mason answered for him. "You heard Sax. They'll be on the ground soon and we don't know why they're here. They might try to come in and while we'll never get everyone moving in time or be able to hide the evidence that they were here." The soldier gestured to the countless plates of food on the tables and the buffet area.

"Alright, then we hide everyone here." Digby jumped up on his chair. "I'm sorry to disrupt everyone's dinner, but our enemies have just landed an aircraft at our door. There isn't time for all of you to move so I ask that you all stay right where you are and remain as still and quiet as possible."

Two hundred or so blank faces stared up at him before someone spoke. "Who are you?"

Digby's eyes bulged, realizing the downside of keeping himself hidden was that no one knew he was really the one in charge. He shook off the mistake and tried his best to introduce himself. "My name is Lord Graves, and I am the one who has protected this place from the shadows."

A number of faces turned to Alex and Mason, since they had been the only ones who had been working with Deuce in the open.

"What he says is the truth." Mason backed him up. "Graves has been integral in keeping this place safe, but for reasons we don't have time to go into, his involvement has been kept quiet."

"Yeah, so um, everyone just do as he says for now." Alex tried to help. "We don't have much time."

His words were unimpressive but the serious tone that he delivered them in seemed to tell the room that now was not the time to argue. The majority of the people responded by putting down their cutlery and pushing away their plates before making an effort to hold still and keep quiet. Only a few needed more proof. Fortunately, Mathew and James as well as some of the other survivors that Digby had arrived in Vegas with backed him up. The room obeyed his orders after that.

"That's better." Digby nodded. "And make sure someone sees to the children so none accidentally blow our cover." Digby watched as a few people made a point to attend to the younger members of the group.

Speaking of children... Digby swept his eyes across the casino floor to look for Hawk and Alvin. Neither boy was in the crowd. *Now just where did they get off to?*

Unfortunately, Digby's search was put to an end when Deuce

showed up. Clearly, he had been in the middle of getting dressed when Sax had found him. The man was still tucking in his shirt while Sax tied his tie.

He rushed to Digby as soon as he saw him. "What do you need me to—"

Digby cut him off before he could finish his question. "Get out there and greet our unexpected guests. Try to stall if you can."

"Oh man, oh shit." Deuce seemed to be struggling to handle the sudden intrusion, but nodded nonetheless. "I'll do what I can."

Taking a few of his men as well as Sax, the casino's fictional leader rushed to the door. Digby made a note of the puzzled expressions he got from the tables across the room. The interaction had clearly shown who was really calling the shots but a number of survivors were still skeptical. He frowned and took charge regardless.

"Parker."

"Yeah, boss?" The pink-haired soldier made a show of standing at attention.

"Get to the stairwell and make sure none of the stragglers are wandering around. There's bound to be a few that haven't come down for dinner and I don't want them making an appearance at the wrong time."

"Gotcha." She saluted and dashed off in the direction of the stairs that lead to the guest rooms. Digby turned to Rebecca next.

"Becky, prepare to hide everyone in case the Autem bastards decide to enter."

"I'm on it." She ran to the entrance of the dining area. "I can put up a blank wall in front of us. The illusion should hold as long as everyone here understands what's happening." She turned back the second the words left her mouth, clearly realizing how hard that would be considering that most of the people in the room didn't know anything about magic.

Digby cringed, immediately regretting his decision to keep the existence of their abilities from the rest of the survivors.

"Alright, everyone, I have something to tell you that's going to be hard to believe, but my associate here is an illusionist." He gave the room a moment to take that in, surprised when not one survivor batted an eye.

Alex stepped closer to whisper up to him. "Um, illusionists are kind of a thing here in Vegas."

"What?" Digby stared down at him from the chair he stood on.

"Not like, the magic type. But just people that do tricks that look like magic." Alex shrugged. "They perform all over the strip."

Digby did his best to work out the concept. "So they're like jesters or actors?"

"Kinda."

"Alright, then." Digby tried to work in that new bit of knowledge into his explanation. "Rebecca here is a master illusionist, and she's going to produce an image of a wall where the entrance of the dining area is so that our enemies will be unable to see us. What I beg of you is to simply accept the illusion as truth. She may be a master, but she is also sensitive to those that doubt her performance." He looked down at her. "Will that do?"

"Maybe." She shrugged. "My Waking Dream spell has ranked up a few times, so it's relatively stable."

"Perfect." He hopped down from his chair and rushed from the entrance. "Come, Alex, we must be ready to act if things go south. We'll hide behind the gambling machines so as to not draw untoward attention to the dining area." He glanced back to Rebecca. "Keep them hidden."

She nodded as he left her behind.

"Wait, where's my staff?" Digby stopped short and turned to Alex. "Surely you've not had the time to destroy it yet." He glanced at his HUD to confirm before giving him time to answer.

MP: 198/198

"Good." He would have gained back the thirty mana that had been infused into the staff if it had been destroyed.

"We chipped off part of the hardened blood at the top of it, but that's it. It's by the new forge now, I'll grab it and meet you back by the slot machines near the entrance."

"Thank you." Digby nodded and left the artificer behind as well before sprinting to the casino floor.

Reaching the first row of machines, he ducked behind one and peeked around the side to catch a glimpse of Sax waiting by the door. The sound of a kestrel's engines shutting down could be heard from outside. He arched an eyebrow. Skyline's airships were relatively quiet.

They must have landed close to the entrance.

Digby ducked low, placing his hand on the floor to support himself. Looking down, he read the letters of the word 'luck' that were tattooed across his fingers. He gave a silent thanks to the man he'd stolen the arm from.

I'm going to need all the luck I can get.

A feeling of dread swelled as he noticed motion near the door. The image of black uniforms became clear through the glass.

Damn!

Skyline's guardians were coming in. He almost would have rather that they be from Autem, since they seemed more focused on building their empire up than tearing the rest of the world down. Instead, they left that task to their hired goons in Skyline. His body tensed at the possibility that these guardians might be Bancroft's top squad that Easton had mentioned days ago.

Digby flicked his eyes back toward the dining area where the survivors were hiding. All he saw was a blank wall. Rebecca had already done her part. He squinted at the illusion, afraid for a moment that someone inside might doubt their eyes enough to unravel the spell. After a few seconds he looked away. The illusion seemed stable enough.

"I assure you, we don't know anything about any escapees." Deuce entered the casino along with a group of five guardians.

Escapees?

Digby's mind raced. They must be looking for Hawk and Alvin. Considering that Vegas was somewhat close to where they jumped from that aircraft it made sense that Bancroft might have his men check in on the nearest settlements. If that was the case, their location might still be safe. Digby relaxed a little. They might just take a look around and leave.

The guardian in charge stepped past Deuce. Digby eyed the man.

Guardian: Level 30 Holy Knight

Great, another one of them. Digby lamented the fact that he kept running into the class. It seemed that Skyline preferred to use their designation as squad leaders. He swept his eyes over the rest of the group.

Guardian: Level 22 Artificer
Guardian: Level 20 Pyromancer
Guardian: Level 25 Rogue
Guardian: Level 21 Cleric

Damn. It was definitely Bancroft's favorite squad. He remembered seeing most of their classes back on the base when he'd watched Skyline's commander pass by with them in tow. He made a point to keep the rogue where he could see him, considering the man almost certainly had the ability to conceal himself.

The knight stopped short and turned to Deuce. "I hope you'll understand that I can't simply take you at your word. You have only recently taken over as leadership here and the escapees that we're looking for could be hiding here under your protection. Now, the individuals I'm looking for are two children and a man. He's rather pale so he would stand out in a crowd."

Deuce attempted to stand in his way. "We haven't had any groups like that arrive today."

"That may be, but we have to make sure regardless." The guardian placed a hand on his shoulder before passing him by again. "You understand."

Digby slipped around to the other side of the gambling machine he hid behind as the guardian trespassed on the casino floor. A part of him regretted not staying in the dining area where he could hide with the others. Surely Autem's people had seen his picture and would recognize him if they spotted him.

Running the numbers, he questioned if he could win in a fight if the need arose. He had most of the group beat in terms of levels, but the knight still had a few on him. That was when he realized something important.

Wasn't there six in that squad back when he'd seen them with Bancroft? Alarm bells sounded in his head as he remembered who was missing.

The illusionist!

He'd completely forgotten that Bancroft had an illusionist under his command. If the man was missing now, it was obvious that he was up to something. The tricky devil could either be concealed or casting a Waking Dream. Digby smirked. At least the illusionist didn't know where he was hiding and couldn't possibly be sneaking up on him. Then again, that begged the question, where was he? Digby didn't get a chance to find the answer before a hand settled on his shoulder.

Digby suppressed a yelp as he spun around to find Alex. He immediately narrowed his eyes at the artificer for startling him. A part of him wished he'd put more points into perception like Rebecca had. No one was going to sneak up on her.

Alex gave an apologetic nod and passed him his staff while making sure to remain hidden. Digby claimed the item and examined the fragments of crystalized blood at the top. The jagged formations extended from the metal head of the staff in a way that might serve as a mace. He felt the weight in his hand, finding the weapon a viable option for potential maiming.

With staff in hand, Digby turned his attention back to the intruders.

"Quite a place you have here." The knight in charge continued to play nice with Deuce.

"Yes. We were lucky that Rivers had gathered so much in the way of supplies before we were able to wrestle control of the settlement away from him." Deuce downplayed the murder spree that Digby had gone on to claim the place.

"How many people do you have here?" The knight was clearly probing for information.

Deuce did his best to mislead the man. Digby just hoped no one had a lie detection spell like Rebecca. The conversation continued for a few minutes more without too much worry until he realized how close they were standing to the sun goddess statue at the center of the floor. From where they stood on, the stone figure that kept the revenants at bay was only fifty feet away. Digby couldn't be sure if the Guardian Core would detect the statue's enchantment or not, but if it could, then it wouldn't take much for them to realize how important it was.

Maybe none of them have their HUDs activated like the guardians back on the base... He brushed aside that hopeful thought as soon as he'd had it. There was no way Bancroft's top squad would be so careless while searching for him and the escaped children. No, they would be on high alert.

Again, the question of where Hawk and Alvin were passed through his head. They hadn't been in the dining area when he'd left it, and if they happened to wander onto the casino floor now, their cover would be blown for sure. He clenched his jaw. All he could do was hope that Parker would be able to catch them before they did anything stupid.

Of course, almost on cue, that was when a voice shouted from across the floor.

"I'm here!" Alvin ran toward Autem's guardians with Parker and Hawk chasing after him. They slowed when it became clear that it was already too late.

No! Digby reached out from where he hid as his deceased heart sank.

"That's what I thought." The knight simply drew his sword and swiped it across Deuce's chest. A spatter of crimson painted the gambling machines nearby. The injured man fell back, clutching his wound. It wasn't fatal but the next attack would be sure to finish him.

"Stop!"

The word surprised Digby even as he realized that it had come from his mouth. Bancroft's men turned in his direction all at once. He stood and glanced back to Alex. "Hurry and heal Deuce."

Alex nodded and pulled a flask from a pouch. It glowed momentarily as he slowly walked toward their fallen accomplice.

"There you are, Graves." The knight raised his sword in his direction. "The commander has been looking for you."

Digby ignored the knight's comment and reached out to Alvin instead. "Why?"

"Because Autem is right." The child stepped closer to the knight.

"They're lying to you." Lana appeared through the illusionary wall that kept the dining area hidden, clearly unable to remain in hiding.

The spell unraveled in an instant, revealing Rebecca and the rest of the survivors. The few that were armed were already standing with guns drawn, just a handful of Mason's combat volunteers with barely a weeks' worth of training. They stepped forward in a futile show of force. With her illusion gone, Rebecca stepped up to stand with Mason. She cast Regeneration on Deuce to make sure he would pull through.

Lana kept running only to stop short as the knight flicked his sword in her direction. She stared daggers at him. "Get out of my way."

"I don't think so." The man held his ground.

Digby continued to ignore him while approaching Alvin. He held his staff low against his side with the bottom dragging on the floor to avoid looking threatening. "Come back to us. You can't trust Autem, or Skyline for that matter."

The boy shook his head. "All they want to do is rebuild the world better than it was. You can't be the good guy if you're trying to stop them."

"You don't understand." Lana tried to back Digby up.

"Neither do you." Alvin turned to her. "You can come too. Autem will take you in. We can still be together."

"I don't want to live under Autem's thumb. And neither does the rest of the world." She dug in her heels in defiance. "I can't go with you."

The hurt on Alvin's face was clear. He must not have expected his sister to turn him down.

"You can't save everyone." The knight placed a hand on

Alvin's shoulder as he shifted his focus to Digby. "I don't suppose you'll turn yourself in."

Digby narrowed his eyes, his blood boiling at the realization of how far gone Alvin was already. "Do you know who I am?"

"I do." The knight let go of Alvin's shoulder. "I reckon you're the necromancer that broke into Autem's R&D building. Level twenty-eight, if the guardian core is reading you correctly. Your name's Digby, am I right?"

"That's Lord Graves to you." He raised his staff to hold it upright before slamming the bottom down on the floor. "And if you think I'm letting you take that child, you are sorely mistaken."

Interpreting his words as an order, Mason stepped forward and gestured for his handful of armed men to fan out. They each took up a position to target the squad of five guardians. Digby held up a hand to stop them. Their guns wouldn't do much against them, and there was a chance they could hit Alvin. Not to mention things might get out of hand fast if bullets started flying. He looked to the dining area and the two hundred or so survivors trapped there to watch things unfold.

He glanced to his HUD.

MP: 198/198

It wasn't enough. At least, not without the help of Asher and his horde. With the dead in the mix, he could win easily. Unfortunately, they were currently at the other end of the strip. He could call Asher and tell her to bring the horde along, but he was sure they wouldn't make it in time. The guardians could probably kill half of the people in the dining area before he was able to stop them. He wasn't even sure he could beat them.

No. A fight was out of the question.

Before Digby could make a move, he picked up the flow of mana with his blood sense. That was when he remembered the illusionist that was unaccounted for.

Damn.

Digby snapped his attention in the direction of the sensation, finding nothing. He arched an eyebrow. He must have picked up the illusionist recasting Conceal to remain hidden. If that was the case, all he had to do was look in his direction and the spell would fail. The only question was, where was he? Digby's vision darted to the statue of the sun god, realizing how vulnerable it was. His only solace was that Bancroft's men couldn't have known about it. Unless Alvin had told him.

"Don't even think about it." Digby focused on the area as the guardian flickered into existence. The illusionist looked surprised for a second but quickly regained their composure.

"Did you place it?" the knight shouted to his man.

"It's set." The illusionist sprinted away from the statue as they pulled something from a pouch. Digby couldn't tell what it was, other than the fact that there was a red covering on one end. The answer became obvious the man flicked open the top and thumbed a button underneath. To his horror, the center of the sun goddess detonated in a blast of stone fragments.

"No!" Digby leapt back as the top half of the statue toppled over. At the same time, a few more explosions could be heard in the distance, somewhere further down the strip.

The knight snapped his sword into the magnetic sheath on his back as if he had finished with the task that he had come to do. "We aren't so impulsive to try to take you and your Heretics out now. Sure, we'd win, but not without losing a few of our own in the process. I know that much. Besides, there isn't much point in risking our lives when there's a nest right here on the strip that can do the job for us."

Digby's eyes bulged at the realization of what the explosions in the distance meant. "How did—"

The knight cut him off. "How did we know about the revs?" He nodded. "I'll give you one guess."

The answer was obvious.

"Rivers." Digby grimaced like the name had tasted foul on his tongue.

"He was quite proud of how his men cleaned up this city." The knight grunted. "The guy actually thought we should be impressed. Probably would have kept his mouth shut if he knew we've had a plan in place to free the monsters and take him out if Vegas ever became a problem."

Digby cursed Rivers. The damned fool had doomed the city with all of his incessant bragging. Bancroft's men must have stopped at the other end of the strip and set their explosives at the doors of the revenant hives before coming to investigate his settlement. Dread sent a chill up his spine. Even after his horde had gorged itself on the revenants within, there were still enough of the creature in there to kill his people several times over at night.

Digby's mind spun at a million miles per second. Without the sun goddess, the revenants would be on them within the hour and his horde would be too slow to help. He snapped his attention back to the squad of guardians as they headed for the door. Their illusionist picked up the rear. They must have planned to destroy the statue from the start. The knight was right; why fight when they can simply let the revenants destroy them instead?

But how did they know?

The bottom dropped out of Digby's stomach the instant it became obvious.

Alvin.

Digby chased after the guardians as they led the boy toward the door. Focusing on the child he confirmed what he feared.

Guardian: Level 8 Mage

Digby squinted at the child's hand, finding a golden band around his finger. He shoved his hand in his pocket to pull out the ring that Alvin had given up. "A fake!"

The boy had tricked him. Alvin must have contacted Bancroft and told him everything.

"How could you?" Digby stomped forward. "You've condemned your own sister to death."

Alvin turned back to look him in his eyes. "She condemned herself by staying with you."

"This isn't you, Alvin." Lana rushed to Digby's side with tears streaming down her face. "Please, don't leave me. You're all I have left. I'm your family!"

Alvin simply turned away, only stopping when another voice called out.

"Wait!" Hawk rushed toward the entrance as the guardians opened the doors. "Take me with you."

Digby staggered, leaning on his staff as the boy's words cut like a knife in his heart. "Not you too." Hawk turned back for a second before running in the opposite direction. Digby reached out. "I'm sorry."

This time, the boy didn't even look back before taking a place at Alvin's side. Digby rushed forward only to stop when one of the guardians lobbed a Fireball at his feet. Hawk and Alvin vanished through the doors a second later.

Digby stared at the door through the flames burning before him as Lana dropped to her knees beside him. The woman cursed Autem and Bancroft with every fiber of her being for what they'd done to her family. The sound of the kestrel taking flight followed. It was too late.

Too late for everything.

The settlement's location was known to Bancroft. Probably Autem and Henwick as well. Even worse, a swarm of revenants were coming.

Digby looked back to the broken statue behind them.

They were doomed.

It wouldn't be long now.

CHAPTER THIRTY-FOUR

Digby stared at the doors of the casino in disbelief.

Hawk was gone.

Was it my fault?

Did I drive him away?

Lana slammed her fist on the floor beside him in frustration wrought by the betrayal of her brother. Between sobs, she cursed Autem for driving a wedge between them. Digby wanted to blame them too, but a nagging voice in his head told him he held a share of the blame.

He'd tried so hard to understand others and he'd come so far. At least, he thought he'd had. Regret swam through his mind as he opened his maw and brought up Hawks' ring that he'd tossed inside earlier. He hadn't been wrong to take it. He was sure of that. Yet, maybe he should have worked harder to make the boy understand. Maybe he should have been more sensitive.

He scoffed at the thought.

Sensitivity wasn't his style. That was why he liked Hawk. The boy hadn't been bothered by his rough edges or demanded that his feelings be handled with care. It made having the child around tolerable. Then again, maybe that wasn't a good enough reason to forgo the consideration.

His downward spiral was interrupted by Alex.

"What do we do?"

Digby snapped out of his thoughts. It didn't matter what he'd done to push Hawk away. No, all that mattered was that he intended to get him back. Either that, or he'd die trying.

"Get the door barricaded." Digby stood back up. "Those revenants will start to trickle down to this end of the strip within the hour. Once one of them starts screeching, we'll be buried in the foul creatures. Barring the doors won't stop them, but it will slow them down." He held a hand down to Lana. "I understand how you feel, but now is not the time to let your despair drag you down."

"What do you need me to do?" She reached up to take his hand. The anger in her eyes told him all he needed to know. She wasn't going to give up without a fight either.

"Be ready to treat the wounded. You're going to have your work cut out for you."

"What about us?" Deuce climbed off the floor with Alex's help. He was still clutching the wound on his chest that he received from Skyline's knight as it stitched itself back together.

Digby answered him with a wave of his hand that told him to follow as he rushed back to the rest of the survivors. He ran through their capabilities in his head on the way. If they were going to survive the night, he was going to need to leverage everything they had.

With a thought, he beckoned to Asher. His feathered zombie master was still with the horde on the other end of the strip across from where the hive had been trapped. To protect the living, he was going to need the help of the dead. Asher answered back over their bond.

The horde moves.

Digby sent a thought back to praise her. A second order reminded her to keep the horde in line. The Revenants wouldn't attack them as long as they didn't attack first. He sent a mental command to his destroyers as well, since Asher lacked control over his rare zombies. With a little luck, the undead behemoths would resist the temptation to eat any of the revenants until he wanted them to. Otherwise, the swarm might tear his horde apart before they could arrive. As it was, his horde wasn't large enough to defend the casino alone. All it could provide was back up.

Unfortunately, that was also slow. The revenants would strike first. Somehow, the survivors in the casino would have to hold them off long enough until help could arrive.

Digby burst back into the dining area and leapt back up onto the chair he'd stood on before. He dropped the end of his staff down on the table beside him to make sure he had the room's attention. "Alright everyone, listen up!"

All at once, his accomplices rushed to stand around him. Mason, Sax and Parker stood to his left, while Rebecca and Alex stepped to his right. Deuce and Elenore slipped into the middle. The speed at which they fell in line was not lost on him, causing a strange feeling to swell in his chest. Up until his death and subsequent resurrection, he'd never known what it was like to have people willing to follow him. The impulse to flee the responsibility passed through his mind, before he shut down the instinct.

Beyond his accomplices stood two hundred confused faces. Convincing them to follow along was going to be the real challenge. He started again.

"Alright, I know all you have questions and I'm going to do my best to answer all of them when there is time. However, right now, we are in imminent danger, and I will need all of your cooperation if we are going to survive."

"Who are you again?" a voice shouted from the back.

Digby rubbed at the bridge of his nose. "I already told you. I am Lord Graves, and I am the one who secured this settlement for all of you."

Several other people chimed in with questions.

"Hear him out." Elenore held up a hand to quiet the crowd.

Deuce backed her up. "Yes, if it wasn't for Graves, we would all still be living under Rivers' thumb. And we would still be giving our children to those Autem guys. Without Graves, we wouldn't even know that Autem was a threat until it was too late."

"Indeed." Digby tried his best to stand tall. "But while I may have rid you all of that braggart, Rivers, my trustworthy apprentice, here..." He gestured to Alex, getting an appreciative nod from the artificer in return. "...has discovered an unfortunate parting gift left behind by Rivers. One that Autem has just weaponized against us." Digby spoke quickly to save valuable time. "His high-cards had trapped tens of thousands of revenants in the buildings on the other end of the strip, and that explosion you heard in the distance was the sound of those monsters being released. They will begin to attack soon, so we must make use of the time we have."

Silence swept over the room as concerned faces stared back at him. Then the same voice from the back spoke.

"What's a revenant?"

"What?" Digby's mouth fell open realizing that most of the people in the room had not been trained in any way to deal with the monsters. It was likely that the only people that would recognize the word were the members of Mason's volunteer combat force.

"The shriekers," Deuce corrected, using the word they'd been using before Digby had arrived. "They're those pale vampire zombie things."

"They are called revenants." Digby stomped a foot on the chair beneath him. "They are most certainly not zombies. I shan't have you giving my kind a bad name."

"What do you mean by your kind?" the same voice from the back asked.

"Ah..." Digby's mouth fell open for a moment, realizing the topic that he'd accidentally brought up. He closed his mouth again before he put his foot in it farther. Then he shook his head and thrust a finger out at the crowd. They were going to have to hear the truth eventually. "Listen here, you. We do not have the time to discuss who among us may or may not be a zombie. But suffice it to say that there are a number of facts that you all have not been privy to due to their rather unbelievable nature. I shall list them as follows, and I repeat, I will answer questions when everyone is safe. So keep your mouths shut until then."

The crowd remained silent.

Digby held up a finger. "Number one, magic is real."

Rebecca cast an illusion of Fireball so all could see before snuffing it out between her hands like a powerful wizard. Obviously, she could have cast a real Fireball but it wouldn't have been as easy to dispose of. The crowd gasped regardless.

"Indeed." Digby nodded as a few hands went up. "Again, no questions until we survive the night. All you need to know is that the cause of this apocalypse is also magic. Magic that Autem ensured would kill as many people as possible, so that they could move in and rebuild the world in their image." He held up a second finger. "Number two, the dead are not our enemies."

Confused expressions filled the room.

"As members of this settlement, I, Lord Graves, promise that you shall never fall prey to the appetites of the dead, for I have the power to control the hordes. Unfortunately, the same cannot be said for the revenants, which is why the swarm heading our way is a threat. I have gathered a moderate horde of zombies to defend us but we will still need to do our part to survive this night until they arrive. My point is, do not fear the dead. Hungry as they may be, they are your allies."

Mason and Alex backed him up, making sure everyone understood before Digby moved on.

"Now that everything's out in the open, this is what I need." He dropped his gaze to his trusted accomplices. "Mason, have your combat force take up arms and meet me at the main entrance. Deuce and Elenore, gather all the noncombatants and take them upstairs to the rooms. Barricade the stairs. If we aren't able to hold the front, make sure nothing gets through to the rest of the humans. Rebecca and Lana, you're on medical duty. The curse acts fast at night, so get a couple enchanted flasks from Alex to make sure no one who gets bit turns. I don't want any of our fallen joining the other side."

Alex pointed to himself. "Shouldn't I do that, since I'm the one that can purify water?"

"No, the task I need you for is too vital for our survival to put you on water duty. Rebecca and Lana can stop back with you to get more when the water's enchantment fades or they run out." Digby furrowed his brow. "How long does your purify spell last?"

"Fifteen minutes."

"Alright." He glanced back to Lana. "Set a timer and make sure to resupply when needed." Digby turned back to Alex. "I need you to focus on the sun goddess. We can't win even with the horde as back up. The best we can hope for is to buy time for you to work your magic. If there is a way for you to use your abilities as an artificer to salvage the effect of that statue, even if it's weaker, then do it. Increasing the balance of life essence could be enough to solve everything. The swarm would simply back off."

Alex nodded. "I don't know how to do that, but I will try."

"There is no try, only do!" Digby quoted something Rebecca had once said as she jumped into the conversation.

"Should I be on water duty?" Her tone wavered a little. "Wouldn't I be better in the fight?"

Digby shook his head. "We have plenty of gun and ammunition. It will certainly take a mountain of bullets to exhaust the revenant's healing ability, but we should be able to hold them back without you. I know your spells are good for offense but they're demanding on the mana and this fight is going to be about endurance. Keeping our soldiers on the battlefield is more important. Just make sure to meditate when you get low so you don't run out of MP." He glanced at Alex. "Same goes for you."

Everyone nodded as a nervous caw bled through the bond he shared with Asher. A thought, more complex than normal, followed.

The swarm hunts soon.

Ready the living.

With that, Digby stepped down off his chair and strode into the casino floor.

"Everyone move. You know what to do. The swarm will be upon us." He slammed his staff down and spun toward the entrance. "We best be ready."

CHAPTER THIRTY-FIVE

Digby stood behind a hastily built barricade of tables, chairs, and gambling machines, waiting for the first of the revenants to arrive. The rest of the casino's access points had been securely blocked back when Rivers had occupied it, leaving the main entrance and one side door as the only remaining weak points.

In front of the barricade, Tavern stood, wielding two crude short swords that had come from the forge. With the promise of free reign of the bar, they were ready to defend the front line until their bones were crushed to dust. The infernal spirit's skeletal form had drawn quite the attention when Digby had summoned them, but they also served to display a bit more proof that he really was the Lord of the Dead that he claimed to be.

The survivors waiting with him tensed as the first threats reached the entrance. Pale faces and bat-like snouts squeaked against the glass as the revenants pressed on the doors. A chorus of screechers drew more as soon as they became aware that there was potential food within the casino.

"Hold your fire." Digby held out a hand to Mason and the rest of his combat volunteers. There was no need to break the glass until it was close to failing already.

Behind him stood thirty men and women. The entirety of the

assault force that Mason had spent the last few days training. Judging from the expressions of terror on their faces, they still had a long way to go. Though, the fact that they had volunteered and had yet to flee spoke to their credit. They were certainly braver than Digby had been back when he'd been a mere human in a similar situation. Yes, they would do fine.

He glanced at his HUD to make sure he'd absorbed the mana he'd spent summoning Tavern.

MP: 198/198

Making his mana last was going to be the real challenge. At least he could Leach some MP from Tavern since the infernal spirit didn't have any spells to cast with it. Though, even with that, it wouldn't go far. Especially since he had put the skeleton's most recent bond point into perception, which only granted a modest increase.

Digby glanced back at the broken sun goddess statue as Alex and Parker gathered its pieces. At least, with its enchantment gone, his absorption rate had returned to what it normally was at night. If he could hold out until his horde reached them, his limited mana supply wouldn't be a problem. Once his back up arrived, he could Leach all the mana he needed from the dead. Unfortunately, according to the updates he'd received across his bond with Asher, his deceased army was moving slow and easily distracted.

It was going to be close.

"They're getting through!" Mason shouted as the glass of each of the doors began to crack under the pressure of several dozen revenants. He and his men raised their weapons.

"Hold." Digby reached out his hand. "Let them in and fire when they are several bodies deep so that your shots might pass through to hit multiple targets."

"Listen to Graves." Mason stepped to his side and leveled his rifle at the doors. "Guns aren't the best weapon against these things, but do it just like practice. Aim for center mass and be generous. A few wounds won't be enough to exhaust the mana that powers their healing ability, but a dozen or so might, so pour it on." He patted a cart that had been wheeled in. "We have plenty of ammo. And I have a team loading more magazines as we speak."

The first of the doors gave way to add a period to the end of his statement. A gunshot rang out from behind him as one of the nervous volunteers opened fire prematurely. The bullets peppered the first few revenants while shattering the glass of another two doors. The swarm outside surged in.

"Stay focused!" Mason shouted to bring his soldiers under control as the creatures poured in and fanned out in the entryway. "Now!"

Digby flinched as rifles barked all around him. He'd never liked guns, though, the hell they rained down was impressive nonetheless. Crimson sprayed from the creatures as they sprinted across the entryway to reach them, bullets bursting through the backs of the first line only to thump hard into the enemies behind them. The sheer amount of damage became too much for their mana system to repair. Many tumbled to the floor to become obstacles for the rest to leap past.

"Rotate!" Mason shouted as his volunteer soldiers in front fell back to reload, only to be replaced by another row of gunners.

The revenants didn't skip a beat, still rushing forward. Some may have fallen, but others simply shrugged off the damage. Some of the fallen even clawed their way back to their feet as their wounds closed.

Digby raised his staff to meet the first wave that darted for the barricade. Holding the shaft of the weapon horizontal with both hands, he cast Decay twice, allowing it to hit an area of effect rather than focusing on a single object. The spell wasn't suitable for offense, but since the creatures generally lacked a relevant will attribute, Decay still served to give them reason for pause. A blanket of necrotic power swept across the oncoming swarm as a dozen screeching voices cried out in protest. Many shrank away at the sudden blast of pain, their skin turning black and flaking away.

With his staff in hand, it only cost him sixteen mana.

Mason's volunteers took care of the rest as a group of five men stepped forward with shotguns. The weapons blasted hellfire at close range into any creature that failed to back away. The rest of the gunners followed up, leaving the entrance filled with over one hundred bat-like corpses.

A cheer came from the volunteers, trailing off to silence as more revenants crowed into the entryway. Their feral eyes locked on the casino's meager combat force as slathering mouths chittered and screeched.

Digby narrowed his eyes at the endless swarm.

The fight wasn't anywhere near over.

No, it was only just beginning.

———

Alex scrambled to gather pieces of carved stone from the floor. Gunfire from the entrance filled the air with a constant volume of nerve-racking pops to remind him of the pressure.

"Pass me what you can," Parker shouted over the sounds of battle as she helped gather everything.

"I think this is all of it." Alex shoved several handfuls of rubble at her. Sweat ran down his forehead as he looked down at the remains of the sun goddess. The statue had been cracked in half, leaving its legs standing where it had been and its torso laying on the floor beside them. Its midsection was barely more than dust and pebbles.

Alex dropped to his knees and placed his hand on what was left of the goddess's head, hoping that it might still have a shred of its previous enchantment. He focused with everything he had and glanced at his HUD.

Nothing.

He checked the other pieces as well but there was nothing left. The enchantment had been destroyed.

"Shit!" Alex cursed his magic. There wasn't anything he could do. He just didn't have the spells.

"We have to be able to do something." Parker picked up one of the larger chunks of stone and made an attempt to place it back on top of the legs. "What if we piece it back together?"

Alex let out a mirthless laugh. "There isn't enough of it intact and we don't have the time."

"You don't have any spells that can fix it?" She leaned closer.

Alex picked up a couple loose stones to hold in his palm. "None that I've learned so far."

Without warning, Parker jumped forward and grabbed his shoulder. "Okay, then we just need to teach you something new."

"What?" Alex dropped the stones from his hand.

She yanked him away from the statue. "Come on."

"Ah, okay." Alex followed her out.

Parker darted toward the front lines, sliding to a stop near Digby as he unleashed a wave of Decay spells to drive back a few revenants. Alex skidded to a stop behind her.

"What the hell are you doing here?" Digby shot them a sideways look.

"Where's Sax?" Parker shouted over the gunfire.

"He's getting another load of ammo." Mason dropped an empty magazine to the floor and reloaded.

"Gotcha." The pink-haired soldier leapt away from the barricade and sprinted back toward the casino's armory.

Alex followed, unsure what she had planned. He would have asked but given the situation there wasn't time. Instead, he vaulted a railing and made a break for the armory. They nearly crashed into Sax as he exited the supply room pushing a cart full of loaded magazines.

Parker didn't give him a chance to ask questions either. "You got glue back there?"

Alex's mind screeched to a halt at the insanity of her question. The statue was in a thousand pieces. Glue was not going to cut it. Sax panted and pointed to a shelf full of medical supplies. Parker was moving before Alex had the chance to stop her.

"Let's see." She swept her hand across the shelves as she scanned the contents. The word 'glue' was repeated under her breath before she snatched up a box of liquid bandage. "This'll do."

"We might want to rethink—" Alex started to question the

point of her actions but she was moving again before he could finish speaking.

"No time, come on." She blew through the door that led back onto the casino floor.

Alex let out a confused sigh and followed just in time to run into a pair of revenants that had gotten past the barricade. He hit the first with an Icicle without hesitation as Parker drew one of her daggers and planted it in the other creature's chest. She leaped back up a second later, leaving her weapon in the revenant to ensure it expired. From there, she sprinted to the dining area where they had eaten before the attack.

Alex hopped the railing outside and followed her in as she vaulted the bar at the back. He furrowed his brow. They had moved all the alcohol elsewhere, so there was nothing back there but a bunch of stemware. Despite that, Parker didn't skip a beat, grabbing several wine glasses and lining them up on the bar.

"Okay what are we doing with those?"

She answered him by setting one glass on its side and snapping its stem with the butt of her remaining dagger. She did the same to the others before tossing him a bottle of liquid bandage. "Start gluing."

Not wanting to waste time, Alex did as he was told while raising his concern. "What is this going to do?"

"You learn new spells by accomplishing related tasks, right?" She grabbed another few wine glasses without waiting for an answer. "Well, I've seen Harry Potter and I'm betting there is a spell out here in the real world that can repair broken things. The only question is, how many wine glasses do you need to stick back together for you to learn it?"

"I've tried to force myself to learn spells before. Back when I was hiding in California, just after I escaped Seattle. I tried to guide the Heretic Seed into giving me something that could be used for combat by chopping wood. It got me nothing." He held onto a mended glass with both hands and slid it to the side to make sure it stayed together while he moved it. Letting go, he left the glue to set and moved on to another glass. "I'm not sure the Heretic Seed can be manipulated like this."

"Sure, but aren't you an artificer?" She snapped the stems off another few glasses. "Shouldn't that give you an edge when trying to learn something that relates to your class? I mean, I'm definitely not an expert on magic, but I've played enough boardgames over the last couple weeks, so it kind of makes sense, right?"

Alex's mouth fell open. He'd been obsessed with using the Seed to gain the strength to fight before. That had been all he'd thought about. He wanted to be strong enough that no one could ever take advantage of him the way people had in the past. He wanted to be powerful, yet the Seed had denied him that wish from the start. Instead, all it had given him was the ability to heat objects.

What if that was never my purpose?

A memory flashed through Alex's mind of shooting one of River's high-cards a few days ago. He hadn't liked the way it felt. Actually, he'd nearly thrown up. Killing was necessary to survive in the world. He knew that much. There was no avoiding it. He always assumed he would get used to it. That when he did, the Seed would finally grant him the power he'd thought he wanted.

What if that isn't the power I'm meant to have?

What if I've been holding myself back by wanting it?

Alex squeezed a drop of glue onto the broken stem of a glass and placed it back together. There was something calming about the act, despite the gunfire echoing through the casino behind him. He held the glass in place and stared at the damaged section in the middle. The crack almost seemed to fade away as the glue set.

It felt right.

"I'm not meant to destroy." The words slipped out before he realized he was speaking.

"What?" Parker checked one of the glasses that he's finished with.

"I think I was meant to do this." He pieced another glass back together. "I think I'm supposed to fix things. Maybe even make things better."

"Are you having a moment here?" She arched an eyebrow at him.

"Kinda." He focused on the task in front of him, finding some kind of connection with the act of mending what had been broken.

He wasn't just fixing things.

He was returning them to the way they should be.

Alex reached for another glass. "You might be a genius, Parker."

She took a little bow behind the bar. "I know."

———

Rebecca slipped through the combatants as gunfire erupted all around her. The sound blended with the screech of a dozen revenants. Lana kept pace close behind her.

"Medic!" Mason shoved a wounded volunteer out of the way as he pumped a round into the skull of a revenant that was climbing over the barricade.

"No, no, no!" The injured man fell back, clutching his forearm. The terror in his voice was evident.

"I've got you." Rebecca leapt to his side, taking one of Alex's flasks from Lana. "Here, drink."

The man's skin grew pale as his eyes darted between her face and the flask, clearly skeptical that its contents could save him from turning. They had seconds at best. Rebecca shoved the flask into his mouth, not giving him a chance to protest. The metal rim clanked against his teeth as his canines began to extend into jagged fangs.

"Don't you go rev on me now." She dumped as much water as she could into his mouth, watching as his transformation slowed to a stop, leaving him mostly human. She cringed as she tried to pretend he didn't still have a wicked set of fangs. Apparently, the curse could be cleansed but the damage it had already caused couldn't be reversed.

"You okay there?" Lana jumped in, pulling a small flashlight from a pocket to shine into in his eyes, which had now become a weird shade of brownish-yellow.

A moment went by where he said nothing. Rebecca sucked in a

breath, ready to Icicle him if he made a move to attack. Then, finally, he spoke.

"You saved me."

His words came out with a lisp as they passed through his retransformed teeth. The volunteer soldier stared up at her as if she was his personal savior. It was probably going to take time for them to figure out the extent of the changes, but for now it seemed like he would be alright.

"Okay, then." Rebecca relaxed and patted him on the shoulder. "Looks like you're good to go." She shot Lana an awkward look as they helped him to his feet and handed his gun back to him.

That was when a quiet alarm sounded from a watch on Lana's wrist. "That's it, we need to refresh the enchantment on the flasks. This one should be good for another five minutes at best."

"I'll go." Rebecca nodded. "You stay and handle any bites."

It only made sense for her to go. Lana didn't have a way to defend herself. Leaving her with the combatants was the best option. A few revs had already made it past the front line and were running loose somewhere on the casino floor. At least if Rebecca went, she wouldn't be defenseless. She just had to make sure to be quick.

Kicking off, she made use of every point of agility that she had to dart across the space toward the broken sun goddess statue. She skidded to a stop, surprised at how fast she had reached it. Unfortunately, the artificer that was supposed to be working on it was gone.

"Damn it, Alex."

He should have been finding a way to restore the statue. She'd seen him a few minutes ago at the barricade with Parker but she'd assumed they had gone back to the sun goddess by now. Rebecca thought back to why they'd been there, remembering they were looking for Sax. Without hesitation, she turned on her heel and sprinted for the armory. Hopefully, they were still there.

There wasn't time to search the entire place for them.

Rifles barked behind her as she weaved between slot machines like a deer through the forest. The physical prowess of a Heretic was something she still wasn't used to. After spending so long locked in a luxury apartment, just being able to run free was a new experience. Let alone being able to sprint at top speed without getting tired. She burst through the door of the armory, reaching the center of the room in only a few strides.

"Shit."

Alex wasn't there either.

"I really should have given him a radio." She spun and darted back out of the room with an annoyed huff only to have a pale form plow into her the instant she passed through the door.

The world spun as she flew several feet and slammed into a slot machine. The air in her lungs rushed out all at once. Glass shattered on impact as pain radiated through her shoulder. A broken shard must have slashed her as she fell. She hit the ground a second later, just as her attacker leapt for her throat.

A mouth full of jagged teeth and a pair of eyes the color of burning embers streaked toward her. A wild screech declared victory.

"Back the hell off." She put an Icicle through the revenant's left eye before it could reach her. The corpse fell beside her, flailing. Its flesh bubbled and spat as it tried to close around the Icicle. A moment later it went limp. She punched the corpse once for good measure. Pain lit up her shoulder as she moved.

"Fak!" Rebecca clutched a hand over the wound, assuming there was still a piece of broken glass stuck in it. Craning her head to the side, she assessed the damage.

"Oh no…"

There was nothing stuck in the wound.

It was so much worse.

A recent line of punctures ran across her skin in a pattern matching a row of jagged teeth. She snapped her head to the side, finding a trickle of blood running from the dead revenant's mouth. Its teeth were bright pink.

"Shit no."

She cast Regeneration in hopes of slowing the curse down. For a normal person, the change was near instant at night, taking less than thirty seconds to take hold. As a Heretic, her constitution was significantly higher, but no one had ever tested the limit. How long could she last, a minute? Two?

"I have to find Alex fast."

Rebecca resisted the urge to run in a random direction to search. Instead, she pushed herself up from the floor and held perfectly still. There was no point to running without a destination in mind.

"Where would he go?" She breathed her words slowly, listening to her breath as it passed through her lungs. The sound blended with the steady thump of her heart. Her heightened senses reached out from there as the pain in her shoulder seemed to eat into the rest of her body. The curse was moving, yet she remained where she was.

Gunfire threatened to drown out the sound she was searching for. Her chest burned like a fire in her lungs as the curse spread. She ignored it and focused on the world around her to filter through the noise. All she had to do was sift through the distractions. She picked them away like weeds. The gunfire. The screeching of monsters. The crunch of broken glass.

That was when she heard it. The distant voice of the only one that could save her.

"Pass me another thing of glue."

Rebecca snapped her eyes open.

"There!" She was running before the word had even left her mouth. Her eyes scanned the casino floor to zero in on Alex's location. The curse flooded her body, biting at all that she was. Her chest burned as the power chipped away at her mana system, like a predator cracking into an egg. It was as if the curse was trying to get at something inside. Something within the core of her mana.

Her soul.

"What did Digby say the Seed had called it, a spark?"

She shook off the question and focused on Alex's voice. It grew clearer with each labored step. He was close. So close that she could taste his blood.

"Wait, no. That's not right."

Rebecca slapped herself in an attempt to force the foreign thought from her head. She was not about to let the curse win.

Tumbling through the dining area, she crashed through a row of chairs, coming to a stop laying on the floor by Alex's feet. The artificer looked down at her with a stupid yet delicious looking face.

"Ah, hi Becca."

Without a second thought, she reached up and clawed her way up the bar he stood by to grab hold of his shirt with both hands. Then, she shouted in his face. "Cleanse me, goddamn it. Before I tear your fucking throat out with my teeth!"

She promptly fell back to the floor as soon as she was finished. The pain in her chest was so great that it started to cloud her senses. It felt like she was disappearing. Like the curse was bleeding into her mana. Then, a sudden cool rushed into her. She reached toward the source and pulled it close, drinking it in. The world began to return, or more accurately, she was being pulled back to it.

"Okay, drink it all. That's right." Alex knelt next to her as she realized she was chugging a flask with the entire spout shoved in her mouth so that her teeth dented the metal. Water ran down her chin and neck.

"You still sane down there?" Parker leaned over the bar above her.

"Yeah, shit, Jesus." Becca started to stand up. "That was not... good."

"That's an understatement." Alex helped her up. "I thought you were going to kill me for a second there."

"I think I almost did." She steadied herself on the bar as she regained her balance. "I got bit."

"I could tell." He nodded.

"What the hell are you doing here?" She glanced to the side at a line of wine glasses that took up the counter of the bar. "Shit, never mind. I don't want to know. Just give me some more purified water."

"On it." Parker grabbed a pair of water bottles from behind the bar and slapped them down in front of Alex.

"Two should be enough before you need more." He cast his spell and pushed them over to her.

Becca snatched them up and motioned to go just as her tongue caught something sharp in her mouth. Feeling around, she found that her canines had grown. She grabbed one of the wine glasses, the bottom falling off as she held it up to check her reflection. Baring her teeth, she found a slight point at the tip of her canines.

"You okay?" Alex eyed her sideways.

She blew out a relieved sigh. "Yeah. But another few seconds and I might have ended up with fangs."

"That would have been weird." Parker set another few wine glasses on the bar.

She turned away from them and headed back out onto the casino floor. "That's the world we live in now."

CHAPTER THIRTY-SIX

Digby released another wave of Decay spells as more revenants rushed the barricade. The creatures screeched and screamed, but more continued to come.

"Get back, you!" He slammed the jagged form of necrotic blood at the end of his staff into the head of a revenant that was clawing its way over the gambling machines. The impact dazed it, but not before it had time to sink its teeth into Mason's hand. The soldier tore himself free, leaving the creature open for another whack. Digby cracked it straight in the mouth. He smirked as a few jagged fangs flew through air. "Try biting someone now."

The combat volunteers unleashed hell around him again to drive the creatures back while adding to the writhing pile of dead and dying revenants that filled the entrance. Rebecca arrived just in time with another stock of purified water to cleanse Mason's bite. Digby did a double take, noticing that the soldier had spontaneously gained a slight point to his ears. Beyond that, there seemed to be no lasting effects.

"Don't trample us, bro!" Tavern howled from the ground, somewhere in front of the barricade. The skeleton had lost everything below their ribs in the fight, leaving them swinging their swords at the legs of the revenants while the creatures stomped over them.

Digby glanced to his HUD, debating on if he had enough mana left to resummon the skeleton to allow his minion to reform.

MP: 62/209

Over the last few minutes, he'd only gained one level despite taking part in killing many of the creatures. Unfortunately, it seemed that the Seed only gave him credit for the ones that his Decay spells were directly responsible for dealing the final blow to. The rest were finished off by the continuous rifle fire, of which he received no experience. Not that it mattered right now. Gaining a level wouldn't have granted him more mana to use anyway. He'd have to wait until he absorbed more to reach his new total. Considering there were no bare patches of earth to bury himself with or time to meditate, he was running out of options. His remaining mana wasn't going to go far, and he had already leached what he could from Tavern mere minutes ago. Any more and he would risk collapsing the infernal spirit's mana system. At best, he could make it through one or two more waves of revenants with the MP he had. After that, he would be out of the fight. Tavern would have to make do as they were.

At least his Decay spell had reached rank B during the fight. With the added boost, it was actually becoming a solid attack against the revenants. Especially since it hit a much wider area now. Granted, the carpet was starting to look a bit threadbare after being caught on the edge of its radius. Unfortunately, even with the increase in power, it was only a matter of time before their defense fell apart.

Another revenant screeched and lunged over the barricade, taking down one of the volunteers. Lana and Rebecca rushed toward him with enchanted flasks in hand. Despite help being nearby, the panicked volunteer fired a wild spray of bullets into the gut of the creature.

"Hey!" Digby jumped toward the danger to shield Rebecca as several projectiles burst from the revenant's back. All but one were stopped by the plates of bone under his clothes. The last tore through Rebecca's thigh, causing her to drop the flask in her hand as her leg buckled.

The revenant spasmed as the bullets that were still lodged in its gut shut down its healing. A flailing limb cracked Lana in the hand. The sound of fingers breaking was audible over the gun fire behind them. Her flask hit the floor as well. Sucking in a breath and shoving her injured hand under her arm, she reached for the container.

"Shit, he's turning." Mason spun to aim his weapon at his own volunteer as the man's face contorted into a wild snarl. For a moment, it looked like the soldier would fire, yet, he hesitated.

The newborn revenant didn't waste the opportunity.

A hand snapped around the barrel of Mason's weapon as the bones within popped and cracked, its fingernails transforming into claws. Mason opened fire, seconds too late. The creature jerked his weapon to the side. A bullet slammed into the floor, sending bits of carpet into the air.

Another four revenants took advantage of the moment, each climbing over the barricade. They all crouched in preparation to pounce into the formation of combatants. Digby swung his staff at one, not wanting to spend the mana to drive them back. Another blast of Decay probably wouldn't kill them anyway. No, they would only return with more at their back.

The volunteers behind him unloaded their weapons at the creatures, obliterating the heads of two of the threats. A call to reload was heard but the remaining revenants were already leaping for whichever throat they could sink their teeth into the fastest.

It was all falling apart.

With no time to do anything else, Digby threw out his arms in the direction of the two revenants that had gotten through as well as the volunteer that had just turned. His mana dropped as the creature's movements slowed. A sound like twigs cracking snapping under foot came from their bodies until they froze in place with blood trickling from their eyes. The crimson streams solidified before they reached the floor.

"What did you do?" Rebecca cast Regeneration to heal her wounded leg.

"Blood Forge." Digby kicked one of the creatures off a volunteer to make sure he'd stopped the revenant before it had done any harm.

"But you didn't open your maw." She stared at the crystalized blood coming from the corpse's eyes.

Digby held out a hand to help her up. "Common revenants usually have a will attribute of zero. That's why Decay is so effective against them. The same goes for Forge. There's nothing stopping me from turning every drop of blood in their body into a million tiny needles."

"That's horrifying." Lana held out her hand so Rebecca could repair her broken fingers.

"Indeed." Digby smirked. "It will stop one of these things in their tracks but it's not an economical use of mana."

"I'm sorry I hesitated." Mason tightened his grip on his rifle as the rest of the volunteers avoided looking at their fellow combatant laying on the ground with frozen tears of blood spilling from his eyes.

"It's understandable." Digby nodded to the soldier. "He was one of your men. It's only natural to hesitate when ending the life of one of your own." He placed his staff down and reached for the deceased volunteer's rifle. "But now is not the time for regret; we have more coming and I'm nearly out of mana."

Digby tried his best not to let on that they were doomed as he leveled the strange weapon at the entrance of the casino. He didn't like guns. They were crude and dangerous, but clubbing monsters with his staff wasn't going to get him very far.

The clawed hands of a dozen more revenants climbed over their dead to rush the barricade. Digby opened fire. All he could do was fight until he had nothing left. Behind him, the volunteers did the same. His rifle thumped against his shoulder in a steady rhythm as it punched holes into the pale forms coming toward him. He gripped the gun tight to keep the weapon's movement from climbing to the ceiling. The scent of smoke and blood filled the air, yet the revenants continued to pour in.

He checked his HUD, hoping his mana value had changed.

MP: 14/209

Tearing his gaze away from the number, he grabbed another container of bullets from the corpse of the dead volunteer at his feet and shoved it into his rifle. It clicked into place and Mason reached over to pull a knob on the weapon's side to ready it to fire. Again he took aim, this time hesitating as a much larger clawed hand shoved its way through the entrance, followed by an enormous bat-like snout.

Revenant Bloodstalker, Rare.

No! The face of the creature sent a rush of terror through his mind. A memory of being torn in half by one of the fiends back in California flashed through his mind. He'd beaten it in the end, but only with the help of a kestrel and his necrotic armor.

How did it get here?

Digby had been sure that the hive at the other end of the strip hadn't had any uncommon or rare types. It must have been drawn by the sounds of battle. Digby shook his head. It didn't matter how. He had to do something or it would tear everyone apart. He shoved his fear down and opened fire, sending every bullet he had into the beast's monstrous face. The projectiles hardly dealt any damage. Certainly not enough to shut down its healing.

The bloodstalker winced for an instant as the wounds healed. The creature's claws tore through the corpses of its kind on the floor as it opened its mouth to unleash an ear-splitting screech.

"That's it." Digby threw his empty rifle aside and prepared to activate his necrotic armor. At least with that, he could slow it down.

The revenant barreled forward like a boulder launched from a trebuchet, only to come to a sudden stop before reaching the barricade. Digby hesitated before calling his armor forth. The bloodstalker's face contorted with panic as it struggled to dig its claws into the floor. Then, to his surprise, it was simply dragged, kicking and screaming, back toward the door.

That was when Digby caught a glimpse of something behind it.

A massive, meaty hand, covered in bone armor, was wrapped around the foot of the bloodstalker. The arm it was attached to could barely fit through the broken doors of the entrance. It was as thick as a tree trunk. Digby's eyes widened as a second hand reached in to feel around, eventually snagging the bloodstalker's other leg.

"Oh god! What is it?" one of the volunteers cried as they stumbled back in fear.

Digby smiled as a thought flowed across the bond he shared with Asher.

We have arrived.

The bloodstalker unleashed a scream louder than anything he had ever heard as the two arms pulled it back outside, where the feet of something huge stood. Digby followed the leg up to its highest point, only managing to find the monster's knee. The Heretic Seed told him what he already knew.

Zombie Destroyer, Loyal.

Digby had spent enough time on the other end of the strip to recognize the biggest member of his horde. Another ear splitting scream came from the bloodstalker as it was pulled upward out of view. It was followed by the sound of tearing flesh. A shower of blood flooded the ground outside.

Revenant Bloodstalker defeated. 3,692 experience awarded.

A second destroyer's feet stepped into view as revenants continued to rush the entrance past them. It simply dropped to its knees and looked through the doors. Every single one of Mason's combat volunteers recoiled in horror as the monster's face came into view. Plates of bone covered its visage, with a pair of horns extending from its forehead. Two milky white eyes searched for prey as it grabbed a handful of revenants and awkwardly scooped them toward its mouth.

"Good lord." One of Mason's men immediately threw up as the behemoth shoveled the creatures in and chomped down. At least four revenants were caught inside, each screaming with all that they had left as their bodies were crushed. A severed leg dropped from the creature's teeth.

"What is it?" another volunteer shouted again with abject terror in his voice as a crowd of zombies moved in to block the entryway, preventing any more revenants from getting inside.

"Are they helping us?" One of the men stepped closer to the barricade, clearly confused by the scene.

Digby let out a wicked laugh. "I told you, the dead are on our side."

A white streak of feathers darted over the heads of the horde, landing on the barricade in front of Digby. A happy caw told him everything he needed to know. Reinforcements had arrived.

"Good girl." Digby held out a hand, enjoying the looks on the faces of the volunteers as she hopped up his arm to his shoulder. He immediately snatched up his staff and cast Leach with his remaining fourteen points, to receive another forty-two back from Asher. She nodded in response, sending a thought across their bond.

More to give.

"That's alright, you've already brought me enough." He cast Control on several of the zombies that had come to their aid and cast Leach repeatedly to drain a small amount of mana from each. Considering that most of them were sure to have an intelligence close to zero, he thought it best not to get greedy. He didn't want to accidentally unravel the mana systems that kept them active. Granted, with the intelligence bonus of his Control spell, their mana capacity would grow to nearly fifty each once they absorbed more.

Repeating the process of casting Control on another group, he Leached what he could from them as well. After that he was, getting close to full. Not to mention he had plenty of minions now, all absorbing mana for him at once. As long as he kept them around, he could cast as much as he wanted with little wait time. He couldn't help but feel powerful with the knowledge that his horde could support him in such a way.

That was when a message from the Heretic Seed burst his bubble.

2 Common Zombies, lost.

"Damn." The revenants were attacking the horde outside. The battle was yet to be won. They had only slowed the swarm down. He turned back to Mason and his volunteers. "Stay here."

They nodded, clearly not wanting to go near the dead that filled the entrance.

Brandishing his staff, he opened his maw on the floor for added style and forged a small platform to raise himself up and over the barricade. He hopped down on the other side, casting Leach again to get a little more mana before marching forward.

"Clear the way." He waved a hand to the side as Asher sent a compel into the horde to back him up. The dead parted without hesitation, revealing a swarm of revenants outside, picking at the horde that stood between them and the humans inside the casino. Digby tried not to tremble as he approached one of his destroyers. As loyal as the behemoth might have been, it was still utterly terrifying that something that big could even exist. As it was, it stood taller than the second floor of the casino. He craned his neck up. "You there, big fella."

The destroyer looked down at him with a vacant expression.

"Pick me up." Digby hoped the giant was smart enough to understand that it should handle its master with care.

The towering monstrosity knelt down and scooped him up, jostling him significantly before he was able to get his balance. Asher cawed in a brief moment of panic as he almost fell. The destroyer raised him over the horde where he could survey the scene. At once he saw the problem. His horde stood over three hundred deep, but the revenant's numbers were far greater. Even worse, now that the dead stood in their way, the creatures had begun to rule the zombies as hostile.

"I can't have that." Digby raised his staff and cast enough rounds of Leach spells to bring his mana to full. Then, he turned to the destroyer holding him up. "Bring me to our foes."

The enormous monster stepped forward, dragging its feet to avoid stepping on the zombies around its legs. Instead, it just waded through them to gently push them aside like waves at the beach.

Looking back, Digby noticed the lights of several hotel room windows behind him. The silhouettes of dozens of people, pressed up against the glass to watch as he commanded the horde from his place in the destroyer's hand while Asher perched menacingly on his shoulder. He was definitely going to have some explaining to do.

"Well, no sense trying to pretend I'm something I'm not." Digby shrugged as his oversized minion held him out over the swarm of revenants that filled the street.

Hundreds of clawed hands reached up, many climbing over one another in an attempt to reach him. Their fingers swiped through the air just below his perch as he held out his staff and opened his maw. There was no need to even cast a spell. Instead, he thrust out his hand and willed the gateway to his void to grow, spending the mana to increase its size until he had just a few points left.

The revenants beneath him cried out in panic as their writhing mass of bodies began to sink. Digby stared down to watch as they were claimed by a sixteen-foot opening in the ground. They flailed and struggled as the pool of necrotic blood claimed them. He snapped his maw shut when the majority were inside, severing over a dozen arms that were still reaching up for purchase.

A rapid string of messages filled his HUD. He ignored them, and spread his hand out wide to Leach more mana from his minions. Only about a minute had passed, but with so many members of the dead absorbing mana all at once, they had replenished enough to keep him going. The emerald death essence drifted up to him like smoke from a fire as it swirled around him. His mana system drank it in to bring him back to full just in time for the revenants below to push into the space where he had consumed the creatures that had come before.

"Fools." Digby smirked as he opened his maw and pushed it to its limit once again. He let out a wicked laugh at the sight of the creatures flailing for rescue. Reaching high into the air as if holding his prey's fate in his palm, he snapped his hand shut. His maw followed suit, claiming another twenty or so enemies. Again his HUD lit up with messages.

Reveling in the power that the horde's support granted him, he drew out his arms and let his laughter swell into a wild cackle that echoed through the street. The moment faded as the revenants released a collective shriek across the length of the strip.

"What's this now?" Digby arched an eyebrow.

Their clawed hands and vampiric faces shrank away in retreat all at once. The horde of the dead grabbed at any that failed to move fast enough, pulling them back. Digby egged them on, compelling them the feed and turning the street into a bloodbath. A glance back showed him the silhouettes of the onlookers in the windows. Many turned away in horror, while others seemed to be cheering.

"That's right, you best retreat." Digby held out his staff over the fleeing revenants, prepared to draw in more mana from his minions. "Remain and I shall devour you all."

That was when he realized that they weren't running from him. Digby arched an eyebrow as two of his common minions fell dead as a result of his continued Leaching. He ceased his casting immediately, running some quick math.

Why didn't they have enough mana?

He craned his neck back toward the casino entrance.

Unless…

It seemed that Alex had found some success with his task of restoring the sun goddess's area effect.

Digby patted his destroyer's shoulder. "Take me back."

The behemoth raised him up and waded its way back toward the entrance of the casino. He took the moment to look back over the Heretic Seed's messages.

55 Active Revenants defeated. 5,060 experience awarded.
You have reached level 30. 6,626 experience to next level.
You have one additional attribute point to allocate.
Guided Mutation: resource requirement for the Emissary's
mutation, Limitless, have been met.
Accept? Yes/No
Guided Mutation: resource requirement for the Emissary's
mutation, Apex Predator, have been met.
Accept? Yes/No

Digby's eyes widened at the sheer quantity of good news. It was about time. Dropping his additional point into intelligence as usual, he willed the Seed to tell him what resources accepting both of his available mutations would cost him. The requirement for Apex Predator was simple enough at just fifty viscera, while Limitless would cost a bit more, needing the consumption of twenty flesh, forty bone, twenty sinew, and twenty mind. Neither mutation's requirements overlapped, so he accepted them both.

Limitless was a must have, considering it could enhance his strength far beyond what had been previously possible even with activation of his necrotic armor. He grinned at the prospect of using both at once. He would just have to make sure he had the mana and void resources to repair whatever damage the ability might cause.

Apex, on the other hand, wouldn't do anything to increase his power, but it would certainly make finding food more convenient. Hell, he might even be able to eat human meals, which would be a huge step in the right direction in coexisting with the humans of his settlement. Not to mention it would make him feel a little more like he belonged in the world of the living. It was easy to forget that had been his goal originally, what with all his villainous cackling and devouring of his enemies.

Thinking about the prospect of regaining his humanity, it was good to remind himself that it wasn't too late for him. If the Heretics Seed's copy of himself was to be trusted, he might learn just how to do that if he could gather the rest of its fragments.

Digby commanded his overgrown minion to lower him down

as he reached the entrance of the casino. Asher sent out a compel to let him through without him even having to say anything. The horde blocking the doors simply cleared the area to join the rest in the store where they feasted upon the revenants that had been unable to flee.

Standing on his toes to see over the rows of gambling machines, he caught a glimpse of Alex and Parker standing by an intact sun goddess statue. The artificer gave him a simple thumbs up while Parker threw out both arms to the restored stone figure standing beside them.

How the hell did they do that?

Digby couldn't help but grin at their accomplishment. They had come through when it counted. The revenants may have been loose on the strip again, but with the statue's enchantment restored, the casino would have nothing to fear beyond the occasional lightwalker that could bypass its effect.

Mason and Rebecca met him as he approached the barricade, while the rest of the combat volunteers peeked out over the top. From their expressions, it was clear that they had realized how easily he could kill everyone in the building. All it would take was a single word to his horde.

Digby hesitated, unsure if he had taken things too far outside in the street. After what the humans had just witnessed, accepting him as any form of leader to their settlement might be beyond their capabilities. Hell, after the display he'd just put on, trusting him not to bite anyone was probably a bit much. Fortunately, Mason spoke up in his defense as a part of the casino's leadership.

"Quit hiding back there. Trust me, I know how hard this is to get used to." He slapped a hand on Digby's back hard enough to shove him forward. "But this guy has saved my ass more times than I can count at this point, even if he is dead."

"Indeed." Digby tried his best to appear friendly, even giving the soldier a playful elbow in the side as payback for the slap. "And might I remind you that I have been walking amongst you all for days, and the only person I've eaten in that time was Rivers." Digby cringed as soon as the admission left his mouth. He had meant it as a reason that they should feel indebted to him for dealing with the man that had been extorting them, but it might have been best to leave out the fact that he'd eaten the man.

An awkward moment went by where everyone continued to hide before, one by one, they began coming out to approach him. They made a significant effort not to look outside to where his horde was eating, but beyond that they seemed to be comfortable enough with him being there. Actually, now that he'd fought to protect them, he couldn't help but notice an element of respect. Sure, it was laced with fear, but still, it was progress. At the very least, the battle had put an end to whatever skepticism they might have had about magic.

As the volunteers began to relax, he noticed a collective reluctance to look in the direction of the revenants that he'd killed by crystalizing their blood. At first, he wasn't sure why, since there were plenty more corpses in the entrance and a few more shouldn't make a difference. The reason became obvious when he thought about things from their perspective. One of them had been human when the battle started. He had been one of their own. Not to mention, Digby had been the one to kill him.

Trying to understand how they felt, it seemed best that the man be given a proper burial rather than letting the horde eat the corpse. Unfortunately, with everything going on outside, it didn't seem prudent to drag the man out to a patch of bare earth. Cremation wasn't wise either, considering they were inside. Instead, he just nodded to himself and slipped through the volunteers to crouch down by the man's body. The eyes of everyone followed him, clearly worried that he might simply dig in for a meal.

"This man fought for the lives of everyone here." He placed a hand on the corpse's chest and cast Decay repeatedly until the body crumbled to dust. "He doesn't deserve to be eaten like a common revenant."

Rebecca and Mason stepped to his sides, each placing a hand on his shoulders to give a gentle squeeze in support of the act.

Digby glanced back at them. "What was his name?"

"David Peters." Rebecca lowered her head while Mason placed a hand over his heart.

"I think he was a fast food worker before all this."

"It doesn't matter what he did before. He died protecting this city." Digby opened his maw and pictured a shape in his mind. Then he cast forge.

The other volunteers gathered around him as tendrils of black blood coiled through the dust on the floor to gather the man's remains before spiraling up into the air. Focusing on the deceased man's name, Digby formed the mixture into a rectangular obelisk with the name of the deceased engraved into its surface. He added a circle around the text, pulling a design element from the Heretic Seed's HUD.

Digby stood as soon as the improvised headstone was finished.

"This man was the first to give his life for the future of this world. I hope that he is the last, though I suspect that will not be the case." He lowered his head. "Our enemies know where we are, and they will not simply forget about us."

"He's right." Lana slipped through the group. "As horrific as the monsters outside our doors are, Skyline and Autem are worse."

The volunteers gave a somber nod, clearly realizing that their victory over the revenants was nothing compared to the fight ahead. Digby let the facts sink in without saying more to avoid adding to the pressure. Then he shook his head, there was enough to worry about.

"But for tonight, we have won the fight." Digby tried his best to give them hope. "Now, let's say we clear out of the entrance here while my horde deals with the corpses. Because I'm pretty sure none of you will want to watch that, if you know what I mean." He patted Asher on the side and gave her an order to manage the clean-up process. She nodded and flapped back to the horde outside.

Mason looked away as the dead began to come in through the doors to drag out the corpses. "Yeah, I don't want to see any of that."

Digby smirked at how squeamish the soldier was after everything he'd seen. Rebecca shook her head as she stepped closer to him and headed back toward the dining area, apparently still hungry despite the scene outside. Digby shrugged, remembering that their dinner had been interrupted earlier.

"Thanks, man." Tavern emerged from under the pile of bodies as the dead cleared the area. Digby shook his head at his skeletal minion and recalled the infernal spirit back to the oversized diamond in his pocket.

With the fight over, he decided to join Rebecca and the others. At the very least, the volunteers could use a drink to calm their nerves. The rest of the humans, led by Deuce and Elenore, began to filter out from the stairwell that led to the upper floors where they had been hiding during the battle. He felt their eyes on him as soon as they did.

I guess it will take a bit more to earn everyone's acceptance.

Digby continued into the dining area with the volunteers, hoping to set an example of human-zombie cooperation. He stopped short as soon as he saw what waited for him at the back of the eatery.

"How?"

Dishes littered the tables full of partially finished meals, while the bar at the back was full of wine glasses. His eyes stared past it all, locked on the mirror behind the bar as a familiar face looked back from an open Mirror Link.

Lana ran past him without hesitation.

Digby held his ground.

"What do you want, Alvin?"

CHAPTER THIRTY-SEVEN

"Surrender."

Alvin spoke as if it was their only option as his face filled the large mirror behind the bar of the dining area. Hawk stood behind him with a new guardian ring clearly visible on his finger like he was trying to rub in the fact that Digby hadn't been able to stop him from getting his magic back.

"I repeat, surrender." Alvin pushed for obedience again.

"I think not." Digby folded his arms and approached the image.

Hawk stepped forward, almost getting in Alvin's way. "If you think those monsters on the strip are all we have to throw at you, then you're wrong."

"Hey, be careful what you say." Alvin gave him a sharp look. "Just let me talk to my sister."

Digby arched an eyebrow at the interaction.

Hawk rolled his eyes. "Relax, what are they going to do about anything? It's not like I'm going to tell them that Bancroft has figured everything out by now and that Easton has been captured." Hawk immediately locked eyes with Digby with a smug smile plastered across his face.

"Hey, stop." Alvin's mouth dropped open in shock as Hawk began speaking as fast as he possibly could.

"Bancroft is attacking at noon tomorrow. I'm fine, just do what you can to get away!"

Alvin shoved Hawk aside and snapped his eyes back to Digby, clearly realizing he had just allowed the boy to warn an enemy of a plan to attack.

"Like hell I'm running away, you brat." Digby swiped a hand through the wine glasses on the bar, sending several smashing to the floor. "I'm coming to get you."

The mirror immediately went blank, reverting to normal and leaving him staring at his own face.

Hawk hadn't turned his back on them at all. He must not have intended to take Autem's side from the start. No, he was just acting as a spy. His reason was obvious. That little idiot was trying to show Digby that he could be trusted. He must have convinced Alvin to contact his sister with the intent of getting a message to Digby. It was the most careless and dangerous thing the boy could have done.

This is my fault.

Digby placed a hand over his mouth. If he hadn't been so curt with the boy, he might have been able to make him understand. Because of his needlessly argumentative attitude, Hawk had placed himself in danger yet again.

No. He stopped blaming himself before he spiraled out of control. It didn't matter who's fault it was or how stupid Hawk's plan was. It worked. It was obvious that an attack would be coming, but he wouldn't have known it would be so soon if the boy hadn't taken things upon himself. Hawk had bought them a chance, one that they couldn't ignore. They could yell at each other later.

Digby spun around to lock eyes with Rebecca and Mason. Alex and Parker stood behind them while Deuce and Elenore joined the group. The rest of the casino's inhabitants filled in around them. Everyone stared at him for a long moment, then he dropped his hand from his mouth.

"We attack tonight."

"What?" Rebecca shook her head, clearly struggling to understand what he meant despite it being obvious.

"The plan we've been working toward, we do the heist tonight." Digby threw his arms out beside him.

"We aren't ready for that." Mason stepped forward. "We barely made it through the last hour."

"And we won't make it through the next day." Digby started pacing back and forth in a manic display of insanity as everyone watched. "If we allow Bancroft to attack us tomorrow then we'll either all die, or suffer such a setback that we'll be unable to mount any kind of legitimate resistance until it's too late. We don't have a choice, do you see? We've already lost. Our only chance to come back from the edge is to reclaim the Seed's fragments tonight. I know how reckless and insane it sounds, but we still have to try." He stopped pacing and turned to the others before repeating his original declaration. "We have to attack the base tonight with what we have and hope for the best."

"And how do we do that without the kestrel or more time to grow the horde?" Rebecca folded her arms as she stared at him with as much skepticism as she could muster.

"Oh, don't be like that, Becky. You know the deal by now. This is what we do, so get on board and help. I need your brilliant mind working on this."

"Fine." She sighed and stepped forward to stand beside him as if joining his side of the argument.

"You too, Alex. Get over here." Digby pointed to the floor at his other side. "You're my apprentice, you don't get a say."

"Okay, but I'm expressing my reluctance now." The artificer joined them.

"No one cares about your reluctance." Digby brushed his comment aside and addressed the group. "Alright, we have about two hours before we have to leave if we're going to make it to our enemy's stronghold before dawn. Once there, we shall need to steal the Heretic Seed's fragments, provided they are actually where we think they are, rescue Hawk as well as Easton and Campbell if they're still alive. Oh, and we should probably abduct Alvin while we're there. Not to mention we'll need to do enough damage to both Autem and Skyline to slow them down enough to buy time for everyone here to evacuate to a safer location."

"You want us to leave Vegas?" Elenore stepped forward.

"Our enemies may not give us a choice in the matter." Digby lowered his head. "As much as I want to stay here, it may be safer somewhere else. As long as we take the sun goddess over there with us, we can secure another location right quick." He raised his eyes back up. "Now, who has any ideas on how to do as much damage as possible to our foes?"

"We'll need to transport the horde in something since they can't walk to the base in time." Parker spoke up.

Digby scratched his head. "Can we use the cargo vehicles like we intended to do with the destroyers before?"

"There's plenty of tractor trailers down at the loading dock." Deuce stepped forward. "We used them to move supplies back when Rivers had just taken over. If we loaded the trucks up, we could deliver your entire horde right to their gates. About twenty trucks should do it."

Digby paced a few more steps. "That would certainly be one hell of a distraction, which we'll need now that we've lost the kestrel. We'll have to slam all twenty vehicles right into their walls. In the ensuing chaos we might have a shot at springing Hawk. It will be risky, but there's a chance we could make it to where they're keeping the Seed's fragments as well." He pointed back to Deuce. "Take your men and gather the vehicles. My minions should be able to drive them if I cast Control to increase their intelligence. No need to risk any of our people."

"I'll go too." Alex jogged to stand with Deuce. "If the dead are driving, they will need protection. As we already know, the base isn't just going to let them drive up to their door. Parker and I can weld on whatever we can to reinforce the cabs while Asher helps Deuce's guys load the horde into the trucks."

"Indeed." Digby nodded. "Get them some helmets too."

"I'm on it." Sax raised his hand from the back.

"Excellent." Digby clapped his hands together. "The rest of you, gather your things and be ready to move. You will evacuate at dawn, and don't wait for us to come back. If we make it, we will meet up later. If we don't, well, survive the best you can."

Everyone got moving when Digby clapped his hands.

The next hour was a flurry of activity. With everything on the line, the entire settlement pitched in. Digby did what he could to help out, but was ultimately forced to take guard duty. The sun goddess provided everyone with room to work, but it wasn't absolute. The majority of the revenants might have kept their distance, but there were a few lightwalkers loose in the night that could ignore the statue's effect.

Fortunately, dealing with them was child's play once the rest of the swarm had cleared out. Digby stood watch to exterminate anything that tried to get close, while everyone else worked like mad to get everything ready.

Alex and Parker assembled a team to support their efforts in armoring the trucks that Deuce's men brought in. Nineteen vehicles in total. Their effort dismantled parts from dozens of abandoned cars, such as their hoods and doors. They repurposed every bit of metal they could to weld it together into armor plating. The hastily assembled reinforcements looked like rubbish but they would at least hold out for the few minutes they needed to approach the base.

While they worked on the front of the vehicles. Asher and Tavern loaded up the cargo compartments in the back. Digby's two destroyers each got their own chariot, since they were too big to fit together in one truck. As it was, they had to crawl in and lay down.

Thankfully, a good number of the common zombies managed to mutate by consuming the corpses of the revenants that had been killed in the recent battle. Digby made a point of organizing them to help each other to eat. The result gave him five armored brutes, twenty silent lurkers, fifteen gluttons, and thirty leaders. They didn't have a need for that many leaders to control the horde, but Digby welcomed the help regardless. To his surprise, the effect was noticeable, causing the horde to move with significantly more organization.

Taking into account the fact that the dead would not be

returning from the attack, Rebecca suggested equipping the lurkers with a harness of explosives. Digby reluctantly agreed. With the horde's level of organization, they could be sent in to rush their enemy's weak points to be detonated remotely by Rebecca or Alex. Once she told Mason of the plan, he sent for Sax, who returned with several dozen bricks of some sort of putty-like substance. A label on the outside read C4. According to the Seed, it was a form of high-explosive.

When they were finished, Digby had Asher distribute the uncommon zombies into the horde and load twelve of the trucks with the dead. There was room to fit more but, after seeing the defenses that Skyline's base had first hand, Digby assumed some of their attack vehicles wouldn't reach the gates. It only made sense to spread the horde out to keep the lion's share of their forces from being destroyed by mere bad luck if the wrong truck was stopped.

Their preparations took just under two hours. Digby winced as he checked the time. If they left immediately, they would reach Skyline's base around an hour before dawn. It was certainly cutting it close. Considering the odds were stacked heavily against them, there was no sense in bringing any of the combat volunteers to take part in the assault. Instead, they would drive the trucks through the more complicated streets on the way there and hand the job off to Digby's minions once the roads opened up enough for the dead to maneuver the vehicles without issue.

Mason would have to follow the caravan in a vehicle meant to transport humans, something called a bus. That way, the living could head back to Vegas to evacuate with the rest of the settlement before the assault started.

In the end, the only living members of the attack team were Alex and Rebecca. Digby was glad to have them by his side. The quest was certainly a lot for the three of them to handle, but amidst the chaos provided by his minions, they had a shot. Especially considering how far they had come. He tried his best to act confident as the trucks began to head out.

That was when Alex pulled up in the bright red Mustang that he had claimed days before. Digby arched an eyebrow at it as his apprentice rolled down the window, wearing a leather jacket underneath body armor. The sword that Digby had stolen a few days ago sat beside him. If it wasn't for his ridiculous blue hair, he would have looked like one of Skyline's men. Despite that, the artificer leaned out the window toward him.

"Get in, loser, we're going to war."

"Just who are you calling a loser? You half-wit." Digby slapped a hand on the hood of the vehicle in argument.

Alex held up a hand. "Sorry, it's a—"

"This is not the time to explain memes to the eight-hundred-year-old-zombie." Rebecca put a stop to the conversation as she jogged out of the casino's entrance wearing a pair of tights and a t-shirt under a bulletproof vest. Digby approved of the look, feeling it appropriate for a burglar.

She popped open the passenger side door and pulled the seat forward. "Now get in, we need to get out ahead of the convoy to get into position before the assault starts. I'll conceal the car and we'll loop around back to where we escaped the other day. We can slip in before the chaos starts."

"Sounds good." Digby climbed into the cramped space behind the front seats. He had to shove his staff in at an angle so that it stuck out the window.

Alex glanced back. "You good back there?"

"I'm dead, remember?" Digby tucked one of his legs up in an awkward position that would torment any normal person. "I don't get uncomfortable."

Before they headed out, he leaned forward over the artificer's shoulder and called to Deuce. "Make sure everyone gets out safely!"

The man rushed to the window to see them off. "You just be sure to make it back."

Elenore pushed her way past him. "You damn well better. We're going to need you if we're going to survive more than a few days out there."

"I think you'd be surprised." Digby chuckled. "The people here are far more capable than one might suspect."

"To be honest, I think you three had something to do with that." She nodded to herself before adding, "Thank you."

"Don't thank us yet." Digby pointed to the casino behind her. "I'm not done with everyone in there. If you think they're capable now, wait 'til you see what they become after I get the means to grant them more power."

"I'd like to see that." She gave him a hopeful smile. "Good luck."

With that, Digby slapped the back of Alex's seat to tell him to step on the gas. The car lurched forward with enthusiasm as the artificer tightened his grip on the wheel.

Digby gave him a pat on the shoulder. "How about you show me how fast this thing will go?"

Alex smirked. "Say no more."

CHAPTER THIRTY-EIGHT

Becca's projected body materialized in the cab of one of the assault trucks. Asher cawed at her from a perch on the dash as one of Digby's undead minions drove.

The zombie turned to look in her direction before nodding and looking back to the road.

"Well, that's... a little unnerving." The thought nearly threw off her concentration enough to cause her to drop through the seat of the truck and fall out the bottom. Fortunately, she was able to refocus her mind before sinking too far. Not that it would have mattered. Nothing could actually hurt her while she was projected. She just hoped her body would be safe while she wasn't using it.

Getting into the base had been easy. Thanks to Alex's choice in cars and his lead foot, they had pulled ahead of the assault trucks by an hour, leaving them enough time to get in position for the assault.

The only obstacle had been what to do with Alex's prized Mustang. Becca had kept it concealed while they approached the base, but the cameras on the wall would see it as soon as they left it behind. If they allowed that to happen, someone was sure to wake Bancroft to notify him of the breach. Fortunately, Digby solved the problem the same way he dealt with most things, by eating it. Alex

434

had looked like he might cry when the vehicle sunk into the necromancer's void.

It was technically possible to get the car back out, but after it had been submerged in the soup of deceased corpses, she was pretty sure it wouldn't run. It was just as well. If Easton and Campbell were still alive, the car wouldn't be big enough to fit everyone once they grabbed Hawk and Alvin. Securing a larger transport was necessary.

Once they'd made it over the wall, the three of them had headed straight for the same bunk house she and Digby had hidden in last time they were there. Apparently, no one had thought to look inside it, because the headless body they had left on the floor was still there. It didn't smell great, but none of the other bunkhouses near it were in use so no one had noticed. That was where Becca had parted ways with the others.

Splitting up was risky, but there wasn't time to stay together. Fortunately, the base was fairly quiet at night. Beyond the front gates and the airfield, there was minimal activity. It made sense, considering that most of Skyline's operations had to take place during daylight hours to minimize the possibility that the revenants might get in the way.

Now, sitting in the cab of the lead attack vehicle next to its deceased driver, she smirked. It was clear that Skyline wasn't expecting a full-scale assault. Checking her map, she found that the base was nearly in visual range. It wouldn't be long now.

Of course, she could have gone with Digby or Alex, but it was decided that her abilities would be better spent to increase the chaos of the assault. After reaching rank B with her projection spell while searching for Dig in the desert, she had gained the ability to cast Waking Dream and Ventriloquism while her body was elsewhere. None of it was capable of hurting anything, but her illusions still had their uses. Taking that into account, there was more value with having her take part in the attack. Especially when she could whip up a few illusionary brutes or a few dozen extra zombies to add more chaos into the attack. With that, Digby and Alex might have a shot at getting their jobs done behind enemy lines without being captured or killed.

Becca went over the steps in her head.

First, Alex had to make it to the airfield and secure a kestrel. That seemed to be the best option for escape, considering they had gotten their last one shot down. Granted, the task was not a simple one. The artificer would need to find a guardian with flight authorization and kill them to unlock one of the crafts. Hopefully he could get it done under the cover provided by the assault.

Second, Digby had to free their people. By now, Hawk must have been taken prisoner after his warning, meaning he would be in a holding cell. That actually helped the situation, since Easton and Campbell were sure to be held in the same building. That just left Alvin, who was probably on Autem's side of the base. Getting him would be a challenge.

Last, they had to meet back up and make it to that gold elevator in the research and development area. Once there, they would need to kill the seer. Hopefully, Dig could learn more about what was on the other side of the elevator by casting Talking Corpse on the woman. Hopefully the Seed's fragments really were there.

There were a lot of ifs in there.

Becca started to chew on her thumbnail, realizing that it wasn't any more real than the rest of her. The whole night was a big if. What if they couldn't find Alvin? Would they leave without him? What if the Seed wasn't on the other side of the elevator? Or worse, what if there was more security on the other side that they couldn't handle? Shit, what if Henwick was on the other side?

When she'd brought up these questions with Digby on the ride over, all he'd done was laugh them off and remind her that everything had worked out so far. He would have been able to convince her if it hadn't been for the fact that his voice had been shaking the entire time. Despite all his talk, he was clearly terrified that they would fail. It was a feeling that she could relate to.

The odds were not good.

Becca shook off her worries and leaned out the window. The lights of the base were beginning to come into view. It was time to get to work. Being careful to maintain her focus, she slipped her projected form through the window of the truck and climbed up onto the roof of the cab. One of the upsides of not being real was that she didn't have to worry about safety as the road streaked by below her.

Asher flapped out from the window behind her and took to the sky. It was probably a good idea. The bullets would start flying soon and the feathered zombie master was too valuable to be in the line of fire. As long as she stayed high enough, it was unlikely that anyone would notice her in the night sky. Not to mention, having a general that could command the troops from relative safety was a clear advantage.

Hopping to the truck's trailer, Becca crouched down and placed her hands on the roof to help maintain her focus.

Then she tried something new.

As a projection, she usually materialized wearing whatever her real body had been. She couldn't change what her body itself looked like, but there was technically nothing stopping her from changing her clothes. Looking down at the projected recreation of the leggings that Mason had looted for her, she decided she could do better. They might be more comfortable than pants, but they weren't exactly intimidating. That was when she asked herself, what would Digby wear?

Her form blurred as her answer materialized around her to match an image in her mind. A long coat of black fabric with a hood that hid her face solidified into existence to change her into a terrifying visage of death. The illusionary garment trailed behind her to flow with the wind. She made point to thicken the fabric to increase her size and distort her form further.

"That will do." Becca laughed, feeling a little like Digby. Clearly, his theatrical nature had rubbed off on her.

Raising her head, she locked her eyes on the front gates as the trucks following behind hers spread out into a row.

The response from the base was instant, spotlights shining from a dozen gun turrets.

All Becca could do was hope that Digby could handle the rest. A swell of dread rolled through her stomach, remembering the look on the necromancer's face as she placed an illusion on him to help him traverse the base. Despite all his talk and posturing, there had been desperation in his eyes.

It was the look of a man that was about to bet everything on one last gamble.

She shook off the thought, trying to pretend that her life wasn't a part of that gamble.

Becca locked her eyes on the front gates just as the night was shattered by a thousand bullets. There was no turning back.

All that was left was to play the hand they had been dealt.

CHAPTER THIRTY-NINE

Mitchell Carter ran for cover as two towering zombie destroyers tore through the men in the base's processing area. He should have been out there with them, but it was easy enough to see that it was pointless. The behemoths simply grabbed his fellow guardians off the ground three at a time and stuffed them in their mouths like a handful of Cheetos. Kestrels fired one barrage after another, bullets chipping bone from the monster's armored heads. It was going to take so much more than that to bring them down.

Carter kept running, there was nothing he could do.

They should have pulled back and regrouped long before the trucks plowed into gates.

What the hell is Bancroft thinking?

The commander should have given the order to regroup. It was like the brass didn't give a shit about the men outside. Sure, the low levels were expendable but there were still plenty of men like himself that had the potential to become so much stronger. He cursed the level cap that had him stuck at fifteen.

Carter shook off his frustration.

Skyline hadn't gotten to where it was by lifting up the weak. If they had decided he wasn't strong enough, then he just had to show them how valuable he could be. It was also possible that something had gone wrong, otherwise, the commander would have entered the battlefield by now. The man was level sixty, for fuck's sake. There was no reason for him to stay in the admin building with his men dying outside.

With that in mind, he took the situation for what it was and kept running, all the while telling himself it was a strategic retreat. After all, he couldn't prove himself to anyone if he was dead. He wasn't a fucking coward, and he wasn't just running for his life.

No, of course not!

He was running with purpose. If he could make it inside the admin building, the commander was sure to be there. Clearly something had gone wrong. The fact that Bancroft hadn't issued any more orders was evidence enough. Carter smiled. If that was the case, the commander might even need his help.

I might even get a promotion if I played my cards right.

Carter smirked as he sprinted for the entrance of the admin building. Everything would make sense once he was inside. He was sure of it. At least, he was sure of it until he reached the door and pressed his guardian ring against the unlock panel beside it.

ACCESS DENIED

"What?" His heart leapt up into his throat.

The admin building certainly had areas that would not allow a level fifteen to enter, but not the main doors. He was sure of it. He'd even been inside before.

"Why would they lock us out?" Carter spun back to the chaos behind him, realizing that the dead were still coming. "There would be time to worry about the door later."

With legs shaking, he stared out across the processing area as the dead spilled onto the base in a wave of insatiable hunger. Carter ripped his sword from the magnetic sheath on his back. They were almost upon him despite the distance he'd run from the fight. His only saving grace was that they had begun to spread out.

"Fucking die!" He slammed his blade down hard to split one of the creatures' heads in two. It staggered another few steps before falling flat on its back. "And stay dead!"

Killing the thing reminded him that he wasn't easy prey. He struck down another two as a third tried to flank him from behind.

"Not so fast." He deftly uppercut the zombie in the chin with a Kinetic Impact. Regret hit him immediately when the monster's head detonated in a shower of gore that left him with blackened brain tissue stuck to his cheek. Despite that, a calm began to quell the fears that had plagued him moments before.

That's right, Skyline won't be beaten by this weak-ass horde of zeds.

His confidence faded as soon as a chorus of howls erupted from a few of the trucks laying on their sides in the processing area. Nearly two dozen of the dead darted from their trailers.

"Good god, they're running." Carter's eyes widened as the Guardian Core labeled them as lurkers. He'd heard of them, but hadn't actually seen one in action yet. "How are they that fast?"

At a full sprint, the monsters rushed past the guardians that were still fighting in the processing area as if they had no interest in them. The sight sent Carter's mind speeding into a wall.

Why aren't they attacking?

It was like they were moving with purpose, each heading in a different direction, straight toward the surrounding buildings. Carter took a step back as one of them ran toward the administration building that he stood beside. He readied his sword only to falter when he noticed what the monster was wearing beneath its tattered shirt.

Is that... C4?

He caught at least six rectangular packages strapped to the lurker's chest along with a coil of wires.

"Shit! Where did that necromancer get that much ordinance?"

Carter turned to run just as the monster reached the doors that he had been unable to open when he'd tried a moment before. He had to get away.

He dove behind a jeep that was parked outside just as the sound of a raven's caw echoed through the sky. In response, each of the wired zombies detonated simultaneously.

Carter screamed as debris slammed into the vehicle he hid behind, nearly knocking the jeep over on top of him. Bits of cement and broken glass fired out from the epicenter like a hail of bullets. If it hadn't been for his Barrier spell, he would have been killed. As it was his, head was still spinning. Despite that, he shoved himself up and got to his feet and coughed on the cloud of dust that swept through the air.

His jaw dropped as the scene came back into view.

The C4-strapped zombies had run straight for every vulnerable point of the base's entrance area. One of the armories was gone, as were a number of security stations and turrets. One of them had even breached the admin building that he was standing beside.

He snapped his head to the gaping hole in the building that he'd been unable to get in a moment before. The security door had been torn apart, allowing a pair of walking corpses to wander in through the opening.

Carter jumped into action, telling himself that he was trying to protect the command building. Cutting them both down, he stepped inside. He wasn't sure how many zombies could have gotten in. He hadn't seen any more but he had to make sure. He had to move. Protecting the building would show the commander how valuable he was. This was his chance.

The fact that it was sure to be safer inside the building was an added bonus.

Making his way toward the Command center, Carter cut down another three common zombies. On his way, he didn't come across any of his fellow guardians. It was like everyone had been sent out to deal with the threat at the gates.

Something is definitely wrong. Otherwise, there would be more of a presence.

Bancroft must have been in some sort of trouble. Something was disrupting their communication and preventing him from giving orders to keep their defense organized. At the very least, they could request some back up from the guardians on Autem's side of the base. Then again, the wall that had been raised at the start of the attack to divide their area probably meant that they had no intention of helping.

They really must see us as expendable.

He shook his head and pushed forward. With or without

Autem's help, Skyline would fight back. He was going to make sure of it.

"Things will make sense when I find Bancroft and show him what I'm worth." He kept moving, all the way to the command center's doors.

Assuming his guardian ring lacked the access level needed to enter, he punched the unlock pad beside the door anyway. The act helped him vent some of his anger. In response, the light above the panel blinked red.

"That figures." He opted to bang on the heavy metal door instead. The commander would probably be pissed, but someone had to tell him how disorganized the fight had become at the front. Plus his persistence showed his dedication.

"Commander! I'm here to help and have a report from the gates."

The doors remained closed, as if no one was listening. He banged again with as much strength as he could muster. No one answered. Carter started to fear that the command center was empty. That Bancroft had somehow been killed.

That would be bad. Then again, if Bancroft had fallen, someone would have to take over. He allowed a momentary fantasy of taking control of their forces. His indulgence was chased away when a woman in a nineteen-fifties hairstyle strode into the hall behind him.

"You there, what are you doing?"

"None of your busi—" Carter shut his mouth the instant his HUD informed him that she was a level forty seer. He'd assumed that she was just some secretary or something.

"I'm sorry, ma'am." He saluted immediately, realizing his error. "I have a report for the commander that I was attempting to deliver."

"Stand aside." She stepped up to the access panel and raised her hand to reveal one of Autem's rings. "Some things take a woman's touch." She gave him a look that made it clear she had acknowledged his earlier reaction.

Carter jumped out of the way, not wanting to get on a high-level guardian's bad side. Behind her, another three guardians followed into the hall. They were dressed in the same Skyline uniform he was. She must have picked them up as an escort on the way there. With the woman taking charge, Carter fell in line behind her while trying to think of something to say that would make him look good. The heavy security door hissed and slid open before he could get a word out. His eyes widened the instant he saw inside.

Enormous monitors surrounded the circular room like the bridge of a futuristic battleship. Each held a view from a different camera on the base, most of which were filled with his fellow mercenaries fighting to hold back the ravenous dead. He froze when he saw the man standing in the center of it all.

Bancroft.

The commander watched as it all unfolded, his face stoic as if immune to the horrors of the attack. A squad of six guardians stood behind him. Carter had heard of them. Squad Zero. They had been hand-picked by Bancroft himself to lead the hunt for the necromancer that was now attacking their base.

Carter couldn't help but feel that they could have done a better job. All the more reason they needed someone like him leading the team. His mind crashed to a halt a second later when he looked past the squad to the back of the room, where a pair of young boys sat.

Why are there kids here?

"What in the Nine's name are you doing, Charles?" The seer walked straight through the door of the command center without hesitation.

Carter pushed past the three guardians that were with her, making sure to find somewhere prominent to stand.

"Stay out of this, Kristen, I know what I'm doing." Bancroft barely looked at her, let alone Carter.

"I will not stay out of it." She added a very proper harrumph as she stamped a foot. "Skyline is in complete disarray out there. Honestly, it's like you're trying to sacrifice your men. I have a good mind to report you to..." She trailed off, glancing back to Carter as if she had been about to say something she shouldn't in front of him.

"Now, let's not go getting the big man involved here. I assure you I have everything under control." Bancroft appeared calm despite the battle raging outside. The evenness of his tone irritated Carter. It was like he didn't even care that Skyline was being humiliated.

"Have you seen what's happening out there?" The seer threw a hand toward the monitors. "I'd hardly call that having things under control."

Carter couldn't help but agree. At least someone was finally speaking up about the commander's error in judgement.

"I realized what it looks like, but I am this close to getting Graves right where I want him. We may lose some men, but I will win in the end. Trust me, everything will fall into place. My opponents have no idea of the trap they're walking into."

The seer seemed to relax. Carter did the same, surprised how easily the anger at nearly being sacrificed faded. He was still irritated by the implied insult that he was fodder to be thrown away, but at the same time, he had to give Bancroft credit. The man clearly had a plan in the works. One that must have required luring this necromancer into a false sense of security. Just the fact that he was able to sacrifice some of his men showed that he was on another level, like an apex predator in an ocean of smaller fish. It was a level that Carter needed to reach to stand as an equal.

He just wasn't there yet.

That was okay, he just needed to work harder. He could get there. He had been a wolf among sheep his whole life. If anyone could reach that level of power, it was him. He just needed to prove himself.

His hopes for the future were interrupted when one of the other guardians pointed to one of the monitors. "Sir, we have an eye on one of the targets."

Carter flicked his gaze to the screen, finding a guy in his early twenties running through the base. At first glance, he looked like one of Skyline's personnel due to the armor he wore and the sword on his back. Then he noticed the blue hair.

Who is…?

"That's the necromancer's artificer." Bancroft paused before smiling. "Or is it?"

"What?" The seer shot him a confused look.

"Think about everything Graves has done for a second." His tone soured as he mentioned the necromancer's name. "That damned zombie has won so far through misdirection and lies."

"And?" The seer continued to stare at him.

"Simple. If he's sending one of his men out in the open like that, it can't be an accident." He narrowed his eyes at the screen. "It's bait." Bancroft let a smile creep onto his face. "I've spent more time than you can imagine thinking about how Graves works. And right now, he isn't fighting a war. No, that isn't his style." The commander shook his head. "This is a game of chess. Graves is trying to draw our attention away from something."

"Would he really sacrifice such a powerful piece?" The seer stared at the blue-haired artificer on the screen. "Letting us take one of his Heretics would be a devastating blow."

"Not if that Heretic isn't real." Bancroft sounded smug.

"You think Graves has an illusionist?" The seer seemed to be considering the idea.

"Think about everything Graves has gotten away with." Bancroft's tone grew confident. "The only way that makes sense would be if he has an illusionist on his side. It's obvious that Ms. Alvarez has unlocked the class." He glanced to the seer as if questioning something. "For all I know, you might be her in disguise. Even those guardians you brought with you could be fake."

Panic flooded Carter's mind. He couldn't let the commander think of him as some sort of rando that might be an imposter. He cleared his throat. "Sir, I can assure you I am a loyal member of this organization. And I am willing to submit to whatever test you decide is appropriate."

"There's no need for that." The seer held up a hand. "Just asking the question would have been enough to break an illusion spell." She swept her hand across the room. "I don't see any spells unraveling here, so I think we are safe. Unless Ms. Alvarez has gained the ability to trick my senses as well as the Guardian Core's analysis. Besides, illusions are rarely useful in battle once you suspect that your opponent knows you have the capability. If anything, the realization that they have access to that type of magic renders it useless. I only wish I had thought to analyze her back when she was standing right in front of me."

Carter relaxed as she continued.

"But that still leaves the issue of what to do about him." The seer jabbed a well-manicured finger at the blue-haired guy on the monitor. "We can't just make assumptions and do nothing. Even with my perception, I can't see through an illusion by looking at a camera feed."

"No." Bancroft frowned. "However unlikely, we should still investigate." That was when he turned to Carter and the rest of the low-level guardians in the room. "It looks like that artificer is heading for the airfield. It's probably a waste of time, but head over there and make sure we have nothing to worry about."

Carter froze, unsure what his best option was. The commander had given him a direct order. It could be his chance to show his value. Then again, if Bancroft was right, it was probably a waste of his talents. If he made his way to the hangar only to find that that Heretic was a fake, he'd have accomplished nothing. Even worse, this might be his only chance. He might never be in the same room with the commander again.

He couldn't take that risk. He was too capable to spend his time running pointless errands. Carter glanced at the other three guardians that had been following the seer. They all looked hapless, like they weren't ready for a fight. Like they were nothing more than weaklings or grunts. That settled it. He would leave the task to them.

"Excuse me, sir." Carter stood at attention. "I trust your judgement and agree that the artificer on the feed is intended to draw our attention away from something more important. Respectfully, I request to remain here to assist in case you require additional support to take down this necromancer." He fought the urge to apologize for his interruption for fear that it might make him appear weak.

For an instant, a vein bulged on the Commander's forehead as if he might start yelling, or worse. The man might just execute him for insubordination. Dread bubbled up in Carter's stomach as he realized he might have overstepped his position. He let out a sigh of relief as soon as Bancroft spoke.

"Very well." He gestured for the other three guardians to move on to the mission he'd previously assigned. The commander waited until they were gone to continue. "What's your name?"

"Guardian Mitchell Carter, fighter class. Level fifteen, sir."

Bancroft pointed to the squad standing behind him. "Go with my men to the brig. It's one building over from here. I have two prisoners there that I want brought to me. Once you return, I should have what I need to set things into motion."

"Thank you, sir." Carter's heart raced. This was the chance he was waiting for. "I won't let you down."

"See to it that you don't." Bancroft turned away as Squad Zero, the top guardians in Skyline, accepted Carter into their group and led him out of the command center.

The next few minutes were a blur.

Carter could hardly believe how powerful Bancroft's top squad was. Each man simply ripped through every walking corpse in their path. Before he knew it, he was already standing in the brig as two prisoners were dragged from their cells. One seemed to have worked as a communications officer. He'd seen the other slinging slop in the mess hall.

Carter suppressed an excited smile as he zip-tied their hands behind their backs. It didn't matter who they were, he didn't feel bad for them. He couldn't. Not when everything was falling into place for him. Bancroft was baiting a trap of his own and he was getting to play an important role.

That fucking necromancer had no idea what was coming.

CHAPTER FORTY

Alex stumbled into the shadows behind a parked jeep as a deafening cacophony tore through the night. Glancing back, he caught several balls of fire bursting into the air over the top of a building near the front gates. The rapid flash of automatic gunfire followed as explosions mixed with the sound of trucks overturning and plowing through the walls.

"Holy crap, holy crap, holy crap." Alex ducked his head and thanked every deity he could think of that he was far enough away.

A string of notifications flashed through his vision, each telling him a guardian of some kind had been defeated. A sudden wave of sensation radiated through his body as the Heretic Seed attempted to condense the information down to just what was important.

> **21 Level 1 Guardians, assorted classes, defeated. 840 experience awarded.**
> **2 Level 2 Guardians, assorted classes, defeated. 280 experience awarded.**
> **6 Level 3 Guardians, assorted classes, defeated. 1,440 experience awarded.**

4 Level 4 Guardians, assorted classes, defeated. 1,320 experience awarded.

Alex's eyes crossed as the information overwhelmed him. In response, the Seed stopped counting individual levels and condensed its messages further.

50 Guardians of assorted levels defeated. 15,980 experience awarded.
You have reached level 25. 3,806 experience to next level.

"Holy crap!" He had only just reached level twenty-two during the battle at the casino earlier that night. There hadn't been a burst of progress like that since he had been below level ten. For a moment he wondered why the Seed had given him full credit for the kills since he wasn't that close to the battle. Maybe it was because he had worked hard to help grow the horde? Whatever it was, it was three levels worth of points. He dropped them all into will and tried not to think about the fact that fifty people had just been killed.

Was the assault really that effective?

It made more sense when he noticed that the victims were mostly low-level guardians. They would be the first to die in the chaos. The realization brought him back down off the high that the sudden level had caused. It was easy to start feeling confident after gaining so much progress so fast, but in truth, there were plenty more guardians where that came from. Taking that into account, fifty was barely even a dent. The stronger ones must've still been in the fight.

After the initial burst of experience, more messages trickled in at a slower rate. He tore his attention away from the Heretic Seed's readout and kept running. The horde was still going strong, at least, for now. He needed to make use of the diversion while it lasted.

Alex skidded to a stop behind a jeep as multiple squads of armored guardians rushed past him to join the fight. Again, they were mostly low levels. He peeked over the vehicle. Skyline's forces seemed disorganized, mostly just rushing to the frontlines without a clear direction. There was definitely something up. While he didn't know Bancroft well, he understood Skyline's commander enough to know that he wasn't incompetent. No, there was a plan in place. A trap hanging over him ready to spring. That was the only explanation that made sense. He couldn't help but feel like there was noose already around his neck.

Unfortunately, there was no time to worry about what Bancroft was doing. He still had a job to do. That was when Alex noticed a straggler running to catch up to the others. He focused on the man.

Guardian: Level 1 Mage

Leaping out from behind the jeep, he snapped his sword from the magnetic sheath on his back and cast Enchant Weapon. The low-level mage froze as soon as he saw him, his eyes locking on the telltale sign that he didn't belong there, his blue hair. Alex dropped to his knees and rolled as a Fireball formed in the man's hand. The spell flew past him as he shifted his weight and sprang back up to slam the flat of the blade into the guardian's chest. The impact combined with Alex's enhanced strength knocked the guy on his ass.

"Please don't." The guardian held up his hands in defense as Alex flicked the tip of his sword at the unfortunate man. It was clear he understood that he didn't stand a chance. Looking down at his terrified face, Alex couldn't help but notice that he was younger than him. The mage must not have been a part of Skyline long. Another two messages scrolled across his vision to notify him of more deaths at the front gates.

"Give me your hat." Alex held his sword in the man's face.

"What?" The mage lowered his hands a few inches.

"Your hat, give it to me." Alex tapped the mage's chest with the end of his sword so that the enchantment spell sparked against his armor.

"Shit, whatever, take it!" He ripped off his cap and threw it to the ground at Alex's feet.

"Okay, now go and don't tell anyone you saw me." Alex pulled his sword away. "And I suggest deserting Skyline as soon as you can. There might not be much left of it in the morning."

"Okay, okay. I will." The mage scurried back to his feet and ran in the opposite direction, as if taking his advice.

Alex picked up the guy's military style cap and shoved it on his head to hide his hair. In retrospect, blue was not the best choice, but with the detail covered, he could blend in a little more. His armor and sword matched the rest of Skyline, so as long as no one looked to close at him, they might not notice he was wearing a leather jacket underneath.

Of course, that was when he noticed a security camera pointing at him from the corner of a building.

I should probably get moving.

Sticking to the shadows much as possible, he made his way to the airfield. Guardians still rushed around, but considering most of them were new recruits, they seemed more lost than anything else. Especially with the lack of consistent orders from Bancroft. Their disarray made them easy to avoid.

After a few close calls, he found himself outside one of the hangars. The sound of the assault was still going strong. The kestrels inside were already taking off to join the fight from the air. They were probably the only thing that could take down Digby's destroyers. Then again, the kestrels might have some trouble, considering Becca was sure to cast illusions to screw up their aim.

Slipping around the hangar, Alex made his way toward the opening that the aircrafts used to exit the building. The smaller doors were sure to be locked, so it left him little choice of which way to go. He waited for one of the kestrels inside to fly out and darted in under the cover of its shadow. Once he was through the door, he ducked behind one of the few inactive crafts. It looked like there was room for a dozen kestrels in the building, but there were only three left. The rest must have already headed out.

A pair of guardians ran around one of the three crafts on the other side of the hangar. Alex waited for one of them to open the ramp on the back to make sure they had the access level that he needed. One of them rushed to the storage area to grab some sort of suitcase before lugging the thing into the craft. At first, he wasn't sure what they were doing, but then he remembered that Skyline usually piloted things remotely. They must have been hooking up a drone to serve as an access point. That would explain what was inside the case.

Not wanting to have to murder the pair, he pulled down on the brim of his new hat and jogged up to the guardians to get a look at them. The first, standing by the ramp, was a fighter. The one inside was an enchanter. They were both low-level like the others dying at the front gates. Alex slowed. It would be nice if he could get them to run away like the last one, but he was ready to start casting if he had to. It looked like there might be a chance when the fighter turned in his direction and refrained from drawing their sword.

I guess covering my hair was a good idea.

The guardian's lack of awareness gave him an idea. Instead of attacking, he tried to channel Digby by acting like he owned the place. With a little luck, no one would analyze him. "What are you two doing? Bancroft wants this one off the network."

"What?" The fighter hesitated for a second, clearly not following the order, before recoiling in horror. "Shit, he's a Heretic!"

Damn.

Alex reached for his sword and cast enchant as his ruse fell apart before it began. The fighter did the same while activating a Barrier. Alex lunged forward, striking his blade against his opponent's with all his strength.

The blow threw the fighter off balance, nearly knocking his sword from his hand. Alex hoped the difference in strength would be clear. Maybe that would be enough to scare him off. Sadly, they tightened their grip on their weapon and struck back. Alex cast Barrier as well to take the hit. The blade glanced off his arm with a shimmer of blue light without him needing to block. He countered with a solid chop to the fighter's gut. The enchantment on his weapon lit up the guardian's Barrier, but failed to get through.

Shifting his weight on the ball of his foot, Alex twisted to shoulder check the fighter hard enough to knock him over. He cast

Icicle three times to finish him off. The first two shattered against the guardian's Barrier but the third hit home. The man released a gurgled scream as the spell pierced his throat.

Another kill notification joined the others.

Alex may have discovered a new calling in fixing the broken things of the world, but that didn't mean he wouldn't fight back.

Without looking, he launched another Icicle in the direction of the enchanter that was still in the kestrel. A crossbow clattered to the open ramp before sliding down to Alex's feet. The enchanter fell back as chunks of ice fell around him. The frozen projectile must have shattered against his armor. Alex didn't waste the opening, kicking the crossbow away and snatching the dead fighter's sword off the ground.

The enchanter froze in place.

Alex tried again to make peace, holding both blades in the man's direction. "Are you cleared to fly that thing?"

The terrified, low-level guardian, answered with a frantic nod.

"Okay. Take your ring off and set it down beside you." He pointed to the door. "Then get out of here and keep running."

The frightened man yanked his guardian ring from his finger and tossed it aside like it meant nothing to him, reminding him that Skyline's men really were just mercenaries. Alex doubted a member of Autem would have been as cooperative. He lowered his swords and let the man go before walking up the ramp to pick up the ring.

That was when a nervous sounding voice called out behind him.

"Stop right there."

Alex arched an eyebrow as he turned to find another three guardians. Their levels were a little higher than the others he'd seen, but not by much. From left to right, they were levels eight, nine, and ten respectively. The two on the sides were fighters, while the middle was a mage. Taking any of them alone would be easy. Three at once, though, could be a problem. Alex held still. They looked confused, but ready to fight at the same time. One of them kept glancing around as if another threat could come from anywhere.

"Are you real?" the man in front asked. He held his hand out as if ready to cast something if he made any sudden movements.

"What?" Alex didn't understand the question. "What do you mean, am I real?"

"Are you an illusion?" He shouted.

"Oh." Alex nodded in understanding before raising both swords. "Um, I think there's only one way to find out."

All three of the guardians' eyes widened as if they weren't expecting a fight. Alex tried his best not to hide the fact that he was just as confused as they were. He couldn't help but shake the feeling that he was missing something important as the imaginary noose around his neck tightened. The three men stared at him awkwardly before finally making up their mind.

The mage stepped forward as an Icicle formed in the air in front of him. "Take him out."

Alex jumped to the side just before the spell shattered against the kestrel's wall next to his head. He enchanted his new sword as he moved. His Barrier was still active, but it had already taken a hit in the last fight. He wished there was a way to know how many more it could withstand. Another Icicle struck him in the shoulder, bursting into glittering fragments against the defensive spell. There was no use running. Especially when he had the stat advantage.

Shifting his weight, he shoved off in the opposite direction to charge the mage. He swung both swords, the enchantments lighting up their blades like molten steel. They connected with the mage's chest to tear through their armor. A burst of energy erupted from the wound as his spells power ripped at the man's flesh. The cut wasn't deep but it certainly gave the mage some-thing to think about as they fell back and tried to heal.

The fighters came at him next, both swinging for his head.

Alex raised both swords to block. His right held firm but his left wavered, unable to handle the pressure. The best he managed was an awkward deflect. He may have had the stat advantage, but being right-handed, his non-dominant hand wasn't nearly as strong. Not to mention both fighters were using both hands to grip their weapons. Plus, Alex didn't have any practical sword training.

Oh shit. He struggled to get his swords back into something that resembled a viable fighting stance. *This might have been a bad idea.*

Jumping back, he dodged another two attacks before giving in and dropping his left sword. Dual wielding was cool and all, but he wasn't ready to do it effectively. The blade clattered to the floor as an Icicle shot past his head. The mage must have recovered.

Again, Alex fell back. This time, running out of space as he found the kestrel behind him. With nowhere to go, he lunged forward and slashed at one of the fighters. His blade slammed into the guardian's Barrier as the other fighter thrust their weapon into his back. A wave of blue light washed across his vision as his Barrier spell repelled the attack before collapsing.

Running out of options, Alex lobbed a Fireball from point blank range without giving his attacker time to react. The sphere burst on contact, causing the man's protective spell to flash as he fell back screaming. His voice shifted to a hoarse cry. The Barrier surrounding him absorbed the damage, though it apparently did nothing to protect him from inhaling the super-heated air that the Fireball produced.

Guardian, Level 8 Fighter defeated. 750 experience awarded.

Another Icicle shattered against his back before he could finish the fighter off. For a moment, Alex thought his armor had stopped it, but he could still feel the tip of it digging into his skin. It must have pushed through at least an inch. There was no time to throw back a flask to heal it. He glanced at his HUD.

MP: 146/301

Still enough left. Ignoring the pain, he launched a flurry of spells to put the guardians in check. Another Fireball flew at the mage to slow them down while he took the time to aim an Icicle, driving it down at an angle into where his target's shoulder connected to his neck.

Guardian, Level 9 Mage defeated. 850 experience awarded.

The remaining fighter leapt for his side as his sword swiped across Alex's arm. If it wasn't for his defense stat, the strike might have taken his hand clean off. As it was, he fell to the ground and dropped his weapon. He lobbed a Fireball as a distraction and launched an Icicle. The fighter dodged them both before raising his weapon for a finishing blow. Alex cast a new Barrier, unsure if the spell would activate in time.

The sword came down as Alex closed his eyes. He flinched as the fighter's weapon clattered to the floor beside him.

Snapping his eyes open, he found his opponent standing awkwardly with a look of sheer bafflement on his face. He clawed at a black spike protruding from his chest. It looked like necrotic blood.

That was when Digby stepped out from behind him, with Becca's dormant body slung over one shoulder. "Looks like I made it just in time, eh?"

The zombie's appearance threw him for a loop. Unless the plan had changed, he should have been trying to free Hawk and the others. Not to mention he was carrying an unconscious Becca. So much failed to make sense.

Alex pushed himself up and pulled off his chest armor to tend to the wound on his back. After examining it, he tossed back a mouthful of purified water from one of his flasks. "Why are you here? And is Becca okay?"

"She's fine. But I couldn't wake her, nor could I leave her back in the barracks. Plus, we're going to need her." Digby's eyes darted around as if he was processing several things at once.

"What, why?" Alex flexed his arm to see how well his wound was healing. "Where's Hawk and the others?"

"Circumstances have changed." The necromancer shifted his weight and rolled Becca from his shoulder, forcing Alex to jump in to catch her before she hit the ground.

"Hey, wait." His wound stung in protest, threatening to reopen as he caught her. "What changed? What's happening?"

"No time. We have to move now." Digby darted off toward a secure door at the back of the hangar. "This way."

"What about the kestrel?" Alex struggled not to drop Becca as he chased after the manic zombie.

"Leave it, we can come back later." Digby pulled a ring from his pocket and pressed it against a panel to the right of the door, causing it to open.

"Where did you get that?" Alex slowed to a stop, holding Becca like a princess. He checked his watch. Her projection spell should be ending any second.

"I couldn't get to Hawk. There were too many guards at the dungeon. I couldn't even find one alone to kill and take their uniform." Digby stepped out into a hall that connected the hangar to another building. "I had to improvise."

"I do not like the sound of that." Alex tried to catch up.

Before Digby had time to explain, Becca's eyes snapped open.

"Yar! The hell?" She immediately began to struggle, clearly having no idea where she was or why she was being carried.

"Hey, wait." Alex nearly dropped her as she kicked his side. "Quit squirming."

"Alex?" She froze. "What are you doing? Where am I?" She shifted her weight to get her feet on the ground.

"No time." Digby spun back to them. "Cast Conceal, now!"

"Okay." She did so without hesitation before lowering her voice to a whisper. "But why?"

"Yeah, that's what I want to know." Alex furrowed his brow, having no idea what the necromancer had meant by improvise.

"I had to…" Digby trailed off and snapped his eyes to the other end of the hallway just as a security door opened.

Every muscle in Alex's body tensed as the last person he wanted to see, entered.

Bancroft.

The commander of Skyline.

The level 60 tempestarii that could single handedly kill them all.

The man walked down the hall dressed in a black coat that fanned out behind him like a Sith Lord. Alvin walked at the man's side. The same squad of high-level guardians that had attacked them back in Vegas followed.

Alex glanced at his mana, finding it close to empty after the last fight. There would be nothing he could do if a member of the group saw through the fragile concealment spell that kept them hidden. Not even Digby had the power to handle them. They were completely outnumbered and outgunned.

Alex held his breath, not wanting to make a sound that might put them in jeopardy. For a moment, it looked like Bancroft might pass right by. Then, a woman slipped through the group to the front to walk beside Bancroft. Becca gasped as soon as she saw her.

Guardian, Level 40 Seer.

His mind raced as he realized who she was and what it meant that she was there.

"They're here!" The woman stopped short, throwing out a hand to slow the others.

"Thank you, Kristen. I told you everything would work out." A wide smile grew on Bancroft's face before he flicked his eyes to Digby. "There you are, Graves. I hope you don't mind, but I brought in some assistance to deal with your little illusions now that I have figured out what class Ms. Alverez is."

Digby narrowed his eyes at the man. "You really think a seer is enough to catch me?"

"No, but this is." Bancroft raised a radio to his mouth. "Bring them in."

Alex watched in horror as a level fifteen fighter shoved Hawk into the hallway with a sword resting against the back of his neck. The man looked especially mean. Another guardian, the knight that had attacked them in Vegas, brought up the rear, shoving two more men in. Alex hadn't seen them before but based on the descriptions he'd heard from the others, it was Easton and Campbell.

Bancroft held both hands out wide as if declaring victory.

"Looks like I hold all the cards now."

CHAPTER FORTY-ONE

Carter gripped the back of the brat's shirt tight in his left hand to make sure he couldn't wriggle himself free.

What was his name? Carter tried to remember. He knew it was something ridiculous. *Oh yeah, Hawk.* He let his sword rest against the kid's neck to remind him that it was there as his heart raced at the scene before him.

Graves, the necromancer, stood stewing with nowhere to run. The hate in his eyes was practically intoxicating. The other two Heretics looked terrified. After all the chaos and havoc they'd caused that night, it was all for nothing.

Bancroft had done it.

The man had actually trapped the undead bastard. There was no way the Heretics were getting out of that hallway with their heads attached to their bodies. Not with this many guardians ready to take them down. The realization made him forget about everything that had gone wrong that night as Bancroft's orders started to make sense.

It was all a ruse.

The commander really was just luring the stupid necromancer into a trap. The disarray of their forces had been part of the plan.

Bancroft had earned his respect ten times over. It took a strong leader to make that kind of sacrifice to secure victory. He must have had complete and total confidence to let the night unfold as it had. Bancroft had truly understood what they were up against from the start.

The commander had even enlisted that woman from Autem for the effort. Carter still didn't know what a seer was capable of, but having a level forty as well as Bancroft at level sixty there, the necromancer didn't have a shot in hell. More importantly, Bancroft had allowed him to be a part of the whole operation.

His admiration was cut short when Bancroft turned back to him. "Carter, wasn't it?"

"Yes, sir." He yanked back on the collar of his captive rather than saluting.

"May I borrow your weapon?" Bancroft held out a hand as he walked back through the squad that accompanied him. They parted, taking up positions against the wall to give him space. Autem's seer remained in the middle with Bancroft.

"Of course." Carter removed his sword from the neck of the kid he held and flipped it in his hand to pass the commander its handle

"Thank you." Bancroft paused and gave him a smile. "You've done well tonight. I won't forget it. Men with your initiative are rare."

Carter couldn't believe his ears. The commander knew him by name. He had actually proved his value just like he had set out to. His damn level cap was as good as gone. He could reach level thirty, maybe even higher. "Thank you, sir. You can count on me."

"Yes. I think I will." Bancroft held the sword in one hand and reached for Carter's prisoner with the other. "Let me take this miscreant off your hands as well."

Carter let go as the commander gripped the kid's shoulder hard enough to make the boy wince. At level sixty, he must have been insanely strong.

"Don't you dare hurt him!" Graves shouted from where he stood at the other end of the hall. "If you harm one hair on his head, so help me, I will bring all the power of the Heretic Seed down upon you personally."

"Oh hush, Graves." Bancroft turned, practically dragging the child prisoner alongside him. "I won't do a thing to the boy. As long as you surrender."

"Don't do it." Hawk tried to shake himself free. "I knew what I was doing. I knew the risks."

Graves let out a frustrated growl that faded into a defeated sigh before looking down at the kid. "I know, Hawk. I know. I just wish you had let me handle things."

"I know, and I'm sorry." For once the defiant boy didn't argue. "I just wanted you to trust me."

"I do trust you. I always have." Graves reached out toward the kid before letting his hand fall. "But I should have made it more clear instead of pushing you around. I see that now."

Bancroft let out a mirthless laugh and placed the sword against Hawk's neck. "This is all very touching, but it doesn't change the fact that this is as far as you go."

Graves stood quietly for a moment letting the muffled sounds of fighting from the front gates fill the silence before he spoke again. "You're wrong."

"What's that now?" Bancroft arched an eyebrow.

"If you think you can threaten my people and I will simply surrender, you have another thing coming." The necromancer swiped a decisive hand through the air.

The eyes of the two other Heretics widened.

"Dig, wait." The artificer stepped forward.

"Yeah, we can figure something out," the illusionist on his other side added.

"No, we won't." Grave's mouth curled down into a server frown. "I know what is at stake here. If we allow ourselves to be taken, the only hope the world has will die with us." He lowered his eyes to the captive child. "I'm sorry, Hawk, but this is bigger than any one person."

"Fine." Bancroft responded by kicking the back of the kid's leg to force him onto his knees before raising the sword to strike. "If you really want to test me, I assure you, you will regret it."

Graves scoffed. "Like you would really kill a child."

"You think I won't?" Bancroft's grip on the kid's shoulder tightened.

"Charles." The seer interrupted the conflict. "There's no need to hurt the boy." The tension in the hall faded for a moment before the seer ramped it up even further. "Not when we have two adult prisoners to execute first." She gestured to the two handcuffed men behind Carter. "Kill them first if you need to show that you're serious. If he still won't surrender, then execute the child if you must."

Bancroft let out a sigh. "I suppose that is more reasonable." He yanked the kid off the floor and threw him to one of the guardians standing off to the side against the wall. Then he turned back to Carter. "Bring Easton to me."

He acted without hesitation. Carter may have proved his reliability already, but he wasn't going to start slacking now. He grabbed the smaller of the two men that he'd gone to the brig to get earlier and dragged him forward. "Come on."

Easton stared daggers at him as he shoved him into position in front of Bancroft. He kicked him in the back of the legs to force him to his knees, just like the commander had done to the kid a moment before. Carter slapped a hand down on his shoulder to make sure he hit the floor hard.

"If you think Graves is going to surrender for me, you're dead wrong. I'm nobody." Easton spat at Bancroft's feet.

"We'll find out." The commander stepped into position and placed his sword against the man's neck, clearly ready to decapitate him right there if the necromancer didn't give up.

The seer stepped to Easton's other side, just far enough so that she wouldn't get hit by the back swing. Carter couldn't help but be surprised that she didn't move further. Apparently she wasn't squeamish. He stepped back as well, making sure not to go too far either in fear that he might look weak.

"This is your last chance, Graves." Bancroft drew back the sword far enough to take Easton's head clean off.

Carter's breathing sped up in anticipation.

"Go right ahead." The zombie let out a laugh. "You're forgetting who you are speaking to." He locked his eyes with the commander. "I am Lord Graves, the right hand of death. I think the question you all have to ask is, what do you think my Heretics and I are going to do when you run out of prisoners?"

The members of Squad Zero, standing along the sides let out a few laughs at the threat.

Bancroft frowned. "Necromancer or not, you are outnumbered and outleveled. I just wish you had the sense to understand that."

"And you best not underestimate me." A crooked smile spread across the dead man's face as he leaned to the blue-haired Heretic beside him and whispered something behind his hand. The artificer's eyes widened as he snapped his head to the necromancer with a mixture of shock, confusion, and doubt on his face.

"Fine." Bancroft swung just as the Heretic artificer reached out toward him. Carter didn't have time to react before the sword in the commander's hand began to glow.

A crimson torrent sprayed into the hallway as the blade struck.

Carter's mind slammed to a halt in confusion.

Blood covered Easton's face, but… it wasn't his.

The seer staggered back, her eyes wide as she clutched her throat, crimson spraying from between her fingers. She opened her mouth to speak, but merely coughed a mouthful of blood down her front. Her hands dropped to her sides as her head tilted back, hanging by a thread. Then her legs buckled. Her body crumpled to the floor a moment later.

Carter's mouth fell open, unable to understand what had happened.

Bancroft stood, holding his sword at the end of an arc that had just torn through the seer's throat, nearly severing her head. The blade in the commander's hand glowed with the telltale light of an enchantment.

What?

What just happened?

The command that Graves had whispered to his artificer was obvious. He'd told him to enchant the weapon in the commander's hand.

But why?

Was there a way to guide the blade? A way to force Bancroft to switch targets? Did they cast some kind of illusion to confuse him?

Carter flicked his eyes to the woman on the zombie's other side.

There had to be a trick in play.

No. The illusionist stood with a hand clasped over her mouth, looking just as shocked as he did.

That was when he realized that the members of Squad Zero, standing around them, hadn't even flinched. He took a frantic step back toward Bancroft's knight behind him.

"What is happen—" His words were cut off by a sudden spike of agony in his chest. He looked down in horror, staring at the point of a sword. It was coated in blood.

His blood.

"I'm sorry, Carter." Bancroft lowered his weapon. "But I don't think you'll be moving up the ranks after all."

Carter gasped as the sword in his chest was yanked out of his body. He clutched at the wound and fell to his knees as blood spurted from his chest. The taste of copper filled his mouth.

All he could do was choke out one word, "Why?"

Bancroft didn't answer. Instead, he simply turned away like he wasn't worth the time and approached the necromancer. "It took you long enough, Graves. If I kept talking any longer, she would have started suspecting something. As it is, I've been spouting vague statements in fear that she might catch me in a lie."

Carter flopped forward on his face as confusion consumed him.

The necromancer laughed off Bancroft's complaint. "Well, I couldn't very well explain things to my side in front of that seer either. You could have at least provided a distraction so I could get my people up to speed without blowing the whole thing."

Both the illusionist and the artificer erupted with questions. Questions that Carter wanted answers to. Dragging his body along the floor through a puddle of his own blood, the world began to fade.

Carter struggled to hold on.

He couldn't die now.

Not now.

Not like this.

He had to understand.

The darkness closed in as his face lay on the cold, wet floor of the hallway. One word echoed in his dying mind.

How?

CHAPTER FORTY-TWO

ONE
HOUR
EARLIER

Charles Bancroft woke to a sudden chill. He clutched his chest until the feeling faded. His heart raced like it wanted to burst from his body. Something felt wrong, but he couldn't place what.

His quarters were dark and quiet as he sat up in bed.

Kicking the blanket off, he reached for the pocket watch on his night stand. The sun wouldn't be up for another hour and a half. He let out a sigh, annoyed that he was missing out on some much-needed sleep. If he was to lead the attack on Vegas at noon, he was going to need as much rest as possible. After all, a good night's sleep was the foundation of a proper day.

The last thing he wanted was for that necromancer to get the better of him. After what had happened in California and the breach a couple days ago, Henwick might not give him another chance. No, the last thing he wanted was to report anything to the man, other than that he'd captured or destroyed that infuriating zombie. As it was, he'd been holding off on speaking with Henwick until he had a victory to report to get himself out of the dog house.

Especially with Autem growing by the day. If that kept up, Henwick wouldn't need Skyline, or even him for that matter.

Bancroft groaned in frustration as he dropped his head back to the pillow with the hope of letting the dark room lull him back to sleep. He snapped his eyes open a second later.

Something was off.

Something that tugged on his senses. Bancroft pushed himself up on his elbows. His perception was far above average. It was nothing compared to Kristen's, but it was still enough to alert him to a danger that might otherwise go unnoticed.

Bancroft swept his gaze across the shadows of the room, unable to shake the feeling that he was being watched somehow. He tried to convince himself he was wrong. If there was someone hiding in the dark, there would be a sound to betray their efforts. It may be subtle but there was always something, like a quiet breath or a heartbeat.

The flaws in his logic set off panic alarms in his head just as a light across the room clicked on.

"Hello, Bancroft."

Graves, the deceased man that had been the cause of all of his problems, sat casually in his desk chair several feet away. He held a pistol in his hand that looked like he'd taken it off one of his men.

The necromancer waved using the hand holding the gun so that the barrel drifted back and forth with the gesture. If it wasn't for the gravelly British accent, he might not have recognized him. It was hard to believe how much the zombie's face had changed. He almost looked human.

Bancroft sat up straight, unsure if he should ask questions or start casting. With the difference in their levels, there was no way the zombie could expect to beat him. He suppressed the urge to call down enough lightning to burn the monster to ash. As much as he hated to admit it, the infuriating zombie was also clever. If Graves had put himself in harm's way, then there had to be more to the situation. There had to be a reason he'd taken the risk.

He opted to ask questions first. "How did you get in here?"

"Simple, I climbed over the wall at the back of the base. I was supposed to be rescuing Hawk and the rest of my people right now, but I ran into a bit of a snag when your dungeons were guarded a bit too well. That's why, in desperation, I headed back to the barracks and slipped into your bed chamber."

"What about the guard I had posted outside?"

"Oh, he was delicious. Dropped him straight into my void, I did." The necromancer grinned and gestured to the pistol in his hand. "Where do you think I got the gun?"

"Do you really think firearms are going to hurt me?" Bancroft scoffed at the notion. "I'm level sixty, for Christ's sake."

"This?" Graves shifted the pistol's aim to the side to suggest a shrug. "Lord, no. I only wanted to make a point."

"And what point is that?" Bancroft probed for more.

"Simple." Graves twirled the gun around his finger like an idiot before tossing it toward the bed. The zombie raised both hands in surrender as the pistol landed in the blankets at Bancroft's feet. "My point is that I have no intent on harming you. All I want is to talk. In fact, if—when I am done—you still want to destroy me, then you may do as you see fit. Shoot me in the face, strike me with lighting, or call up Henwick to deal with me for all I care. The choice is yours. I'll add that I have no Barriers or defenses that would stop a bullet from penetrating my skull at this range. That would be enough to put me down."

Bancroft tilted his head to one side and picked up the pistol, assuming that the zombie had probably removed the bullets. It was an obvious ruse. Strangely, from the weight, he could tell that the weapon was indeed loaded. He furrowed his brow, trying to figure out the trick. "What if I don't want to talk and just shoot you now?"

"You won't. Not when you can see the writing on the wall just as I can." Graves let his hands fall to the armrests of the chair he sat in. "Autem is growing and, before long, Henwick will have no need for mercenaries. Not when he has a force of loyal zealots at his beck and call."

"And you, what? Think you can convince me to change sides?" Bancroft laughed at the zombie's line of thinking. It was utterly ridiculous. He wasn't wrong about Skyline's situation with Autem, but that didn't mean betrayal was on the table.

"Why not?" Graves offered nothing more than a simple shrug.

"You delusional corpse." Bancroft shook his head. "You have seriously overplayed your hand here. I admit that I have my concerns with what Henwick has planned for Skyline after Autem gains a foothold in the world. But if you think your side is somehow a viable option, you are sorely mistaken. With the amount of power at Henwick's disposal, you are simply no match. That might change eventually, but time is not on your side."

"What if there was a way to even the odds?" The zombie pumped his eyebrows.

Bancroft raised one of his. As stupid as the idea was, he wasn't one to turn down a potentially advantageous proposal without weighing the pros and cons. After all, that was how he originally found his calling. It may have been back in the industrial revolution, but he did have a nose for business. Granted, his ambitions were also what landed him in Henwick's path. If it wasn't for his greed back then, he never would have ended up indebted to the man in the first place. It was a lesson he'd learned well, and one that he didn't intend to ignore now.

Despite his concerns, it still made sense to learn more in case the zombie knew something that could actually present an opposition to Autem's rise to power, if only to report it back to Henwick.

Bancroft kept the pistol aimed at the corpse's head. "And how exactly might you even the odds?"

"Simple, I shall regain the shards of the Seed. With that, I can learn more about this power and how to create more fellow Heretics like myself. All I would have to do is get access to this Babel place where I assume the fragments are held."

"You know about Babel?" Bancroft let his pistol's aim falter.

"I do."

"Then you know there's no way you're getting there." Bancroft raised the gun back up.

"You might be right." Graves sighed. "With the information I have now, I am not fool enough to think that my chances are anything but slim. My original plan was to drown your forces in an army of the dead, but thanks to your little attack earlier, I was forced to act prematurely. Honestly, I'm in a bit of a bind. There are several locked doors, automated weapons, and a seer in my way. Not to mention I don't know anything about Babel itself or what's on the other side of those elevator doors. Even if I was able to make it inside and acquire the Heretic Seed's shards, I would still need to make my escape unscathed." He tilted his head to one side. "And let us not forget that you are holding a young man by the name of Hawk that holds some importance to me, as well as Alvin, Easton, and Campbell. I would have to retrieve them as well."

"Sounds like you have a lot on your list." Bancroft debated pulling the trigger right then, but refrained, despite his more reasonable side screaming at him to do so.

"Indeed." Graves held out both hands empty. "I feel I may have bit off more than I can chew, as it were. In fact, I had a good think about it on my way here. The more I considered what might go wrong, the more I felt like failure was inevitable. To put it in a term I've learned during my time in Las Vegas, here, the odds favor the house as it would seem."

"Maybe now is the time to surrender." Bancroft pushed for the simplest solution.

"I think not." Graves laughed. "I didn't say my goals were impossible, just unlikely. Which is why I decided that the best option was to cheat. And to do that, I think you should join me." He grinned like an idiot. "With you switching to the winning side, all of those obstacles in my way would be removed. You could simply walk us right past that seer and into Babel."

"Again, I will have to remind you that I am not insane." Bancroft locked eyes with the dead man. "Babel is not just a place where dangerous things like the Seed are kept. It is Henwick's home. He would kill you the moment you stumbled in there. Not to mention even I don't have the access codes to get in. So unless you have a way to get that seer to tell you, then I'm afraid you're out of luck."

"Hmm. I think I know a way to get the information out of her. It's a bit messy though." Graves winked as if they had already become accomplices. "I'll admit, I wasn't betting on Henwick acting as guard dog. That certainly does put a kink into the idea.

Although, you could simply contact him and tell him you've captured me. That ought to lure him out long enough for me to slip in and get what I need."

"There is no way in hell that I am doing that." Bancroft nearly shot him just to put an end to the insane conversation.

That was when Graves let out a long sigh that carried the scent of death on his breath. "I was really hoping that you could be reasoned with."

"You should have known better." Bancroft tightened his finger around the trigger, unable to believe the necromancer's stupidity. Even worse, he couldn't believe his own. To think, he had actually thought his opponent was clever.

"Fine then, I have a second offer." Graves' voice went cold. "Help me, or die."

Bancroft tensed. Despite the appearance that he had the upper hand, he couldn't shake the feeling that he was wrong. There had to be a trick. Something that he wasn't seeing. "What happened to giving me a choice?"

"It is still up to you." Graves chuckled. "You can join me or die. That's still a choice."

"Threats don't carry much weight, given the difference in power between us." Bancroft tried to keep the zombie talking, hoping that he might show his hand.

"Oh, but that's where you're wrong." Graves leaned to the side to rest his chin in one hand as if there wasn't a gun aimed at his forehead. "I could have killed you already. In fact, when I was here the other day, I was tempted to slip in here and murder you in your sleep even then."

"Again, I'm not sure you could." Bancroft laughed off the threat. "Even if you had tried to swallow me whole, I would have woken up and escaped before you could. I may not be a seer, but my perception is high enough to alert me to that level of danger."

"I think you'd be surprised what abilities I might have up my sleeve." Graves leaned forward. "Just a few hours ago I killed a revenant by turning every drop of blood in their body into a million tiny needles. I'm pretty sure that would have worked just as well on you." The necromancer's mouth suddenly dropped open as if something important had slipped his mind. "Oh wait, no. You must have a will value capable of resisting a spell like that." His tone grew smug as he arched an eyebrow. "Am I right?"

Bancroft suppressed a gasp as the zombie playfully scratched the surface of a secret that few among the guardians beyond himself and Henwick were aware of. It was the reason he slept with a guard outside his door, and why Henwick spent most of his time secluded. His will stat was indeed high enough to resist almost any spell that might target his body directly, but that resistance wasn't absolute.

Graves flicked his inhuman emerald eyes to him. "But you know, I had some time on the ride here, which I spent going over my abilities. And I have to say something about the Resist Trait that all zombies have stuck out to me. Let me bring it up here, so I can run something past you." His green, inhuman eyes began moving back and forth as if reading something off his HUD. "This common trait grants +5 points to will. Normally exclusive to conscious beings, this trait allows a zombie to resist basic spells that directly target their body or mind until their will is over-powered."

A cold sweat broke out along Bancroft's brow as Graves tugged at the thread in the Heretic Seed's wording.

"So tell me, Bancroft, my friend," the zombie's tone grew entirely too casual, "when the Seed states that the ability to resist a direct spell is unique to conscious beings, what do you suppose would happen if I cast such a spell on an unconscious one?"

Shit. That was it.

Bancroft could practically feel the zombie's cold hands tighten around his throat. Henwick had made a point to keep their vulnerabilities quiet. He had even made sure that the Guardian Core's notifications never made note of the loophole. Keeping the secret had been easy. Until now, Skyline had never faced an enemy with magic of their own. Now though, Graves was right. He could have cast whatever he wanted while he slept and his will would have been unable to resist it. The necromancer could have killed him a dozen times over. The realization sent a chill down into Bancroft's very core.

"I'll take your silence as confirmation." Graves leaned back as if he had already won.

Bancroft shook off his dread. "Why didn't you kill me, then?"

Graves clasped his hands together. "I already told you, I want your help. And you won't be able to do that if you're dead. Also, the fact that I have twenty cargo vehicles full of the dead on track to hit your front gates in fifteen minutes, I'm going to need your help sooner rather than later."

Bancroft's eyes widened. "You're insane."

"Maybe." He shrugged.

"If you think a horde of three hundred is enough to defeat my guardians, then you have another thing coming."

Graves snapped his fingers. "Of course not, but they will have a shot at causing enough of a distraction for you and I to get to work. Especially if you issue orders to your men that will throw Skyline's forces into disarray."

"I won't do anything of the sort." He thrust the pistol in his hand at the zombie. "You should have killed me when you had the chance. We're done here."

"Very well." Graves threw his arms out wide as if inviting him to shoot. "Get on with it then. Shoot me in the face and hand my dismembered corpse off to Henwick. See if I care."

"As long as it shuts you up." Bancroft gritted his teeth and pulled the trigger.

His breath froze in his throat when nothing happened. At first, he suspected the gun, that somehow it had been tampered with. He tried again, before the horror of what had stopped him began to sink in. His finger shook on the trigger, unable to actually pull it. No matter how hard he tried, it wouldn't budge, as if an equal force was fighting against him.

"Do you feel that chill, Bancroft?" Graves lowered his voice to a whisper. "That deathly cold inhabiting your bones?"

"No!" Bancroft shook his head to deny the facts.

"I think introductions are in order." The necromancer spread one hand out in his direction. "I'd like you to meet one of my favorite minions. Best get acquainted, you'll be together for a while."

Bancroft's skin crawled from head to toe as his other hand rotated on its own to wave in his direction.

Graves erupted in villainous laughter. "Say hello, Tavern."

Bancroft recoiled as a horrid presence coiled through his body to slither up his throat. His mouth opened against his will to speak two words in a voice that was not his own.

"Sup, bro."

CHAPTER FORTY-THREE

"You did what!" Rebecca's jaw nearly hit the floor as Digby explained his detour to Bancroft's bed chambers.

"Indeed, I animated his skeleton." Digby waved a hand, trying to move past the fact.

"That's so… wrong." Alex's hands fell limp at his sides as Bancroft stood in the middle of the hall surrounded by a squad of his best men.

"Agreed. I'm not happy about it either." Skyline's commander stood there, with a frustrated look on his face. "Let's just get this done."

"Oh, don't be like that, Charles. May I call you Charles?" Digby threw his arm around the man's shoulder. "You're on the winning side now. So stop acting so glum. And consider that an order." He pulled Bancroft close and lowered his voice. "You wouldn't want to disobey an order, now would you?"

"No." Bancroft forced a smile as he pried Digby's cold, dead fingers off of his shoulder.

"What happens if he disobeys an order?" Alex arched an eyebrow.

"I assume Tavern bites off his tongue." Rebecca folded her arms and nodded.

"Good guess. That seemed the most practical deterrent." Digby clapped at her answer.

Of course, technically Tavern was equally as strong as Bancroft, so the man could stop them by holding his jaws open. Though eventually he would get tired, which was not the case for Tavern. The skeleton would overpower him in the end.

Digby changed the subject as he hopped across the hall to where the nearly decapitated seer lay. "And I must say I am impressed with how you handled our little obstacle here." He poked at the woman's corpse with his foot. "I thought you might hesitate, but you really went right for it."

"I'm not an idiot, Graves. There isn't room to do things half-way. If I'm stuck with you, I'm not going to leave any loose ends."

That was when Alvin threw up, reminding everyone that the brainwashed child was still there.

"Oh gross." Hawk stepped away to keep his shoes out of the line of fire.

"Indeed." Digby grabbed the little traitor by the sleeve when he was finished. "Now you listen here, boy, I am taking you back to your sister and you shall have nothing to say about the matter. She'll find a way to talk some sense into you once we've met up with her."

"But——" Alvin opened his mouth for a second before Digby cut him off.

"No buts, mister. Thanks to you, we have to leave Vegas and find a new home yet again, so I don't want to hear another peep."

"Actually, that's not necessary." Bancroft stepped forward. "All operations concerning your capture have been managed directly by me. With Henwick the way he is, and the situation that Skyline is facing with Autem, I wasn't about to report anything back to him until you were either destroyed or captured. Also, I worked directly with Alvin to place him in your midst and gave him strict orders to keep all information between us. I haven't even issued orders to attack your settlement tomorrow. I was going to do that first thing in the morning."

Digby arched an eyebrow. "Does that mean what I think it does?"

Bancroft nodded. "It means that the only people that know where you have been hiding are in this hallway." He gestured to Easton and Campbell as his holy knight removed the manacles from their wrists. "Considering you were able to get two of your people inside our walls, it didn't seem prudent to share information with anyone that I didn't trust. Especially considering how many new recruits we have. The vast majority would sell us out for a better deal in a heartbeat."

"That's smart." Rebecca nodded.

"And paranoid," Alex added.

Digby stepped closer to Bancroft. "Paranoid or not, I could kiss you, you beautiful bastard."

"I request that you don't." Bancroft held up a hand to keep him at bay before glancing at Alvin and Hawk. "My only mistake was speaking too freely about things while those two were in the room. I truly thought that your boy there had truly abandoned you. Seems he's become just as accomplished a liar as you are."

Hawk stood a little taller.

"That wasn't a compliment," Bancroft added.

"What about everyone else in here?" Alex pointed at the six guardians surrounding them in the hallway. "These guys did just attack us back in Vegas."

"Yeah, I almost turned revenant thanks to them." Rebecca backed him up.

"About that." Bancroft held out a hand toward his men, all of which immediately stood at attention. "We all know full well that the rise of the Autem Empire means that Henwick will eventually throw Skyline away when it is no longer needed. I would be an idiot not to understand that. Originally, I had expected that I would be kept on and given a new command in Autem."

"Not feeling too confident anymore, are you?" Digby arched an eyebrow.

"No." Bancroft sighed. "I have always known that Henwick was involved with another organization, but I didn't know the extent of what Autem was or what his plans for it were. Now that I do, I thought it best to have a contingency plan. Which is why I have made sure to curate at least one squad within Skyline that I can trust. That way, if I ever found myself in a difficult position, I would still have some form of back up."

"And these men are loyal to you, then?" Digby swept his eyes over the six men.

"Loyal to me, no." Bancroft shook his head. "But their loyalty can be bought at the right price."

"Pardon?" Digby furrowed his brow.

"True loyalty is rare and often overrated, which is why I trust those who put themselves above all others. It might sound strange, but there is an element of reliability in that. Unlike Henwick, I have no need for fanatics. I'd rather have a professional that honors their contracts any day of the week. That's why I trust these men."

Digby stared at the man, finding an obvious hole in his thinking. "But why would they defy Henwick for you? Once you leave Skyline, you will have nothing to offer them."

"Very true." Bancroft slipped his hands in his pockets. "Considering the current state of the world, money wouldn't even have a meaning to a mercenary. Which is why I have negotiated a deal on your behalf."

"And what deal is that?" Digby narrowed his eyes, not liking the turn that their budding partnership was heading in.

"Simple. If money has no meaning, then that just leaves power." Bancroft gave him a smug look that rivaled his own. "The deal is that, from tonight onward, myself and my men will provide our services in defeating Henwick. In exchange, you will share the power you gain when you acquire the Seed's fragments."

"You want to become Heretics?" Digby glanced down at the string of black runes that encircled his finger.

"Yes." Bancroft's expression grew deathly serious. "The moment we leave the base tonight, we will be casting off our status as guardians, so an appropriate upgrade will be expected. That means full access to the Seed's power. No level caps, no manipulation of our brain chemistry—"

"And immortality." The squad's knight spoke up.

"Yes, that too." Bancroft nodded.

"I'm starting to get the picture." Digby looked into each

guardian's eyes. "Henwick would never share his longevity with a common underling, now would he?"

Bancroft cleared his throat. "No. Other than myself, and a few other operatives within Autem, I suspect not. And obviously, I will lose that perk the moment I cast aside my power as a guardian."

"Do you really think you have enough leverage to be making demands this early in our partnership?" Digby arched an eyebrow. "Might I remind you that I can order your death at any moment?"

"True, but you won't."

Bancroft seemed unfazed by the facts. "You need my help to pull off this ridiculous heist, and you need the silence of my men to protect your home in Vegas. That's all the leverage I need. The choice is yours, either we all win or we all lose."

"Very well." Digby gave a final nod. "I agree to your demands. Now let us get the rest of this theft going." He grabbed Alex's sword from its sheath and used it to sever the flap of tissue that still connected the seer's head to her body.

"Oh gross," Hawk repeated as Alvin threw up again.

"Sorry, but I still need to have a few words with our friend here." Digby coiled his fingers through the woman's strange hairstyle to carry the head.

"I hope this Talking Corpse spell of yours really does what you say." Bancroft started walking in the direction of the hangar, paying the head no mind. "My men will take a pair of kestrels off the network and get them in the air. We'll send one to Vegas now with your people and have the other circle the base until we are ready to make our getaway."

"Make sure your sellswords keep an eye on Alvin." Digby looked back at the boy as one of the guardian's confiscated the boy's ring. "I could see him running off if you leave him an opening."

"I'll keep an eye on him." Hawk gave a sarcastic salute, clearly enjoying the night's turn of events.

"Alright." Digby gave him a smile. "I'll be counting on you."

"What about us?" Easton caught up as Campbell jogged behind him.

"You both will head back to Vegas in one of the kestrels now, along with some of our new mercenary friends. No need for you to hang around here while we handle this heist."

"Speaking of…" Alex raised a hand. "What is the plan for that?"

"Yeah." Rebecca shoved past him. "From the sound of things outside, the assault at the front gates is starting to run out of steam."

Digby glanced back in the direction of the din, noting that the sounds of battle were beginning to fade. According to his HUD, he'd lost one destroyer and more than half of his other minions. The rest of the horde was probably growing thin as well.

He called to Asher over their bond. It was time they regrouped and prepared to escape. Her voice traveled back to him.

Agreed.

The deceased raven was already waiting by one of the kestrels when they reentered the hangar. She flapped into the airship and sat in Hawk's lap as soon as the boy was seated. Easton and Campbell joined him, both looking nervous. Bancroft's men shoved Alvin into the seat beside Hawk. The brainwashed child struggled for a moment but seemed to give up rather fast once it became obvious that he wasn't going anywhere.

As soon as everyone was settled, one of the mercenaries slapped the button to close the craft's ramp. Digby stood at the rear of the kestrel, making eye contact with Hawk as it closed.

"Don't screw up," the boy called over the sound of the engines starting up.

"Oh, shut up." Digby gave him a playful grin. "I have everything under control." The ramp locked shut a second later.

Spinning back to his fellow Heretics and Skyline's soon to be ex-commander, he clapped his hands together.

"Alright, now let's go rob Henwick blind."

CHAPTER FORTY-FOUR

Digby marched through the hangar with his staff in one hand and the seer's severed head in the other as the two kestrels behind him lifted off. Bancroft fell in line beside him, with Tavern firmly rooted in his bones. Alex snapped a second sword into a new sheath on his back as he took up a position beside Skyline's commander. Rebecca strode up to Digby's side and cast Conceal as the kestrels passed by overhead.

From there, they headed straight for Autem's side of the base, leaving the fading sounds of the battle at the front gates behind them. A wall, fifteen feet high, had risen from the ground to protect the empire's refuge on the base from the dead in case a zombie or two got through. The only openings were positioned at the gates that Campbell had smuggled them through days before. A squad of guards stood at the ready as they approached.

Fortunately, getting in was far easier this time.

Taking the lead, Bancroft walked far enough ahead to exit the effective range of Rebecca's concealment and shouted a command at the guards at the gates. They stood down without question, allowing the concealed members of the group to pass by unmolested. Digby nodded to the guardians as he waltzed by, unable to resist the temptation as a sense of smug satisfaction filled him with an abundance of glee.

Considering how desperate they had been just a few hours ago, it was incredible to see the light at the end of the tunnel.

Bancroft kept right on walking straight into Autem's secure building. Several guards inside were in position to shoot the first intruder that might enter. Even the automatic turrets on the walls spun to life the instant the commander set foot in the entryway. Digby skidded to a stop just inside the door, remembering the hallway's sensors could detect their presence even while concealed. If he tried to pass through while the defenses were active, it would be all for naught.

"Shut it down, I need to get through," Bancroft snapped at the guards.

One of the men tapped away at a keyboard in response. The turrets lowered a second later. Bancroft started walking again without another word, leaving Digby and his Heretics to quietly follow in his wake before the entryway's defenses reactivated.

From there, Bancroft marched onward without stopping. Using his guardian ring's access, Skyline's commander opened every secure door in their path until they stood in front of the golden elevator that led to Henwick's supposed home, Babel.

Bancroft's shoulders sank, clearly feeling the weight of what he was about to do. "Alright, you're only going to have one shot at this. Henwick doesn't generally leave his sanctuary, and when he does, he always returns fast. So don't take any longer than you have to. The only security is a single key code directly on the other side of this elevator." He glanced down at the seer's head. "You sure you can get it out of her?"

Digby held up the head. "The spell won't permit her to lie, so I think so."

Bancroft shuddered at the thought.

"Why a passcode?" Rebecca stepped up to the doors. "Why not more security doors like the rest that use the guardian rings as keys."

"The rings are imbued with a minor enchantment when they are forged. It can't be faked so it works well as a key. However, the door lock needs to have an enchantment to read them and that takes mana."

"So?" Rebecca leaned her head to one side.

"So there's no ambient mana in Babel. That's why a more mundane electric lock is used." Bancroft answered matter-of-factly. "I've only been in one level of the facility, but as far as I can tell, the place has no essence to absorb. Somehow Henwick has found a way to block it."

"Why would he do that?" Digby growled back, caught off guard by the new information.

"The Heretic Seed is powerful, and more importantly, it seems to have a conscious need to give that power to anyone that will accept it. There is a reason Henwick locked it away. Even just a fragment is enough to be dangerous." Bancroft locked eyes with Digby. "You were not the first or the last to use the Seed's gifts. Over the last several centuries, the Seed's power has been held by many, all of which were hunted down by Henwick. That's what he formed Autem for in the first place. To keep this power out of the hands of those that couldn't be trusted. Unfortunately, the closer a Heretic is to the Seed, the more entwined the two become. Even now, there are remnants of those that have held the Seed's power sleeping within its fragments."

"What does that have to do with security and the need to block the ambient mana?" Rebecca furrowed her brow.

"Simple. To keep those remnants from causing trouble, Henwick decided to store the Seed somewhere without any ambient mana so that there was no chance of any of those damned souls finding a way back to the world of the living. That's why Henwick built Babel and is up there standing guard. Again, I don't know the details, but I know the facility took over a decade to build." Bancroft let out a mirthless laugh. "I'm pretty sure he had everyone involved killed afterward too. That way no one can ever infiltrate his sanctuary. As it is, his seer was the only person he trusted with the access code."

"So she was his gatekeeper," Digby assumed.

"Yes." Bancroft nodded. "The Seed is on level one of the facility. Once you're in, you'll find a large room with a door on the far side. The Seed's fragments are through there."

Alex swallowed audibly. "I hate to be the one to ask this, but how long do you think you can keep Henwick away?"

"If I contact him with a Mirror Link and tell him I've captured you, it will take him about ten minutes to get to the brig. Once he sees that neither you or I are actually there," Bancroft frowned, "all bets are off."

"Is it possible for the four of us to beat him if we took him by surprise now?" Alex asked in a hopeful tone. "That might solve everything."

Digby's shoulders tensed. "As much as I would like to take advantage of our situation, that might be getting a little too greedy."

"I'm surprised to hear such a reasonable statement from you." Bancroft folded his arms.

Digby deflated. "As much as I hate to admit it, Henwick would probably kill us all before we had a chance to cast a spell. He's had too much time to grow stronger. I can't compete."

"I agree." Rebecca sighed. "But for the sake of reconnaissance, what level and class is Henwick anyway?"

Bancroft answered her with a laugh. "Your guess is as good as mine."

"You don't know?" Alex looked confused. "Haven't you ever analyzed him?"

"I would if I could." The man shrugged. "But my rank doesn't have the clearance to see that information. All I see is an error message if I try. Though I assume his level is much higher than any of ours."

"Alright then, no attacking Henwick." Digby scratched that option off the list of possibilities. "We will hide until he passes by, and take the elevator as soon as there's no chance of us getting caught."

"Yes." Bancroft scratched at his chin. "And hide in one of the labs, don't try to conceal yourselves anywhere near him. He will see right through any illusion you cast, so make sure he is out of the building before you move. As it is, I'm going to need to cast a wind spell to clear the air in this hall to make sure he doesn't smell the blood coming from my former colleague there." He gestured to the seer's severed head. "I'll head straight for the kestrel we have waiting after contacting him and meet you on the roof of this building. So don't screw around. Get what you need and get out." He handed the seer's ring to Digby and walked over to the woman's empty desk to point to a panel set into the wood. "This is the unlock panel for the elevator. That ring will open it and call the lift."

"Alright, we'll move fast." Digby spun back toward the labs down the hall to find somewhere to hide.

"Make sure you do." Bancroft grimaced. "I'd say I'll leave you behind if you're late, but something tells me that your minion wouldn't allow that."

"Indeed." Digby smirked as he parted ways with his new accomplice and ducked into the laboratory where Rebecca had stolen those warding rods from. It was empty save for a revenant standing in the middle between another set of those floating metal bars.

"Shit." Alex Icicled the creature on reflex.

"Calm down. It's warded." Rebecca rolled her eyes.

"Oh." His vision darted around the room. "This is where you found those rods with the rune work?"

"It is." Digby barely paid attention to their conversation, more focused on the frosted window that ran along the wall, waiting for a shadow to pass by on the other side to tell him Henwick was out of the way.

"Here, help me with this." Rebecca dragged Alex over to the storage unit that held the rest of the laboratory's warding rods and started filling every available pouch on his armor with the things.

"Good call." The artificer followed her lead, emptying out a few more pouches so he could fit more. "If I can experiment with these later, I might be able to figure out how they work and make more. The more I learn about enchanting, the more things start to seem possible. If these little rods can float in the air, I wonder what else I can make levitate."

"Shush." Digby held up a finger to stop them. Normally, he

would have been happy to loot the place right alongside them, but with Henwick's perception being what it was, he didn't want to take the chance that the man might hear something.

Both Rebecca and Alex froze, looking sheepish before making an effort to slow down and be quiet.

That was when every necrotic nerve in Digby's body cried out in panic. It was as if the curse inside him sensed a threat beyond any he'd faced so far. His eyes bulged as a shadow drifted into view on the other side of the frosted window.

Henwick!

The realization that his mortal enemy was standing mere feet away, with nothing but a bit of blurry glass between them, sent an uncomfortable chill down his already cold spine. The shadow moved at an even, almost casual pace, as if the assault at the front gate was no threat at all.

Digby squinted at the figure, hoping to trigger the Seed's analyze ability through the window. If the Guardian Core restricted Bancroft from seeing anything about the man's class or level, then the Seed might have a shot.

Nothing happened.

Damn! The blurring effect of the glass was too much. Digby ground his teeth in frustration, understanding how foolish it would be to try to sneak out to take a peek. Stewing in his frustration, he remained where he was until the shadow had passed and made sure to leave enough time for Henwick to exit the building.

"Alright, move!" He spun back to the door as soon as the coast was clear. Rebecca and Alex ran behind him as he sprinted back to the elevator and pressed the seer's ring to the panel embedded in the desk.

The light above the golden doors came to life.

They piled into the tiny box within as soon as the entryway opened. A control panel with three buttons hung on the inside wall. Rebecca punched the circle labeled, level one.

The doors closed a second later, leaving them to look at the expensive looking oil painting that covered the wall. Scenes of angels looking down on a mass of people below filled each canvas. Digby couldn't help but notice that there were nine of the celestial figures watching from the clouds, their faces full of judgment and contempt.

He tore his attention away from the paintings as the elevator got moving. The motion caused the bottom to drop out of his stomach. He tried his best to ignore the feeling.

Rebecca furrowed her brow after several seconds had passed. "I'm just going to point out that the building we are in is not tall enough for this elevator to still be traveling up this long."

Alex's eyes widened. "And how concerned should we be about that?"

CHAPTER FORTY-FIVE

Digby exchanged awkward looks with his fellow Heretics as the elevator continued its ascent. He tried not to think about where the lift might have been taking them. With magic involved, he supposed they could end up anywhere. The doors opened before he could give it any more thought.

Digby hesitated as soon as he took in the room beyond. Unlike what he expected, it was made of solid stone, like the parking garage he'd been in back in Vegas. The space was cold, with multi colored pipes lining the ceiling. The difference between the opulent, wood paneled, elevator and this new room was jarring.

"It's like a basement." Alex stared up at the simple light fixtures hanging above them.

"Or an underground bunker." Rebecca glanced to the side, obviously checking her HUD. "Bancroft was right, I'm not absorbing any mana after using my Conceal."

"That's unnerving." Digby headed through the entry room to approach a keypad beside a large door. "Alright, let's get this seer talking." He held up the severed head in his hand and cast Talking Corpse. "Hello there."

The seer opened her eyes, immediately narrowing them to slits as she spoke one word with as much venom as possible. "You."

"Apparently this one can do more than answer questions." Digby shrugged.

"That's right." The seer's eyes glanced around clearly trying to figure out where she was before looking down. "Where is my body?"

"You died and your body is cooling on the floor." Digby snapped at the head. "Now let us get on with things."

"Henwick! There are intruders in Babel!" The seer made it clear that she had no intention of cooperating. "I repeat, the necromancer has breached Babel!"

"Quiet you!" Digby shook the seer's head. "Henwick isn't here and I need information." He shoved her toward the keypad. "Tell me the code."

The head scoffed. "I will not tell riffraff like you a thing."

"Umm, what?" Digby yanked the head back as Rebecca stepped in.

"Phrase it as a question, not a command."

"Alright," Digby looked the seer in the face. "What is the code?"

The seer immediately frowned and rolled her eyes. "7825."

"Thank you." Digby reached for the keypad only to stop before pressing any buttons. "Wait, I wasn't specific when I asked that." He raised the head again. "Was that the code to this door or something else."

The seer grimaced. "Something else."

"What was it for?" Digby furrowed his brow.

"My luggage." The seer groaned.

"No one cares about luggage," Rebecca growled. "Just ask for this door's code and be specific."

"Fine, fine." Digby asked again, this time getting a string of twenty numbers. He had to ask her to repeat it twice before he was able to input them all. He tossed her head to Alex as soon as the doors opened.

"Hey!" the seer shouted. Digby debated cancelling the spell but refrained just in case he needed more information from her.

The room beyond was huge, with a metal walkway wrapping around the wall twenty feet up. Sweeping his eyes across the floor he found dozens of large rectangular doors embedded in its surface, most of which were closed. Digby inched his way over to the closest open pit to peek over the side.

A pair of revenants screeched up at him from below.

"Gah!" Digby leapt back from the edge.

"This must be where they have been keeping the specimens that Skyline has been collecting." Rebecca glanced down at the creatures trapped in the chamber below.

"Why would they want to keep them around?" Alex took a peek as well.

"It doesn't matter. We have to move." Digby kept walking. "I wasted enough time with that seer."

"I have a name," the head complained.

"No one cares." Digby scanned the far wall to find the door that Bancroft had said would lead to the Seed's fragments.

Rebecca and Alex nodded and followed him across the room, making sure to stay away from any of the open specimen chambers below. There was no telling what might be in them, nor was there time to be curious.

Reaching the other side of the space, Digby slapped the open button to the side, revealing a stone hall, filled with glass cases of all sizes. Their mouths dropped open in unison. It was like some kind of museum.

At the end of the space was the Heretic Seed.

A huge rectangular case stood, holding close to a thousand glass vials, each containing a tiny black shard. It was as if Henwick had made sure that none of them could come in contact with each other.

"That's it." Digby forced himself forward, having trouble believing that he'd found the source of his power again. He placed his hand on the glass as soon as he reached the case, feeling the shards call to him. No, not to him. To the fragment in his chest. It was as if it wanted to be whole again.

"Now we just need to get it out of here." Rebecca ran her fingers up and down the corner of the case, looking for a seam.

"Can we smash it?" Alex did the same on the other side. "I don't see any hinges."

"It doesn't have any and I'm sure the glass is bulletproof."
Rebecca stepped back. "Shit, the case is too big to steal. Even if we
could move it, we'd never get it into the elevator."

"We don't have to." Digby stepped back and opened his maw
wide enough to swallow the Seed's prison whole.

"Umm, okay, that's one way to do it." Alex moved away from
the shadowy gateway as the entire case began to sink into the black
fluid of Digby's void.

"Is it okay to do that?" Rebecca gave him a sideways look.

"Your guess is as good as mine." Digby gave her an awkward
shrug. "But I don't see any other options." He glanced back at the
rest of the cases in the room, wondering what else might be worth
looting while they were there.

Once the Seed vanished into his maw, he snapped it shut and
went for the nearest glass box. A pair of sparkling red shoes sat
inside. He tried to analyze them but something seemed to be
blocking him. Like the glass had been treated in some way to repel
the ability.

"Oh well." He shrugged and opened his maw anyway. There
was no sense leaving anything behind if he could help it. He could
only imagine the look on Henwick's face when he found out.
Besides they still had a few minutes to spare. With the second case
safe in his void, he moved on to another that held a sheet of red
fabric. He would have tried to take more but opening his maw
wider than its default size consumed too much mana, leaving him
low enough to worry since there was nothing in the area to absorb.

"We have three minutes to get out of here," Rebecca reminded
him.

"Good, plenty of time." He turned and headed back into the
large specimen room and ran for the elevator. "I hesitate to say
this, but things are actually going rather smoothly."

He regretted the comment as soon as the words left his mouth,
because right on cue, a voice called out from somewhere in the
space.

"Hello?"

Digby skidded to a stop. Who was it? A guardian? Worse?

The voice came again, sounding like the source was down in

one of the specimen chambers in the floor. It sounded raspy and scared.

"Is, is anyone there?"

Digby flicked his eyes back to Rebecca.

She nodded.

They still had a couple minutes and it wouldn't do to ignore a loose end. If whoever the voice belonged to had a way of communicating with Henwick, it might not matter that they had time to spare. They might exit the elevator with an ambush waiting for them.

Rushing to the edge of the nearest specimen chamber, Digby stared down into the darkened space to find a shadowy figure.

Guardian: Level 15 Necromancer

"What?" Digby struggled to understand what he was reading. Then a second message came in.

Zombie Master, Rare.

Digby froze as the pieces fell into place. They knew Henwick had needed access to a source of pure death mana to alter the curse. That was why he had originally tried to capture him. Despite that, Henwick had been able to hijack the curse anyway. Digby had assumed he'd found another zombie with enough mana to help. His assumption had been that Henwick had turned one of his own men.

"You're a necromancer?" The zombie master stared up at him, clearly analyzing him as well. "Oh my god, you're him. You're Graves!" He staggered back in shock. "But... how are you here?"

Digby started to open his mouth to answer but the zombie below continued to talk. This time, to himself.

"No, Clint. No, you're losing it. He can't be real. No one is coming for you." The zombie chewed on the ends of his fingers, some of which showed bone peeking out through the tips as if the skin had been gnawed off. "But what if he's real? What if I'm saved?" He snapped his head to the side. "No! Graves can't be here. Henwick wouldn't allow that. Henwick hates Graves. He's a liar and a thief. You're going to die here. You already did."

"Okay… This guy has lost it." Rebecca stared down at the frantic zombie.

"Doesn't matter." Digby shook his head. "We can't let Henwick keep him."

"What?" Alex furrowed his brow as Digby leaned over to speak.

"Excuse me, Clint, was it?"

"Oh yes." The zombie nodded with enthusiasm. "Clint, I'm him."

"Alright then." Digby made his best effort to sound friendly. "I'm sure you have had a rough go of things here, but I am real and I want to get you out of here. Would you like that?"

"Yes yes yes." Clint threw both hands up as if he could somehow reach the edge of his prison despite being nowhere near tall enough.

"Good." Digby lowered his staff down. "Grab on to this and I'll pull you up."

Clint did as he was told, reaching for the staff and grasping the end only to immediately slip off. "Sorry. I'm not strong."

"Damn!" Digby pulled his staff back up. "This won't work. His attributes must have been reset to zero when he died, just like mine were."

"We have one minute left." Rebecca called out. "Any more and we'll be on borrowed time."

"Alright, alright." Digby glanced to his HUD, finding just enough mana for a blood forge. He opened his maw and cast the spell without wasting any more time, sending a tendril of blood reaching down to the deceased prisoner below. A crude ladder formed as soon as it touched the floor. "Can you make do with that?"

"Yes yes yes." Clint stepped onto the first rung, stumbling a bit, but managing to climb without too much trouble. "You can do this, Clint, freedom is close, freedom is here." The zombie master reached up out of the pit as Alex grabbed hold of the tattered uniform he wore to help him up. The zombie immediately snapped at his hand. "No touch, teeth eat!"

"Woah." Alex yanked his hand away before getting bit. "Easy now."

"Hey!" Digby shook a finger at the zombie. "None of that, or I'll put you right back down there."

"Sorry, sorry, my fault, my fault." Clint lowered his head. "I haven't been this close to prey before."

"That's understandable, but these are friends." Digby grabbed his shoulder to guide the unsteady zombie toward the elevator.

"Yes. Friends, not food," Alex added, getting an annoyed look from Rebecca as she held up her watch.

"We're out of time."

Moments later, they piled back into the elevator. Clint immediately snapped at Rebecca in the enclosed space.

"Hey! What did I tell you?" Digby stopped him from making contact.

"Sorry, sorry."

"Actually," Digby grabbed the seer's head from Alex and placed it in Clint's hands. "Here, nibble on that."

"Hey, wait, stop!" The seer complained as he began to chew on an ear.

"Oh quiet, you're dead. It's not like you need skin." Digby made sure Clint was safe to travel before turning to the others. "Someone hit the button." Unfortunately, before anyone could press anything, Clint took it upon himself to lend a hand.

"I'm helping." He thrust one of his bony fingers out to press a button, seemingly at random.

"Shit, get him away from there." Rebecca jumped forward to slap the zombie's finger away from the control panel.

"What did he hit?" Digby got the zombie master under control.

"I think he pressed three," Alex added.

"Damn it." Rebecca hit the correct button to send them back to the base. "Maybe it didn't register."

Digby's hopes sank as the elevator began moving up instead of down. "That's not good."

The doors opened a second later to reveal a new room, this one looking more fitting in style with the fancy elevator they rode in. A dining room fit for a king greeted them like something out of a castle. Tapestries hung on the walls and statues adorned the far side bracketing large windows.

Digby's mind screeched to a halt as soon as he took in the view of the scene beyond the glass.

"Rebecca?" He couldn't stop his voice from shaking. "Is this one of those things that is normal in modern times but seems weird to me because I'm from the past?"

"Jesus fuck, no!" She shook her head with a frantic denial. "This is not normal."

Alex couldn't even form words as he stared, slack jawed, at the window.

The elevator doors closed automatically, leaving the view burned into Digby's mind. A pitch black sky, a landscape of gray-ish-white ground full of craters, and a blue planet floating in the darkness.

Clint added a final statement on the subject whilst chewing on a bit of the seer. "Did you not know we are on the moon?"

CHAPTER FORTY-SIX

"Shit, I need a moment." Rebecca pressed her fingertips into her temples as the elevator began to descend back to the base.

"Oh my god. Oh my god. I was in space," Alex added. "My brain hurts."

"Well, no sense worrying about that now. So Babel is on the moon, at least we know why there's no ambient mana." Digby shrugged off the realization, finding the shock less severe since surprises had become entirely too common since waking up in a strange time after his life as a medieval peasant.

The elevator slowed to a stop and the doors opened to let them back out.

"Alright, no point standing around." Digby held on to Clint as they moved to keep him from lagging behind. The zombie looked as frail as he had been back when he'd first become aware of himself in Seattle. The seer finally stopped complaining about being eaten.

From there, they made their way to the top of the building to meet Bancroft and get the hell out of there. Bursting through the door to the roof, Digby swept his gaze through the skies where several kestrels flew, many firing at what was left of his horde at the front gates. Most of his minions were gone, leaving a small number of zombies and a badly injured destroyer still trying to eat Skyline's forces. From the look of things, the dead had caused a significant amount of damage.

There were corpses everywhere.

"Looks like Bancroft's sabotage really threw Skyline off." Rebecca stared out across the scene.

"They might not recover," Alex added.

"Let's hope not." Digby spun to look for their getaway airship. "Now where is our new accomplice? He better not have left us to rot."

Kestrels flew this way and that, with no way of knowing which one was their ride out of there. All he knew for sure was that none of them were coming down to pick him up.

"Damn! Where is he?" Digby slapped a hand on the edge of the roof as a pained howl from his remaining destroyer drew his attention.

The poor monster had taken some sort of explosive projectile to the face, leaving the horned helmet of bone that covered its head blackened and charred. Another explosion detonated against its armored leg. Digby winced sympathetically as it fell to its hands and knees. White hot bullets streaked through the night, tearing through his minion's back. Despite that, the destroyer pushed itself back up and roared in defiance, its furious howl echoing across the heavens.

Digby focused on his bond with the oversized minion, feeling the heat of the fire surrounding it. He hated that he had to sacrifice the beast, though he knew there was no other way. At the very least, the behemoth had proved how strong the dead could become. Even as its bone armor began to fail, it reached down and scooped up a guardian from the ground to stuffed them in its mouth.

That's right, keep fighting. Make them wish they never crossed the horde.

Digby felt the crunch of teeth on bone across his bond as the destroyer bit down. He didn't shy away, even with the rising heat of the flames that threatened to burn his minion to ash.

Then, he froze.

The same wave of dread that had hit him earlier when

Henwick's shadow had passed by the window crashed over him again. The only difference was that, this time, it was stronger, like an inconceivable power was moving against him. Before he could open his mouth to say anything, the sky above the front gate simply opened up as a blinding light, brighter than the sun itself, shined down. A pillar of energy poured from the heavens to engulf the destroyer below.

Digby fell backward as a surge of real pain flooded the bond he shared with his minion as the light consumed the oversized zombie in seconds. He shut down his bond, feeling like he might burst into flames as well. His minion's silhouette screamed, louder than anything he'd heard. Its pained cry went silent as the blinding light began to fade. A massive skeletal form stood in its place, reaching up as if it had been trying to shield itself from the attack. The figure of charred bone collapsed to dust a moment later.

"Are you okay?" Alex jumped to his side, patting on his clothes.

"Holy hell!" Digby shoved himself back up, only then realizing that smoke was wafting from his body. Whatever that attack was, it had been so powerful that it had bled across his bond. If he hadn't pulled away from the link, he might have expired too.

"We have to get moving." Rebecca grabbed his shoulder to help Alex pull him up.

"No no no no." Clint began to panic. "He knows. He's coming."

Getting back to his feet, Digby placed a hand down on the edge of the roof for support. That was when he saw him.

Henwick.

Digby recognized the man instantly despite being so far away. The man was dressed in white, a tiny speck of light in the dark of the battlefield that had consumed the front gates. Clearly, he had realized he'd been tricked. He squinted as he took in the figure.

Guardian: Level 100 High Priest

"We must flee." Digby shoved away from the edge of the roof and turned his eyes to the sky. "God damn it, Bancroft, where are you?"

His demand bore fruit as a kestrel approached from the other side of the building, flying low to the ground as if trying to stay hidden. For a moment it looked like it might crash into the floor below them. The airship pulled up at the last second, slowing almost to a stop as it spun around to hover at the edge of the building.

"Run, damn it!" Bancroft beckoned frantically from the open ramp on the back.

"Move." Digby grabbed Clint by the shoulder, as Rebecca and Alex sprinted toward the craft. The pair reached the edge of the roof in seconds, both looking back to Digby as he dragged the unsteady zombie master along beside him.

That was when a light began to shine from above.

Digby raised his eyes to the heavens as a pure white glow grew within the clouds the same way it had right before a ray of light burned his destroyer to ash. Then the glow grew, expanding wider and wider until the entire area above the budding that he stood on was illuminated. Digby snapped his eyes back to the kestrel as Bancroft stepped away from the ramp, clearly recognizing the spell that was coming. He shouted something at the cockpit just before the airship began pulling away from the roof.

Digby's first instinct was to shout a command to Tavern to force his former enemy to wait, but Bancroft's judgment wasn't wrong. The kestrel was too valuable to risk it being caught in the radius of the spell. Without it, none of them would be getting out alive.

"Go!" He snatched the seer's head from Clint and launched it to his apprentice. "I'm right behind you."

Alex and Rebecca both turned to the edge of the roof and took a running start to cross the ever-growing gap to the kestrel's ramp. Any normal human would have fallen to their death, yet they both made it with ease. The only question was if Digby could do the same.

"Come on!" Grabbing a firm handful of Clint's shirt, he yanked the zombie master onto his back and activated his Limitless mutation. The sky above grew brighter and brighter as he felt every part of his body stop listening to reason. His feet hit the roof one after another, sounding like a stampede of horses. His deceased muscles felt impossibly light while simultaneously burning from the inside out. He cast a Necrotic Regeneration to handle whatever damage he might cause as he flew across the roof with his zombified cargo on his back.

Clint let out a terrified howl as the sky opened up with a torrent of life essence.

Digby locked his eyes on the ramp of the kestrel as it flew further and further away. Even with his Limitless mutation doubling his strength, he couldn't possibly make it. His skin burned as the power pouring down surged toward the roof.

"I will not... lose... now!" He roared with every ounce of will in his deceased body as he planted his foot on the edge of the roof and opened his maw. Henwick's spell hit the building behind him, tearing through it like paper as it swept outward toward him. He cast Forge just before it reached him.

"We're going to die! Again!" Clint screamed from Digby's back as a post of crystalized blood rocketed up from his maw. He kicked off with everything he had, feeling the crack of bone and the snap of ligaments from within his legs. Light poured from the windows of the building behind him as Digby soared through the air.

"Don't quit on me now!" he commanded his own body to obey as he slapped his free hand down on the edge of the kestrel's ramp. Something in his shoulder popped but he held on regardless. His entire hand went numb as if there was too much damage for him to pinpoint.

Two hands reached down to wrap around his wrist just before his fingers gave way, leaving him staring up at the faces of his fellow Heretics.

"Pull us up, you fools!" He glanced back at the building he had jumped from just as it detonated in a burst of shining light.

Rebecca grabbed the back of Clint's shirt and yanked, making sure to keep her hands away from his jaws while Alex pulled Digby to safety. He rolled onto the floor of the passenger compartment at Bancroft's feet as all the strength he had possessed a moment before faded to nothing. The weight of a hundred boulders settled across his frame as the damage of his Limitless mutation became clear. He cast another Necrotic Regeneration when he realized he couldn't move his legs.

The ramp at the back closed as the kestrel dropped down and sped up.

"You'll never get away with this." The seer's head rolled toward the back of the compartment. "Hey!" she shouted as Clint grabbed her off the floor.

Digby rolled his eyes, still trying to regain the feeling in his limbs.

"Optical Camouflage active," the guardian in the pilot's seat shouted back. "We'll be clear in under a minute."

"If Henwick doesn't shoot us down first." Rebecca rushed forward to the cockpit to take the open seat beside Bancroft's man.

The next few minutes were some of the most tense Digby had ever experienced. Everyone in the kestrel remained deathly still, each waiting for a blast of heavenly light to obliterate them. Digby let out a needless sigh when it never came. He dropped his head back to the floor.

"See, I told you I had everything under control."

EPILOGUE

One by one, the Heretic Seed's fragments surfaced from the black blood of Digby's void.

One by one, the shards were removed from their protective glass vials.

One... by... one... the slivers of obsidian were placed upon the green felt of the poker table within the high-roller suite where Digby had played his first gameI' of cards.

The trip back from the base had been tense but uneventful. With the kestrel's camouflage active and the speed at which it traveled, they had gotten away clean. They had bet it all and won. Henwick might find them eventually, but not today. Not until the Seed's power could be reclaimed. They had gotten to work the moment they returned.

There was much to do.

Digby stepped up to the poker table, its surface piled high with obsidian fragments. Running his fingers across their winnings, he felt the power within calling to him. He let his eyes travel across the room.

Near the wall, Deuce and Elenore stood, both cheerful at the fact that they did not need to leave the city that they had fought so hard to protect. Across the table, Mason, Parker, and Sax stared down at the bounty on the felt, clearly feeling the importance of what had been achieved.

By the door, Clint stood still holding the head of the seer and trying his best to go unnoticed. At the bar sat Bancroft tipping back a glass of bourbon. Digby couldn't be sure if his former enemy was trying to calm his nerves after making an enemy of Henwick, or if the skeletal minion within was indulging in a well-earned reward. Behind him, Rebecca and Alex both slouched into a pair of chairs, clearly exhausted from the ordeal that they had been through that night.

Digby sat down, prompting Asher to flap up to her place on the back of his chair. She cawed as every member of his crew looked in his direction.

"So that was Henwick?" Alex stood up from his chair and stepped to his side.

"Indeed." Digby closed his eyes, remembering the man's image amid the death and destruction that their assault had wrought.

"Did you catch what level he was?" Rebecca joined them at the poker table.

Digby nodded. "Level one hundred."

They both sucked in a breath.

He blew out a long musty sigh in response. "It seems we have our work cut out for us."

Bancroft pushed away from the bar and approached the table to lean a hand on its edge. "You realize all of this," he held out his glass to gesture to the Seed's fragments that littered the felt, "was sealed away for a reason. Henwick wasn't just locking this heretical magic away from the world to stop others from challenging him." He shook his head. "He was keeping a potentially dangerous power contained."

"Dangerous or not, this power is necessary." Digby opened his eyes and raked a hand through the shards. "Regardless, the Seed never belonged to Henwick."

"True, but I doubt he will consider your opinion on the matter." Bancroft let out a breath laced with a shudder. "You realize he is going to be furious."

Digby picked up a few shards from the table, letting them trickle through his fingers as the corner of his mouth tugged up into a crooked grin.

"Good."

ABOUT D. PETRIE

D. Petrie discovered a love of stories and nerd culture at an early age. From there, life was all about comics, video games, and books. It's not surprising that all that would lead to writing. He currently lives north of Boston with the love of his life and their two adopted cats. He streams on twitch every Thursday night.

Connect with D. Petrie:
TavernToldTales.com
Patreon.com/DavidPetrie
Facebook.com/WordsByDavidPetrie
Facebook.com/groups/TavernToldTales
Twitter.com/TavernToldTales

ABOUT MOUNTAINDALE PRESS

Dakota and Danielle Krout, a husband and wife team, strive to create as well as publish excellent fantasy and science fiction novels. Self-publishing *The Divine Dungeon: Dungeon Born* in 2016 transformed their careers from Dakota's military and programming background and Danielle's Ph.D. in pharmacology to President and CEO, respectively, of a small press. Their goal is to share their success with other authors and provide captivating fiction to readers with the purpose of solidifying Mountaindale Press as the place 'Where Fantasy Transforms Reality.'

Connect with Mountaindale Press:
MountaindalePress.com
Facebook.com/MountaindalePress
Twitter.com/_Mountaindale
Instagram.com/MountaindalePress

MOUNTAINDALE PRESS TITLES
GameLit and LitRPG

The Completionist Chronicles,
Cooking with Disaster,
The Divine Dungeon,
Full Murderhobo, and
Year of the Sword by Dakota Krout

A Touch of Power by Jay Boyce

Red Mage and
Farming Livia by Xander Boyce

Ether Collapse and
Ether Flows by Ryan DeBruyn

Unbound by Nicoli Gonnella

Threads of Fate by Michael Head

Lion's Lineage by Rohan Hublikar and Dakota Krout

Wolfman Warlock by James Hunter and Dakota Krout

Axe Druid,
Mephisto's Magic Online, and
High Table Hijinks by Christopher Johns

Dragon Core Chronicles by Lars Machmüller

Pixel Dust and
Necrotic Apocalypse by D. Petrie

Viceroy's Pride and
Tower of Somnus by Cale Plamann

Henchman by Carl Stubblefield

Artorian's Archives by Dennis Vanderkerken and Dakota Krout

APPENDIX

ATRIBUTES AND THEIR EFFECTS:

CONSTITUTION: Attribute related to maintaining a healthy body. Allocating points improves the body's ability to fight off disease and lowers the chance of infection and food borne illness. Greatly affects endurance.

AGILITY: Attribute related to mobility. Allocating points will improve overall control of body movements. Greatly affects speed and balance.

STRENGTH: Attribute related to physical prowess. Allocating points increases muscle destiny to yield more power. Greatly affects the damage of melee attacks.

DEFENSE: An attribute related to physical durability. Allocating points improves skin and bone density. Greatly reduces the damage you take. Defense can be supplemented by wearing protective clothing or armor.

DEXTERITY: Attribute related to skill in performing tasks, especially with hands. Allocating points will increase control of precise movement. Greatly affects control of melee attacks and ranged weaponry.

INTELLIGENCE: Attribute related to comprehending information and understanding. Improves processing speed and memory. Greatly affects mana efficiency. (+4 per attribute point.)

PERCEPTION: Attribute related to the awareness of the world around you. Allocating points improves the collection and processing of sensory information and moderately affects mana efficiency. (+2 per attribute point.)

WILL: Attribute related to controlling your mind and body. Allocating points will increase your dominance over your own existence. Greatly affects resistance to spells that directly affect your physical or mental self. (+1 per attribute point.)

NOTEWORTY ITEMS

THE HERETIC SEED
An unrestricted pillar of power. Once connected, this system grants access to, and manages the usage of, the mana that exists within the human body and the world around them.

HERETIC RINGS
A ring that synchronizes the wearer with the Heretic Seed to assign a starting class.

THE GUARDIAN CORE
A well-regulated pillar of power. Once connected, this system grants temporary access to, and manages the usage of, the mana that exists within the human body and the world around them.

NOTEWORTY CONCEPTS

AMBIENT MANA
The energy present with a person's surroundings. This energy can be absorbed and use to alter the world in a way that could be described as magic.

MANA SYSTEM
All creatures possess a mana system. This system consists of layers of energy that protect the core of what that creature is. The outer layers of this system may be used to cast spells and will replenish as more mana is absorbed. Some factors, such as becoming a Heretic will greatly increase the strength of this system to provide much higher quantities of usable mana.

MANA BALANCE (EXTERNAL)
Mana is made up of different types of essence. These are as follows, HEAT, FLUID, SOIL, VAPOR, LIFE, DEATH. Often, one type of essence may be more plentiful than others. A location's mana balance can be altered by various environmental factors and recent events.

MANA BALANCE (INTERNAL)
Through persistence and discipline, a Heretic may cultivate their mana system to contain a unique balance of essence. This requires favoring spells that coincide with the desired balance while neglecting other's that don't. This may affect the potency of spells that coincide with the dominant mana type within a Heretic's system.

MASS ENCHANTMENTS
Due to belief and admiration shared by a large quantity of people and item or place may develop a power of power of its own.

SURROGATE ENCHANTMENT
An enchantment bestowed upon an object or structure based upon

its resemblance (in either appearance or purpose) of another object or structure that already carries a mass enchantment.

WARDING
While sheltering one or more people, a structure will repel hostile entities that do not possess a high enough will to overpower that location's warding.

INFERNAL SPIRIT
A spirit formed from the lingering essence of the dead.

HERETIC & GUARDIAN CLASSES

ARTIFICER
The artificer class specializes in the manipulation of materials and mana to create unique and powerful items. With the right tools, an artificer can create almost anything.

DISCOVERD SPELLS:

IMBUE
Allows the caster to implant a portion of either their own mana or the donated mana of a consenting person or persons into an object to create a self-sustaining mana system capable of powering a permanent enchantment.

TRANSFER ENCHANTMENT
Allows the caster to transfer an existing enchantment from one item to another.

MEND
Allows the caster to repair an object made from a single material. Limitations: this spell is unable to mend complex items.

ILLUSIONIST

The illusionist class specializes in shaping mana to create believable lies.

DISCOVERED SPELLS:

CONCEAL
Allows the caster to weave a simple illusion capable of hiding any person or object from view.

VENTRILOQUISM
Allows the caster to project a voice or sound to another location.

MAGE
Starting class for a heretic or guardian whose highest attribute is intelligence. Excels at magic.

POSSIBLE STARTING SPELLS:

ICICLE
Gather moisture from the air around you to form an icicle. Once formed, icicles will hover in place for 3 seconds, during which they may be claimed as a melee weapons or launched in the direction of a target. Accuracy is dependent on caster's focus.

TERRA BURST
Call forth a circle of stone shards from the earth to injure any target unfortunate enough to be standing in the vicinity.

FIREBALL
Will a ball of fire to gather in your hand to form a throwable sphere that ruptures on contact.

REGENERATION
Heal wounds for yourself or others. If rendered uncon-

scious, this spell will cast automatically until all damage is repaired or until MP runs out.

DICSCOVERED SPELLS:

NECROTIC REGENERATION
Repair damage to necrotic flesh and bone to restore function and structural integrity.

CARTOGRAPHY
Send a pulse into the ambient mana around you to map your surroundings. Each use will add to the area that has been previously mapped. Mapped areas may be viewed at any time. This spell may interact with other location dependent spells.

CREMATION
Ignite a target's necrotic tissue. Resulting fire will spread to other flammable substances.

CONTROL ZOMBIE
Temporarily subjugate the dead into your service regardless of target's will values. Zombies under your control gain +2 intelligence and are unable to refuse any command. May control up to 5 common zombies at any time.

SPIRIT PROJECTION
Project an immaterial image of yourself visible to both enemies and allies.

ZOMBIE WHISPERER
Give yourself or others the ability to sooth the nature of any non-human zombie to gain its trust. Once cast, a non-human zombie will obey basic commands.

BLOOD FORGE

Description: Forge a simple object or objects of your choosing out of any available blood source.

ENCHANTER

Starting class for a heretic or guardian whose highest attribute is will. Excels at supporting others.

POSSIBLE STARTING SPELLS:

ENCHANT WEAPON

Infuse a weapon or projectile with mana. An infused weapon will deal increased damage as well as disrupt the mana flow of another caster. Potential damage will increase with rank. Enchanting a single projectile will have a greater effect.

PURIFY WATER

Imbue any liquid with cleansing power. Purified liquids will become safe for human consumption and will remove most ailments. At higher ranks, purified liquids may also gain a mild regenerative effect.

Choose one spell to be extracted.

DISCOVERED SPELLS:

DETECT ENEMY:

Infuse any common iron object with the ability to sense and person of creature that is currently hostile toward you.

HEAT OBJECT

Slowly increase the temperature of an inanimate object. Practical when other means of cooking are unavailable. This spell will continue to heat an object until the caster stops focusing on it or until its maximum temperature is reached.

FIGHTER

Starting class for a heretic or guardian whose highest attribute is will. Excels at physical combat.

POSSIBLE STARTING SPELLS:

BARRIER
Create a layer of mana around yourself or a target to absorb an incoming attack.

KINETIC IMPACT
Generate a field of mana around your fist to amplify the kinetic energy of an attack.

SPECIALIZED CLASSES

NECROMANCER
A specialized class unlocked buy achieving a high balance of death essence withing a Heretic's mana system as well as discover spells within the mage class that make use of death essence.

STARTING SPELLS:

ANIMATE CORPSE
Raise a zombie from the dead by implanting a portion of your mana into a corpse. Once raised, a minion will remain loyal until destroyed. Mutation path of an animated zombie will be controlled by the caster, allowing them to evolve their follower into a minion that will fit their needs.

DECAY
Accelerate the damage done by the ravages of time on a variety of materials. Metal will rust, glass will crack, flesh will rot, and plants will die. Effect may be enhanced through physical contact. Decay may be focused on a specific object as well as aimed at a general area for a wider effect.

DISCOVERABLE SPELLS:

ABSORB
Absorb the energy of an incoming attack. Absorbed energy may be stored and applied to a future spell to amplify its damage.

BURIAL
Displace an area of earth to dig a grave beneath a target. The resulting grave will fill back in after five seconds.

CONTROL UNCOMMON ZOMBIE
Temporarily subjugate the dead into your service regardless of target's will/resistance. Zombies under your control gain +2 intelligence and are unable to refuse any command. May control up to 1 uncommon zombie at any time.

EMERALD FLARE
Create a point of unstable energy that explodes and irradiates its surroundings. This area will remain harmful to all living creatures for one hour. Anyone caught within its area of effect will gain a poison ailment lasting for one day or until cleansed.

ANIMATE SKELETON
Call forth your infernal spirit to inhabit one partial or complete skeleton. Physical attributes of an animated skeleton will mimic the average values for a typical human.

FROST TOUCH
Description: Freeze anything you touch.

TALKING CORPSE
Temporarily bestow the gift of speech to a corpse to gain access to the information known to them while they were alive. Once active, a talking corpse cannot lie.

FIVE FINGERS OF DEATH

Create a field of mana around the fingers of one hand, capable of boring through the armor and flesh of your enemies. Through prolonged contact with the internal structures of an enemy's body, this spell is capable of bestowing an additional curse effect. Death's Embrace: This curse manifests by creating a state of undeath within a target, capable of reanimating your enemy into a loyal zombie minion. Once animated, a zombie minion will seek to consume the flesh of their species and may pass along their cursed status to another creature.

HOLY KNIGHT (GUARDIAN ONLY)

A class that specializes in physical combat and defense. This class has the ability to draw strength from a Guardian's faith.

TEMPESTARII

A class that specializes in both fluid and vapor spells resulting on a variety of weather-based spells.

AREOMANCER

A class that specializes in vapor spells.

PYROMANCER

A class that specializes in heat spells.

PASSIVE HERETIC ABILITIES

ANALYZE

Reveal hidden information about an object or target, such as rarity and hostility toward you.

MANA ABSORPTION

Ambient mana will be absorbed whenever MANA POINTS are below maximum MP values. Rate of absorption may vary depending on ambient mana concentration and essence composition. Absorption may be increased through meditation and rest.

WARNING: Mana absorption will be delayed whenever spells are cast.

SKILL LINK
Discover new spells by demonstrating repeated and proficient use of non-heretic skills or talents.

TIMELESS
Due to the higher than normal concentration of mana within a heretic's body, the natural aging process has been halted, allowing for more time to reach the full potential of your class. It is still possible to expire from external damage.

ZOMBIE RACIAL TRAITS (HUMAN)

BLOOD SENSE
Allows a zombie to sense blood in their surroundings to aid in the tracking of prey. Potency of this trait increases with perception.

GUIDED MUTATION
Due to an unusually high intelligence for an undead creature, you are capable of mutating at will rather than mutating when required resources are consumed. This allows you to choose mutations from multiple paths instead of following just one.

MUTATION
Alter your form or attributes by consuming resources of the living or recently deceased. Required resources are broken down into 6 types: Flesh, Bone, Sinew, Viscera, Mind, and Heart. Mutation path is determined by what resources a zombie consumes.

RAVENOUS
A ravenous zombie will be unable to perform any action other than the direct pursuit of food until satiated. This may result in self-destructive behavior. While active, all physical limitations will be ignored. Ignoring physical limitations for prolonged periods of time may result in catastrophic damage.

RESIST

A remnant from a zombie's human life, this common trait grants +5 points to will. Normally exclusive to conscious beings, this trait allows a zombie to resist basic spells that directly target their body or mind until their will is overpowered.

VOID

A bottomless, weightless, dimensional space that exists within the core of a zombie's mana system. This space can be accessed through its carrier's stomach and will expand to fit whatever contents are consumed.

ZOMBIE MINION TRAITS (AVIAN)

FLIGHT OF THE DEAD

As an avian zombie, the attributes required to maintain the ability to fly have been restored.

BOND OF THE DEAD

As a zombie animated directly by a necromancer, this creature will gain one attribute point for every 2 levels of their master. These points may be allocated at any time. 7 attribute points remaining.

CALL OF THE DEAD

As a zombie animated directly by a necromancer, this minion and its master will be capable of sensing each other's presence through their bond. In addition, the necromancer will be capable of summoning this minion to their location over great distances.

ZOMBIE MINION TRAITS (RODENT)

SPEED OF THE DEAD

As a rodent zombie, the attributes required to maintain the ability to move quickly have been retained. +3 agility, + 2 strength.

BOND OF THE DEAD

As a zombie animated directly by a necromancer, this creature will gain one attribute point for every 2 levels of their master. These points may be allocated at any time. 7 attribute points remaining.

CALL OF THE DEAD
As a zombie animated directly by a necromancer, this minion and its master will be capable of sensing each other's presence through their bond. In addition, the necromancer will be capable of summoning this minion to their location over great distances.

ZOMBIE MINION TRAITS (REVENANT)

BOND OF THE DEAD
As a zombie animated directly by a necromancer, this creature will gain one attribute point for every 2 levels of their master. These points may be allocated at any time. 9 attribute points remaining.

NOCTURNAL
As a zombie created from the corpse of a deceased revenant, this zombie will retain a portion of its attributes associated with physical capabilities. Attributes will revert to that of a normal zombie during daylight hours.
+8 Strength, +8 Defense, +4 Dexterity, +8 Agility, +5 Will

MINOR NECROTIC REGENERATION
As a zombie created from the corpse of a deceased revenant, this zombie will simulate a revenant's regenerative ability. Regeneration will function at half the rate of a living revenant. Minor Necrotic Regeneration requires mana and void resources to function. This trait will cease to function in daylight hours when there are higher concentrations of life essence present in the ambient mana.

MUTATION PATHS AND MUTATIONS

PATH OF THE LURKER
Move in silence and strike with precision.

SILENT MOVEMENT
Description: Removes excess weight and improves balance.
Resource Requirements: 2 sinew, 1 bone
Attribute Effects: +6 agility, +2 dexterity, -1 strength, +1 will

BONE CLAWS
Description: Craft claws from consumed bone on one hand.
Description: .25 sinew, .25 bone
Attribute Effects: +4 dexterity, +1 defense, +1 strength

PATH OF THE BRUTE
Hit hard and stand your ground.

INCREASE MASS
Description: Dramatically increase muscle mass.
Resource Requirements: 15 flesh, 3 bone
Attribute Effects: +30 strength, +20 defense, -10 intelligence, -7 agility, -7 dexterity, +1 will

BONE ARMOR
Description: Craft armor plating from consumed bone.
Resource Requirements: 5 bone
Attribute Effects: +5 defense, +1 will

PATH OF THE GLUTTON
Trap and swallow your prey whole.

MAW
Description: Open a gateway directly to the dimensional space of your void to devour prey faster.
Resource Requirements: 10 viscera, 1 bone
Attribute Effects: +2 perception, +1 will

JAWBONE

Description: Craft a trap from consumed bone within the opening of your maw that can bite and pull prey in.
Resource Requirements: 2 bone, 1 sinew
Attribute Effects: +2 perception, +1 will

PATH OF THE LEADER
Control the horde and conquer the living.

COMPEL ZOMBIE
Description: Temporally coerce one or more common zombies to obey your intent. Limited by target's intelligence.
Resource Requirements: 5 mind, 5 heart
Attribute Effects: +2 intelligence, +2 perception, +1 will

RECALL MEMORY
Description: Access a portion of your living memories.
Resource Requirements: 30 mind, 40 heart
Attribute Effects: +5 intelligence, +5 perception, +1 will
Units of requirement values are equal to the quantity of resources contained by the average human body.

PATH OF THE RAVAGER
Leave nothing alive.

SHEEP'S CLOTHING
Description: Mimic a human appearance to lull your prey into a false sense of security.
Resource Requirements: 10 flesh.

TEMPORARY MASS
Description: Consume void resources to weave a structure of muscle and bone around your body to enhance strength and defense until it is either released or its structural integrity has been compromised enough to disrupt functionality.
Resource Requirements: 25 flesh, 10 bone.

Attribute Effects: +11 strength, +9 defense.
Limitations: All effects are temporary. Once claimed, each use requires 2 flesh and 1 bone.

HELL'S MAW
Description: Increase the maximum size of your void gateway at will.
Resource Requirements: 30 viscera.
Attribute Effects: +3 perception, +6 will.
Limitations: Once claimed, each use requires the expenditure of 1 MP for every 5 inches of diameter beyond your maw's default width.

DISSECTION
Description: When consuming prey, you may gain a deeper understanding of how bodies are formed. This will allow you to spot and exploit a target's weaknesses instinctively.
Resource Requirements: 10 mind, 5 heart.
Attribute Effects: +3 intelligence, +6 perception.

PATH OF THE EMISSARY
Demonstrate the power of the dead.

APEX PREDATOR
Description: You may consume the corpses of life forms other than humans without harmful side effects. Consumed materials will be converted into usable resources.
Resource Requirements: 50 viscera

BODY CRAFT
Description: By consuming the corpses of life forms other than humans, you may gain a better understanding of biology and body structures. Once understood, you may use your gained knowledge to alter your physical body to adapt to any given situation. All alterations require the consumption of void resources. Your body will remain in whatever form you craft until you decide to alter it again.

Resource Requirements: 200 mind
Limitations: Once claimed, each use requires the consumption of void resources appropriate to the size and complexity of the alteration.

OVERPOWER
Description: Similar to the Ravenous trait, this mutation will remove all physical limitations, allowing for a sudden burst of strength. All effects are temporary. This mutation may cause damage to your body that will require mending.
Attribute Effects: strength + 100%
Duration: 5 seconds
Resource Requirements: 35 flesh, 50 bone, 35 sinew

MEND UNDEAD
Description: You may mend damage incurred by a member of your horde as well as yourself, including limbs that have been lost or severely damaged.
Resource Requirements: 50 mind, 100 heart.
Limitations: Once claimed, each use requires a variable consumption of void resources and mana appropriate to repair the amount of damage to the target.

Made in the USA
Columbia, SC
25 July 2024

d0ddcf31-d877-48b7-ac12-08d691092ea4R01